Sandy McCutcheon was brought up in Christchurch, New Zealand, but since the early 1970s has lived mainly in Australia. He has worked in a variety of jobs, from sheet metal factory employee and swimming pool painter to actor and theatre director.

Although he is best known as the host of 'Australia Talks Back' on ABC Radio National, Sandy McCutcheon is also the author of more than twenty plays. He has travelled extensively in Africa, Asia and Europe as well as living in Finland and Austria. He has twice won awards at the New York Radio Festival for radio documentary making, and been awarded the International Kalevala Medal by the Finnish government for services to Finnish culture.

A practising Buddhist for the last twenty-five years, he is a passionate campaigner for social justice and human rights and a strong supporter of Community Aid Abroad and Amnesty International, with a special interest in the issues of self-determination for Southern Sudan, East Timor and Tibet.

www.Sandy.McCutcheon.com
Sandy@McCutcheon.com

I0591083

DELICATE
INDECENCIES

DELICATE
INDECENCIES

SANDY
McCUTCHEON

HarperCollins*Publishers*

HarperCollins*Publishers*

First published in Australia in 2001
This edition published in 2002
by HarperCollins*Publishers* Pty Limited
ABN 36 009 913 517
A member of the HarperCollins*Publishers* (Australia) Pty Limited Group
www.harpercollins.com.au

Copyright © Sandy McCutcheon 2001

HarperCollins*Publishers*
25 Ryde Road, Pymble, Sydney NSW 2073, Australia
31 View Road, Glenfield, Auckland 10, New Zealand
77–85 Fulham Palace Road, London W6 8JB, United Kingdom
Hazelton Lanes, 55 Avenue Road, Suite 2900, Toronto, Ontario M5R 3L2
and 1995 Markham Road, Scarborough, Ontario M1B 5M8 Canada
10 East 53rd Street, New York NY 10022, USA

National Library of Australia Cataloguing-in-Publication data:

McCutcheon, Sandy.
    Delicate indecencies.
    ISBN 978 0 7322 6455 0 (pbk).
    1. Terrorists – Fiction. 2. Weapons – Fiction.
    I. Title.
A823.3

Cover and internal design by Darian Causby, HarperCollins Design Studio
Cover photograph by Phil Schermeister/CORBIS
Typeset by HarperCollins in 10.25/13.5 Sabon

For Suzanna

ACKNOWLEDGEMENTS

My thanks to: Bob, Fiona, Anke, and Simon for the introduction to the life of the Libertines. Mario and his Cyberspace Station — www.mprofaca.cro.net/mainmenu.html — a must for any spy! My editor, Nicola, at HarperCollins whose technique with the lash is first rate. John and Nicol for the company and music. Katya in Minsk for the journey to Kimzha. Paul Stepanek for the Czech phrases and spelling. And special thanks to the woman who started it all — Jane Bury — for the school photo of Jane and Teschmaker.

*I seek the love that is more
cruel than pain.*

Isadora Duncan

Love hurts.

Gram Parsons and Emmylou Harris

PRELUDE

He had always known that it would end with the funeral. Having come so far and risked so much he had expected to feel a sense of elation, but instead he was restless and irritable. The feeling was exacerbated by his own act of betrayal. He had made the decision not to return home and yet here he was carrying out one final task for his former masters. Of course the weather hadn't helped. He had not reckoned on there being so much fresh snow at this time of the year. Following the cars from the church to the cemetery he had started to worry that there might be some sign of his labours the previous evening. But when the priest had led the mourners to the grave site it had been through a pristine white landscape unmarred by even a single set of footprints.

He had enjoyed the church service, not because he was interested in the family's sad recollections of their daughter's short life, or because he was religious, but rather that it was leading to the moment when the coffin would be covered with the dense wet soil and he could start his new life. And yet when he stood beside the grave and watched the coffin being lowered, he wondered if the girl was at peace. It struck him as an odd thing to have crossed his mind. He didn't know the girl; had not even known her name until he saw the report of her death in the paper: a young prostitute, stabbed to death by a drunken client. It had taken him only a couple of hours to locate the family and they were exactly what he needed: impoverished working-class folk who, in their moment of grief, were welcoming of the stranger who appeared at their door. They took the proffered card but looked to his face for understanding. Patiently he explained that his charity provided all the burial expenses for those in need and soon he was sipping a cup of tea beside a small gas heater in their rather shabby living room.

The burial service came to an end and again he murmured his condolences to the family and watched as the car he had paid for set out on the journey back to their home. But he remained, hugging his arms around him against the cold. He stood and watched until the council gravediggers filled in the grave and patted the last of the soggy dirt down with the backs of their shovels. And still he stood, appearing to all the world like a man frozen in grief at the sad life that had come to an end so young. He watched as the stone slab was lowered onto the earth and only as the workers hurried away into the approaching twilight did he move.

He walked to the side of the grave and, after removing the bunch of flowers, lifted up the small vase, his fingers probing the small cavity until he located the wire. Gently he pulled at it until he had just enough exposed to extend out of the cavity, over the edge of the grave and into the dirt beneath. Having satisfied himself that it couldn't be seen, he returned the family's flowers to the vase and replaced it in the cavity. Now he was done. He stood up and looked around, but he was alone amongst the gravestones and concrete angels. It began to snow again; large goose-feather flakes from a leaden sky. On the walk back along the path towards the entrance of the cemetery he wondered how long the demon he had buried would lie sleeping — how long it would be before someone returned to raise the dead.

When he reached the gates he was annoyed to find that the old man wasn't there. There was only one car in the car park and it wasn't his. He glanced at his watch. It was well past the time he had arranged to be picked up. Fortunately there was a telephone over at the kiosk by the car park. He set out towards it, then stopped as he saw a man step out of the lone car. To his astonishment the man greeted him in Russian.

'Comrade!'

'Yes?' he replied cautiously. There had been no indication in his instructions about anyone else knowing where he was. Christ, had they learned of his decision to jump ship? Had the old man betrayed him?

The stranger saw the apprehension on his face. 'Relax, Comrade. I'm Krasikov. I bring greetings from the Centre. I am to ask you if you've completed your work.' He raised an enquiring eyebrow.

The man relaxed and allowed himself a smile. 'Yes, Comrade Krasikov, you can tell those in Moscow Centre that the lily is well and truly planted.'

'Congratulations.' Krasikov beamed broadly, then added conspiratorially, 'I hear rumours that there may well be an Order of the Red Star in the offing.'

The deflated feeling the man had been experiencing deepened. He had always dreamed of the rewards that might one day come his way. But there was a bitter irony in them being offered at the very time when he had made the decision never to return home. He tried to disguise his feelings. 'I was simply doing my duty.'

'Talking of which . . .' Krasikov began and fumbled in his pocket. 'I was asked to also give you this.' He pulled the pistol from his pocket.

For a second the man looked at the weapon as though he didn't comprehend. He gaped at the silencer, then up at Krasikov. 'But you said the Order of the Red Star . . .'

'Posthumously.' Krasikov shrugged and pulled the trigger. It always amused him that a dull pop could throw a man backwards in such a manner; it seemed far too inconsequential. He looked down at the man clawing at the snow as though he were attempting to climb a wall. Then he leaned over and fired a second shot into the back of the man's head.

Later he took the body into the city and, after placing a bag containing a small quantity of cocaine in the dead man's coat pocket, dropped the body at the rear of one of the city's sleazier hotels. And, just as he had anticipated, the media and the police treated the murder as yet another gangland slaying.

Krasikov enjoyed his work. He had no idea what the man had done to deserve the sentence he had carried out on behalf of the state, but if the organs decreed him guilty then it was so. Krasikov went straight to the airport for the long flight home where, if there was a Red Star to be had, it certainly should be his.

PART ONE

CHAPTER ONE

Moscow, December 2000

It seemed, the man thought bitterly, that his entire life had been reduced to a series of boxes.

It had been almost a decade since he had announced his retirement as KGB chief with the Moscow Military District. On 11 October 1991 the KGB was abolished and it seemed to Konstantin Ivanovich Laverov that it was a suitable time to get out. The world he knew was already disintegrating around him and, given the unusual speed with which his resignation was accepted, he knew that he had made the right decision. There was, it appeared, to be no place for the old guard in the new pecking order so, suddenly weary of life, he cleaned out his office and packed his personal files and possessions into boxes. He had been taking the last load home to his apartment on Ulitsa Novyy Arbat when he was confronted by two men who flashed badges at him and insisted that he accompany them. It had been a miserable moment. He climbed into the car with the pessimistic thought that nothing had really changed. Retirement, it seemed, was not an option. It surprised him that he didn't feel scared; he just hoped that they would get it over with quickly. His work had always been all consuming, but especially so since his wife had left him over a decade previously. He had worked diligently, putting in the long hours and then trudging home to the empty box that was his apartment where his only comfort was his nightly ration of vodka. It hadn't been much of an existence. He had no real retirement plan other than a vague notion of learning to fly fish, or maybe getting a cat. Nothing really.

But the car journey had not been to prison or ended with a bullet in the back of the head. Instead he found himself being taken to the Parliament and ushered courteously into a small back office. If the destination had come as a surprise, it was nothing to what he felt when he was introduced to the man who wanted to talk to him. Academician Yevgeni Maksimovich Primakov had been one of Gorbachev's leading foreign policy advisors but had now taken over as head of the new foreign intelligence service, the Sluzhba Vneshnei Razvedki or SVR.

Primakov had taken a moment to size him up, his face impassive. Laverov looked older and a little more ragged around the edges than he had expected. Maybe he was ill? There had been no health assessment on his file. The suit was worn and shiny, the old tie tightly knotted around the man's creased neck. The hair, a mousy salt and pepper, had been brushed back a little too severely and Laverov's glasses looked like standard military issue from years before. It was an image that reassured Primakov. The man standing to attention in front of him was certainly not on the take. Those who had accepted some of the more dubious benefits of the new era didn't dress like this.

'I want an older and wiser head, Konstantin Ivanovich,' Primakov explained amiably. 'An advisor. Not an official position.'

He paused, watching Laverov for a reaction. None was forthcoming so Primakov smiled and continued. 'Your pension will be generously increased and we'll probably need to call you in from time to time.'

Still there was no reaction, other than a curt nod of the head. It didn't surprise Primakov. He had selected Laverov because of his stoical nature and the comment in the file that described him as a man who could be relied on not to rock the boat. Still, he wondered that the man hadn't been more grateful.

It seemed so simple at the time, but what it had translated into for Laverov was another ten years of work. Much of the time it was analysis of old archives, sometimes just sitting in on debriefings and, when asked, offering an opinion. Cleaning up other people's Cold War shit was how he would have described it if anyone had cared to ask. Nobody did. Laverov never saw Primakov again, except on television or in the newspapers. By 1996 he had risen to be Boris Yeltsin's Foreign Minister and two years later Prime Minister. Now he was gone and Laverov had no idea who he was really answerable to any more. Everything had to go through Boris Kozlovsky, but it had taken Laverov about thirty seconds during their first meeting to realise he was merely a channel. He restrained himself from asking which department Kozlovsky was working for, but it stood to reason the man had inherited him from someone in the SVR. Just another chattel handed down from person to person. Still, there was an upside. Primakov had been right about the generous adjustment to his pension and Laverov was soon able to afford a better suit and even a second-hand car. He had decided long ago not to question his good fortune. Life had certainly become more comfortable. At least until this latest assignment.

Laverov looked at the pile of boxes. The instructions for this job had been couched in such secrecy that he wondered if somebody up the chain of command wasn't suffering from a resurgence of Stalinist paranoia — locked rooms and an armed guard outside the door at all times. It was just a pile of old boxes.

Laverov waited until Kozlovsky had locked the door behind him before opening the first box. It took him a while to realise what he was looking at, but when he did he knew he was stepping into very dangerous territory.

Moscow, April 2001

Teschmaker arrived in Moscow on the early flight from Vienna, flying into a day that was bleak and drizzly. Out of habit he treated himself to a coffee at Café Margarita and, giving in to his sweet tooth, allowed himself two small *vatrushki*. The sweet cheese-filled tarts were rich and filling and, apart from one Russian restaurant in his home town, nobody made them better than the chef at the Margarita. He acknowledged it was an indulgence and knew he really should be getting on with the job at hand, but he also knew that what lay ahead of him would probably be damp, cold and unpleasant. He helped himself to a newspaper from the rack and ordered a second coffee and a shot of Cristall.

The front page of the *Komsomolskaya pravda* showed a smug George W Bush announcing plans for a new nuclear defence system. The newspaper noted that it seemed clear the Americans were preparing to walk away from the 1972 Anti-Ballistic Missile Treaty. The remainder of the page was devoted to a lengthy interview with Russian Foreign Minister Igor Ivanov and his comments about Bush's policy. It appeared Ivanov welcomed Bush's offer to consult with the allies and with Russia and reiterated Moscow's readiness to agree to major cuts in strategic weapons. Ivanov also said that it was impossible to view the ABM Treaty in isolation from other strategic arms control issues and underlined that Russia remained committed to retention of the ABM accord. The cartoon on page two showed George W Bush building a huge missile defence system while under his nose a nuclear bomb was being towed up the Potomac on a barge crewed by Chinese sailors. Teschmaker turned to the editorial section and smiled at the lingering debate about Putin's revival of the old Communist national anthem and the red flag. It all sounded very back-to-Brezhnev. It seemed that somebody had forgotten to mention to the newspaper's editors that the Cold War was over.

He put the paper down and for a while just sat and enjoyed the feeling of the vodka settling into his stomach, but then, deciding that he could procrastinate no longer, he paid his bill and headed regretfully out onto the street. He would have liked nothing better than to stay in the cosy old café but he knew that if the rain set in it would make his job even harder. Fortunately the weather appeared to be improving; a pale sun struggled to cast shadows and the biting wind that had greeted him on arrival had departed the city.

Teschmaker walked quickly up Tverskoy, heading towards the Chekovskaya Metro. He knew the central area of Moscow extremely well, but his destination out in Volkhonka was unknown territory and he had been forced to consult a map to locate it. As far as he could tell it was several miles south of the city centre and, according to his map, he would have to take the Serukhovskaya Line out to the Sevastopolskaya Metro and from there walk to Ulitsa Kahkovka.

He found the place without any trouble. It was easy to spot because even now, some seventy-two hours later, there was still smoke coming from the rubble. Teschmaker could feel some residual warmth in the bricks. He was about to make his way into the building when a young policeman emerged from inside and officiously directed him to report to the local police chief who was lounging in a police car parked across the street.

The windows were fogged on the inside but as Teschmaker approached one of them was rolled down, allowing an acrid cloud of cigarette smoke to escape. The older, overweight man seated inside made no attempt to get out and greet him, just issued a surly demand for his papers. Teschmaker, having been through this ritual so many times before, stoically fished them from his jacket pocket and handed them over. As he did he caught a glimpse of an expensive gold watch. So the police chief accepted the largesse of the local players. It was the same the world over, he thought gloomily. Probably hasn't had his salary paid in months and is unhappy at being out in the rain. Unhappy to have his career sunk in the suburbs. There was no point in trying to be civil so he stood back and watched as the policeman took his time lighting a fresh cigarette.

'Just an accident,' the man finally proclaimed, glancing in the direction of the ruined warehouse. He had already done his walk-through and realised that there was nothing worth salvaging so had returned to his car while a couple of his men moved through the shell of the building. Going through the motions. He made no attempt to hide his resentment at Teschmaker's intrusion onto his patch, peering at his documentation as though it was written in Swahili.

'You won't find anything,' he said dismissively. 'My office is next to the Metro. You can pick up your papers from there when you're finished.'

Teschmaker shrugged and went off to look around. He had to acknowledge that the results were impressive. All that remained of the rows of washing machines and refrigerators were twisted shells. Pallets of what might once have been food mixers or toasters were now fused pools of glass and blackened plastic. But he also found that the arsonist had been careless.

And it was certainly arson. General Insurance International had been dubious about the claim — a hefty sum on a policy only recently taken out, and with a stipulation that any payout would be in American dollars. Well, that made sense, Teschmaker thought; it certainly wasn't worth burning a warehouse full of electrical goods if you were going to be paid in roubles.

'So, I was right, yes? Just an accident.' The police chief didn't think much of this smartarse foreign insurance investigator. He shoved Teschmaker's papers across the desk and got to his feet, ready to show him the door.

'You know what a rat flambé is?'

'A what?'

Teschmaker ignored him and took a seat. 'A rat flambé. An old Mafia trick. The recipe is pretty simple. One live rat, one small tin of petrol, one box of matches and a pair of gloves to protect your hands. You soak the rear portion of the rat in petrol and light it with the matches. Then you release the rat into the targeted building, preferably into the most highly inflammable area, and remove yourself from the vicinity.'

'Very funny, Mister Investigator, but I'm afraid we've concluded our investigation and found the fire to have been an accident. I don't mind you wasting your own time, but not mine.' He waved his hand towards the door, indicating that his visitor should leave.

'That's a pity. Because you overlooked something important.'

'I'm afraid I can't spare any further time —'

'Then I'll just have to take my little discovery to

your superiors. I'm sure they'll be interested in finding out why you're unwilling to investigate Mafia activity on your patch.' Teschmaker figured it was worth the bluff. He got to his feet. 'I'll show myself out.'

'Wait a moment! What discovery are you talking about?' The police chief's voice was taut and he looked as though he was struggling to refrain from launching himself at Teschmaker. 'I should remind you that it is a serious matter to withhold information gathered from a crime scene.'

'Crime scene? I thought you said this was an accident?'

'Let's say I have developed an open mind on the matter.'

Teschmaker casually dumped the bagged remains of a fairly well-barbecued rat on the man's desk. 'Unfortunately for your arsonist, the rat didn't manage to leave the scene of the crime, and sadly for the rat, it died just outside the building.'

'It doesn't prove anything —'

'So your superiors in Moscow will believe that out here all the rats stink of petrol and are prone to self-immolation?'

For a moment the police chief looked at the rat as though wishing it were Teschmaker, then he returned to his seat. 'I will need you to make yourself available over the next couple of days . . .'

On the police chief's recommendation Teschmaker booked himself into the nearby Sevastopol Hotel. It was not a good choice but at least it confirmed that the local Mafia didn't have a monopoly on rats.

The following morning the owner of the warehouse was dragged in for questioning. He denied having anything to do with petrol, rats or matches. He had been in Petersburg at the time, he pointed out indignantly. His alibi checked out and was enough to save him from being charged, but on the other side of the ledger the rat was enough to annul his insurance claim. He walked out of the police station free but destitute, an angry man. Stupidly he didn't check behind him and so Teschmaker and the now grudgingly co-operative police chief were able to follow him straight to a local gypsy neighbourhood.

Later, while he waited for his flight at the airport, Teschmaker phoned the police chief to ask him if there had been any further developments. To his surprise the man was remarkably upbeat.

'I've just arrested the warehouse owner and charged him with arson and the murder of a local gypsy rat-catcher. I'll post you the documents.'

At the airport Teschmaker remembered another errand that he had promised himself he would attend to before returning home. From his jacket pocket he took a small piece of a jigsaw puzzle. It was what he referred to as a *difficult* piece — one of the hundreds of sky-blue pieces that could only be distinguished from any other by its shape. Wrapping it carefully in tissue paper, he sealed it inside an envelope on which he had previously written the New York address. Before boarding the aircraft he purchased some stamps, affixed them and dropped the envelope in a postbox. Then Teschmaker flew home.

CHAPTER TWO

Russia, February 2001

For many people the twenty-hour train journey from Moscow to Arkhangelsk would have been a journey to avoid. Not for Laverov. For him it was a chance to escape from the claustrophobic room and the boxes of files that he was increasingly thinking of as toxic. He desperately needed to devote some time to thinking. It was also a chance to put some space between himself and Boris Kozlovsky. At first the relationship had been reasonably relaxed, with Laverov handing over a sealed report at the end of each week and Kozlovsky seemingly uninterested, spending more time attempting to impress Laverov with his successes with the foreign women he picked up in the Arbat. But as the investigation dragged its way into the second month Kozlovsky had become increasingly antagonistic towards Laverov, openly suggesting that maybe he wasn't up to the task and, at the same time, prodding him for more details. It occurred to Laverov that Kozlovsky knew very little about the substance of his task and he wondered why the man was now showing interest.

The only time the antagonism flared into outright hostility was when Laverov requested permission to make the journey to Arkhangelsk. He hadn't mentioned the trip in his report, preferring that it contained only what he knew, not what he surmised or hoped to discover.

'Arkhangelsk?' There was a look of incredulity on Kozlovsky's face as though Laverov had requested a trip to the moon. 'There is no provision in my budget for you to travel anywhere.'

'Then please request it from your superiors.'

'I'm afraid I can't do that without providing a detailed explanation of why it is necessary.'

'You know I can't do that without compromising security,' Laverov replied testily.

'Then I can't get you authorisation.'

For a moment Laverov looked at the younger man, wondering just how far to push, but decided that it would be better to short-circuit the discussion. He shrugged and got to his feet. He would request the travel authorisation in his next report, thus taking the entire problem out of Kozlovsky's hands.

'At your age you are lucky to have a job at all, Laverov,' Kozlovsky said quietly as Laverov went to the door.

Laverov felt a surge of anger but again kept himself in check, deciding to include a comment about Kozlovsky's attitude with his next report.

When he returned to Kozlovsky's office the following week he made no mention of the travel request and endured Kozlovsky's smug remark about everybody being happier now that Laverov was concentrating on the job at hand. For his part Laverov made no comment, content to hand over the report and leave.

It was the following week that the shit hit the fan. Kozlovsky was livid.

'You went above my head.' The voice was dangerously pitched, the tone accusatory.

'You refused to do your job.' Laverov kept his cool, aware by Kozlovsky's reaction that he had won if not the battle then at least this skirmish.

'You didn't turn up to work on two days this week. I hope you can explain?' Kozlovsky waved a file at him. 'I have all the details.'

'Good, then you'll know that I was following other lines of enquiry.' It irked Laverov that the young man had been checking on him, but he was certain that Kozlovsky had no idea what he had been up to.

'You are being paid to sort some old files, not make enquiries.'

Laverov smiled and, knowing that it would rile the young man, pulled up a chair and sat. 'I take it from all your foaming at the mouth that my request for travel has been approved?'

There was nothing for Kozlovsky to do but capitulate, but he did so with bad grace and, as he handed an envelope over, added a sting in the tail. 'Yes, you can go. I've booked your tickets. I couldn't get you on a plane so it's going to have to be the train, I'm afraid.' There was a slight smirk on his face as he added, 'I hope you aren't too put out, but I have you on the train that leaves at one in the morning.'

Laverov didn't give a damn what time the train departed. A victory was a victory. In fact the time suited Laverov. The trip was thinking time and it no longer mattered to him when he did his thinking.

He arrived at the station in plenty of time and found that Kozlovsky had gone out of his way to make the long trip as unpleasant as possible by booking him an aisle seat in the rear smoking carriage. Laverov ignored the seat and installed himself in a comfortable chair next to the window in the dining car and ordered a strong coffee. He knew from long experience that after three in the morning the staff would be playing cards in the kitchen and wouldn't bother him until breakfast time. And, in the unlikely event that he was hassled, he had a letter of authorisation that would have intimidated a Lefortovo prison guard let alone a state rail employee. It had intimidated Laverov. When he first opened the envelope he had given it a cursory glance to check that it was in order. The signature at the bottom had pulled him up cold and not for the first time he wondered what the hell he had gotten himself involved in. Instinctively he patted his jacket pocket to check that he hadn't left it behind. Reassured, he settled in and turned his mind back to the boxes.

There were far too many dead people in the boxes. It had taken two months so far and he was still under halfway through them. The first part of Laverov's task — checking the files off against a microfiche index — had been relatively simple and he was quickly able to confirm that several were missing. But the second task — finding any of the people mentioned in the files — was proving more difficult. The majority of the people appeared to be called 'name deleted'. There were other common threads: they had all worked on or been associated with the same project; they had, for the most part, lived in one of the closed cities; and, even though some of them had been relatively young at the time the files were compiled, they had all suffered the same fate — death. It was as though an illness had reached out and claimed them all and Laverov had enough knowledge of the old days to know where that illness came from. To complicate matters, every reference to what the actual project was had been carefully removed. There were also a number of people who were referred to by code names. It was obvious from the context that they were all *agent-boyevik* or combat agents. He suspected by the code names that some of them were not Russian nationals. In several of the heavily censored files he had found a cross-reference to a file which supposedly contained the real names of the agents. That file was one of those that was missing.

Eventually, in frustration, Laverov had asked for a meeting with Kozlovsky and requested a list of everyone who had been given access to the files over the previous five years. Kozlovsky had curtly declared it impossible but to Laverov's surprise the list was waiting for him in the locked room the following day. It was very short: General Lebed, Boris Yeltsin, General Igor Rodionov, Yevgeni Primakov, Oleg Rusak, Vladimir Putin. Presidents, prime ministers, members of the

Duma and ex-defence ministers. Laverov had stared at the list for a long time, trying to make sense of it. Was it possible that the missing files had been removed by one of these people? If so, why was he being asked to investigate them? Or was he? Anyone with a reasonably developed sense of survival would quietly slip their investigation into reverse after seeing those names. His instructions had been unusually vague: check for missing files and attempt to verify the existence and nature of the project. They appeared to imply that the original creators of the files were no longer amongst the living; something it seemed that they had in common with the subjects of their files.

Hopefully, in the next few hours without distraction, he could fathom out answers to the seemingly endless list of questions that his investigation had thrown up. What had the project been? Was he right in assuming it was past tense? Given that some of the code names suggested foreigners, wasn't it logical to assume that the project had involved another country or countries? What was it that the authorities wanted to discover from his analysis of the files? Simply that some were missing? No. If that was the case then there would have been no reason for them to authorise this trip. And the deaths? Had it been a medical research project? Germ warfare? A virus escaped from a lab? His mind tossed up objections to the various scenarios that presented themselves. He knew that beneath the surface of chaos there had to be a reason — a line of logic. Despite his best efforts his mind kept coming back to the central question. What had the project been? Without that information he was blundering around in the dark. He went back to the list of people who had requested access and checked the dates of each request, but again there was nothing significant. Dead end.

Yet there were chinks of light. A few weeks earlier he had come across a real name. Mikhail Lvovich Tarasov was mentioned as a supply officer who was to be investigated because he had known name deleted in the closed city of Krasnoyarsk-45 and had also come in contact with name deleted again in Chelyabinsk-70. Laverov had gone to the state archives and, to his surprise, managed to locate Tarasov's service record. According to the documents he was alive, being paid a pension and living in the village of Kimzha in the province of Arkhangelsk. He was seventy-six years of age.

Laverov ordered another cup of coffee and watched as the train moved through a snow-covered countryside illuminated by icy moonlight. They had stopped at several stations as they made their way out of Moscow but now the towns were increasingly infrequent. It was, he thought as they sped through a sleeping village, as though he were journeying back in time. The further from Moscow they travelled the more the stations looked as though they belonged in another century — wooden buildings lit yellow by flickering lamps. Further out the pure white expanses were broken only by the deep shadows of forests and timber plantations. This was not a world Laverov knew, but he found himself fascinated by the idea that inside the distant farmhouses entirely different lives were being lived out. Different dreams and fears. Yet somehow they were connected. No, he corrected himself bitterly, they might as well inhabit another universe for all they would care about his concerns.

He took off his glasses, tucked them into his jacket pocket and settled back in his seat. Eventually the constant rocking of the train and the white world unfolding outside the window lulled him into a troubled sleep.

Out of the past came a chimera, shape-shifting: his long departed wife. Behind her a bust of Lenin, suddenly animated, smiling knowingly. His mother, for a moment, washing him in a hip bath, her skin smelling of the rough soap an aunt supplied to them. His wife, drinking with Lenin. Primakov's face, close up, demanding that he hand back the key. What key? The one his wife has handed to Lenin who has changed into a marshal's uniform? He has no key, he shouts, and waiters turn on him, fingers to lips, eyes darting messages of silence. You never had a key, his wife sneers, no longer in a restaurant with Lenin but in a limousine whose driver turns and smiles. It is Kozlovsky, his face marked by a long scar down one cheek, the blood dripping. Laverov shouts that they are all mad, jerks in his sleep, his head hitting the cold glass window, and wakes to the sound of an argument at the other end of the dining car.

Laverov fumbled for his glasses then peered blearily at his watch but was unable to focus. The large clock on the wall was easier to see but the hands, stuck on 12.45, looked as though they hadn't moved since Brezhnev was a boy. He turned stiffly in his seat and watched as a guard and one of the bar staff struggled to move a drunk soldier out the door.

'They're bleeding us dry,' the young man shouted. 'You can't deny that.'

'Move or we'll put you off at the next station.' The guard attempted to twist the drunk's arm behind his back, but the man slipped from his jacket and dived back behind a table where another soldier was asleep, one hand clutching an empty vodka bottle.

'Fucking traitor!' the soldier swore quietly. 'If you like the fucking Yanks so much why don't you piss off out of the country?'

The guard exchanged glances with the waiter and then, deciding that neither of them were fit enough to manhandle the young man, took a wallet from the soldier's jacket, extracted a couple of notes and handed them to the waiter. 'Give him another bottle.' He tossed the wallet and jacket on the table and turned away.

As he moved up the carriage he noticed Laverov was awake and paused by his seat. 'Sorry about that, Comrade, he'll be less trouble asleep.'

It had been a while since anyone had addressed Laverov like that. He smiled at the man. 'What was his problem?'

'Same old story. Nobody loves the military any more. Girlfriend went off with some foreigner and all this new democracy and free market stuff is a plot by the Americans to weaken and humiliate us.'

'He could be right.' Laverov yawned. 'Hasn't done much for me, I can tell you.'

'Me neither.' The guard stepped aside as the waiter returned with a small bottle, then lowered his voice. 'I feel sorry for the young slob. Not much for his generation to look forward to now. The sooner we get someone like Zhirinovsky in charge, the sooner we'll get the country back on track.'

Laverov shrugged, unwilling to get involved in a political argument, especially over a right-wing maniac like Zhirinovsky. But, along with the majority of Russians, he agreed with the diagnosis of the country's ills. Democracy and free markets, which a decade earlier had been touted as the way forward, had given birth to ugly perversions of these institutions and opinion polls now showed that profound doubt and even despair about Russia's future was widespread. They also revealed that anti-Americanism had permeated the whole society and was probably more deeply entrenched than at any time in Russian history.

Laverov watched the guard move away then turned to the window. Outside the moon had set, leaving the countryside enveloped in a cold darkness.

CHAPTER THREE

It was a long flight, across continents, time zones and date lines. He arrived jetlagged, groggy and ill-prepared for what awaited him. As usual his wife, Gwenda, failed to meet him at the airport and so Teschmaker took a taxi. He always resented the taxi ride from the airport. Though there had been years of talk and shilly-shallying, the city bypass road was still just lines on some city planner's sketch pad. Having to drive north through Claymont then east onto the Mitchell Freeway and finally back south to Gower seemed a waste of both time and money. It was possible to wend your way through the secondary roads but when he had tried it once, some years before, he had encountered over twenty sets of traffic lights before he stopped counting. Mind you, it was hardly the cab driver's fault there was no direct route. He tipped and thanked the driver, who nevertheless still didn't offer to get his case from the boot. Screw you, he thought and headed inside.

Gwenda was upstairs packing. On the dining room table, propped up against a vase so he couldn't avoid seeing it, was a letter from General Insurance International. Gwenda had, of course, opened it. The letter was brief and straight to the point. The company had over-extended itself in the re-insurance market and due to an over-abundance of natural disasters they were closing down several divisions. International Investigations was the first to go. Thank you for your eighteen years of service. Please accept the enclosed severance pay, entitlements and generous redundancy package. No right of reply. For a moment his mind went blank. Gwenda had, as usual, closed the curtains as if preparing for an air-raid blackout. It contributed to the claustrophobic feeling he always experienced in the house and, in his own act of rebellion, he crossed over to the window and pulled them apart.

For a long time he stood, numbly staring at his own reflection. It was not a sight that pleased him. The synchronicity of his features didn't seem to be any compensation for a face which someone in the office had once described as 'giving new depth to the word bland'. And the body? Gangly like a poplar in winter. The cold winds that stripped the leaves had taken a fair amount of his hair as well. He ran his fingers through the remnant vegetation and told himself lamely that looks weren't everything. He was fit. But his subconscious wasn't about to accept this false optimism and shot him down with 'fit for what?'. Teschmaker, well used to standing back from the internal bickering, shrugged at his reflection. Outside it was pitch black. There was nothing there so he pulled the curtains closed again.

By the time he had returned to the table and read the letter a second time, Gwenda was waiting in line to have her say. She delivered her situation report with military brevity. Incompatible. Still had her life ahead of her. Martin's prospects didn't look promising. He could have the house and the BMW. He could have his name back. Yes, she would be just fine, not, as she noted acerbically, that he had cared to enquire. Oh, and by the way, she was going to keep the beach house and her Audi. Yes, there was another man. Someone who was not always away on business. Yes, she had been sleeping with him for the last two years. No, she corrected herself, not sleeping; *staying awake*, she added cruelly. And the rest was none of his business. She would file for divorce. Her bags were packed. She would close the door herself, thank you.

An over-abundance of natural disasters. Teschmaker thought the phrase was ill-chosen, odd. Surely that's what insurance was for? Another man? That came as no surprise as, right from the beginning of the marriage, they had both practised serial infidelity. Gwenda would file for divorce? His wife had always filed things. A bureaucratic high-flyer, she had latched on to Martin during his ascendancy. He supposed he must have been a good catch from her perspective. The right school, the right university, good social connections and lots of money. She had taken his name and filed it next to hers. She had shelved any notion of offspring as an unworkable intrusion into her own career path and invested instead in a wardrobe and accessories that consumed far more than any children would have. She had, Teschmaker reflected as he wandered around the house, marvelling at the efficiency with which she had cleaned out her cupboards, a well-filed mind. He paused, raised the blind and stared out the window. But there was no solace there. Even the garden — Gwenda's garden — was neat rows of lettuces filed alphabetically next to leeks. Cabbage next to carrots. The zucchinis alone in a row of their own.

'We don't belong in Gower,' she never tired of reminding him. She had grown up in the old-money enclave of Milton and aspired to Charlottewood. 'Even Drayfield would be better than Gower. Who lives in Gower?'

'We do,' had been his stock reply, uttered with increasing weariness over the years.

'That may be fine for you, but I don't belong here.'

And where did he belong? Nowhere, really. Redundant. Another odd word. A euphemism. I've just become garbage; he thought, no, not quite accurate. I have just been *labelled* garbage. I have been filed under junk, refuse, detritus.

Teschmaker felt light-headed, amused by the absurdity of the situation. He had just completed another successful case, come home to his successful marriage and someone had tossed a rat flambé into his life. For a while he sat, nursing a glass of scotch, wondering if he should torch his own home and whether the insurance was in his name or Gwenda's. But then, in a sudden energising surge of anger, he realised that it had never been his home. It was Gwenda's and he had simply been filed in whatever department Gwenda required him for at any particular moment. He was listed most often under finance and least often under sex. He was there to provide the additions to the jewellery and costume department and, when she had physical cravings, he was to satisfy them on demand and with the least attendant fuss, romanticism or stickiness.

In the few moments that the anger gave him before the jetlag cut back in, Teschmaker strode around the house opening and shutting cupboards and doors. 'Not mine!' he shouted. 'Not my house!' He didn't recognise any of it.

Teschmaker's mid-life crisis came upon him like a cyclone, unannounced. There were no warning signs, no gradual approach. Weatherproof, he had sailed on calm seas or flown high above storm clouds. For him there had been no gradual erosion of his self-confidence, no depression, no self-doubt, no impotence. Like a tropical depression the crisis had formed quickly off the coast of his life and swung inland, hitting hard and catching him unawares. And, like an unprotected building, the structures of his life were torn away in a single instant. The tsunami that followed the initial onslaught swamped him, then tossed him like so much flotsam, depositing him in very unfamiliar territory. Howling like a mad animal he lurched from room to room, barely comprehending the significance of the empty drawers and cupboards. Gwenda's decamping had obviously been well planned and executed over a number of days. But all Teschmaker saw was emptiness. Finally, lurching into the eye of the storm, he shattered the empty scotch bottle against a wall and stumbled towards the laughably labelled master bedroom — but the bed had the smell of Gwenda. No, he corrected the description, it had the smell of whatever expensive French perfume she had last purchased. Eventually he slept on the couch.

It was late the following afternoon when Teschmaker awoke. He fixed himself a cup of coffee and wandered from room to room until coming to a stop before the mirrored door of the wardrobe in his bedroom. He sat on the bed and stared. The man looking back was drawn and tired, somehow absent. The sandy-coloured hair, receding from his forehead, seemed to reveal even more of his scalp than it had the night before. The blue eyes were ringed — racoon eyes, lined in unhappy purple. And the brow too, wrinkled. He was looking old and worn out. 'I'm becoming my father,' he snarled at his reflection. It surprised him because his self-image . . . He stopped the train of thought, realising that he didn't really have a self-image. All of his life, professionally and personally, he had spent being curious about others — never about himself. Then it occurred to him that he was buried beneath all the possessions. He looked around. Everything in the room had been chosen by Gwenda. What had he bought? What belonged to him? Even more than that, what did he really need or want?

With a sudden cold logic and determination he walked around the house again, hunting for *his* things. Things? Is that how I define myself, he thought, and it occurred to him that he had a chance in that instant to do something extraordinary. At this moment in his life he had no calls on him, no need to work, and he could use the time exactly how he wanted. It was at that precise instant that he decided on the strategy to change his life completely. He would clear away all the junk, all that was extraneous, and then maybe what remained would truly be his.

In a prolonged bout of inspired madness Teschmaker stripped the house to the bare essentials. With the fanaticism of an ascetic he pared away at his life, ridding himself of anything that he did not recognise as part of himself. Slowly he became aware of a pattern emerging from the chaos. He was removing colour. The single bowl and plate he retained were white. All that remained of the cutlery was a silver knife, fork and spoon. The blue and green ceramic-handled sets were consigned to the growing pile of discards. Out went the paintings, the television, stereo, CDs, radios, excess sheets and linen, lamps, books, clothes, shoes, rugs, sofas and two of the coffee tables.

'Did someone die?' The van driver from the Catholic charity office had never seen such a donation. When he first arrived, he thought someone was playing a joke on him. Outside the house, covering the driveway and spilling over onto the lawn, was what looked like the home's entire contents. He was based in South Pendle, where they stacked the working classes in neat concrete boxes and furniture was bought from sales catalogues or second-hand warehouses. It took him a couple of minutes to realise that the welded conglomeration of old engine components he was looking at was in fact a functioning lamp stand. In South Pendle they would have stripped it down for the parts. He had walked around the side of the house to find the owner digging up what looked like a particularly neat vegetable garden. 'Did someone die?' he repeated when he finally got the man's attention.

'Something like that,' Teschmaker replied vaguely. He was exhausted. It had taken him several days but once this load was gone he was done.

'I'll shoot back and get the big truck and a couple of guys to give me a hand,' the van driver said.

'And help yourself to the vegetables.' Teschmaker indicated the pile of produce he had strewn over the backyard. But the driver was gone.

It was dusk by the time they were finished. Teschmaker, rejoicing in the absence of the blackout curtains, stood in the centre of the empty lounge room and watched the truck's tail-lights disappear out the gate. Upstairs, in his study, he opened the wardrobe door and grinned at the sight of the five shirts, one jacket and one raincoat. All neat, all tidy. All his. The old master bedroom was now empty and the remains of his world resided in a couple of packing cases. To one side of the study he had put what had been the spare bed. The only other furnishings were his desk with his computer, a phone and an easy chair. Beside the computer was a bottle of scotch.

Over the next few weeks he left the room only for food or to replenish the scotch. It was, he convinced himself, the hub of his universe. In moments of clarity he recognised that he was down, but he also knew that he was not out. He had no notion of where his life would now lead him but was convinced that if he stayed put long enough something would occur to point him in the right direction. It was only a matter of time, he told himself. A matter of riding out the storm.

But the storm had a long way to run.

The phone had rung only a couple of times. The first time it was Max, his counterpart in Britain. Lost his job as well. Damn bad form, he whined, given the years of service. Beyond the call and all that. Given their all. Any sniff of an opening in your neck of the woods? Just thought I'd ask. No, nothing around. Plenty of time on our hands to look though, eh? There was more like that, then a rambling monologue about his son's dismal school results.

Teschmaker listened for a while, contributing the odd grunt to reassure Max that he understood what a rough time he was having.

Gwenda? Left you? Damn it all, just when you need them, eh?

Not at all, Teschmaker replied.

Oh well, I suppose you're enjoying replacement therapy?

What?

Replacement therapy. You know, out with the old, in with the new. Haa Haa.

No, not looking. It was true. He hadn't thought of Gwenda, thankfully. Hadn't thought of a replacement.

And he didn't think about it until the next time the phone rang.

Sally was one of Gwenda's circle. Married to James with a regulation set of children and an annoyingly affectionate spaniel named — for some convoluted reason Teschmaker had never cared enough to fully understand — Mozart. Sally, bored with her lot in life, had made a habit of flirting with Teschmaker at dinner parties. A couple of times, in her cups, she had suggested she would rather enjoy a fling with him. I am a woman of *elastic* virtue. Name the hotel. Name the day and I'm yours, *daaarling*. Teschmaker had always executed a gracious retreat.

'I was just thinking of giving you a call,' he lied. 'I thought I might take you up on that offer.'

'Really,' Sally purred. 'And just when I had decided you were a very cold fish. What brought about this sudden rush of blood to the loins — Gwenda away on holidays?'

'Actually, more than holidays. She's done a bunk.'

'Done a bunk?' The purr vanished abruptly.

'De-camped, abandoned ship, done a runner, flown the coop.'

'Gwenda has left you?'

'Exactly.'

'But I need the two of you to make up a table . . .'

'Sorry. Bad timing, huh?'

'What on earth did you do to her?'

'Not enough, if I remember right.'

'I take it there is another man?' This, gentler, digging.

'Oh, several. Heaps of them.'

Silence.

'How could you? I mean, *really*, how could you?'

'How could I *what*?'

'Suggest that you and I might . . . I shudder to imagine what you had in mind.'

'Really, Sally? You were always saying you would like nothing better than a quick horizontal rumba.' He could feel the ice forming at the other end of the line but hadn't the sense to stop. 'Don't even need to waste money on a hotel now I have the place to myself.'

'You are forgetting that I am Gwenda's friend. I could never betray her like that. I feel sorry for you, Teschmaker.' The line went dead.

Well, screw you — or not, as seemed more likely. He poured a large scotch.

Blundering idiot, he castigated himself, while at the same time wondering how he could repay Sally for her about-face. What had she been after anyway? Forbidden fruit, was that it? As long as he was married he was desirable, but now what? Was he a threat? Or simply an uncomfortable reminder of her own hypocrisy? Hadn't wanted to go to bed with her anyway. Liar. Replacement therapy, huh! The last thing he needed.

But the demon was on the loose. Out of the bottle. No, that was a genie, or was it a djinn? Letting the djinn out of the bottle. Djinn and tonic, Sally? Not gin, scotch . . . and he realised he had drunk a little too much on an empty stomach. Food, he told himself sternly. A man cannot live on bed alone. But instead of the kitchen, his feet were betraying him, leading him unerringly astray. The bloody little book was somewhere. He fossicked through the box of possessions that he had quarantined from his cleansing of Gwenda's house. Not there. Then he remembered and retrieved it from where it was hiding guiltily at the back of his desk drawer.

Picking the right woman was important. He flicked through the notebook, his hunger for food now running a very poor second place to an urge that he had suppressed for so long. Nothing wrong with a little companionship, he counselled himself. Some of the names in the notebook were so old he had trouble remembering the faces that went with them. Katherine? Arizona at Christmas. Bridget? No, that was a London number. What was it — four, five years ago? Too long. Too far. Pity. He remembered the very pleasant evening that had nearly ended up in her Swiss Cottage apartment. That was a pattern that ran through many of the names on the list: nearly. He seemed to be fine at the preliminaries. Hopeless at completion. But then, he had never been much of a hunter because of the lack of nerve when . . . going in for the kill — could he call it that? The stalking, the ritual dance; not a problem. But there was something in him that hesitated on the threshold.

He ran his finger down the list. Margaret Ellis. No. Someone called Poppy. He searched but failed to retrieve anything. Jane. Teschmaker laughed. Jane someone. She was a hangover from his teenage years. How had her name made it into the book? Mandy . . . The name brought a smile to his lips and his hand reached for the phone. Smart lawyer. Resolutely single. They had run into each other in Buenos Aires while on a case; she was defending and he was giving evidence for the prosecution. Despite their opposing positions and her subsequent loss in court, Amanda Duggan had taken him out to dinner at the exquisite Au Bec Fin in Recoleta. Ex-pats. Strangers in a strange land. The conversation and wine had flowed easily. Mostly he listened. Mostly she talked. As usual he had been a little reticent about taking things any further but Mandy had called the shots. They spent three days in the nearby and splendidly elegant Alvear Palace Hotel.

The phone rang about three times before switching to the answering machine.

'Hola! You've called Mandy and Rodolfo. Neither of us is available right now, but leave a message and we'll get back to you.'

Obviously Mandy was no longer resolutely single and, so it appeared, had been back to Argentina.

He turned the page, but then turned back. Jane. What had happened to her? The memory of his childhood girlfriend was fuzzy. Part pleasure, part discomfort. Something nagged at him, some unpleasant association. Jane who? Damn it! Couldn't even remember her surname.

He sipped the scotch and was about to put the book down when he saw Irina's name. Talk about replacement therapy writ large! He had met her a few years before in the Austrian Alps, while resting up after a gruelling three weeks at the trial of a man who had conspired with his wife to fake the theft of her diamond necklace. The couple had fallen out over the insurance payout and the woman had reported her husband to the authorities then skipped the country with half the insurance money and the diamonds, leaving her irate husband behind to face the music. Teschmaker had found the case depressing and so decided to perk himself up with a few days in the snow.

He had left Vienna late in the day and by the time he arrived in the mountains it was dark and snowing. Somehow he took a wrong turn and ended up in a village far from his intended destination. Luckily he found an inn and managed to convince the landlord to give him the last available room. The man watched in silence as Teschmaker filled out the registration and, when he proffered his passport, waved it away with a dismissive gesture. 'No use for those around here.' His dark eyes sparkled. He appeared to be part Asian and Teschmaker wondered if this small valley had been on Ghengis Khan's travel itinerary.

Upstairs, Teschmaker located his room. As he opened the door he had the oddest sensation of having stepped back in time. He was not surprised by the lack of a television set because at that time few of the small mountain villages had satellite receivers. But the absence of a phone and radio reminded him of just how far off the beaten track he had strayed. He unpacked and went downstairs in search of a drink.

It was a large establishment and when Teschmaker commented to the landlord that it was surprising they were so fully booked the man explained that such an occurrence was rare. Teschmaker had arrived during the Festival of the Wives — an event that took place every ten years. Accepting Teschmaker's offer of a flask of wine, the landlord — a garrulous type whose dark eyes were as sunken in one direction as his bulbous nose protruded in the other — was expansive on the topic.

'For decades we have suffered from an exodus of young women,' the man sighed. 'Unlike the local men, who take over the family farm or business, or work in our timber mill, the women are lured away by the bright lights of the city. The problem became so serious that there came the day, just after the end of the war, when not one man in the village could find a wife.'

'A problem indeed,' Teschmaker commiserated. He had no particular interest in the subject but was finding it pleasant enough just to sit in front of the log fire and drink the wine.

'Indeed.' The man nodded sagely and sipped his drink. He was staring so deeply into the fire that for a moment Teschmaker thought he had forgotten the conversation. Then with another deep sigh and heave of his shoulders the man turned back to face him.

'My father and some of the other council members discussed the problem and came to the conclusion that if things continued in such a way the village would die. Nine hundred years our families have been here. Generation after generation.' He swilled the red wine in his glass, examining it as though he could see the generations swirling before his eyes.

'A long time by any standards,' Teschmaker offered, but the landlord hardly seemed to hear him.

'They organised a competition and advertised it worldwide through small newspaper advertisements. Women were invited to send in a photograph and a two-hundred-word explanation of why they would like to marry a local man and live in our village. Even back then there were many countries where the women had few prospects and that first year we had hundreds of responses. A selection committee went over the entries and chose the twenty winners, who were notified. The government immigration officials were hesitant at first and even threatened to block the women at the border, but finally agreed on condition that any couple married under the scheme signed a pledge to remain in the village for the rest of their lives and that the village council must act as guarantor. Since then we've been holding the competition every ten years.'

'Fascinating.' Teschmaker refilled the man's glass. 'And what reasons do the women write for wanting to live in your village?'

'Nobody really knows.'

'But I thought you said they wrote two hundred words.'

The landlord shook his head. 'Most of them don't speak or write our language so we just look at the photographs.'

The two men sat in silence for a while, listening to the crack and spark of the fire, watching the patches of soot burning themselves out on the blackened stone. Eventually Teschmaker asked how the men were selected.

'All the single men of marriageable age buy tickets in a lottery and then the twenty winners are drawn from a barrel. Tomorrow, the day of the festival, the winners will gather in the village hall and be introduced to the women. The local brass band plays for exactly one hour during which dancing is encouraged. When the band stops the men sit in a row and then it is up to the women to decide which man they want.'

'The men don't have a say in it?' Teschmaker asked, his interest growing.

'Not officially, but technically there is a chance during the dancing for them to tell the women what they have to offer. Unfortunately in practice it is unusual for anyone to speak the same language.'

'What a strange custom!' Teschmaker laughed. 'Surely marriages to foreigners, let alone those founded on competitions and lotteries, must run into a lot of problems?'

'Problems,' the landlord said darkly, 'are not permitted. The government in Vienna has stipulated that if the Festival of the Wives causes problems it will be banned.'

The following morning Teschmaker found himself in the rather odd position of being the only male at breakfast. Of the twenty women in the room, none appeared to be the slightest bit hungry. Some picked nervously at their food, while others sipped juice or coffee and stared morosely out at the tattered remnants of the storm. He wondered what was going through their heads. What circumstances had brought them to this moment, to this place?

Over a passable bowl of porridge and some excellent coffee, Teschmaker amused himself by trying to guess their nationalities. More than half of the women were obviously Asian. Two Pakistani or Indian women glanced at each other across the room, as if checking whether mutual support would be possible. He counted off the others: one Chinese woman, a Malay, two Korean, three olive-skinned women with distinct Slavic features, four Filipino and a lone Japanese. Two Latino women sat at the same table, while nearest to the window a slender Eurasian with short slicked-back hair was flicking distractedly through a magazine. The remainder looked European or American, though Teschmaker could not imagine why an American would aspire to marry into this particular village. He glanced outside. The snow had stopped and a weak sun was battling its way through clouds that seemed intent on shredding themselves on the surrounding peaks.

After breakfast Teschmaker wrapped himself up in his coat, scarf and gloves and trudged through the snow to the community hall, a log building that stood alone on a small headland jutting out into the river. Below it, down the bank, the snow had been swept from the surface of the ice and several young children were practising their figure skating. Even from a distance Teschmaker could see that they were all of mixed race, living proof that twenty years of competition winners had left their genetic mark on the village.

Inside the hall the marriage candidates had been seated facing each other in two neat rows of ornately decorated chairs. Each chair seemed to have a totemic significance: bear, wolf and other animal skins, and indeed entire heads, adorned some chairs, while others represented swans, owls and gothic images of what Teschmaker took to be forest or valley nymphs and goblins. The rest of the village's adult population was crammed onto plain wooden benches at the back of the hall.

Teschmaker had expected a festive atmosphere and so was surprised to feel the level of anxiety that pervaded the hall. Then he saw the cause of the concern. There was an empty chair on the male side of the room. One man was missing. Twenty women. Nineteen men. In an attempt to strike a calming note the band picked up their instruments, but their warm-up was cut short by the appearance of the village mayor. He quickly explained that the problem caused by the unexpected death of one of the candidates in a logging accident had been solved. A second ballot had just been held and a new candidate chosen.

'I'm sure you will join me in welcoming him. A man, dear to our hearts, who so tragically lost his own wife to illness only a year ago.'

A collective sigh went through the crowd and then scattered applause as a man made his way through the body of the hall to take his seat with the other candidates. The man, stooped and walking with the aid of a stick, was in his seventies.

The band struck up but for a few minutes nothing happened. People wrung their hands in embarrassment and exchanged quick glances, but it was the floor that was receiving the most attention. Finally a large bearded individual got to his feet. The audience applauded wildly and, flustered, the man turned and did an awkward clown-like bow to his supporters. Emboldened he marched across the room and then, as though changing his mind, veered away from the woman before him and stopped in front of one of the Filipino women.

Avoiding his eyes, the woman rose to her feet and let herself be led onto the dance floor. Despite his size the man danced superbly and for the next few minutes he spun her around the floor to the accompaniment of a lively polka. Encouraged, the other men began to make their moves and soon all but two people were dancing. The remaining woman, flaxen-haired and of European appearance, simply shook her head when the old man shuffled over to her. Her refusal elicited murmurs and a few boos from the onlookers.

Though those around him found her behaviour unacceptable, Teschmaker grinned at the stalemate. The woman obviously intended to sit out the entire event. Eventually the mayor intervened and spoke sternly to her, but she ignored him. The anger in the crowd was growing and it was only the intervention of the local policeman that stopped several of them approaching the woman to remonstrate with her. For her part she simply sat, impassive, unmoving, steadfastly refusing the old man's and the mayor's entreaties.

When the music stopped the couples returned to their seats and the mayor called for quiet. 'The time has come for the women to choose,' he said, 'and for us to open our hearts and welcome them into our little community.'

As the applause died down all but one of the women stood up and walked over to where their prospective husbands were seated. For a moment or two they paused, glancing more often at each other than at the men. Then the Filipino woman who had been the first to dance returned to her dancing partner and beckoned to him to join her. Suddenly, as though afraid that the man they had selected would be snapped up by someone else, the remaining women moved forward. There was a brief altercation between the two Pakistani women as they both approached the youngest of the men. The boy looked little older than eighteen or nineteen, gangly but fresh-faced and smartly dressed. In the end he took the hand of the taller of the two women; her rival spat out some remark and turned to the two remaining men. She glanced at the old man but chose the other, a dark individual in his thirties.

At this point the mayor and the local policeman moved in and firmly escorted the young blonde woman to her feet. She struggled but was unable to break free. Sensing that she was trapped, the fight seemed to go out of her and she joined the others now standing in front of the makeshift altar that had been erected on the bandstand. A priest, who Teschmaker hadn't noticed in the crowd, rose and made his way forward to perform the quickest wedding ceremony he had ever witnessed.

As the priest raised his hand to pronounce the assembled couples legally married the blonde woman swore loudly and slipped from the policeman's grip. Before the startled crowd could react she had run from the hall. Pandemonium broke out.

'Calm. I insist we have calm!' shouted the mayor. Slowly the noise abated and people took their seats. 'She will be dealt with,' he said. This was greeted with shouts of approval.

'I pronounce you man and wife,' said the priest.

It was beginning to snow again as Teschmaker returned to the hotel. Outside a police car's blue light was strobing through the large feathering flakes. On the rear seat he noticed a large rusty anvil and a length of rope. It struck him as odd, but once he entered the inn he forgot all about it, his attention captured by the mini-siege that was developing inside.

'She's locked herself in her room,' the landlord explained.

Teschmaker decided to avoid the excitement and took himself off to the dining room for a late lunch.

He followed this with what he intended to be a short catnap, but it was early evening by the time he opened his eyes. In order to wake himself up, he lit a cigarette and stepped through his window onto the fire escape. As he smoked he watched the activity down on the river. By the light of two tar torches some men were cutting a large hole in the ice. Ice fishing at night? This was, he chuckled to himself, a truly strange village.

Walking into the bar he found himself in a conference of war. The town council, the policeman and the priest were huddled over their schnapps, the woman's refusal to accept her husband being their only topic of conversation. The mood was black and ugly and Teschmaker suddenly knew that the scene he had observed from his window was not a preparation for fishing at all. Above the bar was a smoke-stained sign: 'There is no drinking after death'. It seemed appropriate to the moment.

'She refuses to open her door,' the landlord informed him as he gave Teschmaker a shot of schnapps. 'In fifty years this has never happened. If the government officials heard about this . . .'

'Is she unwilling even to talk with you?'

'I wouldn't know about that. You see, nobody knows her language.'

'I do. I'll speak to her for you,' Teschmaker offered. He had heard her swear earlier and recognised it as a Russian dialect.

The landlord turned to the local councillors and conveyed Teschmaker's offer. It was accepted unanimously.

'Her name is Irina. Tell her she has one hour. If she does not agree to come out and go to her husband in that time, then we'll come in and get her. Tell Irina that her behaviour is jeopardising the tradition of our festival.'

'And what will you do if she refuses to cooperate even when you get her out?'

'Leave that to us.' The landlord shook his head slowly, as though such an outcome were impossible to comprehend.

Up on the first floor Teschmaker knocked gently at the door. There was no reply. For a moment he worried that she might have pre-empted the villagers and taken her own life, but then he heard a muffled sound from inside the room. At least she was still alive.

'Hello, Irina?' He paused then continued in her native tongue. 'I heard you speak earlier. You come from near Murmansk, don't you?'

'Who are you?' The voice was firm, fuelled by anger rather than fear. She obviously had no idea of the fate that awaited her if she refused the marriage. The idea of a young woman ending her life in the freezing waters of this place was repugnant to Teschmaker.

'I'm a friend. I need to talk to you.'

The sound of her mother tongue was enough to convince her and Teschmaker heard the bolt slip free. He went in and shut the door behind him.

'I think she now appreciates the gravity of her situation,' Teschmaker reported as he came downstairs. 'She said to thank you for your patience and she will be out of the room within the hour time limit you set.'

'And will she go to her husband?' The policeman tossed back his schnapps and held out his glass for another. 'Will she keep the old man warm?'

'I'm afraid you are going to have to ask Irina that,' Teschmaker replied solemnly.

For the next fifteen minutes he drank with the local men then excused himself to go to the toilet. Letting himself out the rear door he made his way around to the front of the inn and found that Irina had followed his instructions perfectly. She was waiting for him in the police car where Teschmaker's bag shared the back seat with the anvil and rope.

'The key to your room,' she said and handed it to him. 'I shut the window behind me.'

'Thank you, Irina.'

As he eased off the handbrake and let the police car roll silently down the hill away from the inn, he dropped the keys out the window. 'I think I'll consider myself checked out,' he said.

When they arrived in Vienna they dumped the police car, then Teschmaker made contact with Irina's embassy and arranged an appointment for the following day. Later he phoned the hire-car company and reported that his car had broken down and gave them the name of the village. The car company apologised profusely. Later still, he and Irina enjoyed an intimate dinner at a smart restaurant and then booked into a small comfortable hotel.

'You could be my husband,' she said after they had made love.

'No,' Teschmaker laughed. 'I'm afraid not. I am a very married man.'

He closed the notebook. The scotch and the late hour were closing in on him and though he knew it would have been sensible to get some food into his stomach, he opted instead to make his way to bed. As he fell asleep the image in his head was not of Mandy, Sally or even Irina, but Jane.

CHAPTER FOUR

The metal-studded tyres were fighting a losing battle with the ice. Several times on the ten-minute ride from the train station the taxi slewed sideways, the driver swearing profusely at the failure of the snowplough drivers to keep the road in better condition. He also swore at whoever was responsible for the weather. Laverov had checked the forecast before leaving Moscow and had been expecting fine conditions, minus twenty-three degrees Celsius with a wind chill factor of minus twenty-two. But someone had forgotten to tell whichever department was in charge of dispensing the weather to this part of the country. It was considerably warmer: minus eight or nine and snowing. Very pleasant.

He steadied himself against the door as they slid sickeningly, narrowly avoiding a car broken down in the middle of what Laverov assumed was supposed to be a road. The driver made some cutting remarks about the unfortunate motorist's mother and her nasty predilection for sex with a variety of endangered wildlife. For his part Laverov offered no comment, but gripped the seat more firmly and attempted to peer through the small hole that the driver had scraped in the ice-covered window. He caught a glimpse of one of the few functioning street lights, but apart from that nothing. The driver must be navigating by instinct rather than sight. Fortunately the ice, snow and lateness of the hour meant that there were few other vehicles on the road. Welcome to Arkhangelsk, Laverov thought and gritted his teeth as they bumped over something. A kerb? A body? No, probably not. Nobody with any sense would be out on the streets now including, it seemed, Volodarsky, the first deputy police chief, who Laverov had requested meet him at the station. Something more important must have cropped up, he told himself, unconvincingly. Arkhangelsk looked as though the majority of the population had abandoned it to the winter. Very sensible.

The check on the weather had been as far as his research went. Never having been anywhere in the Arkhangelsk Oblast, Laverov found himself wondering if they had any daylight at all in winter. Situated on the Severnaya Dvina, near its mouth into the White Sea, Arkhangelsk was as far north as Laverov ever wanted to go. Despite his deep-seated antipathy towards hotels, the people who owned them, ran them or even stayed in them, he experienced a sense of relief as the taxi entered the better-lit city centre and slid to a stop in front of the Business Centre Hotel on Voskresenskaya Ulitsa. He wondered what overtly romantic person had dreamed up the name. Maybe in the new capitalism era

'Business Centre' was considered sexy? Though not even mildly romantic his room turned out to be comfortable, and after a single medicinal shot of vodka he drifted off into a dreamless sleep.

The following morning was the first time in some years that Laverov had managed to be up, dressed and breakfasted before sunrise. His feat was somewhat diminished by the latitude — this far north the winter sun didn't put in an appearance before 10 am. Even then it was, at best, a fleeting appearance. Its desultory attempt to mount the sky was abandoned by midday, followed by a hasty descent; the entire event usually over by 2.30 pm. Not much of an effort, Laverov thought gloomily as he looked out at the leaden sky; it was doubtful the sun would bother putting in an appearance at all today. The night's snowfall had blanketed the city and it was a fair bet that there was more on the way. Oh well, what couldn't be avoided must be confronted. He heaved on his coat and headed out into the cold.

The first deputy police chief of the Arkhangelsk region finally deigned to grant him an audience, but not until he had left Laverov sitting in an unheated waiting room long enough to understand that functionaries from Moscow were not going to get preferential treatment in his fiefdom. The man was in his mid-thirties, elegantly dressed, with a complexion and body that owed a lot to sun lamps, obsessive work-outs and possibly a steroid or two. Despite his relative youth and fitness, it was immediately apparent that Volodarsky liked to present himself as a world-weary individual who had seen it all.

'I expected someone younger,' he murmured as though to someone else. 'Pleasant train trip?'

It was too pointed. Too obvious. He even sounded like Kozlovsky. Laverov nodded and, sensing that there was no point engaging in pleasantries, plunged in. 'I need to arrange transport to Kimzha.'

There was silence for a moment as Volodarsky narrowed his eyes and studied Laverov.

'Kimzha . . . Kimzha . . .' He repeated the name a couple more times, rolling it round his mouth to experience the flavour. By the look on his face it was not to his taste. Then he heaved a sigh, thumbed through a folder on his desk, extracted a sheet of paper and made a pretence of reading it. Finally he looked up.

'It's a pity you didn't tell me that before you left Moscow. The only access is by river and . . .' he glanced out at the snowflakes feathering past the window, 'this time of year, well . . .' He shrugged. 'They're frozen. You could come back in spring, after the thaw. I'm sure we could assist then.'

I am a brick wall, the man was saying, beyond which you shall not pass. Go back to Moscow. Stop wasting my time. There was nothing subtle about the obstruction nor the confidence with which it was delivered. He sat back in his chair like a headmaster who, having chastised a pupil, awaits his departure. But to his surprise Laverov didn't appear inclined to play the pupil's role.

'I'm also a very busy man,' the policeman added. Still Laverov sat, a slight smile on his face. Volodarsky began to feel unsettled. 'And so if there is nothing else . . .?'

Laverov took the letter from his pocket and handed it over, almost apologetically. 'I was asked to show you this. It probably won't help. Certainly can't unfreeze rivers but . . .'

He left the sentence unfinished and made a pretence of cleaning his glasses while Volodarsky read the document. The point at which he saw the signature was obvious. He sat up and fixed Laverov with his eyes.

'I should have been informed that this was presidential business,' he snapped. 'I would have had you met.'

'Oh, that wouldn't have been necessary. I can see how busy you are.' Laverov put his glasses back on and smiled generously.

Unaccustomed to feeling uncomfortable in his own office, Volodarsky carefully folded the letter and put it back in the envelope. Kimzha? It was nowhere. During winter there were two, three hundred peasants there at most. Half the houses were abandoned. There was the church of course, but that was hardly likely to interest anyone but a student of architecture. He composed himself, handed back the envelope and made a valiant attempt at a friendly smile. 'Of course, I shall do what I can.'

'That would be most kind.'

'You must understand that these are difficult times. Crime is getting out of control.' He indicated the pile of folders on his desk. 'So much crime and so few resources.'

The lack of resources obviously didn't extend to his personal wardrobe: the suit was imported, the shoes beneath the desk Italian, and the ostentatious gold watch nicely matched to a pair of eighteen-carat cufflinks.

'In Soviet times everything belonged to the people. The change has created the situation where things have ceased to be "ours" but didn't become "mine". They're nobody's. Now people have no qualms about destroying something that was created by other people to buy a bottle or support themselves.'

Laverov listened to the suddenly expansive policeman, wondering why he was getting the all too familiar lecture on the breakdown of the post-Soviet state. Maybe it was like the snow outside the window, he thought gloomily, something that had to be endured. He made a sympathetic clucking noise and nodded. Times were tough. They always had been. As the policeman ladled out the statistics to support his argument, Laverov tuned out. The man was getting kickbacks. Nothing new or surprising in that. He resented Moscow? Everybody outside the capital did.

After a time the lecture came to an end and Volodarsky, perhaps feeling he had demonstrated that he was a loyal servant of the people, came full circle. 'So may I ask what you are seeking in Kimzha?' The tone was friendly now, inclusive. Two professionals getting stuck in, shoulder to shoulder. He had already made a mental note to see what he could find out about Laverov, just to cover his own back.

'I need to interview a man named Tarasov.'

'The man is a resident? It's not a popular winter destination.' Volodarsky's grin confirmed that he also had well-placed friends in the dental profession.

Laverov had never seen such perfect teeth, except in the advertisements on television.

'He moved there several years ago. He's a very old man.'

'Ah . . .' Volodarsky nodded knowingly. 'Digging up the past, eh?' He reached behind him for a file, flicked through it and ran his finger down a list of names.

'Ancient history. More of an archaeologist than a policeman,' Laverov offered, more in a spirit of conciliation than humour. The over-hearty laugh that his remark elicited seemed to indicate that he was making progress.

'Mikhail Lvovich Tarasov?' Volodarsky read from the file. 'Moved to Kamenka six years ago. Stayed a few months and has been registered in Kimzha for the last five years.'

'That's the man. Any idea why he chose Kimzha?'

'It's not a retirement village.' Volodarsky snorted, his expression making it clear what he thought of the place. 'Masochism or in-laws.'

'In-laws?'

'There's no other Tarasov on the register but his file says he was married to a Marina Fyodorova Vetrov, now deceased.'

'And?'

'Her brother, Ivan Vetrov, was a timber worker who lived in Kamenka a few years ago.'

'Lived?'

'Died. I know the name because he and his wife were killed in a house fire. I figure Tarasov probably came to collect whatever survived the fire and decided to stay. So what has this Tarasov done that brings someone like you halfway across the country?'

'He may have known people who knew other people,' Laverov said obliquely, wondering what kind of person Volodarsky thought he was.

Sensing that he was going to get precious little out of his taciturn guest, Volodarsky closed the file. 'Let me get my driver to take you back to your hotel and I'll see what I can organise.'

'You can unfreeze the rivers?'

'In the old days, if the bosses said it was unfrozen . . . Now, unfortunately, we have to deal with reality. There is a *zimnik* — a temporary winter road — that the lumber factory at Kamenka maintains to supply its winter maintenance crew. It's only used once a fortnight but it could be accessible if the weather clears. The problem is finding a vehicle. There are plenty on the books, but those that are still in working order tend to get stolen. Even those that aren't repairable . . .'

'Are stripped for scrap?'

Volodarsky nodded.

This was not unexpected. Russians had taken to recycling in a big way. Anything that wasn't bolted to the floor was considered fair game and if the floor was wooden — well, it usually went too.

'We had an entire locomotive taken last year. And just last week . . .' He fished another file from his desk. 'A local thug decided that he would take a kilometre of electrical cable right off the power lines. So unlucky, really — the one day the power was working. Eleven thousand volts. Killed him instantly, leaving him fried and hanging from a safety harness. Of course the lines went dead and another group of enterprising thieves took four hundred metres of copper wire during the night without disturbing the body.' He glanced down at the file again and frowned. 'No, not quite right. It seems they took his boots.'

Any doubts about the strength of his improved relationship with Volodarsky were quickly dispelled when Laverov arrived back at the hotel. His room had been upgraded and a bottle of vodka was sitting on the bureau — compliments of the management. So the police chief had the hotels in his pocket as well. Still, Laverov thought as he opened the bottle, it was probably less risky than cutting down power lines, and a hell of a lot more lucrative.

Later, fortified by lunch and another shot of vodka, Laverov took advantage of an unexpected break in the weather to take a brisk walk through the city. Turning from Voskresenskaya into Troitskiy Prospect, he followed the tramlines to Karl Libkneht and on down to the embankment. It was, even in winter, an interesting city. Old wooden houses, survivors of an earlier era, sat oddly alongside modern concrete apartment blocks and office buildings. Off the main thoroughfare the tramlines and overhead wires were replaced by streets lined with poplars, now stripped of their leaves. When he reached the embankment he was in another world again. The expanse of the Dvina lay frozen in front of him and from between the clouds a low sun sent a single spear of light onto the snow-covered ice. The noise of the trams and traffic was lost behind the wind crackling the ice in the trees and the crunch of the snow beneath his feet. A couple of hardy skiers shot past him, fiercely working their sticks and trailing small clouds of mist from their heavy breathing. A lone man, all fur coat and astrakhan, walked behind him. Down here on the exposed banks of the Dvina the cold was intense, so Laverov turned back to the city through Pomorskaya with its quaint old stone buildings. He glanced up at the metre-long icicles hanging from their eaves, imagining them breaking off in the spring. But spring and the danger of accidental death by icicle was a long way off and as he turned back into Troitskiy Prospect the clouds returned, and with them the snow.

On the steps of the hotel Laverov paused and looked back along the street. The man in the astrakhan hat had developed a sudden interest in architecture and was examining the front of a nearby building. Poor sod probably had less idea of what he was doing than Laverov did, but the exercise would have done him good. He would most likely be stuck in a car for the rest of the day, or at least until they concluded that Laverov wasn't going to venture out from the hotel again.

As it turned out Laverov didn't leave the hotel for the next forty-eight hours. Twice Volodarsky rang to assure him he was on the case but was having difficulties getting a vehicle, problems with drivers being ill and, of course, the weather. Laverov had to concede that at least he was telling the truth about the weather. The snow showers had combined to produce blizzard conditions with — if the television report was to be believed — little hope of respite in the next few days.

However, the morning of the third day Laverov awoke to clear skies and a drop in temperature down to minus twenty-five. As if on cue the phone rang.

'I have a driver and a tracked vehicle.' Volodarsky sounded a little too crisp; the friendliness gone from his voice. Laverov wondered what had happened in the interim. Maybe the effect of the letter was wearing off and the man was simply too busy to play transport nanny to a southerner. Maybe he was just busy; snowed under.

'When can we leave?'

'The driver is collecting supplies and I have to confirm the accommodation. How long do you intend to be in Kimzha?'

'A couple of days at the most.'

'Vladimir Almukhamed is not the regular driver but he works as a log hauler during the summer and knows the area. He'll be at the hotel in an hour.'

Vladimir was still wearing the astrakhan hat and if he had ever worked as a log hauler it was a long time ago and with a different body. His hands looked as though they hadn't touched anything more wooden than a pencil. Still, Laverov thought as he settled back in the cabin, it was warm, the man didn't appear to be talkative and there was a bottle of vodka jammed in between the seats. *Compliments of the Kamenka Timber Company.* It seemed news of his letter of authorisation had spread.

It was one of the slowest journeys Laverov had ever made. Vladimir exchanged the minimum of pleasantries, clamped on a pair of earphones, plugged his walkman into the cigarette lighter on the dashboard and retired into whatever music was on his collection of CDs.

After winding their way through the outskirts of Arkhangelsk they followed a country road for a few kilometres and then, after passing through what looked like a deserted village, slowed down to a crawl. Laverov had no doubt that the roads would usually be in dreadful condition, but snow was a great leveller and the passage of a recent snowplough had left them with an almost smooth ride. He was about to tap Vladimir on the shoulder and ask why the reduction in speed when the reason became obvious.

There was little to mark the entrance to the temporary road and they could easily have missed it if someone had not tied a red flag to a snow-encrusted larch on the right-hand side of the main road.

'The *zimnik*!' Vladimir bellowed above the music in his headphones.

'How far is it?' Laverov mouthed, not bothering to put any effort into shouting.

'Four hundred kilometres.'

'How long?'

'What?'

'I said . . . how . . . long?' Laverov repeated.

The headphones came off one ear and for a moment Laverov thought he heard a snatch of Madonna.

'About ten hours they tell me. Maybe more. Depends on the weather.'

They tell me? Laverov was concerned not by the man's lapse from the flimsy cover story he had been fed about being a lumber hauler, but by the implied admission that he had never travelled the route before. Four hundred kilometres along a temporary road in the middle of winter was not to be undertaken lightly. *Ten hours?* He hoped that Vladimir had brought along enough CDs.

He fished a cigarette packet from his pocket and lit one. Instinctively he rolled down the window but the sudden blast of sub-zero air was an immediate reminder that they could all make mistakes. He quickly closed the window and resigned himself to travelling in a smoke-filled cabin.

Within a couple of hours they had lost the daylight, but despite the recent heavy snow the road was in reasonable condition and it appeared to Laverov that they were making good progress. He wondered what Vladimir was on, for apart from two desperately cold stops to urinate he drove without a break, choosing to eat, drink and smoke on the move, all without a hint of the exhaustion that Laverov was feeling merely as a passenger. Mostly they travelled through dense forest, but occasionally ventured across what was presumably, in the warmer months, boggy marshland. At each point where they had to re-enter the forest, the red flags were clearly visible in the headlights. They looked brand new. Above them the aurora borealis glittered and shimmered, sending wave after wave of intoxicatingly beautiful curtains of light across the narrow band of sky between the trees.

With great restraint Laverov held back from the vodka for the first few hours, but eventually relented, telling himself it would distract him from the growing numbness in his rear. To his relief and surprise

Vladimir declined the offer that, given the circumstances, he felt impelled to make. They drove on into a strengthening wind from the north. They were still travelling under a clear sky but the wind whipped up the fresh snow on the road in occasionally blinding flurries. It seemed to have no effect on Vladimir, who sat on the same speed for hours, not even slowing for the stretches of ice or the infrequent but deep track marks left by a previous traveller on the road. Eventually the vodka worked its way through Laverov's system and he dozed off, hypnotised by the endless white road through the forest.

He awoke just as they came out of the trees onto a flat expanse of land. Laverov peered through the dark at what he hoped was the confluence of the Mezen and Kimzha rivers.

'There,' Vladimir said quietly, pointing to a couple of pinpricks of light slightly to their right. 'Kimzha.'

Sometime in the last hour he had taken off his headphones and for the first time was looking haggard and worn. Above them the night had clouded and a few desultory snowflakes feathered their way to earth.

'Fifth house as we come into the village,' he announced confidently.

The idea of getting out of the snug warmth of the truck and going into a cold house seemed like madness, Laverov thought as he peered at his watch. It was twenty minutes past midnight. But when they located the large, two-storey log house a few minutes later, he was relieved to see that the lights were on and smoke was drifting up into the falling snow. He mentally awarded a Red Star to the police chief back in

Arkhangelsk. They stumbled through the snowdrifts to find the door unlocked and the house both clean and warm. A couple of beds had been made up and, after stoking the fire, they went straight to sleep.

The morning, when it eventually arrived, did little to disperse the cold mist that had enveloped the village in the night. It looks like my head feels, Laverov thought grumpily as he sipped the hot coffee after breakfast. As a cook Vladimir was a better driver.

'I'm going out for a while.'

Vladimir made to rise but Laverov gestured firmly that he should remain where he was. 'You might as well relax here. I hope this won't take too long and we can rest for the day and then head back tomorrow.'

He left before the driver could protest.

Kimzha was not what Laverov had envisaged. Somehow the last two centuries had passed it by and here, in this unlikely and inhospitable part of the world, he was suddenly in a Russia he had only read about. Despite the cold he stood transfixed by the sight of a farmer atop a pile of silage on a horse-drawn sledge. The horse's breath jetted dragon-like from its nostrils into the frost. There were no bells on the horse's traces and the apparition slid past in silence, vanishing into the gloom. Ahead of Laverov stood an exquisite church. He had thought that the huge log houses were impressive, but this was something from a fairytale: five towers and cupolas over a massive log structure. Above the square sanctuary flared four barrel gables, each with its own tower and cupola, the entire building held together by a tall central tower, its crowning cross lost in the mist. Hopefully, if his meeting with the elderly Mikhail Tarasov went smoothly, he would have time to visit the church.

Laverov didn't hold much hope of getting anything useful from the retired supply officer. Apart from the man's advanced years, and the problems that might cause his memory, his position would not have allowed him access to whatever secrets were buried beneath the mountains of files back in the locked room in Moscow. On the other hand, it seemed strange that Tarasov had chosen to hide himself away, so far from the rest of the world. The story about his brother-in-law may have been true and may explain the reason Tarasov came to the area, but it hardly explained his bunkering down in this isolated village.

It had been Laverov's intention to ask the first person he met to direct him to Tarasov's house, but apart from the farmer and his horse there wasn't another soul in sight. Laverov trudged down the street until he saw a woman hurrying along in front of him. The sweet yeasty smell that wafted in her wake suggested that she was delivering freshly baked bread.

'Excuse me,' Laverov called and the woman turned and waited for him to catch up. 'Sorry to disturb you, but I am looking for someone. I wonder if you can help me?'

'There's not many of us to choose from so it shouldn't be too difficult.' The face, wrapped in a woollen scarf, was lined and leathery but the smile was as warm as the bread smell that surrounded her.

'Tarasov, Mikhail Lvovich.'

The smile vanished from the woman's face and she crossed herself. 'He's not here.' There was no warmth in the voice now. 'Go back to Moscow.'

The woman scurried off along the street and turned down a small alley between two of the large wooden houses.

Laverov was stunned. It wasn't just the woman's claim that Tarasov was no longer in Kimzha but the look on her face — as if he had enquired after Stalin or the Devil. 'Shit,' he swore quietly, 'now what am I going to do?' And why had the mention of Tarasov elicited such a response? He shook his head and, pulling his coat tightly around him, walked on towards the edge of the village, following the tracks of the horse and sleigh. As he expected the farmer hadn't gone very far and he came across him at the open door of a small barn. Here the smell was not of yeast or bread but of dung and animals. The farmer was unloading the last of his load into a feed tray. From the relative warmth of the barn, half a dozen cows turned their large soft eyes in his direction and then returned to their feeding.

'Good morning,' Laverov said as he approached, determined not to get off on the wrong foot with the man and startle him.

The man grunted something and dug his fork deep into the silage. 'I thought there was foreigners about.'

'News travels fast even in Kimzha, eh?'

There was no reply for a moment as the man laboriously stripped off a pair of filthy gloves and proceeded to roll a cigarette. He lit it and then, as though suddenly remembering that Laverov was there, handed him the tobacco pouch. 'Hard not to notice when you make as much noise as you did last night.'

Laverov smiled. 'You don't miss much.'

'Not a lot to miss exactly. Place is pretty quiet, unless the priest has been at the vodka or the old witch Evdokia is in one of her moods and decides to take it out on her husband.' He spat in the snow.

'She gives him a hard time?'

'So she thinks. Poor fellow was killed in a logging accident over ten years ago. Evdokia has never forgiven him. She has a drink from time to time and the next thing you know the whole village can hear her yelling at him.'

'Sounds entertaining,' Laverov said lamely.

'Just the two of you this time?'

Laverov's fingers were freezing as he fumbled with the cigarette papers. 'So how could you tell there are only two of us?'

The man looked at him as if he was truly stupid. 'Only two sets of footprints, I reckon.'

'Ah . . .' Laverov nodded and tidied up the end of the cigarette. He hadn't really wanted one but didn't think the man was going to be able to avoid him while a stranger was holding his tobacco. 'I met a woman just now with some bread —'

'That's Evdokia.' The farmer exhaled a cloud of steam and smoke. 'You're lucky that she didn't give you the evil eye.'

'I think she did.' Laverov lit his cigarette and drew in a mouthful of acrid smoke. It tasted like the stuff the farmer was feeding his pampered cows. 'I said I was looking for Tarasov and she —'

'And are you?'

'What?'

'Looking for Tarasov?' The farmer held out his hand to retrieve his pouch.

'I only want to talk to him.'

The man thought about that for a moment as he tucked his tobacco away in his trousers then said dryly, 'Could be a little difficult.'

'Why?'

But the man knew he had the aces and he wasn't about to play them until he was good and ready. 'You are a policeman?'

'Retired.'

'Once a cop always a cop, I say.'

Laverov shrugged.

'You're not from Arkhangelsk either, I can tell by your accent.'

'Maybe you should have been the cop.' Laverov removed a strand of coarse tobacco from his tongue.

'No. I never liked cops.'

'Understandable,' Laverov said. Over the years the Soviet police had done little to endear themselves to the average Russian. 'So why would it be so hard for me to talk with Tarasov?'

'Wouldn't be too difficult if you were Evdokia.' The man spat again.

'Why is that?' For a moment he wondered if the farmer were simple, but then felt a chill run up his spine when he realised what the man was saying. 'You mean he's dead?'

'They don't get much deader.'

Laverov was suddenly furious, thinking of the deputy police chief in Arkhangelsk. That bastard must have known all along and had probably derived a great deal of pleasure from playing him for a sucker and sending him on a wild-goose chase to Kimzha. He forced down the impulse to swear out loud. 'Been dead long?'

'Does it matter? Dead is dead.'

'It matters.'

'I thought you lot were all one big happy family.' The man eyed him quizzically then added slowly, 'Stupid bastards came out in the middle of the last big storm. Said they just wanted to have a talk to him.'

'And . . .?'

'Seems he didn't want to talk to them. Shot himself. They buried him the next morning.'

'That would be . . .?'

'Yesterday. The ground was as hard as granite. Bastards should have left him till spring. Tarasov wasn't going anywhere.'

'Shit.' Laverov took a long drag and studied the cigarette's glowing tip. He could see the red flags, the fresh tracks in the snow. The temporary road — the *zimnik* — was carrying more traffic than this frozen hole warranted. Had there really been trouble getting a driver? Or were they keeping him on ice while the sanitation squad came in and cleaned up?

'Where is Tarasov buried?'

'There's only one graveyard. You can't miss it.'

'Beside the church?'

'Behind it.'

'Thanks for the smoke.'

'It'll kill you,' the man said dryly and retrieving his pitchfork started tossing the last of the silage into the feeder. Behind it the cows chewed their cud, clouds of steam billowing from their nostrils.

The driver Vladimir was not happy at the order to dig up the grave. Neither was the priest. But Laverov, fuelled by anger, was as impervious to their protests as he was to the cold. There was a stalemate while the priest remonstrated with him about desecrating the graveyard and Laverov countered by producing his letter of authorisation. The priest appeared singularly unimpressed by President Putin's signature, but when Laverov produced the remainder of the previous night's bottle of vodka he was granted access not only to the graveyard but also the priest's telephone. This latter concession was important as it was the only telephone in Kimzha.

'I need a pathologist and your best forensic team,' Laverov said as soon as he had Volodarsky on the line.

Volodarsky paused before replying and Laverov had the distinct impression that someone else was with him. Eventually he responded, 'What the hell is going on out there?'

'Tarasov is dead and I want an autopsy.'

'Dead? How?'

'Apparently he shot himself.'

'Then there's no need for an autopsy. I suggest you make your way back to Arkhangelsk and I'll look into it and forward the details to you.'

I bet you will, Laverov thought. Nice clean death certificate. No messy story of visitors arriving when the road was supposed to be impassable. 'No. I'm staying until I've seen the body.'

There was another pause and this time Laverov could hear a muffled conversation taking place.

'You're digging up the body?'

'As we speak.'

'You need authorisation for that, Laverov.' The tone was now openly hostile. 'I insist you stop immediately. I'm sending a team to —'

'I have all the authorisation I need,' Laverov said quietly and hung up. As an afterthought he pulled the phone socket from the wall and crushed the plug beneath his boot.

'The ground is frozen solid.'

Vladimir appeared to be making slow progress. Around him in the fading light stood a group of seven or eight locals. A bottle of vodka was being passed from hand to hand. There was no sign of the priest.

'Keep digging,' Laverov ordered and turned to the villagers. 'I would like one of you to take me to Tarasov's house.'

Old ways die slowly, he thought, as several of the older residents stepped forward. Authority only had to be assumed to work. He could have been a coal worker from the Ukraine, but if he used the right tone he knew he would be obeyed. He pointed to a fit-looking middle-aged man. 'What's your name?' He kept the tone official but friendly.

'Medvedev, Valentin Mikhailovich.'

'Then, Valentin Mikhailovich, you shall be my guide.'

There was nothing outside to distinguish the log house from any other in the village, but inside it was a different story. In the years that Tarasov had lived in the house he had occupied only a couple of the rooms: a living room and a bedroom. Both had been completely trashed.

'Must have been a very friendly chat,' Laverov said to Medvedev who, having taken off his cloth hat, was turning it nervously in his hands. He stood in the doorway, obviously shocked by the scene in front of him. 'Have you any idea who did this?'

The man crossed himself. 'No, sir.'

Laverov looked at him for a moment. No, he wouldn't know anything. Nobody ever did. He turned on the lights and spent the next hour sorting through the mess. It appeared that nothing had escaped the visitor's attention. Chairs had been smashed and their stuffing removed, drawers had been emptied of their meagre contents and even the wallpaper had been torn from the walls to reveal the sacking behind. This too had been slashed. He stooped and picked up a silver cigarette case. It was empty but undamaged. Whoever had done this to Tarasov had obviously been in a hurry if they had overlooked such loot. Laverov slipped the case into his pocket. The remains of Tarasov's life didn't amount to much — old newspapers, a few books and the bare essentials of existence. In the bedroom clothing had been tossed onto the floor and the single bed stripped and overturned, its wooden frame twisted, the headboard broken in two. Laverov wondered what they had been looking for and if they had found it. He supposed not. The violence of the search was too extreme, as though carried out in frustration. He also wondered why they had left the place in such a condition, knowing, as they must have done, that he was on his way and would inevitably end up here. Maybe that was it. Maybe they were saying 'look what we can do'.

In the wreckage of what had been a bedside table he found a torn photo of a young woman. The photograph must have been about fifty years old. The eyes looking out at him, faded and yellowed, held no answers, only questions. He held the pieces of the photograph together and turned it over. Whatever had been written on the back had long departed into illegibility. Some scraps of paper caught his eye but again revealed nothing. A postcard from Prague with a picture of the Charles Bridge, but no words on the back. The postmark indecipherable. Nothing.

Laverov was about to investigate the kitchen when Medvedev tugged at his sleeve. The man looked alarmed.

'What?'

'Sir . . .' He pointed to the ceiling.

'What is it?' Laverov demanded impatiently. Then he realised why the man was looking so agitated. They hurried outside into the now dark afternoon. The beating sound was growing louder and the throaty cough of the engine was unmistakeable.

The Hind came in low and fast over the village, its landing lights beaming down through the snow that swirled up from the rotor's downdraught. Damn it! He hadn't even considered the possibility that they would use a helicopter.

Medvedev stood transfixed on the doorstep, the look of hatred in his eyes a link back to some long-remembered and unforgiven incident. Whatever it was suddenly empowered him. Taking Laverov's arm, he propelled him down the steps and around to the side of the house. For a second they were illuminated in the fringe of a spotlight strong enough to cut through the flurries of snow. The sound of the Hind was now deafening and Medvedev had to yell to make himself heard.

'Come on! We have to get away from here.'

Laverov nodded and plunged after him, floundering through a snowdrift that lay across the laneway. When they reached the street that led to the graveyard he turned and watched as the helicopter circled the house. 'What the fuck do they think they're doing?'

But before Medvedev could answer the building was hit by two rockets fired in quick succession.

'Cleaning up the mess.'

The payloads had been incendiary and within seconds the village was illuminated by the flames roaring from the old wooden structure.

'Come on, I have to see the body before those bastards get there.'

But Medvedev shook his head. 'You want to end up like the house?'

Laverov peered at the man through the dark. He couldn't be serious? But then he felt Medvedev take his arm again and he was steered firmly towards the church.

'The body can wait. We have to make you disappear.' He pushed Laverov up the steps in front of him and then slipped around to open the heavy wooden door. 'Don't worry, they won't find you here.'

The only illumination in the sanctuary was from a small electric light that had been installed inside an older oil lamp with red glass. It looked out of place. Laverov followed Medvedev across the sanctuary floor to a small room at the rear. From there a ladder led up into a hole in the ceiling. It hardly looked like a secure hideout but he followed the man up until they came to a landing. A second ladder continued up, but Medvedev paused and pulled at what looked like a solid piece of timber. To Laverov's surprise, it moved to reveal a small niche in the wall.

'Inside,' Medvedev ordered. 'It's cramped but there's a seat. Just keep still and quiet. I'll be back for you after those pigs have gone.' And with that he closed the opening behind him, leaving Laverov to fumble for the seat.

He found a small wooden stool and sat, getting his breath back, calming his mind. After sitting in the dark for a couple of minutes he realised that the small cubbyhole was not as black as he had first thought. In front of him a small observation slit had been cut in the wall, through which — if he leaned forward and pressed his face against the logs — Laverov had a view down over the village.

The burning house was out of his line of vision to the right, but a pall of smoke drifted across the houses in his view. Then the lights of the helicopter illuminated the cemetery. The lone figure of Vladimir, if that was indeed his real name, was signalling to it to land. The small circle of villagers who, just minutes before, had been curious onlookers were nowhere to be seen. Hopefully they were locked safely in their houses, he thought, though the image of Tarasov's house in flames caused him to wonder if inside was indeed the place to be. The Hind came slowly down into a whirlwind of snow, its blazing lights creating a circle of light that reminded Laverov of the small glass snow-domes that the Moscow peddlers sold to tourists in the markets. You shook them and inside a miniature snowstorm swirled around a tiny model of St Basil's.

As the helicopter settled four men armed with machine-pistols jumped onto the snow and fanned out across the graveyard. Laverov sat back, suddenly scared. Obstruction or interference he could deal with — indeed had come to expect — but this was a very different game and one in which he suspected there were no rules. Below him the helicopter cut its engines and he heard the rotors slowly feather to a stop, leaving the village muffled in what now felt like a dangerous silence.

Twice in the next hour he thought he heard voices and occasionally a sharp cracking sound. His first reaction was that it was gunshots but he then realised it was probably coming from the blazing timbers in the remains of Tarasov's house. Now that the Hind's lights had been extinguished the only illumination was the flickering glow through the cloud of smoke that hung like a pall over the village. Despite the growing intensity of the cold Laverov didn't dare move around so he wrapped his coat tighter and made a conscious effort to move his toes within his boots in order to keep his circulation going.

For another hour he fought against the cold and his own fears, then he must have dozed off for the next thing he knew he was abruptly awoken by the sound of loud voices close at hand. There were people in the church.

He heard someone climb the ladder and held himself absolutely still as the person paused on the landing directly outside his hiding place. Then, to his relief, the steps continued up the next ladder to what he assumed was the bell tower. Heavy boots sounded on the wooden floor above before the searcher descended again, moving straight on past him.

Laverov let out his breath and leaned stiffly forward to check through the observation slit. The smoke from the fire still blanketed the area and light snow was falling from the darkness above. The Hind sat silently, but now the internal lights were on and as he watched a man came down the steps onto the snow and lit a cigarette. He paced impatiently as he smoked and constantly surveyed the perimeter of the graveyard. Then he spotted something and signalled to someone inside the chopper. Another man came to the hatch and stood watching as two armed men emerged from the dark and trudged towards them, their weapons held casually at their sides. With a great sense of relief Laverov realised they were preparing to depart. The engines coughed into life and a few minutes later the machine struggled into the air.

For what seemed like an eternity Laverov listened until he could no longer hear the Hind and the village had returned to silence in the angry orange light of the burning building. But still he remained seated while his mind played through every paranoid scenario it could imagine. They had left men behind. Another machine was on its way. The *zimnik* would be under observation and he would be killed as soon as he left the village. For a moment he wondered if he could repair the telephone connection he had so hastily destroyed. But he knew there was nobody he could ring. Given that the Hind had been working if not under the command of then at least with the tacit approval of the police chief in Arkhangelsk, he was the last person to contact. It was probable that Volodarsky was only a bit player in the drama, offering logistic support. Would they send more men by road? They would certainly have decided on some way of dealing with him. And who were they? Under whose command? A renegade group of the armed forces? Such a thing was possible given the low morale in most of the regular units. Many had not been paid for months and conditions were grim, and while there were few who remembered the painful fiasco of Afghanistan there were other open wounds, the Chechen campaign not least.

There were too many unanswered questions, Laverov conceded. The cold was killing him and he could no longer sit still. But just as he was struggling to his feet he heard a sound down in the sanctuary. He lowered himself onto the seat and waited. Someone climbed the ladder and then the entrance to the hidden space opened beside him, allowing light from a hand-held kerosene lamp to flood in. Holding it was Medvedev, his face drawn and grim.

'Come,' he said shortly. 'They've gone for the moment but I don't trust them not to return.'

'Who were they? Army?'

'Not the army I used to be in.'

He preceded Laverov down the ladder. Waiting at the foot of it were the priest and the farmer Laverov had met earlier in the day. Medvedev introduced him simply as Dimitrov. Without explanation they plunged out into the dark and cut across the graveyard.

'What happened to the body? Did my driver manage to dig it up?'

'Your driver was one of them,' the priest said. 'They disabled your truck and took him with them. They took the body as well.'

'I needed to see it —' Laverov began.

'No. I saw it before it was buried. Nobody needs to see such things.'

'And had he shot himself?'

'In the back and in the neck? Hardly,' the priest snorted.

'But why? What was Tarasov to them?'

'Nothing,' Medvedev said as they came out of the graveyard into a lane behind a row of houses. 'Tarasov was just an old man. Forget about him. It's you they're after.'

'Then why did they stop searching?'

'Because one of our young men went for a long walk into the forest. They followed the footprints for a while and decided you wouldn't survive the night. There's nothing out there for hundreds of kilometres. Nikolai doubled back through the trees and was home long before they were.'

They had come to a stop at the rear of one of the houses and they waited as the farmer climbed the steps and knocked gently. The door was opened and a plump woman let them in and ushered them through to a large kitchen. It was a relief to Laverov to be out of the cold, but more welcoming was the sight of the food and vodka on the table. The woman left them and for a while the men ate and went over the night's events.

The thing that struck Laverov most was the intense dislike of outsiders in general and the authorities in particular. Eventually he felt compelled to ask why they were assisting him.

The farmer, Dimitrov, having eaten was rolling a cigarette. He paused and looked at Laverov with a broad grin. 'If you were one of them we would take you out in the snow and let you freeze to death. But these people want you dead so much, it seems you must be one of the angels.'

Some angel, Laverov thought as he helped himself to a shot of vodka. Fool, yes. But not an angel. 'I take it they'll keep an eye on the *zimnik*?'

Medvedev nodded.

'But I can't stay here . . .'

'Where do you think you could go?' There was something in the priest's tone that sounded as though he were scoffing at this outsider. He had been drinking quite heavily since they had come into the house and now was sunk back in his chair looking decidedly morose.

Laverov ignored his remark. 'I have to get back to Moscow and I figure there is no way to do that other than through Arkhangelsk.'

'You could get to the railway station at Lomovoje — ' Medvedev began.

'How? Your angel has wings all of a sudden?' The priest rolled his eyes. 'Or maybe he could ski?' He turned on Laverov. 'You ski, do you?'

Dimitrov waved his hand in a placatory gesture. 'There is another way.'

Medvedev grinned. 'My thought exactly. I take it you have some warm clothes our angel can wear?'

Laverov didn't know whether it was the vodka or the warmth but he sensed he was missing something. 'What are you talking about?'

'Come, I'll show you.' Dimitrov picked up a lantern and led the way out the back of the house to a small shed. He slid a piece of timber out of the way, swung the door open and indicated that the others should step in. The place was obviously used as a storehouse. Garden implements competed for space with a couple of fuel drums, an old rotary hoe and some horse tackle that looked as though it belonged in a museum. The farmer stepped through the clutter and started to toss aside a pile of sacks at the rear of the shed. There was a chuckle from Medvedev as he uncovered a shiny black Lynx snowmobile.

The priest exploded. 'That's the one that was stolen from the timber company.' He grabbed Dimitrov by the shoulder and angrily swung him around. 'You swore to me that nobody in the village had anything to do with it.'

'Calm down, Father.' Medvedev pulled them apart. 'Nobody in the village knows about it except us.'

'That's not the point. It is theft and, in case you've forgotten, it's a sin.'

'The timber company hasn't paid us for last summer's work. So we liberated it. If they want to play the new age capitalists then they must accept everything from the capitalist system, not just the bits that they like.' Dimitrov shrugged himself free and began to clear a path for the machine.

'Property is theft.' Medvedev chuckled wickedly. 'This is property — we stole it.'

But the priest was not to be placated and, rather than become an accomplice, chose to stomp off. But he didn't go far; when they returned inside to complete their preparations they found him muttering to himself and nursing the vodka.

It was just before midnight when they set off. There had been a coin toss to select who would drive Laverov, the decision falling in favour of Medvedev who seemed pleased with the outcome. Warmer clothes were found, extra fuel strapped on board and the storage compartment under the double seat was packed with provisions. By the time everything was judged to be in order Laverov was exhausted and beginning to feel dubious about the entire undertaking.

Dimitrov, attempting to set his mind at rest, pulled out a map and pointed out the route he and Medvedev had been discussing. 'See, you'll stick to the rivers — the Kuloj, the Pinega and then from Ust' Pinega cross-country to Lomovoje. There's a train station there and you'll be on the express to Moscow before they realise you've left Kimzha.'

'How long?'

'The going is flat and, apart from snowdrifts, should allow you to maintain well over fifty kilometres an hour.'

'Have you ever travelled that far on one of these things?'

Medvedev let out a throaty laugh. 'Never. It will be a real adventure, yes?'

Laverov was still unconvinced. 'Won't they be watching the rivers?'

'Why should they? They don't know we have the Lynx.'

Despite his disapproval the priest gave them a drunken blessing and the quiet of the winter night was shattered as the Lynx roared to life. They could hear the damn thing in Arkhangelsk, Laverov thought grimly as he pulled a pair of goggles over his eyes, adjusted the scarf around his mouth and clambered on behind Medvedev. He didn't have time to wave goodbye because the snowmobile lurched forward and as they accelerated along the road all he could think of was hanging on for dear life.

They seemed to be travelling far too fast for safety and he felt that it was only a matter of time before Medvedev lost control of the machine. Yet the man appeared to know what he was doing, slowing each time they came across larger snowdrifts, and though they tilted alarmingly as they descended the bank of the Kuloj they didn't come to grief. Once on the frozen river Laverov began to relax and found, to his surprise, that he was actually enjoying the motion of the machine. The ice was covered by wind-compacted snow which rippled across the surface much like the desert sand Laverov had seen in travel documentaries. For a while the ripples caused the snowmobile to rock gently, but as Medvedev grew accustomed to the conditions and increased their speed the rocking stopped and they sped through the night, leaving a cloud of snow crystals in their wake.

He hadn't realised that he had fallen asleep until Medvedev shook him gently.

'You want to stay outside and freeze, Comrade?'

Laverov, suddenly aware of the silence, looked around. They had stopped by a small wooden hut in a clump of birches just up from the river. From inside the structure came a faint yellow light.

'Where are we?' Laverov asked.

'On track and on schedule — just south of the Kuloj settlement. I did a large arc around it and picked up the river again.'

'I mean . . . here. What's this place?' He got groggily off the machine and suddenly realised how cold and stiff he was. He stumbled and Medvedev took his arm.

'A loggers' summer hut. There's everything we need.'

Within fifteen minutes they had the potbelly stove roaring and laid out a couple of tattered mattresses they had found on the hut's single bunk. As they sipped coffee and wolfed down several slices of bread and jam, Medvedev talked glowingly about the snowmobile's performance, expressing surprise at its fuel economy.

'Of course we travelled pretty slowly, but I reckon we got about one hundred and fifty kilometres out of the tank . . .' He went on for a while about the Rotax 580cc engine but all Laverov could think of was how delicious the jam tasted and how inviting the mattress looked. Eventually they blew out the light and, despite having slept on the journey, Laverov went straight into a deep and dreamless sleep.

The morning was over when they woke. What there was of the sun had begun to slide from the sky and to the north a bank of clouds looked as though it was marshalling its energy for an assault on them later in the evening. They decided to move on immediately.

It was just as the sun was about to set that they ran into the problem. There was no warning. They didn't hear a thing. Coming round a slow bend in the Pinega River, Laverov, who had been nestled in behind Medvedev, knew nothing about it until the machine suddenly turned sharply, slid sideways and came to a halt.

'Fuck!' Medvedev yelled.

About a hundred metres in front of them a storm of snow was backlit by the sun, creating a rainbow halo of flying crystals. It would have been beautiful if not for the fact that the halo had a malevolent heart. At its centre was a helicopter gunship.

Laverov glanced along the river banks, but there was no way they could make a dash for it. Any forest that may once have been there had long ago been clear-felled. And it was a pretty good bet that beneath the snow lay a maze of tree stumps and old logs. There was nowhere to run. Medvedev had come to the same conclusion and with a shrug of resignation switched off the engine. They sat and watched as the gunship came slowly towards them and then settled on the ice. The hatches opened and a man in civilian clothes stood in the hatchway while three armed men dropped down into the snow. The men fanned out and advanced towards them, their weapons raised.

'Fuck,' Laverov said quietly.

CHAPTER FIVE

Jane? He peered at the faded photograph. Yes, it was definitely Jane. Just when he had stopped thinking about her, Teschmaker had found her amongst some personal papers tossed into one of the packing cases during his whirlwind cleansing of the house — his exorcism. Now, sailing on calmer waters, he had started to investigate just what had survived the massive clean-out. Putting things in order, he told himself. Cleaning up my act. There had been the normal collection of unfiled but now useless expenses claims — a hotel phone bill in this country, a currency exchange charge from another. Jane had come as a surprise.

For a moment his memory still refused to divulge her surname but then it came to him. Morris. Jane Morris. What had become of her, he wondered. Had she made something of herself, as his mother used to say. Teschmaker laughed bitterly. Successful self-creation was a rare skill indeed. He slid the photo onto his desk, intending to come back to it, but his imagination was hooked. Jane Morris. In the picture she was fourteen or fifteen years of age. And — he looked at his child-self — so was he. Their birthdays were only one week apart and it was because of this special bond that he and Jane had fallen in love. It had been a short and painful affair lasting probably no more than six or eight weeks. 'My first girlfriend,' he said out loud. Of course there was Ginger, but he had only been seven. He stored away the memory of Ginger for later retrieval.

The love affair had started at Jane's birthday party and lasted until the school holidays and a protective father took her away from him. He remembered the party and her mother's inappropriate fare — individual jelly rabbits with strawberry ice-cream, bread-and-butter triangles sprinkled with hundreds and thousands. Did such things still exist? Jane had been mortified and only regained her composure by raiding her mother's drink cabinet and adding a large quantity of gin to the otherwise innocuous fruit punch. It was a sleep-over party and they had, after the parentally supervised 'lights-out', played spin the bottle. Kissing Jane — not his first kiss, but the first one during which he tasted anything. The first one in which his tongue had been electrically engaged by another. Jane was a good kisser. Late in the night, when the other kids were asleep, she had sat down on the floor beside his sleeping bag and, emboldened by her consumption of gin, taken his hand and slid it inside her nightie so that he could feel how big her breasts were. The illicit nature of the experience had burned itself into his subconscious and even now, so many years later, he liked nothing better than the first touch of a woman's breasts while she was still clothed. A week later, at his own birthday party, they had another opportunity to further their new-found passion for bodily exploration and during the course of a late-night rendezvous Teschmaker had experienced his first spontaneous orgasm. It had been a revelation to both of them. It might have gone on if not for Jane's father . . .

Teschmaker picked up the photograph and studied it again. It was hard to imagine that he was the same person as the freckle-faced young man. In contrast, Jane at fifteen was no longer a girl but a young woman and he could imagine how she must look now. No, he told himself, you have no idea. She may even be dead. She may have developed leukaemia, died in a car crash or been disfigured and lived a short life in dreadful isolation. A more likely scenario was that she had grown up into a beautiful and successful woman, married, had two point three children and returned to whatever career she had carved out for herself. Teschmaker remembered her as self-confident, bright and with an at-times acerbic tongue. She was probably even more sensual as an adult than she had been as a provocative teenager.

There was something more, another memory, less well remembered, from his later teenage years. They had met once, by accident. He had been playing pool in a pub and had seen Jane at another table, had gone over and said hello. For some reason she had treated him very coolly. He remembered trying to get her interested in playing but she didn't know the rules and was, he realised, only spending time with him in order to infuriate the man waiting for her at the bar. He was a bit player in someone else's movie. There had been stories too about Jane being a hot little number in the ski hut with the older boys from university, but he couldn't recall the details. He sat with the photograph for a long time and eventually decided that, having nothing better to do, he would see if he could locate her and make contact. An amusement? A distraction? It didn't really matter; it was something to do.

In the morning Teschmaker awoke feeling better than he had in weeks. As if to complement his mood the weather had improved. It was the first day of summer. Where to start in his search for Jane Morris? The natural thing to do was to use the same spiral technique he had always employed in his insurance investigations — start at the centre and work outwards. But where was the centre?

A quick glance in the phone book showed him there were hundreds of people with the surname Morris. And, he counted carefully, forty-two with the initial J. He dismissed the notion of simply phoning them all. Her parents? Then he remembered the other bond between them: they both had fathers who had absconded. Jane's had gone not long after their short romance, vanishing in some quickly hushed-up scandal. Teschmaker's father was less decisive, disappearing for long periods to make his special pilgrimage to the bottle. On the odd occasions he returned home it was courtesy of the unfriendly constabulary or the over-friendly social workers who saw him through his seasonal dry spells in some clinic.

Eventually his father had settled into a Salvation Army hostel in the small country town of Austin-on-Lees which, by happy coincidence, shared a wall with the local pub.

Alexi Teschmaker's initial dismay at the strict instruction that no inhabitant of the hostel was to cross the threshold of the hotel was soon forgotten when, employing some long-hidden talent for joinery, he constructed a small hatchway that opened onto the side wall of the saloon bar where the tall bottles of beer were always chilled and ready. 'It even saves on having to buy a fridge. They keep the milk for my cornflakes in there as well.'

Teschmaker retreated from the recollection. He didn't mind memories as long as they remained ice-thin and over the years he had become a master at skimming over them. Darkness lurked beneath that surface and he had no intention of voyaging down in that direction. The Morrises had lived in Hitchon — his mind skipped adroitly back to the problem of tracing Jane — Hitchon, the suburb he had grown up in. Jane's mother had survived whatever scandal had engulfed her husband but she would probably be dead now. Jane's father had never reappeared and Teschmaker had grown up knowing that his whereabouts was not a subject discussed in polite society. He was probably dead as well. Then it occurred to him that Jane had suddenly switched schools. She had received a scholarship to Milton.

There were four residential suburbs that saw themselves as being a cut above the rest. Charlottewood, Milton and Drayfield boasted old money, old homes and tree-lined streets, and then there was Lakeside. You could buy your way into Lakeside, or be posted there to one of the embassies. And if you lived in any of *the* suburbs, there were only two schools: Milton and Drayfield. Nothing else came close. Milton College was an exclusive girls' school. The name was etched into his memory because of the scandals that had rocked the private school sector at the time. Three members of the equally exclusive Drayfield Boys' College were caught in a compromising situation in a girls' dormitory at Milton. The boys were suspended for a term, escaping expulsion as much on the grounds that they were members of the rowing eight as that their fathers were old boys and pillars of the society. The entire affair would have been hushed up by the tight-knit conservative establishment if it had not been for the incident in the chemistry lab. Three weeks after the initial incident a girl from Milton was rushed to hospital after an accident which the newspapers described as being of 'a sexual nature'. The broken test tube was removed from her vagina and she was quietly transferred to another school. The female chemistry teacher who — so it was stated in a leaked report — had been involved in the incident retired from teaching and moved overseas. At the same time several other girls were removed from the school by concerned parents who felt that the scandal might harm their daughters' career prospects. Unfortunately the media turned the scandal into front-page news which included an embittered disclosure from an unnamed girl who claimed that she was not the first to be expelled for pregnancy and yes, the father was a student from Drayfield. She wasn't certain which one because, so she claimed, it had been dark at the time and they had all consumed a fair amount of alcohol. The final blow was the death of the headmistress. She gassed herself in her car, leaving an extremely explicit diary which recorded her distress not only at general events but at the fact that the chemistry teacher with whom she had been having a liaison for five years had been betraying her with several of her students. Paradise lost.

'Good morning, my name is Jeremy Barclay, I'm phoning from Barclay, Lim & Brean. I'm currently handling an estate that includes a bequest in favour of a woman who is only identified as "my good friend Jane Morris from Milton College". I wonder if you would oblige me by putting me through to someone who can confirm that a woman by that name did indeed go to Milton, and if so possibly apprise me of a way of contacting her?'

The administration office at Milton was most obliging. Within minutes Teschmaker had more information than he had bargained for. The loquacious librarian knew everything there was to know about Jane Morris.

'Of course we are all very proud of Jane. Not only was she school captain and dux but she went on to get the university medal and . . .'

'Actually all I —' Teschmaker began but the librarian was in full flight.

'There are so few girls who excel right across the spectrum but even back then Jane showed she was one out of the box. Do you know, her two hundred metre butterfly record still stands?' Teschmaker had to admit he had been unaware of that. 'And the three years she was in the debating team are still the only time that we won the inter-college debating three years in a row. And of course we have all followed her career with great interest.'

'I'm sure you have. But all I really need to know is how to get in touch with Miss Morris.' Teschmaker repeated his story about the bequest from a deceased estate.

'Unfortunately we don't give out our old girls' addresses but I believe she now runs her own company.'

'Really?'

'Oh, yes. A *very* successful consultancy firm, from what we hear. Mind you, she no longer goes under her maiden name. After graduation she married Oliver Sinclair. That is *the* Oliver Sinclair . . .' The librarian allowed a generous pause into which Teschmaker inserted appropriately appreciative clucking noises. 'They were married in the College Chapel and there is the loveliest photograph in the yearbook.'

'And they are still married?'

He vaguely remembered Sinclair suing one of the tabloids for running a series of paparazzi shots of the magnate with some anorexic starlet or model, and of course there had been the famous incident with the Bulgarian diva. Sinclair could never have been called good looking but his wealth and power ensured that nobody ever used the word dumpy, at least within earshot. His face, round and full, was graced by the most outrageous walrus moustache that Teschmaker had ever seen. Mind you, as they hadn't been fashionable for as long as he could remember, he had seen very few. So Jane had married The Moustache . . .

'I should certainly say so.' Marriage breakups obviously were not a Milton thing. The woman's tone indicated how much she disapproved of even the veiled suggestion of divorce. 'After all, she is a Milton girl and I'm sure you are aware we strive to instil the highest standards of behaviour in our charges.'

'Thank you,' Teschmaker said. 'You have been of great help.'

'Not at all. It's been a pleasure.'

Oliver Sinclair? Well, she certainly had done okay for herself. Sinclair was one of the national success stories. Having taken on his family's already booming tube-making business a couple of decades back, Sinclair had diversified and, with the assistance of some canny takeovers and a measure of good luck, now had an empire with offices in three continents and interests in everything from telecommunications to aerospace industries. The magnitude of his wealth was a well-kept secret but his very public partying was as legendary as his trademark moustache. There had been an incident a few years ago which had captured the headlines. Sinclair had thrown a huge birthday bash for himself, the centrepiece of which was a private concert at one of the most upmarket resorts on an island famous for the opulence of its hotels. He hired a full orchestra and at great expense flew in a brace of internationally renowned opera singers. Apparently his birthday concert went off without a hitch. The trouble began with the after-show party. It had been billed as an enormous beach party but the five hundred or so musicians and guests soon spilled over from the beach. Someone decided that the sea was a little chilly for skinny-dipping so started the move to an adjoining resort which boasted the biggest outdoor pool on the island. The resort's unsuspecting guests were awoken in the middle of the night and peered over their jasmine and bougainvillea-draped balconies to witness what one journalist described in a frenzy of purple prose as 'an orgy that would have made Petronius blush'. All attempts by the resort's outnumbered staff to bring proceedings to a halt failed and — according to dozens of eye-witness reports — they, along with many guests and onlookers, actually joined in the debauchery. There was no police presence on the island and so it was only the natural limitations of the human body and the advent of dawn that brought things to a close.

It is doubtful that even Oliver Sinclair's vast wealth would have been sufficient to cover up such an event. Over the next few days it seemed that almost every visitor at the resort had video footage of what the tabloid press labelled the Birthday Bonkathon. One academic achieved his five minutes of fame on the talk-show circuit when he proclaimed the event the largest sustained mass copulation in modern times. The police played down reports that traces of methylenedioxymethamphetamine had been found in the punch served to guests on the night.

For his part Oliver Sinclair made no public comment. He made no comment at all; a fact that led several critics to suggest he had friends in high places covering up for him. It was only when the Minister for Immigration became involved that it came to light that Sinclair was missing. It transpired that one of the opera singers, a Bulgarian soprano travelling on a restricted visa, had failed to leave the country. Further investigation revealed that, as far as anyone could tell, she had even failed to make it down for breakfast on the morning following the party. On inspection her room was found to have been trashed in a manner the visibly shocked resort manager described as 'worse than the excesses of a certain notorious rock band'. The sheets were taken away for the forensic teams to examine and, to the embarrassment of everyone involved, the amateur video footage of the orgy in and around the pool — which up until that point had been digitally manipulated to disguise individual faces and genitalia — was revisited in an effort to establish the presence of Sinclair or the singer. Though it produced extraordinary evidence of both human inventiveness and stamina, it failed to reveal a single body part identifiable as belonging to either of the missing couple. The only result from the exhaustive police investigation was that three officers were recommended for immediate stress leave.

When a local fisherman's wife reported her husband's failure to return from a four-day fishing trip the police were slow to connect the events. By the time they did the woman had gone to the media, who were not as slow on the uptake and soon had several helicopters searching the area.

Nobody who saw the initial footage would ever forget it. It was hard for even the most politically correct to ignore the Bulgarian soprano's ample bosom and propensity for displaying an over-generous cleavage in her operatic performances. So the sight of her stark-naked imposing figure at the prow of the fishing boat raising a single defiant finger to the TV crews ensured massive ratings for the nightly news. 'The Flight of the Valkyrie!' the tabloids gleefully chorused. Most of the time Oliver Sinclair remained well below decks and as neither the fisherman nor the soprano seemed inclined to heed the attention of the media or instructions from the police helicopters a 'Bulgarian Stand-Off' ensued. In the end it took a boarding party of immigration officials with a warrant for her deportation to bring the tryst to a close.

Sinclair's enemies complained that the magnate had bought his way out of trouble and that the poor fisherman, in jail awaiting trial for obstructing the police in the course of their duties, was taking the rap for him. This point of view gained some credence when, a couple of days later, the singer was very publicly deported. She was farewelled at the airport by Oliver Sinclair and a small string quartet he had hired for the occasion. In a particularly poignant gesture he had bailed the fisherman and flown him and his wife down for the occasion.

Teschmaker's most enduring memory of the event was a remark made by Sinclair at the impromptu press conference held after the flight had departed. 'What were her final words to you?' asked an eager reporter, at which Oliver Sinclair had laughed long and hard. Finally, wiping the tears of mirth from his eyes and tweaking the ends of his moustache, he looked straight down the barrel of the TV camera and said with a perfectly straight face: 'I wouldn't know, would I? I mean, you have to understand the Diva speaks not one word of English and I not one of Bulgarian.'

Oliver Sinclair . . . Teschmaker wondered how Jane Morris fitted into such a world. Finding her would not present much of a problem as the Sinclair mansion — or 'Oliver's Taj' as it was referred to with varying degrees of sarcasm or envy — was a city landmark. Though he had been born and bred in a blue-blooded Charlottewood family — *the* Charlottewood Sinclairs — he had caused a scandal by eschewing his birthplace and buying a large plot of land on a rise overlooking the city's Botanical Gardens. A flurry of writs and protests ensued as various groups objected to what they saw as the bypassing of numerous planning and zoning regulations. In the end money and highly paid lawyers won the day for Sinclair. There were also those who objected on aesthetic grounds, but their arguments — based as they were on subjective judgments or architectural philosophy — soon retreated from the front pages and found themselves a home in obscure textbooks and university lecture notes. 'Palladio meets Gaudi — conceptually a post-modernist nightmare', as one professor of architecture so succinctly put it, was hardly the news grab the TV cameras were after.

As he did a web search for Jane and Oliver Sinclair, Teschmaker paused to wonder what it was in him that was fuelling his desire to find Jane. The initial stimulus had been the photograph and his natural curiosity. But now he realised his aim had grown; no longer was it simply the desire to locate and meet her. In fact, meeting her was slipping further and further down his agenda. What he really wanted was to know who she had become. They had both started from a shared base, socially, educationally, financially. Was discovering who she was now going to give him a clue about himself? He dismissed the notion. It would have made a nice neat piece of socio-psychological profiling, but it wasn't true. He was simply curious. And as long as he remained focused on her, his own demons would stay where they belonged — fettered deep underground in his subconscious.

'It's only because she's there,' he said out loud. 'Just like a mountain.'

The WebFerret search engine signalled that it had reached the outer limit of its parameters and recovered five hundred sites that contained references to Oliver Sinclair. That would be more than enough, Teschmaker thought. He refined the search, excluding the business and financial references, seeking only newspaper reports. Again there were five hundred. He clicked on *Find key word within results* and typed in the name 'Jane'. This time the WebFerret returned one hundred and eighty-three matches. Teschmaker poured himself a small glass of scotch and sat back to begin the long task of sifting through them.

The extraordinary thing about the articles on Mrs Sinclair was her absence. If the social columnists were to be believed, she was something of a mystery woman. Right from the early days, following the much publicised and photographed wedding, she seemed to have retreated into her husband's shadow. There were very few photographs that showed the couple together. This was even commented on by one society columnist who cattishly ascribed it to the disparity in their height and shape: Why would a pretzel pose with an olive? One photograph, a paparazzi shot, was of the two of them boarding a plane for a high-level meeting that Oliver Sinclair was to attend at a trade delegation in Moscow. Then there was a gap of several months before she was captured again at her husband's side as he received an award from the President for services to industry. Teschmaker peered at it. Even in this photograph Jane appeared to be a reluctant participant. Her dress and pearl choker spoke of wealth and style, but there was something about the averted eyes that drew him in. He slid the cursor over Jane's face and clicked to zoom in, but the image lacked definition. He returned it to normal size and stared at the photo. He had kissed those lips. His eyes went down to her neck. He must have touched it but he had no conscious memory of doing so. The breasts. He remembered her breasts. In the photograph they were obscured partially by shadow, partially by her husband's shoulder as she clutched his arm. Teschmaker remembered her nipples. He tried to imagine how they might be now. Had they been suckled by children? Did her roly-poly husband suckle them? Teschmaker felt the stirring in his groin and the thrill of pleasure as his erection pressed against the confines of his clothing. Do you still like them being touched, he wondered. He gulped at his scotch and clicked down to the next article.

Studying the photographs it became evident to Teschmaker that Jane had instituted a deliberate policy of avoiding the eye of the camera. There was a short report that mentioned a child, a girl named Melanie Louise, travelling with her parents to a conference at which her mother was giving a paper. Teschmaker read the article carefully, making notes of the few details included. The conference had been held in Washington almost a decade ago and hosted by an organisation called the Institute for Strategic Analysis. According to the report, Jane Sinclair's paper was expected to be a major contribution. She was not quoted directly but Oliver was, joking that he was pleased to be going along as babysitter. The accompanying picture was of Melanie and her father. No sign of Jane.

Teschmaker, released from the surge of sexual tension, was suddenly focused. He did a search on the Institute for Strategic Analysis and found an enigmatic website that simply pointed interested parties to a list of published research material available for purchase on receipt of a valid credit card number. Teschmaker scanned down the list but saw no sign of anything by Jane Sinclair. He made a quick note to himself to investigate her field of study and take a look at her thesis from the university. For the moment he had enough to go on. He knew where she lived and that was the centre from which he would spiral out until he had built a complete picture of Jane Sinclair.

Before switching off the computer he clicked back to the photograph of Jane with Oliver. He peered at the screen, trying to see what it was that she saw with those eyes. Why did she turn away? Was it shyness? He could hardly imagine that the outgoing teenager and apparently successful academic had become a shy mature woman. Was it simply a trick of the light, the camera catching her at the wrong moment? No; his instincts told him that she really had no desire to join her husband in the limelight he appeared to thrive in. And what did she think of his very public antics? Was she, as the librarian had suggested, a fine upstanding member of the community imbued with all the qualities that Milton College had instilled in her? The eyes seemed to be saying something. But tired, and with slightly too much scotch under his belt, Teschmaker knew he wouldn't find the answer by staring at the monitor.

CHAPTER SIX

Life is very strange, Laverov thought as he took his seat aboard the Czech Airlines flight to Prague. It was a notion he had been thinking about a lot in the last two weeks. For the first time in years he felt invigorated, as if the *Weltschmerz* that had insidiously invaded his life over the past decade was in retreat. Maybe it was the sense of danger that now surrounded his investigations, or that he had allowed himself to become involved to the point where he genuinely wanted to track down the ghosts he had unknowingly released. And they were still ghosts. For so long they had remained trapped in the files, safely hidden beneath black-ink erasures and the censor's scissors. In opening those boxes he had given them light and energy and now it seemed they demanded his attention. It was true that in the years before he had retired there had been some danger, but Laverov had never had the luxury of concentrating on a single case. It had always been a situation of competing demands — murders, rapes, robberies — all requiring more time and manpower than he had at his disposal. And there had been the politics of his own survival. The Party matters, the bureaucratic intrigues, the fight for resources. Now, for the first time, he could maintain a single focus and — if recent events were any guide — he had been granted backing, resources and a freedom of movement that previously would have been unheard of. Now all he had to do was follow the ghosts.

He settled back in the seat, relieved to see the doors close without a last-minute passenger arriving to take the seat next to him. Laverov had never enjoyed flying; not that he had done much. Maybe that was the reason for his unease — lack of experience. The few flights he had taken had all been with Aeroflot — not an ideal introduction to aviation. This time, however, he was relaxed, not by the fact he was flying ČSA — though that was a plus — but rather that his fear of flying had paled into insignificance next to what he had recently survived. He accepted a boiled sweet from the hostess and fastened his seatbelt. Was he still afraid of dying, he asked himself, after the evening on the Pinega River when he truly thought he was going to die? The answer was yes.

He and Medvedev had sat silently as the soldiers approached, knowing that there was nothing they could do to avoid capture. But it hadn't been capture at all.

'Which of you is Laverov?'

'I am.' Laverov stepped forward.

'Your friend can go. We'll transport you from here.'

Medvedev looked stunned for a moment and then shook Laverov by the hand. 'I don't know who the bastards were who were trying to screw you, but if you meet up with them give them one for me.'

He turned with a look of slight disbelief to the soldier. 'I can go?' He obviously expected to be shot in the back, for he zig-zagged wildly as he drove off.

The soldiers laughed and escorted Laverov to the waiting helicopter. Inside, the civilian shook his hand and indicated he should take a seat. He offered no name and Laverov asked for none. He checked that Laverov was securely strapped in and then, before taking his own seat, passed him a headset with a small microphone attached. Laverov put it on and watched as the soldiers prepared for takeoff. They went through their routines and settled into seats at the far end of the aircraft.

'The President apologises for the security lapse. It's being rectified as we speak.' The man's voice in the headphones sounded eerily disembodied and gave Laverov the feeling that he was speaking to someone else. 'Fortunately the deputy police chief in Arkhangelsk has a well-developed sense of self-preservation and though he was taken in by the criminal elements at first, he had the sense to do some checking.'

'Volodarsky? I thought he was in with them.' His own voice sounded frail and razor thin.

'There is a lot to criticise him for, but be thankful he contacted the authorities in Moscow. Your name is red-flagged and any enquiry gets passed right to the top.'

Laverov steadied himself as the helicopter lurched; he felt as though it was drifting sideways. Then he heard the pitch of the rotors change; as they bit into the cold thin air the machine lifted clear of its own miniature snowstorm and into the now dark sky.

'Why? I really have no idea what's going on.'

There was a sound like a chuckle. Maybe it was static. Then the man leaned over and handed him a slim folder. 'For your own protection. The less you knew the safer you were.'

'The last couple of days have stretched my definition of safety.'

'You were the tethered goat. We wanted to see what predators came sniffing around.'

Thanks, Laverov thought, I'm stranded in the middle of nowhere, damn near killed, dragged through the wilderness on a 'liberated' snowmobile and now I'm being called a goat?

'And who came sniffing?'

'Read the file. I'm afraid it stays with me.'

Laverov opened the folder and spent the next twenty minutes reading a report that left him feeling cold and sick. If the information was accurate then what he had been through was child's play compared with what the man he was reading about was capable of. The man was also one of the names on the list of those who had requested access to the documents in the boxes he was studying in Moscow: the ex-member of the Duma, Oleg Rusak.

'The money that bought him his seat in the Duma was Mafia money. God knows how many people were killed along the way,' explained the voice in Laverov's headphones.

'But why go into parliament when he had his own crime empire?'

'Who knows? Power? Vanity? Contacts?'

'So with all this —' Laverov pointed to the folder '— why not just arrest Rusak?'

'Because he is after something we are after.' There was a long pause and then the man added, 'We hope he can lead you to it.'

'Rusak is listed as one of the people who sighted the documents I'm studying in Moscow.'

'Yes. We suspect he is responsible for the missing files.'

'I need to know about the project referred to in the files, otherwise I'm flying blind.'

This time the silence was longer. Then the man took back the folder. 'I'm sorry, I can't tell you more at this stage.'

'It makes my job nearly impossible,' Laverov protested.

'It would make it harder if you knew the full picture.'

That didn't make sense. Blundering around in the dark was easy? Since when? It had damn near got him killed. 'Why?'

Again there was a burst of static in his headphones. It might have been a laugh.

'If you knew the whole picture I doubt you would want to be involved.'

'I have a choice?'

'Well, let me say that I think the time has come to untether you.'

No need to keep the goat tethered once the predator has got the scent. Not a nice position to be in. He was about to suggest that they should find someone else but he had the distinct feeling that retirement was not an option.

'What is Rusak like? Everything in there is fine but it doesn't tell me much about his personal likes and dislikes.'

'He's a sadist in the real sense of the word. He likes inflicting pain and watching it inflicted by others. There has been a suggestion that Rusak is making snuff movies and certainly he has been involved in importing S&M porn from wherever he can get it.'

'You're suggesting that he doesn't do this just for the money . . .?'

'Money is the last thing he needs. He does it for kicks; some sort of sick addiction.'

There was a sudden change in the noise of the rotors and Laverov leaned sideways and peered through the small window. Below them was an unfamiliar landing strip. They landed with a rather solid bump and five minutes later he was being bundled across the tarmac to a waiting military jet. The civilian wasn't coming along on this leg of the journey but he explained that Laverov would be escorted safely back to Moscow.

'Study your target. Get to know everything about him but don't get too close yourself. We have our own man on the inside and he says there is a chance Rusak may be going to the Czech Republic. We need to know why.'

Thanks, Laverov thought bitterly, now I'm an untethered goat with a mission.

* * *

In Moscow he continued his searching through the boxes of documents. He knew it could take months but he worked longer and harder than before, aware that every day he remained in the dark was another day that Rusak was moving further away from him. There was one consolation. The surly and suspicious Kozlovsky had been quietly removed; his replacement was an elderly woman who, like Laverov, was old-school KGB. Anna Naryshkin did her work, filed his reports and made him the worst coffee he had ever drunk. It was just like the old days.

It was a week after his return from the north when Laverov discovered 'The Professor'. At first he thought he was just another inconsequential player, but as he cross-referenced the code name against the project locations he found the name listed more than once and every reference carried a notation pointing to a major file on the man. But that file was missing. Then Laverov came upon a travel authorisation on which someone had scrawled the words: *Who granted this and why?* It appeared that the Professor had left the country. Laverov was about to toss the file to one side when he noticed the date and destination. The application was for travel to the Czech Republic. Just as interesting was the fact that the date of the travel request was exactly one week after Rusak's application to view the files. It raised the very interesting possibility that the Professor had been tipped off. He could not have been unaware that the project had developed a very high mortality rate. He was warned;

he fled. And later some bureaucrat was reprimanded for authorising his decampment to the Czech Republic.

Two days later Laverov had the man's name and address. He was living in Mariánské Lázně — Marienbad — under the name Karel Schmidt.

Ruzyně airport is seventeen minutes from the city centre and the driver from the Russian Embassy, obviously under instructions not to talk, made the journey in silence. This was fine by Laverov, who was enjoying the scenery and feeling elated at being a tourist even if only temporarily. He would have been content to drive around all day, taking in the sights and tasting the local *pivo*. Unfortunately the driver took him straight to Praha-hlavní nádraží where he deposited Laverov, breaking his silence only to inform him that he had a two-hour wait for the next train to Mariánské Lázně. Laverov had been supplied with what felt like a generous amount of local currency so, not having eaten on the flight, he went to the restaurant on the top floor and treated himself to *drštková polévka*, tripe soup, and the *pivo* he had been craving — a mug of excellent Budvar, the original and only real Budweiser. It certainly tasted nothing like the sweetened cat piss a visiting American had once insisted he try in Moscow.

The 190-kilometre train trip to Mariánské Lázně took only three hours but instead of being allowed to relax he was interrupted several times by a couple of officious conductors who questioned his reservation, his ticket and his passport. The only problem Laverov could see was that he was Russian and these Czechs had long memories. He was relieved when they finally pulled into the station.

Why had the Professor chosen this place, he wondered. Maybe he had a health problem. Certainly his colleagues who remained in the Soviet Union had developed one, Laverov thought grimly as he bordered trolleybus No 5 along Hlavní třída to the town centre. The resort itself looked tired and worn, a far cry from the romantic vision Laverov had in his head after reading the Goethe elegy that had added to the town's fame. The yellow facades were weathered and in need of a touch up and the rundown atmosphere of the town was not assisted by the chill wind and low cloud that shrouded the surrounding wooded hills.

After checking in at the Hotel Atlantic he strolled across the road, climbed a set of stairs to the Jalta vinárna and ate a reasonable meal. As he ate he consulted a tourist map of the town and decided that as it was just after 5 pm and the evening looked as though it was promising rain, he would take a taxi. He wrote down Karel Schmidt's address on a napkin, finished his beer and went down to the street. The promised rain had been downgraded to a misty drizzle.

'You're Russian, no?' The taxi driver was young and despite the cold was dressed in jeans and a T-shirt with the word Xtasy emblazoned across the front in bright green letters.

'How can you tell?'

'Your clothes,' the taxi driver said sympathetically.

Was it that obvious? After his experience with the conductors on the train he had hoped to avoid the Russian label. Fortunately the taxi driver was too young to remember Dubček and the night of

28 August back in '68 and seemed happy to practise his stilted Russian on his passenger.

Karel Schmidt's house was nestled amongst pine trees with a view down over the town. Laverov had no real idea what the man had been running from but it looked like the kind of place he would have chosen had he been in Schmidt's position.

'Could you return for me in an hour?' Laverov handed the driver a reasonable tip and watched as the notes were carefully counted.

The young man nodded. 'I'll be back and wait for you.'

Laverov paused until the taxi had gone then opened the latch on the gate and walked up the stone steps to the large gabled cottage. It looked like a miniature version of a Swiss chalet. The place was in darkness. After knocking and getting no response, Laverov walked around the side of the house. Two shirts and a pair of trousers hung damply from a line. They looked as though they had been there for some time. He spent a few minutes investigating the backyard. The place was tidy and well looked after. A small woodshed was well stocked and smelled sweetly of pine resin and at the rear of the house a neat terraced garden looked as though it was ready for the coming spring.

Laverov knocked on the rear door but again there was no movement from inside. He tried the handle and to his surprise found it open. Maybe one of the benefits of living in Mariánské Lázně was not having to worry about locks, he mused; in Moscow they would steal the door. He swung the door open and called out. Nothing. He stepped through the entranceway and fumbled for a light switch but there didn't appear to be one. Then his hand brushed a cord; he pulled it down and a small low-wattage globe flickered to life.

'Oh shit.' He gazed in disbelief at the scene in front of him. It looked as though a tornado had struck the place — a replica of the sight which had greeted him in Tarasov's house in Kimzha. Laverov stepped over the remains of a chair and made his way gingerly to the other side of the room and pulled open the curtains. Night was falling quickly and he wanted to keep an eye on the front of the house so that he could see the lights of the taxi when it arrived. He turned back to the scene of devastation and began to carefully pick his way through the wreckage.

Each room of the house had been treated in the same manner; the entire place had been pulled apart and smashed to the floor. There was something odd about it but it took Laverov a while before he realised that what he was seeing was not the evidence of a thorough search but a rampage of destruction. Worryingly, he also found traces of dried blood on the floor of the bathroom.

In the kitchen every plate, saucer, jar and bottle had been smashed. The contents of the fridge were scattered amongst the debris and to his horror he found the body of a ginger cat — its head had been completely obliterated. Laverov crouched down and studied the cat in an attempt to work out how long it had been dead. He guessed no more than a day, maybe two at the outside. It was as he was about to stand up that he noticed the newspaper cutting. The top portion of the paper was badly stained but holding it under the light Laverov realised that he had just had a stroke of luck. The clipping was from a Moscow newspaper and showed a short overweight man with an outrageously drooping moustache. He was flanked by a tall elegant woman on one side while on the other, grinning at the camera, was Oleg Rusak. The paragraph below described 'the friendly welcome extended to the industrialist Mr Sinclair and his wife by parliamentarian Oleg Rusak'.

The peculiar thing about the photograph was that someone had used a blue pencil to circle one of the figures — that of Mrs Sinclair.

CHAPTER SEVEN

He had forgotten just how grotesque Sinclair's home was.

Teschmaker had decided to ease himself into the surveillance, as though it were a treat to be savoured in small portions rather than devoured in one sitting. Consequently he had avoided the front of the mansion, opting rather to take a stroll through the Botanical Gardens and reacquaint himself with the house from the face that it presented to the public. It was not exactly as he remembered it, but then he acknowledged that he was viewing it with a very different mind-set from when he had last seen it, being more interested now in its effect on those who inhabited it rather than its exterior. But despite his altered focus the exterior still had the power to instil in him a sense of disquiet. In the intervening twenty years the trees had grown and now the alternating yew and cyprus softened the impact of the building's grotesquely sculptured facade. The arcs of columns appeared to mirror the semicircles of trees, as though they had grown as stone shadows of their living counterparts. The huge concave windows, shadowed by the curved entablature which supported the domed roof, seemed to Teschmaker like grossly hooded eyes, sunken and misshapen. The domes — which ranged from cruel mockery of the golden onions of the Kremlin to perverse beehives — had been softened by pollution, lichens and moss over the years and now looked less harsh than he remembered. The much-criticised roof sculptures that were in fact chimneys still stood like ancient travellers from Greece and Rome lost between the domes, their sooty apertures as intriguing as they were bizarre. In the early morning only one of the six chimneys was actually in use, but the sight of the smoke pouring from Medusa's mouth brought a smile to Teschmaker's chill face. Was Jane in there by the fire in a dressing gown? Was she drinking coffee from a bowl? Was her child still living at home? Melanie would be fifteen now. It hadn't escaped his notice that this was the age Jane had been when they had enjoyed their short romance.

Returning to his car Teschmaker drove around to the cul-de-sac where huge gates guarded the entrance to the mansion. The gatekeeper's house, constructed in the style of a Karelian slab church, differed from its ancient ancestor in that the slabs were hewn not from spruce or birch but hard red granite carved to look like timber. Knowing he would attract no attention, Teschmaker pulled in behind an early morning tour bus which was lingering while its occupants took photographs. Walking over to the gates, he peered down the driveway past the gatekeeper's house. If the twin scoops on the Botanical Gardens side of the building had resembled giant eyes, then the single scoop at the centre of this side was a gargantuan mouth, the columns like broken teeth spat out onto the lawn in front of it. The multifaceted windows bubbling up and out from the huge brass front door glinted in the morning sun like crystallised saliva while the driveway snaked towards him like a probing tongue. It must, Teschmaker thought, be a very strange sensation to walk up that driveway and through the entrance. One would feel engulfed by the house. Consumed.

Again it was obvious that the trees had grown but here, set back on the garden's boundaries, they had failed to soften the impact of the architecture. The sweep of columns leading from the house to the gateway increased in size as they arced in, producing an almost dizzying reverse perspective. Teschmaker wondered what had inspired such a grotesque statement. The columns nearest the gate were crumbling, obviously meant to look like the shattered remains of some ancient structure, but the nearer the house they got the more intact and larger they became. It was as though Sinclair were saying 'I have reversed the process of decay'.

Teschmaker was walking back to his car when he heard the hum of an electric motor. He turned to see the huge iron gates slowly opening. Moving quickly he got in and started the engine. As he did so, a royal blue Rolls Royce purred out of the driveway, a uniformed chauffeur at the wheel. Although the rear windows were tinted Teschmaker thought he glimpsed two people in the back seat. He had not intended to do more that morning than check out the house, but decided that he might as well tag along and at least get an idea of Sinclair's routine. There was also a good chance that Jane was one of the passengers; if so, he might save some time and find out where it was she had her office.

To his surprise the car did not turn into Fitzgerald Drive and head towards the central business district but cruised up the slip road onto the Mitchell Freeway. Intrigued, Teschmaker slotted himself into the traffic, allowing a two-car buffer between him and the Rolls. Even though it was just after the morning peak hour there was still a fair amount of traffic on the road, but most of it was heading in the opposite direction, into the city. For a moment Teschmaker thought they must be heading out to one of the industrial suburbs, maybe to one of Sinclair's factories in Claymont or South Pendle, but they turned off at the Belmont exit, dived under the freeway and headed towards the river that divided middle-class Belmont from the upper-crust enclave of old money that was Charlottewood.

As they crossed the Charlotte River Bridge and entered broad tree-lined Lombard Avenue, Teschmaker was forced to slow down. There was now only one car in front of him and he knew it was a fair bet that someone like Sinclair would employ a driver trained in spotting any kind of surveillance. He dropped further back but kept the Rolls well in sight. Ahead the Rolls signalled and made the left-hand turn into Haycroft. This was unfamiliar territory and Teschmaker knew he was certain to be noticed. Then, as the chauffeur pulled in at the side of the road in front of a high wall that almost completely obscured the bluestone house beyond, Teschmaker saw the answer to his problem. Two houses further along the street on the same side was a discreet 'For Sale' sign. He drove past, parked and taking a notebook from the glove box got out and made a show of writing down the number of the real estate agent. In the meantime, the chauffeur had gone to the rear of the car and was opening the door. Teschmaker felt a surge of excitement. Surely this would be Jane.

It was and it wasn't. Dressed in a Milton College school uniform the young woman was, even from a short distance away, the spitting image of her mother. For some reason she was being dropped off. Her father remained in the car. Then, as Teschmaker pretended to look at the house in front of him, he saw a tall, elegantly dressed woman come over to the car. There was no doubt in his mind. This was Jane. The rear window came down and she exchanged some words with the man Teschmaker suspected was Oliver Sinclair. Jane straightened up, took the girl's elbow and guided her in front of her through the gate in the fence.

Teschmaker was jubilant. He was feeling an almost childlike pleasure in uncovering who Jane had become, and now he not only had a centre to start from but the added mystery of why she was apparently living in a separate house. There had been not a hint or whisper of marital disharmony in any of the press clippings that he had scanned. Though given Oliver Sinclair's playboy lifestyle, it surprised him that the gossip columnists hadn't speculated on the possibility. It was as though Jane was a no-go area and the media left her alone. Strange, he thought.

A black Ford cruised slowly past, the lone occupant taking a long look at the house for sale. Out of your price range, Teschmaker thought. Even the bottom end of this market would drive Mercedes or BMWs. He waited until the Rolls had pulled away then got back in his car and tried to decide on his next move. He was tempted to wait and see where Jane went to, but knew he had been a little too exposed to risk picking her up from his present position. The other option was to go and get some breakfast. Ahead of him the Ford driver turned around and came slowly back along the street. He probably wants to have a closer look, Teschmaker thought, so decided to get out of the man's way. The breakfast option won the day.

Later in the morning he decided to see if he could track down the consultancy that the librarian had mentioned. He instituted a computer search of listed company directors but Jane Sinclair was not registered. On instinct he deleted Sinclair and replaced it with Morris and was immediately rewarded. Jane was one of two directors in a company called Strategic Options. The other director was listed as Sarah Norrby. Teschmaker smiled. The old girlfriends had got together. Sarah's parents had migrated from Sweden in the 1950s and at school the two girls had become inseparable. Outside of his contact with Jane, Teschmaker had met Sarah only a couple of times and once made the mistake of asking her out. It had been in the aftermath of his romance with Jane and Sarah had given him short shrift. 'How could I go out with you? What would Jane think?'

What on earth, Teschmaker had thought. Would she even have cared? At that stage Jane had stopped taking his phone calls and started going out with a creep from university who smoked a pipe and wore a duffel coat and brothel-creepers.

Brothel-creepers. Suede shoes with thick rippled crepe soles. Teschmaker's father was wearing them the stormy last night they visited Ginger Mick at the Miners' Rest in Keynes. They had been on holiday together, father and son in the old miner's hut the family had purchased some years before. The holiday was a ritual, a repayment for the neglect, made up for by over-indulgence and a week of being spoiled rotten. His father, Alexi, was in those days a tall man whose stoop still lay some years in the future. Under his shirt the pallid flesh was soft and smooth, a marked contrast to a face worn and creased by too much sun, cigarettes and booze — a cartographer's nightmare of rivulets, ravines, small pockmarks, craters and stubble. High cheekbones were the only sign of his Russian heritage and the eyes — deep dark pools, liquid, rheumy, forever darting over your shoulder looking for another chance. At ten, Martin loved his father. Loved him, and understood that a week was all he was good for. More than that and he would be back on the bottle, ranting and lecturing him about his mother's selfishness.

'You want to go see Ginger?'

They always did. It was just a matter of timing. They had been inside the shack all day, stoking the fire, playing cards; breaking only to make sandwiches or dash out into the rain for an armful of firewood. The wood and fibro cottage shuddered and creaked in the wind and when the heavens opened up the drumming on the roof was deafening. Whenever the rain was really heavy they played the game of pretending to be shouting to each other, feigning puzzlement at the other's inability to hear. They laughed until their stomachs hurt and yet they also mouthed words that would otherwise have been left unsaid. *I love you*, his father mouthed.

You too. Martin formed the words silently. Wanting to scream them.

'Can I have a sarsaparilla?'

'You think you're old enough?' His father made his usual joke.

They checked the fire, put up the spark-guard and, after wrapping themselves in their oilskins and scarves, plunged out into the wild west-coast night. As they entered the forest the storm seemed to retreat, the tossing tops of the trees creating a zone of eerie dripping silence. His father, torch in hand, strode fast over the soft forest floor while Martin loped along behind, keeping his eyes fixed on the path, aware of the roots that snaked out and curled around themselves, sometimes holding small pools in their folds. Even on dry days the litter of beech leaves was soft underfoot. Now, glistening and wet, it squelched beneath his father's thick crepe soles.

A few minutes later they emerged from the forest onto the cinder path that led across the railway tracks to the town's main street. There was electricity but the few remaining houses set between the railway and the main street had, by some unspoken convention, opted for kerosene lanterns. The soft golden glow of the lamps slipped out between tattered curtains and escaped through gaps in weatherboards long past their replacement date. Mining for gold had fizzled out some years before and the few remaining ore wagons, now rusted to the tracks, held nothing but ragged weeds. The coal bunkers were empty but a large floodlight still illuminated the yard, silhouetting the water tower, the remnants of a canvas hose flapping from a gantry above their head. A train signal, rusted at half-mast, had slowly tilted over during the years of neglect and now stood like some uneasy sentinel.

Teschmaker shivered, pulled the hood of his parka around his face and stepped carefully over the lines and rotting sleepers. 'Watch out for trains!' his father laughed, waiting for him in the lee of the signaller's hut.

A century before the main street of Keynes had been a bustling centre, boasting a bakery, draper, dentist's and doctor's rooms, two general supply stores, a whorehouse, postoffice, two banks and six hotels. Now it had shrunk to one general store and, flanked by empty shells of buildings, the dilapidated Miners' Rest. The nearest police station being fifty miles away, trading hours were regulated by demand rather than statute. Stepping around the potholes in the road they climbed the steps onto the hotel verandah. It was only six thirty, but from the array of coats and oilskins already hanging on the old brass hooks it appeared that the entire town was ensconced for the evening. Martin and his father shook the rain off their wet-weather gear, hung them up and made their way into the thick smoky atmosphere of the pub.

Since the West Coast Highway bypass had been built a decade earlier, few people bothered to make the detour to Keynes. There was nothing there. The locals, unable or unwilling to sell their homes, had banded together, like shipwreck survivors, and yet accorded Alexi Teschmaker and his son some respect for swimming against the tide of history. They greeted them cheerfully and returned to their drinks. Martin found himself a seat and watched as his father went up to the bar. He was frightened of the hotel owner, a huge man with the roundest face he had ever seen. Somewhere in a shady past he had lost the sight in his left eye and it now seemed to have a life of its own, flickering and darting uncontrollably. On account of this he had picked up the nickname Flecker-eye-Pig. Usually he was addressed simply as Flecker-eye but didn't seem to mind what you called him as long as you paid for your drinks as they were served. Martin didn't like looking at him but was, at the same time, fascinated. Flecker-eye must have sensed it and was given to walking up behind the boy and tousling his hair. Martin turned his chair sideways, which took the hotel owner out of his direct line of sight but left him in a position to see if he was being advanced upon.

'Evening, Alex, nice drop of weather.' Flecker-eye fixed Teschmaker with his good eye. 'The boy let you out, huh?'

'Yeah.' Alexi grinned. 'As long as I buy him a sarsaparilla and let him flirt with Ginger.'

'Like father like son, huh?'

'Not quite. I'll have a bottle.'

Flecker-eye poured the sarsaparilla, dropping in a couple of ice blocks and a blue straw. 'Ginger's not in yet.' He flipped the top off a tall bottle of beer and inverted a glass over the neck. 'But she'll be here.'

Father and son didn't talk much in the pub, content to sip their drinks and listen to the chatter around them. The locals were a strange bunch, all of whom they knew by sight but only a few by name. The Couch brothers, red-haired twins in their sixties, were the last of the old-style prospectors. Secretive and monosyllabic, they huddled in the far corner of the pub, staring into the fire, dreaming of ore bodies. Neither man had ever married and both were so shy with women that they even avoided looking at Ginger, though local gossip had it that one of them had slept with her twenty years before and the other brother had beaten him severely and not spoken to him for over a year. It was probably true.

Peter Svoboda had spent years in the merchant navy before running foul of the authorities over the importation of some forbidden substance. Seven years in a correctional institution had given him his land-legs and he had turned up in Keynes with all of his worldly possessions loaded into the back of a battered Rolls Royce Silver Cloud. It took him five years to restore the car and they were still waiting for him to put the cladding on the back of his house. Svoboda never left town yet always had cash in his pocket. Rumour had it that he kept a sizeable stash of money buried somewhere nearby.

Old Jack and Mary Verdugo ran the store. Simon Chalk told everyone he was a poet, but nobody had seen a word he had written, and of course there was Ginger.

If Ginger Mick had a real name certainly nobody in Keynes had ever heard it. Her attitude to her personal history was pretty casual. Sometimes she would claim to have worked in the 'US of A' and at others she would sigh and say how much better times had been when she was in Paris. The truth was that she had probably never been out of the country, but nobody cared. Everyone in town loved her and most of the men were occasional clients. 'Everyone's welcome but nobody's free,' she liked to chime. Now over forty, she was the first to admit that she was past her prime but 'I've still got it and it works for me. How about you hon?' When the main road bypassed the town so did Ginger's passing trade but, to the relief of most of the town's dozen or so men, she had decided to stay. Martin Teschmaker was seven when he first met Ginger. She had proclaimed him 'adorable', bent to kiss him and then, in a moment of bliss that remained with him for years, she turned his head to give him a good look straight down the neck of her low-cut dress before pulling his head in to her ample bosom.

'Another sars?' His father's voice interrupted his fantasising.

'Sure.' He glanced at the amount of beer left in his father's bottle and was relieved to see that he was on his good behaviour, sipping it slowly, making it last.

As his father rose and headed to the bar there was a flurry of movement at the door and the subject of Martin's musing swept in. Ginger, her teased-up red hair flecked with rain, held the door open and ushered in a stranger. Silence engulfed the room like a wave.

After dark, midweek, lousy weather and someone had driven into Keynes?

'Everybody! This is Malcolm,' she announced. The man, mid-thirties, obviously from the city, glanced around nervously, a look on his face as though he had walked into a waxworks display that had suddenly come to life.

'Hi.' The voice was pinched and a little too high-pitched.

'Unfortunately Malcolm's car has run out of gas.'

There was a general sigh in appreciation of the unfortunate nature of the situation.

Ginger beamed, playing the house, playing the moment. 'I told him that fortunately the general store sells petrol.'

Nods of agreement and someone called out, 'Exactly right.'

Ginger paused for quiet then, winking at Old Jack and Mary, continued, 'Unfortunately, it seems that the general store is closed and won't be open until tomorrow.'

'Yes, tomorrow . . .' came the chorus.

'So,' Ginger worked herself up for the climax, 'Malcolm has agreed to stay here for the night.'

There were cheers all round as Ginger guided her catch to a table and, not wanting to let him out of her clutches, signalled to Flecker-eye for previously unheard-of table service.

Martin was disappointed that Ginger hadn't come over to say hello but sensed that something else was happening. He turned to his father to ask him what was going on but his father pre-empted him, touching him on the arm and whispering, 'I'll order us a couple of chops and chips. I think we're in for some fun.' He wasn't wrong.

It took Ginger Mick less than three drinks to get Malcolm up the stairs. As she shepherded him in front of her she turned and made a furtive bow to the crowd below, giving them a thumbs-up. She vanished from view and there was a scurry of activity. Martin watched in amazement as a blackboard was rapidly erected at the back of the bar. Peter Svoboda, being the most agile, clambered up on a chair and hooked a string to a small ring hanging down from a hole in the ceiling. Flecker-eye had moved quickly from behind the bar and was collecting bets from the patrons.

'What is it?' Martin asked, pointing to the object now hanging from the string. It appeared to be a large penis cut from plywood and painted in gaudy Day-Glo pink.

'Shh, just watch.' His father took five dollars from his pocket and pressed it into Flecker-eye's hand. 'Number three.'

'Why does everyone rate poor Malcolm so low?' Flecker-eye feigned innocence.

Behind the bar the dart scores had been erased from the blackboard and replaced with a large zero at its centre, above and below which ran a line sectioned off with small marks scaled from one to twenty in both directions. The penis — Martin was now convinced that it was such — was suspended alongside the central zero. Drinks were recharged and the bar fell silent. Mrs Hong made a rare appearance from the kitchen and signalled to Martin's father that he would have to wait for the food until the fun was over. She handed Flecker-eye twenty dollars and took a stool at the bar.

For a while nothing happened but then there was a murmur of excitement as the wooden penis shuddered then lurched up and down. All eyes were on it. As it came to life, Peter Svoboda, who was positioned beside the blackboard, added a mark in blue chalk at the upper and lower points reached. For the first few minutes it bounced up and down between the one and two . . . then a cheer from Martin's father as it touched the threes. But that was as good as it got. Unfortunately five people had bet on the same number, however his father still pocketed fifteen dollars and bought them both another drink when their meal arrived.

A little later Ginger came down, followed a few minutes afterwards by a flushed Malcolm, blissfully unaware of the entertainment he had provided. He took a seat near the Teschmakers and Ginger joined him.

After the meal and his father's second bottle of beer, Martin was getting bored. Ginger had ignored him all evening and he was finding the smoky atmosphere tiring. But just as he was about to tug at his father's sleeve and suggest they go, Ginger came over and, bending down, slowly planted a big kiss on his cheek.

'Can I borrow your dad for a moment, hon?'

'Sure.' She could have anything she wanted.

For a moment Malcolm looked miffed as he saw Ginger heading up the stairs with another man. But then he saw the wooden penis.

'Just watch.' Flecker-eye had appeared beside him, a wicked grin on his face.

Peter Svoboda returned to the scoreboard and with a theatrical flourish produced a piece of different-coloured chalk — red. The penis came to life, jerking up and down between the numbers two and three. Then a cheer went up as the tempo increased and Svoboda was making red chalk marks between five and six, then seven and eight. Finally, as the bar cheered hysterically, the penis hit a huge ten. A large red chalk mark underscored the triumph, the only thing redder being Malcolm's face as he suddenly realised the significance of the small blue marks beside the number three.

Years later, visiting his father in the hostel, Teschmaker asked him about the incident.

'Did you really ... you know ... with Ginger Mick?'

'Did I ever! The two of us jumped up and down on that bed until we thought the frame was going to break.' Alexi laughed at the memory and then doubled over with the cough that was soon to kill him. 'She was something, wasn't she?'

'You never ... you know?'

'With Ginger Mick? No, son, she was your girl. I never even took my bloody shoes off.'

Father's shoes ... brothel-creepers.

Have I changed that much? Teschmaker stared into the now highly polished bathroom mirror, trying to find answers in the face that confronted him. He looked older than he felt, but then he had thought that for at least a decade. Yet somewhere behind the mask was the boy who had boulder-hopped up the creek beds with his father, sat in the Miners' Rest and blushed each time he caught a glimpse of Ginger's cleavage. The same eyes had been bewitched by Jane ... Eyes that were now, he reminded himself, a lot older. A fact which had been brought home to him by Sarah Norrby, Jane's best friend and business partner, who not only hadn't recognised him but had barely given him a second glance when he called in unannounced at the registered office of Strategic Options Proprietary Limited.

The office was a compact modern two-storey building in the middle of the new Angus Street development in Lincoln. It had been a squalid inner-city housing estate until a decade ago, when the investors had moved in, relocated the tenants to the suburbs, and revitalised the area. After a short tussle with a feisty receptionist Teschmaker had managed to get ten minutes with Sarah Norrby on the pretext of enquiring about the company's ability to profile investment possibilities in Poland. He had left the office with more information than he would have expected without forking out a hefty fee, and the conviction that Sarah and Jane were plugged into a very lucrative business. He learned nothing new about Jane, beyond the snippet that she was often away for extended periods so should he require further information he would need to make an appointment. Jane, he was told, would be the person to see as she specialised in the Eastern European region. Unfortunately she was out of the office at present. Would he like to make an appointment? He said he'd think about it. Sarah handed him a business card with the number to call if he decided he did want an appointment with Jane; Teschmaker slid it into his wallet and thanked her. Not once did Sarah show a glimmer of recognition. Mind you, he had introduced himself as Dennis Burke from Consolidated Mutual Funds.

Have I changed that much? He pulled himself away from the mirror and, suddenly feeling very alone in the empty house, contemplated going in to the Russian Quarter for a meal. But he opted in the end to go only as far as the kitchen where he cooked himself a plate of mashed potatoes topped with two poached eggs — comfort food. He ate slowly and then spent an hour tidying up, disinfecting and scrubbing down the benches.

Later in the evening he fiddled around arranging the pens and pencils on his desk in the study, trying to convince himself that it was time he got on with his life and either introduced himself to Jane or gave up his pointless investigation. After all, what was he investigating? He had set out to find her and that he had done with relative ease. So now what? Something in him hesitated at committing to a meeting. That was a very different situation, containing as it did the possibility of rejection. And, he convinced himself, he had not really got close to her. Not close enough to observe her sufficiently to see if introducing himself to her was what he really wanted. Maybe it was a hunting ethos. He had read something about the hunt being more thrilling than the kill. Maybe the entire episode was an aberration brought on by his sudden change of circumstances. The cleaning-out of the house had been a pretty drastic step. He surveyed the remnants of his life only to find that their sparsity still gave him an intense sense of satisfaction. And the house was so clean now. Every surface scrubbed and disinfected. The place sparkled and shone like never before.

He poured himself a scotch and sat for a while, wondering about Jane. He could call her in the morning. But the idea made him nervous. Damn it, he castigated himself, why are you making a big deal about it? It's only a phone call. But the doubting side of his brain hit back immediately. What would he say to her? What was there to say?

'Hello, you probably don't remember me but . . .'

'Hi, I've been following you all week . . .'

Damn stupid. He grimaced at his train of thought, suddenly embarrassed by his inability to confront her. Maybe he would simply suggest they catch up over dinner sometime and leave it up to her. There was no conceivable reason why she should be the slightest bit interested in renewing their acquaintance. It had, after all, been a very long time ago . . .

Just before heading for bed he had an idea which, fuelled by the scotch he had drunk, seemed like a way of passing the responsibility to Jane. He opened his wallet and took out the business card Sarah had given him. There would certainly be nobody at Strategic Options Proprietary Limited at this time of night.

The voice on the machine was neither Jane's nor Sarah's, but it invited him to leave his name, number and the purpose of his call.

'This is a message for Jane. It's Martin Teschmaker. I've been working overseas as an insurance fraud investigator but I'm back home having a break . . .'

Damn, that sounded awkward and it wasn't exactly the truth. He felt suddenly self-conscious but knew there was nothing he could do but blunder on. 'I was wondering if we could meet for dinner one night, or coffee? Something . . . I guess I would just like to catch up.' The thought flashed through his head that there might be a time limit on recorded calls so he quickly left his phone number and hung up.

For Christ's sake, why did I do that? Stupid, I bet I sounded like some dumb idiot on the make. Oh well, he laughed bitterly at himself, at least half that statement is true.

He hadn't expected a quick response. Indeed he was half convinced that he would never hear from Jane at all. So when the phone woke him the next morning he was not only surprised but unprepared.

She didn't waste time on niceties. 'You have a bloody nerve!'

'What?' He shook his head, trying desperately to focus his mind.

'You fucked up my life once before. You think I'm going to forget that?'

There was nothing half-hearted about her anger. He was getting both barrels, point blank.

'Hey . . . hang on. It's me, Teschmaker —'

'I know who the fuck you are. Believe me, if I could forget you I would. You have some nerve, thinking you could weasel your way back into my life. I don't need it, especially right now. Not ever.'

'But Jane —'

'Just fuck off out of my life. You ring me again and I'll fucking kill you.'

PART TWO

CHAPTER EIGHT

It was like looking for three grains of rice in a snowdrift. In the old days the KGB would have brought in a flame-thrower and melted the snow. If the rice ended up cooked, so be it. But these were not the old days and Laverov was no longer in Russia. Here in the West he had to work with — what had Moscow said? Kid gloves. A ridiculous expression. It was more like attempting to pick up a needle while wearing mittens. He had been in the country for ten days and though things had gone well initially, he had come to a grinding halt now. The first of his targets had been simple to find and he had located her in the first week. But of the others there was no sign.

The odd thing was that despite the lack of progress his mood had improved considerably compared to how he had felt before leaving Moscow. On the day he left he had been ready to toss the whole thing aside and cop the consequences. Uncharacteristically he had unburdened himself to Anna Naryshkin — not the details, of course, but the feeling. She hadn't said much but she had done him the service of listening. That was a change for Laverov who had spent the previous days being briefed by people who seemed more intent on displaying their skills than hearing his concerns.

Anna Naryshkin made him a final cup of coffee before he left for the airport. If he had survived it and Aeroflot, Laverov figured he could survive anything.

'Don't go messing in things, Konstantin Ivanovich.' Anna shook her head, as though aware that these men just couldn't help themselves.

Messing in things? He shrugged it off. It was what he did; what he had always done. 'I'll write to you,' he joked.

'Sure you will. Now run along or you'll miss your flight,' Anna said and for the first time reached out and touched his shoulder.

'The orders come from the highest office,' the functionary who escorted him to the airport had intoned solemnly, pausing to check that the less than subtle message was being understood. 'Failure will not be tolerated.'

Great. So they would kill him if he failed?

'You will locate the targets, ascertain from them the location of the package and then eliminate the targets.'

Perfect plan. And he would live exactly how long after returning? No doubt there would be a medal. It always looked good when they buried you with a medal. And Laverov had no doubt they would bury him. Why not? Everyone else connected with 'the project' appeared to be dead. Except the surviving grains of rice. The woman in the photograph from

Karel Schmidt's house in Mariánské Lázně had been easy to identify. Basic detective work had taken him in a single step to the Professor. And from there things had fallen into place, except for the connection to Rusak which still remained a mystery.

'For security purposes it is felt that you should avoid any contact with our embassy.' The functionary was working his way down a check list. 'Unless in an extreme emergency.' The man glanced over his sheaf of notes in a manner which indicated that extreme emergencies were something unsavoury and not to be contemplated. 'And it goes without saying that you will do nothing to bring yourself to the attention of the local security and police.'

Very sensible, as long as killing three people wasn't against the law. Laverov placed his hand over his heart, his face a deadpan mask of sincerity. 'I'll do my best,' he replied.

Oblivious to Laverov's mocking gesture, the man put his papers away, took Laverov by the shoulders, embraced him and kissed him on both cheeks. 'The motherland is entrusting you with a sacred duty.'

God, he thought glumly as he boarded the plane, where do they find these people? Rejects from Mosfilm?

Sometime in the middle of the night he awoke to find they were landing in Dubai for fuel and a change of crew. The passengers emerged from the plane, stiff and bleary-eyed, into a hot desert night. Arab police carrying machine-pistols eyed them suspiciously as the officious cabin crew herded the passengers across the orange-lit tarmac into a marble-floored transit lounge.

143

The turnaround time, they announced, would be two hours. Islamic law forbade the consumption of alcohol. Have a pleasant evening.

Fuck you too, Laverov said under his breath and headed for the men's room. That turned out to be a mistake. When he returned to the lounge it was to find that another flight had landed and discharged its human cargo. The place was swarming with Indonesian and Sri Lankan guest workers whose bodies and plastic bags had commandeered every available seat. For a while he paced the lounge, stepping over bodies and ignoring the stares of curious locals who appeared to have nothing better to do at 3 am than stand gawking at the infidel zoo inside their glass cage. Fuck you as well, Laverov thought. He had never warmed to Arabs. Not since Afghanistan. You try to help some godforsaken dust bowl of a country and get your arse kicked for it. Chalk another one up for the Americans, outspending the Soviets yet again. They must be really proud of what their CIA-supplied arms and money had done. They and the Taliban deserved each other.

It dawned on Laverov that he was getting extremely grumpy. As an act of rebellion he purchased a postcard of a mosque, addressed it to Anna Naryshkin and wrote: *Having a wonderful holiday. Love, Uncle Charles.*

Standing on the Charlotte River Bridge, Laverov wondered if Anna had received the card or if it had been intercepted and she was now being questioned about who Uncle Charlie was. Maybe it had been a foolish whim. Paranoid, he told himself, you're getting paranoid, then consoled himself with the thought that in his game paranoid people lived longer. He stared down at the quickly flowing waters below and let his mind flow with it. A little way downstream a plump duck came in for a waterski landing, fluffed its feathers and trod water. To its right a trout flickered past, heading for the cover of the weeds. It had been another fruitless day. He had tailed the woman from home to work and back again and then wasted time in the Russian Quarter, making his way around the cafés on the off chance that he may spot Rusak. Back in Moscow they had assured him that the man they had inside Rusak's organisation was travelling with him and that it would be only a matter of time before he made contact and alerted them to Rusak's whereabouts. A matter of time? What did that mean? Weeks? Moscow's man might well have been uncovered, be dead or both. He may be in bed with a head cold. Anything could have happened. And in the meantime he would . . . what? Follow the woman? It seemed pointless. Her routine hardly varied. She went to work, she came home — end of story. And Laverov still had no idea of the Professor's whereabouts. All of which begged the question of why Rusak was here. Why and where?

Then there were the phantoms. He had become spectacularly adept at chasing phantoms. There was the jogger he had noticed several times running down the street where the woman lived. He made a habit of pausing at the same tree each morning and performing ridiculous-looking stretching exercises. The tree was opposite the woman's house. Laverov had spent an entire day tracking down everything there was to know about the man. He turned out to be a mortgage broker who enjoyed golf, was married and having an affair with the receptionist in his office. Dead end. He had reached a similar conclusion about the driver of a red Mitsubishi pick-up — she had been house hunting. Then there was the dark blue BMW. Nice car — a 318i E46, a serious motor. The driver turned out to be an ex-insurance investigator whose wife had recently left him. Probably house hunting as well; according to his neighbours in Gower he had recently cleared out most of the contents of his current home. Phantoms. Dead ends.

Laverov went back to contemplating the water boiling beneath the bridge. Downstream the duck attempted to swim against the current and then gave up. Sometimes that was the best option.

Teschmaker turned his attention to his study. He opened the first box and was immediately confronted with a film packet containing nothing but negatives. He took a strip and held it up to the light. It took him a few seconds to work out that the images were holiday snaps he had taken of Gwenda in Cape Town on their only joint holiday overseas during the entire marriage. Her reverse image, almost all reds and oranges, was holding a flower. It was probably a hibiscus — he had a vague memory of her being presented with one on checking into their hotel and her insisting that he take a picture. The photograph, even compensating for its reverse, strangely blue image, seemed stupid, inconsequential. Had he ever had a print made? He supposed so. Why save the neg now?

No reason. And somebody had left fingermarks on it. Not neat. Not tidy. He tossed the packet in the wastepaper bin.

Next he came upon a shoe box. He knew what it contained but he opened it anyway and plunged his hands into the dozens of small pieces of a jigsaw puzzle. This was no ordinary jigsaw. He selected a piece at random and examined it. The glue that had been used to attach the canvas to the hardboard sheet so many years before had stood the test of time — a thoroughly professional job, and one befitting the painting by Matthias Zywitza. It was, he thought, probably the most expensive jigsaw puzzle ever made. The original painting had been valued at US$80,000, but that was a couple of decades ago and Zywitza's work now fetched astronomical sums. The circumstances of Zywitza's death at the hands of his gay lover had been an added bonus. What would it have been worth now — two or three million dollars? Teschmaker laughed and located an envelope, slipped the jigsaw piece inside and sealed it. Normally he posted the individual pieces from outside the country but decided that, on the balance of probability, an envelope bearing a local postmark was hardly going to give the game away. The postmark was only local from his perspective. To the recipient it would be yet another untraceable foreign posting.

Teschmaker checked inside the box — there were still at least two hundred pieces left even though he had been mailing them with relative frequency for almost twenty years. In that time at least half the pieces had gone, usually individually but sometimes, when he was feeling particularly malicious, he would send a full packet. He had no idea if the recipient was still alive, but he knew he would continue the postings until all the pieces were gone. The slower the revenge the sweeter it is, he thought as he picked up the pen from his now well-organised desk. He addressed the envelope with quick neat letters and placed it in his jacket pocket, ready for posting. He ran his eye over the desk. Pen, paper, ruler — all lined up correctly.

Eventually his mind came back to the thought that had been circling his consciousness like a wolf around a wounded lamb, waiting for the right moment to strike. Jane. Her phone call had upset him more than he cared to admit to himself. A rejection — yes, that he could have coped with. Indeed it was what he had expected. But the vehemence of her attack had startled him. He went over and over everything he could dredge up from the past but nothing fitted. Whatever it was, she had it wrong and that irked. He didn't mind that she didn't want to see him. But the anger? *You fucked up my life once before. You think I'm going to forget that?*

He slammed the door shut on the line of thought and headed for the bathroom. The place was a mess and he spent the next half- hour placing his few toiletries in their correct places. *Believe me, if I could forget you I would.* He washed his hairbrush and comb, rinsed his toothbrush and scrubbed the stains and traces of dirt from its handle. Then he squeezed the half-empty toothpaste tube from the bottom up and rolled the empty foil tightly so as to leave the remaining part of the tube plump and even. He washed the outside of the tube for good measure, paying special attention to the cap. *Just fuck off out of my life.* The soap was a problem. It had become wet and gelatinous underneath and no matter how he washed it and patted it dry it continued to leave marks on the sink. In the end he threw it out and opened a new one. Once everything was clean he spaced things out so there was enough room between the comb and the brush, the toothpaste and the toothbrush, that he could pick each of them up without disturbing the item next to it. Order. Tidiness . . . and no thoughts of Jane. But she insisted. *You have some nerve, thinking you could weasel your way back into my life.* Each time he relaxed his guard she was there worrying at his heels, demanding attention. She was, he decided eventually, an untidy part of his life that needed to be cleaned up. She was wrong to be angry at him and once he had cleared up her misconceptions about him then he could stop worrying about her. Fucked up her life? Oh, yes — how?

In the morning Teschmaker rose early and, after making himself a sandwich and a thermos of coffee, climbed in his car and headed towards what — despite the lack of definitive proof — he was mentally tagging as 'Jane's house'. The traffic on the Mitchell Freeway was light so early in the morning and he made good time to the Belmont exit. Across the Charlotte River Bridge the joggers and power walkers were out in force, many of them accompanied by dogs that looked as expensive as their owners' designer clothes. He drove slowly along Lombard Avenue and left into Haycroft. Cruising past the high-walled property he did a U-turn, parked under the shade of a large leafy oak, poured himself a coffee and settled down to what he hoped would be a short wait. It was a good location. He had an unimpeded view of the gates in the wall and at the same time was not in direct line of sight of any of the neighbours. The last thing he wanted was some neighbourhood watch vigilante phoning the police and reporting him as a suspicious loiterer.

A few returning fitness freaks sweated past but they seemed absorbed in their exercise or involved with whatever it was they were listening to on their headphones — none of them gave him a second glance. One man paused by a tree and pushed against it with one arm and then the other. Pointless. He then did a series of toe-touching exercises that presented Teschmaker with an unpleasantly intimate view of his rear. Cellulose in lycra.

By eight thirty Teschmaker began to wonder if Jane might be away, or if the house was not her normal residence after all. Maybe she wasn't separated from Sinclair but simply divided her time between the two houses. However, at five minutes to nine the gates swung open and he heaved a sigh of relief. Jane, dressed to go out, secured first one and then the other gate before reversing out of the driveway in a light blue Saab 900i. Teschmaker guessed it was probably a 1988 or '89 model. He had expected something a little more modern, a little more swish. Jane stopped and closed the gates before driving off in the direction of the freeway. It was frustrating. Twice now he had seen her and both times had failed to get a good look at her. Teschmaker prided himself on his ability to 'read' people — the subtle markers, the body language. All he had managed so far was a momentary sighting of the woman and he craved more.

He began to reverse out then, sensing rather than seeing a car, slammed on the brakes just in time to avoid backing into an approaching vehicle. His attention on Jane had been absolute and he had failed to see a black Ford coming along the road behind him. He cursed but accepted the angry glare from the driver. It was actually an advantage having the black Ford between him and Jane as it gave him a useful buffer and lessened the possibility that she would notice him on her tail. There was something about the black Ford . . . and then he remembered, it was the same car that had been in Haycroft Street the first time he was there. He had assumed then that the man was a prospective buyer of the house that was for sale across the street from Jane's; now his naturally suspicious nature, honed over the years as an insurance investigator, went on to full alert. He castigated himself for the lapse in attention and for not having checked the rest of the street as he normally would have done. In the insurance field he had always worked on the premise that anyone who thought they could defraud the industry would do so, and many times in his work he found that others, usually the local police, had a watching brief on the same individuals he was after. Crooks were crooks and often were involved in more than insurance fraud. But there was something — a vague feeling — that this man was not with law enforcement. The alarm bells weren't ringing but Teschmaker decided not to dismiss the coincidence of the black Ford being in the street a second time.

Trusting his instincts, Teschmaker slipped back a couple of car lengths. If he was right, the Ford would follow Jane and all he had to do was to shadow it and he would still be on her tail. He slowed down and pulled to the side long enough to allow an anxious commuter, obviously running late for a nine o'clock start, to overtake him. It was a calculated risk but the worst that could happen was he might lose sight of Jane and now that he knew that she lived in Haycroft Street he could always pick her up again. The bigger question was: why would anybody be following Jane? The absurdity of the question in light of his own actions made him laugh out loud. Another old boyfriend? Someone else who had 'fucked up her life'? Maybe Sinclair suspected she was having an affair and was having her followed. There were, he realised, many reasons why Jane might be under surveillance. It could also be — a wild notion, he acknowledged — that the man was her bodyguard; he had learned over the years that the rich had some pretty crazy ways of spending their money.

Two cars in front of him Jane's Saab increased speed and turned up the on-ramp for the Mitchell Freeway, heading for the city. Both the black Ford and the commuter followed. Nothing surprising in that. The odds were that ninety per cent of cars on the roads at this time of day would be heading into town.

Jane sat on the speed limit and within fifteen minutes moved into the exit lane for the city centre. The commuter in front of Teschmaker continued straight on. There was now no doubt that the black Ford was following the Saab. Teschmaker had to admit the driver was acting like a real professional, keeping well back and even switching lanes from time to time. As they reached the CBD and the heavier traffic along Raddle Avenue, the man allowed a small car to act as a buffer then changed lanes, keeping Jane in sight from a different vantage point. Each time they approached traffic lights he closed up, allowing no possibility of her leaving him stranded. The man's abilities not only made Teschmaker wonder who he was working for but caused him additional difficulties. At times three and sometimes four car lengths behind Jane, he ran the real risk of losing both of them, or being pulled over for running a red light. Fortunately he made it through the city without incident.

It was now clear that Jane was heading for her office, and as they turned into the new business area of Lincoln the Ford slowed down, letting Jane get well ahead. Eventually, a block away from her office, the man pulled into a loading zone and waited. Caught off guard, Teschmaker could see nowhere to stop and was forced to keep going. He drove past, acutely aware that if the man in the Ford was even half as good as he suspected, he would recognise Teschmaker's car as the one that had nearly pulled out in front of him twenty minutes or so earlier. Well, it couldn't be helped. As he drove by he saw Jane getting out of her car in her office car park. Knowing that he could make no further progress with her, Teschmaker switched his attention back to the Ford and decided to see what the other driver was playing at. He drove quickly around the block and as he turned the corner back into Angus Street was relieved to see that the black Ford was still in the loading zone. A small trendy-looking coffee bar seemed the ideal place to park, but the vehicle spaces were all full. Then he spotted a space in a parking bay outside an advertising agency, reversed into it and sat with his motor running under a sign that promised that unless he was a client his car would be clamped and towed away.

Teschmaker was about to pour himself another coffee from his thermos when the man in the Ford, obviously coming to the same conclusion Teschmaker had about Jane, decided to pack it in for the morning. Displaying none of his previous driving style, he headed onto the Ring Road. Slotted in two cars behind him, Teschmaker assumed the man was going back in the direction of Jane's home, but before the turn for the Mitchell Freeway the Ford veered off, taking the underpass in the opposite direction, following the signs to Lakeside. Teschmaker, confident that the man had no idea he was being followed, dropped back a couple of car lengths just to be on the safe side.

The commonly accepted stereotype was that only two kinds of people lived in Lakeside: over-paid media stars and diplomats. The thought of the media raised a possible explanation of the man's attention to Jane Sinclair — an exposé. Somebody had discovered something about Jane that, because of the notoriety of her husband, would make great copy. He could see it — the investigative reporter backgrounding the victim before a paparazzi-style photographer zoomed in for a few revealing shots. But again it raised more questions. What on earth could Jane be involved with that would cause the media to shadow her daily routine? And why now, given that to date she had been left alone by the media, probably due to Oliver's connections?

They rounded a couple of corners and came to the long slow descent that is Federal Boulevard. Here the mansions — rumour had it — went up by half a million dollars a block up to the crest of the hill where the American Embassy perched behind its splendid lime-washed walls. Before they reached the edge of the lake the Ford turned left and slowed down. Teschmaker realised he was too close and again was nearly forced to drive past. Fortunately a taxi pulling out of the ornate Thai Embassy slotted in front of him, providing a small buffer — enough for Teschmaker to see the Ford drive up to the security boom gate of a slightly less salubrious building. He glanced at the street sign. Scanlon Drive. There was a red oval plaque on the wall beside the gate but he was past before he could read what was written on it. At the end of the street, Teschmaker stopped, pulled out his street directory and looked up Scanlon. There marked on the map in small red letters were the words: Embassy of the Republic of Romania.

Knowing there was nothing more he could do here he checked his watch. It was now getting on for ten o'clock. He was beginning to get hungry but the sandwich on the seat beside him was looking less and less appetising. Remembering the coffee bar opposite Jane's office he turned the car around and retraced his route back towards the city, intent on having a snack and attempting to make sense of the situation. The black Ford's destination was an intriguing and unexpected development. How many times a year did anyone think about Romania? Teschmaker glanced at the envelope containing the piece of the jigsaw which he had addressed the night before and thrown into the car, meaning to post it somewhere outside the city. The intended recipient, now living in New York, was a Romanian, Bela Manolescu. It was only a coincidence — but a strange one nevertheless.

Food, I need food, he thought as he turned into Angus Street. But as he did, Teschmaker saw Jane's Saab pull out of the office car park. 'Damn!' he swore and reached for the sandwich.

In stark contrast to the way that Jane had driven before, Teschmaker now sensed she was aware of the risk of being followed and was doing everything she could to minimise that risk. Whereas before she had been content to sit on the speed limit, now she varied her speed and twice pulled into the side of the road as though going to park then sped away again. Fortunately Teschmaker had opted to stay well back, but even so it took all his skill and a fair dose of luck to stick with her. Having managed that, he was unsure if he had also managed to stay undetected. There was a heavy flow of traffic on the roads but despite her ducking and weaving he remained three to four cars behind her. Teschmaker was even more confused now. The notion that she was concerned about being followed was intriguing enough, but what could possibly explain her behaviour now? Had she deliberately learned to drive like this? Why? Or was she just a gifted amateur? There was, he thought, a lot more to Jane Sinclair than he had anticipated and he felt vindicated in having decided to follow her for a few more days.

After weaving their way around the city, Teschmaker watched as Jane made a second trip down Raddle Avenue. This time, however, she appeared to be dawdling, looking for something; then, with a sudden burst of acceleration, she cut through a gap in the traffic and shot down the ramp into the Empire Hotel car park. Her strategy, if it had been such, worked perfectly. Teschmaker, in the wrong lane and three cars behind, had no chance of replicating her manoeuvre and was forced to drive past. Fortunately there was a parking space half a block on but it was a good five minutes before he was able to walk down into the car park. There was no sign of Jane's Saab. He saw immediately that he had been outwitted. The car park entrance was on Raddle Avenue but the exit lane came out a block over on Hepburn Avenue. Jane had simply driven in and straight out the other side. Deciding to cut his losses, Teschmaker took the elevator up to the lobby and climbed the flight of stairs to the nearest restaurant.

An hour later, though not happy at his lack of progress in keeping tabs on Jane, Teschmaker had at least managed to have an early lunch. He returned to his car, removed the parking ticket from under the wipers and drove home. All in all, he thought later as he poured himself a scotch, the day had not been a complete waste of time. He had established that Jane was being followed by someone associated with the Romanian Embassy, and that Jane was probably aware of it and, when it mattered, took great pains to evade him. It was probably some clash of commercial interests, Teschmaker surmised. Maybe her business had stepped on someone's toes somewhere along the line. Anyway, it was enough to sustain his interest and tomorrow he decided he would do the whole thing again.

For the next three days Teschmaker followed Jane's movements but not once did he spot anyone following her and she did nothing more than go between work and home. Whatever reason the car from the Romanian Embassy had for following her, apparently it no longer existed. By Friday Teschmaker was ready to give the whole thing away, except for the fact that he couldn't get her angry attack on him out of his mind. Her accusation that he had ruined her life and then hanging up with no explanation riled him. He followed her to work, got a space outside the coffee bar, parked, found himself a table and ordered a strong latte.

Maybe he should just walk up to her and demand an apology. Or write her a letter and ask her to explain. *Stay away from me or I'll kill you*. That was just plain stupid. The one thing he was now certain of was that he wasn't going to drop the matter. She had stained him and he would rub away at it until there was no trace of it remaining.

Teschmaker's musings were cut short by Jane's reappearance in the car park across the road. She emerged blinking into the sunlight and stood a moment, checking the street as though aware that there were times when she was followed. Or was he reading his own knowledge into the situation? He watched as her gaze took in the cars parked outside the coffee bar, but if she recognised his dark blue BMW she gave no sign. Teschmaker slipped five dollars under his coffee glass and moved quickly back to his car. To his surprise Jane was not walking towards her Saab but to an older VW Golf parked at the rear of the lot. He waited until she was almost at the end of Angus Street before he followed.

It had not occurred to Teschmaker that she might switch cars and even now he was uncertain if this was a deliberate ploy or had some less devious explanation. Maybe she had done the same on other days and he had missed her. Maybe — the thought suddenly struck him — the Romanian had also used more than one vehicle. No, he consoled himself, he was getting far too paranoid and totally without reason. But he checked the rear-vision mirrors. There were several cars behind him, none of them a black Ford. However, erring on the side of caution, he made a mental note: a cream-coloured delivery van, a beaten-up Mitsubishi Magna and, quite a long way back, a compact late-model maroon Mercedes and a couple of taxis. He switched his attention back to Jane. The Golf was a diesel version and fortunately had less acceleration than her Saab, but she was driving as she had several mornings earlier, switching lanes and taking a very circuitous route to her destination.

Teschmaker checked behind him again and was relieved to see that none of the cars behind him appeared to be the same: a taxi, a Toyota Landcruiser and an old Renault. There was a lot of traffic now and he concentrated on Jane. He realised that, with a few variations, she was going through the same routine as before and so he decided to take a risk. As they approached Raddle Avenue he peeled off to the right, heading for Hepburn. It was probable, he reasoned, that she would use the Empire Hotel car park in the same manner she had three days previously and so he threaded his way through the mid-morning traffic and double-parked opposite the hotel exit. Just as he was beginning to think he had jumped to the wrong conclusion, the VW Golf appeared out of the car park and headed north. 'Gotcha!' he said out loud.

Confident she had lost any tail, Jane drove the full length of Hepburn at a more relaxed pace. From there she took the Ring Road, joined the Mitchell Freeway and then, to Teschmaker's surprise, took the Claymont exit onto the Airport Freeway. Maybe she was going to meet somebody. But that didn't explain the change of cars. You don't change to a down-market vehicle to pick up a visitor off a plane.

Jane sailed past the airport exit and headed for the country. At least I was right about that, he congratulated himself.

Beyond the airport the traffic was very thin and Teschmaker dropped well back giving her plenty of space, only speeding up when she vanished around a corner. Within twenty minutes they were beyond the city, cruising at eighty kilometres an hour along a slowly winding country road. A pick-up truck with bales of fresh lucerne in the rear overtook him, but given the long stretches of road it was not a problem. Teschmaker would have no difficulty spotting the Golf if it turned off the main road as the side roads were invariably crossroads running in a straight line to left and right. And they were all unsealed so, given the recent dry weather, he would easily see the dust trail behind her car.

Thirty minutes later the car and truck in front of him slowed down as they drove straight through the tiny village of Daleborough and on towards Landsbury Crossing. Teschmaker glanced at the fuel gauge and was relieved to see that he still had more than half a tank. He had not anticipated such a trip and he just hoped that wherever Jane was going it was not much further. He didn't have long to wait. A couple of kilometres past Daleborough the road started to wind up the Landsbury Valley, giving him beautiful views over the patchwork quilt of the plains below. Fields of green, brown and the occasional yellow of sunflowers or rape flowed away as far as the eye could see. Ahead of him the pick-up signalled and then turned off down a dirt road, leaving only him and Jane on the road. A couple of minutes later he climbed around a corner and saw her stopped at a gate. It was too late to do anything so he drove by, relieved that she was too busy with a padlock even to glance in his direction.

Around the next corner Teschmaker pulled to the side of the road and waited. Give her a couple of minutes, he thought, then drive past and have a look. There was obviously no way he could go in but he was intrigued by her destination. He had always seen her as a city girl. Sure, she had been a social skier and probably done a bit of bushwalking, but a hobby farmer? No, that wasn't Jane. But then the thought occurred to him that maybe she had a lover living here.

As he drove back he slowed down to a crawl, allowing himself a good look at the property. Set well back from the road, protected by a steel gate and dry-rock wall, was a two-storey stone house surrounded by large trees. The place, if the grounds were any indication, was extremely run down: long grass had already gone to seed, dead branches lay where they had fallen and the house looked as though none of the shutters had been opened in years. It had all the attributes of an abandoned dwelling. To the left of the gate was a makeshift letterbox constructed from a plastic pesticide container cut in half through the middle. It was full of leaves. Underneath hung a sign: Gormenghast RMS 143. Teschmaker wondered how long it had been since the Rural Mail Service had delivered anything here, and what kind of person would name a house Gormenghast.

Jane obviously wanted to deter any casual visitors for she had not only closed the gate but re-fastened it with the padlock. It seemed a strange thing to do if her behaviour was above board. He couldn't imagine any of the local farmers bothering with such locks. From the road, the dry-stone walls ran back along either side of the front paddock which, he guessed, must have been almost two acres in size. To one side an old shed leaned precariously, its slow fall halted by the trunk of a large elm. Behind it he could just make out the rear of Jane's car. Why, he wondered, did she feel the need to disguise her presence? The weed-covered driveway led to a turning circle directly in front of the house. Why not park there?

Convinced that he could learn nothing further he drove back to the city, stopping for a moment in Daleborough where he posted the envelope containing the single piece of the old jigsaw puzzle. Today, he told himself, I made progress.

Later he kicked himself for not having recognised the two cars parked opposite his house as he arrived home: a Landcruiser and a compact maroon Mercedes. But at the time his mind had been on other things. On the drive back to the city, in a welcome break from his preoccupation with Jane, his thoughts had gone back to his first meeting with Bela Manolescu.

It was his very first assignment just over twenty-two years earlier. In reality an insurance claim of such magnitude should have been handled by a more senior investigator. But the New York manager of General Insurance International, sensing an opportunity for a weekend away with his mistress, had insisted that Teschmaker would have no trouble with the case.

'It's one of the open and shut variety,' the manager smiled. 'Open the chequebook and shut the case.'

He paused to make sure that Teschmaker had time to enjoy his little joke. Teschmaker smiled diplomatically.

'Mr Manolescu,' the manager continued, 'is a very valued client so don't ruffle any feathers. Go through the forms and pay him the $80,000.'

'Sure,' Teschmaker replied. 'I'll do the paperwork, issue the cheque and have my report on your desk by Monday morning.'

He watched as the manager drove off to tell his wife that he was unfortunately going to be out of town all weekend. 'Sorry honey, something big has come up.'

Later that afternoon Teschmaker checked the address on the Lower East Side and took a cab. At first glance the brownstone apartment looked pretty run of the mill.

Nothing fancy. It didn't reek of ostentation and wealth. Then Teschmaker's eye caught sight of the grilles over the windows — not just the ground floor but also the first and second. That was more like it. The claimant styled himself as an 'art connoisseur' though nowhere in the documentation could Teschmaker see any indication of the man's profession. He must be one of those termed 'independently wealthy', Teschmaker supposed.

The man who greeted Teschmaker at the door was enormous. He was also naked, except for a sarong that was struggling to contain his waist. Bela Manolescu's round face was hung with huge jowls of fat that wobbled around his chin and neck. He took Teschmaker's hand limply in his; Teschmaker extricated his hand as quickly as possible and handed the man his business card.

'Mr Martin Teschmaker. A pleasure. A divine pleasure,' Manolescu murmured. 'Shoes off, if you don't mind.' He indicated the row of shoes and sandals that lay in a neat row to the left of the door. 'Some slippers for Mr Teschmaker, please, Raymond,' he called and immediately a young Asian boy appeared carrying a pair of white slippers. 'Quickly! We don't want his toes to catch cold.'

As Teschmaker leaned over to untie his laces he was very conscious of the two men watching him. Raymond, also dressed only in a sarong, knelt down and, despite Teschmaker's protestations that he could do it himself, eased Teschmaker's feet delicately into the slippers.

'Much better,' Manolescu beamed and, giving Raymond a friendly pat on the bum, sent him scurrying off to fetch refreshments. 'Vodka tonics and something to nibble,' he instructed.

In an overly familiar gesture he took Teschmaker's arm and led him from the hall into a large marble-floored sunroom. The room faced onto an interior courtyard, bereft of direct sunlight but fitted out with a spa and a large couch above which was an array of sun lamps. Teschmaker glanced at the rolls of flesh that circled Manolescu's girth but could see no sign that they had ever been anything but white. The vast expanse of flesh was pallid and unhealthy, the only suggestion of colour coming from the discoloration caused by the veins that struggled to move blood around his protruding belly. Maybe the solar lamps were strictly for his guests.

'A tragedy of immense proportions,' Manolescu sighed as he guided Teschmaker towards a leather armchair. He released his arm and moved around a small coffee table to lower himself, breathing heavily, into a sturdy chair that looked as though it had been custom-built to encompass and support the man's huge form. As he sank down he allowed the sarong to fall open, displaying, with no sense of embarrassment, huge thighs and calves striped with the purple of varicose veins.

'The loss of the painting?'

'It is like losing a beloved child. For a German, Matthias Zywitza's work is so tender you can almost feel the brush strokes. So painterly. And such a rare sense of light.'

'I'm afraid I'm not familiar with his work, but I understand how painful it must be to lose a treasured possession.'

'Do you, Martin? The sense of loss was debilitating. For days I looked at the empty space on the wall, expecting that at any moment the painting would materialise.' He allowed his head to roll back to the chair's headrest and for a moment stared at the ceiling. Then he snapped his head down and looked Teschmaker directly in the eye. 'I hope you don't mind if I call you Martin?'

Teschmaker didn't like it but, remembering his manager's words about Manolescu being a valued client, shrugged in a noncommittal manner. There was something in the way Manolescu looked at him that made him feel decidedly uncomfortable, like a child in the presence of a paedophile. But he suppressed his reaction. Fortunately the awkwardness of the moment was cut short by the return of Raymond carrying a tray of drinks and some wafer-thin biscuits topped with caviar. The young man moved a photo album to one side to put the tray on the table and handed Teschmaker his drink. He then sat at Manolescu's feet and proceeded to pass him the biscuits one by one.

It was such a strange sight, Teschmaker thought: the slightly built Asian man, not much more than a boy really, sitting beside those enormous feet, swollen ankles and bulging thighs. Manolescu sipped his drink and with his other hand casually stroked Raymond's neck as though he were a lap dog or the house cat.

'I'll need you to sign some papers, I'm afraid,' Teschmaker said, placing his drink on the table and swinging his briefcase up onto his knees. 'And I'm required to ask a few questions.'

'Of course, dear boy. Ask away.'

Manolescu passed his drink back to Raymond and pointed at the biscuits. 'For our guest! You are forgetting yourself!'

To Teschmaker's amazement he hit the young man a stinging blow across the face. Raymond blushed, got to his feet, picked up the plate of biscuits and offered them to him. Feeling under some obligation, Teschmaker took one and mumbled his thanks.

For several minutes Teschmaker went through the routine questions about the break-in and the theft, then sat back and took another sip of his drink. 'Well,' he said with a manufactured smile, 'everything appears to be in order. All I need now is a copy of the police report and the receipt from your original purchase.'

'Certainly.' Manolescu prodded Raymond to his feet and indicated he should help him from the chair. 'I'll get them from my study. Can I get Raymond to freshen up your vodka?'

'No.' Teschmaker shook his head. 'I'll be fine.'

As Raymond assisted the lumbering Manolescu from the room, Teschmaker drained the last of his drink. Putting his briefcase to one side, he picked up the photo album and flipped through it. There is nothing quite as boring as another person's collection of happy snaps, he thought. But he was wrong. The pictures were anything but innocuous snaps. The album was a detailed record of Manolescu's sexual exploits with a number of younger men. Raymond featured in a majority of them, sometimes alone, sometimes in conjunction — if that was the right word — with other men. Despite his bulk, Manolescu appeared to be reasonably agile in pursuit of his sexual goals. The photos were not of a particularly high quality and had been taken with a camera that date-stamped every photo. One in particular intrigued Teschmaker. It showed Manolescu standing beside Raymond, proudly displaying the front page of a foreign-language newspaper carrying the big man's smiling photograph. The headline was not clear enough to be read, but Teschmaker guessed that the picture had been taken in Romania where Manolescu reportedly kept a palatial home somewhere outside the Transylvanian city of Braşov. Was it Sibiu? Teschmaker had read it in the file but couldn't immediately recall the name. If Teschmaker had harboured any doubt about Manolescu's vile character the picture put paid to it. The man was not only a lecherous sodomite who preyed on young boys, he was — if the date stamp on the photo was anything to go by — also a liar and swindler.

Based on the date of the photograph and what it revealed, the logical thing would have been to reject Manolescu's insurance claim and hand him over to the police. But that would have been too easy. It was probable that the police could get a conviction, but only for the insurance matter. Checking that Manolescu was not on his way back into the room, Teschmaker slipped the picture from the album and into his briefcase. It may take a long time but Teschmaker knew with certainty that justice would eventually be served.

It was eighteen months before Teschmaker was able to take time off from an investigation he was conducting in Hungary to visit Romania. When the opportunity presented itself he set aside a week to locate Manolescu's Transylvanian home-away-from-home. It turned out to be a relatively simple task as every pretty boy for miles around Braşov knew of Manolescu and his exploits. He found the mansion — not in the pretty town of Sibiu with its cobbled streets and pastel-coloured houses but in Sighisoara, one of the greatest medieval cities left in the world, complete with a walled citadel on the hilltop, secret gateways and passages and a fourteenth-century clock tower. Ironically Manolescu's house was also in the place where Prince Vlad Tepes was born — the man upon whom the character of Dracula was modelled.

Fortunately the mansion was unattended when Teschmaker called and he had no problem forcing an entry and avoiding the rudimentary alarm system. As he had seen in the photograph, the missing painting, supposedly stolen in New York, was hanging above the bed in which so much of Manolescu's lust had been taken out on young boys. Teschmaker quickly removed the painting from its frame and let himself out by the front door. No alarms sounded. No caretakers. No problem.

Within forty-eight hours Teschmaker had located a local craftsman who, for a generous fee, glued the canvas to a hardwood backing and designed and cut it into a two thousand piece jigsaw. Teschmaker toyed with the idea of attempting to reassemble it, but in the end proceeded with his original plan. It gave him immense satisfaction to imagine Manolescu's reaction to opening that first package containing twenty pieces of his beloved painting.

It was a satisfaction Teschmaker had stretched out over the next two decades as he continued to post Manolescu pieces of the jigsaw. Revenge, Teschmaker knew, was sweetest when slow.

CHAPTER NINE

There were two of them. Muscle. No splitting the roles between nice guy and bad guy — both the men were heavy-duty trouble. Even though Teschmaker hadn't noticed the cars outside, the splintered woodwork around the front door was indication enough that he had a problem. A sensible response would have been to do a smart about-turn and beat a hasty retreat. But Teschmaker, drawn by some fatalistic urge, simply walked in. The light was on in his study and so he climbed the stairs and found them there: one in his office chair, the other perched on the edge of the desk. The room had been given a thorough going-over — the single bed was on its side, the bedding tossed in a corner. It was no longer tidy.

'I'd rather you didn't smoke.' It wasn't the most convincing of deliveries.

The man in the chair swivelled it around and made a nonchalant show of flicking the ash from his cigarette onto the floor. He was a big man. Ex-cop? Teschmaker had seen plenty of specimens like him outside clip joints and strip clubs in cities from Rio to Copenhagen. His hair was shaved within a millimetre of its life and his T-shirt sleeves were rolled up to reveal the obligatory tattoos. The men were a matching set. Both had necks that would not have looked out of place on a Brahman bull. The second man pushed himself off the desk, dropped his cigarette at his feet and ground it into the carpet with the heel of his steel-toed boots.

'What happened to your house?' the man in the chair asked. 'Kinda empty, isn't it. Your wife take off with all your furniture?' He laughed and spun the chair back to the desk. 'And this crap? Really, what is a man like you doing with all this junk?' He swept everything within the arc of his arm onto the floor. 'I'm afraid you didn't even have enough for us to trash.' He looked up at his companion. 'Disappointing, wasn't it, Norman?'

'Absolutely, Mr Edwards. Not enough, nothing.' Norman grinned. He seemed quite content to play the apprentice.

'You should have mentioned you were coming. I could have ordered some stuff in —'

Teschmaker would have said more but Norman, lacking anything else to trash, started in with a well-aimed blow to the solar plexus quickly followed by a blow to his face that spun him against the wall. For a moment he held himself up but Norman lashed out with his boot and Teschmaker's feet were whipped from under him. Not content that the message was getting through, Edwards contributed a kick to the side of his face. From that moment Teschmaker realised there was little point in attempting to win them over with his sharp line in spirited and incisive repartee. He was aware that Edwards was talking to him but for a while things were a little hazy.

'Norman, be a decent bloke and help me get Mr Teschmaker off the floor.' Between them they pulled Teschmaker to his feet and pushed him into the chair.

'Now,' Edwards continued, 'all of that was just by way of introduction.' He shook Teschmaker roughly to make certain he was paying attention. 'You're probably wondering what Norman and I are doing here? Natural enough question. I have always subscribed to the belief that *ira furor brevis est* and I'm not normally an angry man. But I could get riled if you don't understand the message that following Jane Sinclair is not a healthy occupation. In fact, we understand that it could prove terminal.'

'Absolutely.' Norman grinned. 'Terminal.'

There was plenty more, but really only variations on a theme. Even in his bruised and groggy state Teschmaker was able to convince Norman and Mr Edwards that he understood the point they were making. 'Terminal,' he assured them. Teschmaker wasn't sure why they needed to drag him down the stairs and prop him up by the front door. Maybe they wanted him to wave them goodbye. Maybe they wanted to make sure he locked up after they had gone. Though how he was supposed to do that given the splintered door frame he wasn't certain. But he leaned there and watched them depart.

'And get some fucking furniture,' Edwards called back from the front gate. 'All those empty rooms will end up giving you the creeps.'

For a long time he stood at the door. Not because he was worried that they might return, but he had the distinct feeling that if he let go of it he would crash to the floor. After a while he knew he had to test his mobility; to his relief he found he could make it up the stairs. He paused in the toilet to vomit and then groped his way to the bathroom cabinet. The sight that confronted him in the mirror was not a pretty one. The split lip looked as though it would swell up somewhat more before it was done and though it had been years since he had sported a black eye, he was reasonably certain that he would possess two of them by morning.

He opened the cabinet and immediately regretted he had done such a thorough job of cleaning everything out of the house. There was nothing on the shelves but a bottle of Eno's lemon-flavoured fruit salts. Teschmaker picked it up and headed for the kitchen. He knew that Eno's were good for an upset stomach but how efficacious they would be for one that had been severely kicked was uncertain. He popped the lid off and found that the remains of the fruit salts had become encrusted on the bottom of the jar. He prodded at them with a teaspoon but they were as hard as rock. But the fruit salts were the nearest thing to medicine in the entire house so Teschmaker persisted. Determined not to be beaten, he filled the jar with water and was depressed to see that the effervescence normally associated with the product had long since given up the ghost. He drank the cloudy liquid anyway and limped off in the direction of the bedroom to put the bed back in some semblance of order. Attempting to lie down was going to be painful, but it beat the hell out of trying to stand up all night.

He didn't sleep well and in the morning woke in even more discomfort than the night before. There is, Teschmaker thought, at least one advantage from looking so beaten up. Nobody was going to ignore him. While it might be a wiser move to take his face and ribs to a medical centre for a little attention, he had a different candidate in mind.

He eased himself as gently as he could into a suit and tie, grimacing at himself in the mirror but acknowledging that the damage looked far more dramatic on a well-dressed individual. Had he been a tramp or a red-neck swampy he would probably not have been afforded more than a second glance. Driving into the city he turned off the motorway and detoured into the Russian Quarter, heading to Shlyapnikov's.

A tidal wave of Russian émigrés had flooded into the city after the Revolution, followed by a ripple or two and then a trickle during the Stalinist years. Though many of the successful Russian businesses now had offices downtown, it was here, around the Petrovsky Markets and in the triangle formed by Guzenko, Vlasov and Fyodorov Avenues, that the heart of the community still lay. Here you could still hear Russian spoken, could drink decent vodka and play chess or, as was Teschmaker's intention, have a bowl of the best borshch in the country followed by a slice of Sharlolka Malakova. The dessert, first created by the French chef Carême for Czar Alexander I, was the speciality of Teschmaker's long-time friend

Aleksandr Yefremovich Shlyapnikov. 'Old friend' would have been a better description for Shlyapnikov was as old as the hills. His weatherbeaten face looked as though it could have been around in the days of the Tzar and Rasputin. He was probably only eighty or so, but instead of playing down his age he had developed the habit of exaggerating it. 'I remember before the Revolution . . .' he would say, keeping a straight face, betrayed only by his twinkling eyes and historical impossibility.

There was no sign of his friend in his usual spot, propped up behind the bar, chessboard in front of him. Neither could he see Shlyapnikov's wife, Zoya Nikolayevna, so Teschmaker took his time over the food and followed it with a cup of coffee. Shlyapnikov's contacts and his ability to worm information out of people were legendary. If something was to be known Shlyapnikov knew about it. If he didn't know he could find out. It made him an invaluable ally. Teschmaker wanted to seek Shlyapnikov's advice about who was who in the Romanian Embassy, but it could wait.

Feeling only slightly more prepared to face the world, he walked back to his car and drove into the business district. It took another frustrating twenty minutes to find a car park and when he did it was a good ten minutes from his destination. He hoped that the enforced walk would loosen up his aching muscles but it didn't. However, it did give him the chance to observe people's reactions to his battered face. Is this how a leper feels, he wondered. The pedestrians flowed around him. A beaten-up Moses parting the waters.

He entered the foyer of Sinclair Towers and, keeping his head down, merged with a group of people waiting for the elevator. He had no idea where to find Oliver Sinclair but it was a pretty fair bet that it would be on the top floor. He was wrong. Workers in cramped office cubicles cast curious glances at him, but nobody asked what he was doing there. Sheep in pens; it reminded Teschmaker of his deep-seated aversion to corporate culture. The first thing he had done when he became involved in the insurance industry was to find a job that took him on the road. Selling was the obvious one, but his dislike of hustling was as strong as his distaste for claustrophobic offices, so he had worked towards a job in investigations only to find that most of the fraud division spent their time chasing paper trails.

The company maintained a small team of investigators who kept themselves aloof from the others. Their offices were often locked and deserted; they would appear from time to time to drop some tiresome paperwork on someone's desk, like teachers distributing exams. The stories about them were the stuff of legends and they thought of themselves as an elite — the industry superstars. And indeed some deserved the superstar tag. People like Marcia Brumpton — everybody's idea of a benign granny — famous for having tracked down a renegade insurance agent through his parrot, a bird with a taste for a particular bird seed that had to be ordered in. Both man and parrot were now behind bars, the parrot in the care of Marcia Brumpton. People like old Harry Stainsworth, who had followed a hunch about a woman whose husband had died in the Soviet Union after being arrested for drunkenness. The wife collected a massive life insurance payout and went about her business, soon marrying again. Harry also went about his business and in Moscow, by bribing the right people, found that the man had not died in custody but had been released with a hangover. Harry took a copy of the man's fingerprints and returned home where, three weeks later, he procured a set of the new husband's fingerprints. They were identical.

Harry's other claim to fame was that he had worked with William 'Wild Bill' Donovan, the man who, along with California-born insurance magnate Cornelius V Starr, had set up the remarkably secret Insurance Intelligence Unit as a part of the Office of Strategic Services, a forerunner of the CIA. Starting in early 1943, they had gathered half-a-dozen top insurance agents, Harry Stainsworth among them, and produced intelligence on the Nazi insurance industry. Most importantly, the unit searched standard insurance records for blueprints of bomb plants, timetables of tide changes and thousands of other details about targets. It was only after the war that it became clear the Germans had also used insurance records as a source of intelligence, but by that time Harry Stainsworth was a legend.

Teschmaker had walked the entire length of the twenty-fifth floor without being challenged. He couldn't believe that Sinclair would allow such lax security. There had to be another lift. Or . . .

He found the door to the fire stairs and managed to slip through and close it behind him without setting off any alarm that he could hear. There was, of course, no way of knowing if he had triggered a warning in the building's central security station, but glancing around he could see no cameras. Above him the stairs continued to a door that was supposedly only able to be opened from the inside — that was unless you forced a credit card into its unprotected edge. Teschmaker grinned at the thought of giving Sinclair a ticking off about his poor security. Slipping through, he found himself in an extremely ornate corporate bathroom with gold fittings and half a hillside of cipolin marble. I suppose the money had to be spent on something, he thought. He paused to relieve himself in a urinal cut out of a single block of marble.

There was always risk attached to a straight confrontation. Once the element of surprise had been expended there was little else to recommend it, but as he opened the door out of the bathroom he realised that he had no alternative. Teschmaker found himself standing at the back of Oliver Sinclair's private office. Sinclair was sitting at his desk, apparently studying a document. For a moment Teschmaker had a rush of panic and considered simply backing out. The man sighed and sat back in his chair.

'You could have gone to reception, Martin.' He didn't turn around. 'I had told them to expect you.'

'I've always been the backdoor type.' So, there had been a security alarm or a camera he hadn't spotted. 'And I needed the exercise.'

'Come around here so I can take a look at what Mr Edwards described as a low-level remedial massage.'

'He has a way with words.'

Teschmaker walked around the desk and eased his still complaining body into several thousand dollars worth of Italian calf leather. It was the first time he had been close enough to get a good look at Sinclair. He was dressed in an open-neck shirt that would have been more at home on a tropical beach and the exposed bit of chest looked as though it had spent a little too long in the sun. He was even smaller than the PR-sanctioned photos portrayed him but then, Teschmaker thought, most people would be diminished sitting behind such a vast slab of mahogany. He also looked older than Teschmaker had imagined: sixty? sixty-five? It was hard to tell. The previously dark brown hair was now salted with a considerable amount of silver but there was no sign of a receding hairline. The eyebrows, prominent because of the jutting brow, were neatly trimmed. The famous walrus moustache was a shade or two darker than the hair, probably cosmetically enhanced. To Teschmaker's surprise Oliver Sinclair picked up a pair of spectacles. That was something the public never saw. He wondered if he used contact lenses in public.

'Look at it this way, Martin, it could have been a lot worse.' Sinclair turned on the rather impish smile that was something of a trademark. Most female columnists considered him to be a jovial little dumpling and, despite his age, his boyish behaviour always guaranteed him reasonably kind treatment from the media. Many of the women journalists thought him attractive. 'I originally decided to have you killed.'

'I'm flattered you thought of me at all.' Teschmaker couldn't understand why but he didn't feel the slightest bit intimidated by the man or his wealth. The bravery of the fool? Probably. 'People usually ignore me.'

'Oh, I thought about you a lot. I have always been pretty broad-minded but there is a certain kind of slime ball that really gets my goat, and you happen to be one of them.'

'I'm afraid you are confusing me with someone else.' Teschmaker shrugged. 'I'm just your regular clean-living guy.'

He decided that the best way to play this was not to be drawn into a fight. Mind you, he was unsure how long he could maintain the facade because, not far beneath the pain and stiffness of his battered body, he was suppressing a great deal of anger.

'No, Teschmaker. Don't play the fool with me. You know my reputation. I like a bit of fun as much as the next man. Probably a little bit more, seeing I can afford it. But I draw the line at this kind of shit.' He slid a 10 x 4 photograph across the mahogany. 'You're a sick man, Teschmaker.'

Teschmaker picked it up and stared at it, trying to understand what he was looking at and why Sinclair thought he would be involved with what looked like a bunch of pretty bent individuals. The photo, taken with a wide-angle lens, was grainy but despite the lack of crisp focus showed more than enough to get the general idea. Several men and women in various states of undress seemed deeply involved in inflicting a great deal of pain on each other. In the foreground a rather weedy-looking individual was curled in a foetal position. Teschmaker couldn't ascertain the person's gender but suspected he was male. The person was naked except for the rope that bound him around his neck and snaked down his back to where his wrists were tightly tied. From there the rope continued on to his ankles, which were tied up against his back. It looked anything but pleasurable.

'Nice rope work,' Teschmaker murmured, and it was — the kind of thing to turn a scoutmaster green with envy.

A woman, her neck collared, was in the centre of the picture, her hands manacled to an eyebolt in the ceiling. Her head was turned away and another woman, dressed only in a leather G-string, was whipping her with a riding crop. In the background an overweight middle-aged male was strapped into a large wooden chair, his feet hoisted on stirrups, a blindfold around his face, and a blurred figure seemed to be attaching metal clamps to his genitals.

Teschmaker looked back at the manacled woman. Was that Jane? He winced in sympathy.

'Natty rope work and some rather unusual appliances but it doesn't ring any bells.'

'Bullshit!' Sinclair snapped. 'You're involved with that bunch of psychos and you've been following my wife. I don't understand what the hell you thought you'd gain by sending me the photos. Did you think I would pay you off or something?'

'You can think whatever you like, Sinclair.' Teschmaker allowed a little of the anger to leak out. 'But whatever your fantasies are, they don't concern me. And next time get your facts right before you send your bully boys around to pick on the wrong man.'

'Crap, Teschmaker, you're talking crap.' Sinclair got to his feet. 'I want to know what the fuck your little game is.'

'My game is about minding my own business and not having the shit beaten out of me by your thugs. If you weren't who you are I'd have you hauled in for assault —'

'You haven't a hope in hell of that happening,' Sinclair snorted.

'I'm sure you're right. But when I last checked there were still some sections of the media that you didn't control. I'm certain they would find my story amusing. Especially if I let them know about your obsession with whips and chains.'

Teschmaker smiled through his cracked lips and got to his feet. 'And now, if you don't mind, I'll let myself out the way I came.'

Clamping his mind shut against the protests of his aching limbs he strode purposefully around the desk and opened the door through to the toilets.

'Oh, one last thing.' He turned back to the room but kept the door open behind him. 'I wasn't following your wife. I was following the man who was following her. I was hoping you would tell me a bit about him but I'm obviously wasting my time.'

He stepped through the door and quickly locked it. Teschmaker knew he had little chance of making it out of the building but decided to give Sinclair's security boys a run for their money. He walked down three flights but on each floor the fire doors were locked. He could open them in the same way he had done on the top floor, but he could smell smoke and where there was smoke . . .

His judgment was spot on. Six floors down the fire door was jammed open by a metal ashtray. A couple of empty Pepsi cans and a hamburger wrapper littered the stairwell. He walked nonchalantly through the door and past a series of open-plan offices to the elevator. Nobody afforded him a second glance.

The elevator arrived half full of people. Apart from a few glances at his battered face, he could have been just another office worker on his way out for lunch. Three times on the way down the lift stopped for people to get on or off but there was no sign of a security presence. They will be waiting in the foyer, he thought. But they weren't. As the remaining people moved out of the lift he felt a gentle tug on his arm. A young boy dressed in some kind of official company uniform looked up at him enquiringly.

'Mr Teschmaker?'

'Yes?'

'Mr Sinclair phoned down and said he had forgotten a couple of things he wanted to discuss —'

'So?' Teschmaker said curtly and strode towards the doors.

The boy, tenacious as a puppy, kept pace with him. 'He was wondering if you had time to come back up?'

'Tell Mr Sinclair,' Teschmaker said gently, 'to fuck off.'

He nodded at the doorman, who swung the door wide for him. The boy, suddenly nonplussed, remained inside.

CHAPTER TEN

It was evening when the doorbell rang. He had spent the afternoon tidying the mess in his study, vacuuming the floor, polishing his desk and neatly arranging his pens and pencils. The front door, however, was another matter. Teschmaker had toyed with fixing it himself but in the end decided it was a job for an expert.

Not until next week, the local handyman's wife told him. Max was doing Mrs Thorstien's bathroom taps, old man Sutton's cracked bedroom window and some renovations for the smart young things who had taken over the old rectory at St Matthew's. 'God knows where they get the money,' she had moaned. 'Not like in our day.'

Teschmaker commiserated with her and asked her to let Max know he needed a new front door. After that he had driven back to the Russian Quarter and arranged for Shlyapnikov to get him a list of personnel at the Romanian Embassy and, if possible, what cars they drove. Aleksandr Yefremovich loved playing the spy and was only too happy to assist as long as Teschmaker sampled Zoya Nikolayevna's stroganoff. Teschmaker had driven home a couple of hours later to find his door repaired rather than replaced and a note from Max tucked under it. *Your friend paid for it.* Since when have I had friends, Teschmaker had wondered. Now it seemed he had visitors too.

'I take it you have no objection to red?' Oliver Sinclair looked a little out of place, awkward, as though he had no idea how to behave in the suburbs. He was still wearing his Hawaiian shirt but had thrown on a navy jacket with gold buttons. He looked like an off-duty commodore from a yacht club. 'By way of an apology.'

Teschmaker glanced over Sinclair's shoulder. A white Porsche Carrera Cabriolet sat in the driveway. No Rolls Royce and no chauffeur. Sinclair was slumming it. He took the proffered bottle of wine, something French, something expensive.

'I'm not sure if I have two glasses but we can look.' He led the way through to the kitchen.

'Edwards said your house was empty.'

'Termites,' Teschmaker responded gravely. 'Ate the lot.'

He located two glasses and retrieved a corkscrew from a drawer. 'We'll go upstairs.'

'Your wife cleaned you out?' Sinclair asked, pausing on the stairs and surveying the empty rooms below.

'No. Everything was chosen by her and when she left I decided I had never really cared for her taste in anything. Haven't got around to replacing it.'

'Clean slate, huh?'

'Something like that.'

Teschmaker swung the study door open. 'Here. It's all a bit cramped but at least there's a chair.'

He ushered Sinclair in, carefully cleared a space on the desk, put the glasses down and proceeded to open the bottle. Oliver Sinclair pulled the remaining chair over beside the window and opened it a small way.

'Mind if I smoke?'

Teschmaker, much to his own surprise, found that he was shaking his head. 'No. Sorry there's no ashtray but the window will do. Here.' He passed him a glass of wine. 'So,' he said, sipping at his glass, 'do you make a habit of having people beaten up?'

'Not usually.' Sinclair produced a large cigar and started to unwrap it. 'And I don't often have to apologise for anything. But I was pretty steamed up about what my wife is going through —'

'She left you?' Teschmaker interjected.

'Six months ago. Trial separation, she called it. I was sent a bunch of those photographs.' He placed the unwrapped cigar carefully on the window ledge, pulled an envelope from his jacket pocket and handed it over. 'Of course I reacted.'

The photographs were of much better quality than the one Teschmaker had seen earlier in the day. Though still with the slight graininess that suggested they had been pulled from a video still, they were well lit and sharply focused. Jane wasn't hard to spot; she would have been hard to miss. In every one of the photographs she was centre frame. Naked or with a studded collar, tied in some, strapped in others, being whipped in two of the photographs and expertly tied in another. In the final of the series she was strapped into the chair Teschmaker had seen in the earlier photo. Spreadeagled with clamped wrists and ankles, she was having clothes pegs attached in a circle around her nipples.

There was something odd about the photographs. Maybe it was just the way they had been shot but in none of them was there any sense of a background. In each one the victim was lit in such a way that the background and indeed the other participants appeared to merge into absolute blackness. Maybe they had been Photo-shopped. 'And you thought I was involved with this?'

Sinclair tugged at the ends of his moustache then took a small silver cutter from his top pocket and clipped the end of his cigar. 'I've been floundering around. Jane wouldn't say a word. Just packed up. I told her I was going to take custody of our daughter but she pointed out that to do so I would have to produce the photos in court. Well, I backed off.' He paused and lit the cigar. 'The thing is, I'm so damn used to getting my own way that I didn't know how to handle this. I hired Edwards and his sidekick to keep an eye on Jane and they reported that you had been following her. I assumed it was because you were involved.' He peered through the smoke at Teschmaker. 'And you tell me you're not.'

'Which I take it you now believe?'

'I did some further checking up. You weren't even in the country when these photographs were taken.'

'I told you, not my scene. Neither is blackmail.'

Sinclair laughed. 'That's the silly thing. I was certain that the next thing would be a demand. You know the kind of thing: your money or we publish.'

'And it didn't happen?'

'Not yet.'

'So why did they send them?'

'I was rather hoping I could interest you in finding out.'

'Really?' Teschmaker was surprised. 'It seems to me that your two head-kickers would be better equipped for a job like that.'

Sinclair shot a wry glance at Teschmaker's black eye. 'They are good at some things.' He took a sip of his wine and turned on the trademark grin. 'But not only did the idiots not bother to run a proper check on you but even Jane has constantly managed to give them the slip.'

'I'm sorry, Mr Sinclair, but if *you* have done your checking properly you will know I'm not a private detective.'

'You're an insurance investigator.'

'Was. I am now an ex-insurance investigator.'

'Same thing though.'

Teschmaker shook his head. It wasn't true. The style and type of work was rarely the same. 'I don't have the temperament for that kind of work.'

'I can pay enough that your temperament isn't too inconvenienced.' Sinclair took another pull on his cigar. 'How did you get into the business in the first place?'

'Insurance?'

'The fraud side.'

It was funny, Teschmaker thought later, that Sinclair's cigar hadn't prompted the memory. It was, after all, due to cigars that he had managed to join the elite band of investigators.

The case was the first loss in the courts that the company had suffered in years. The embarrassing thing was that it wasn't even over a large amount of money: $10,000 — peanuts really. The client, a Britisher, had purchased a case of extremely rare cigars at an auction in New York and immediately insured them against everything from theft to fire. He returned to London where, in under a month and having paid only a single premium, he smoked all twenty-four cigars. The company would have had no problem with that had the man not then filed a claim stating that the cigars had been destroyed in a series of small fires. Naturally enough General Insurance International refused to pay the claim, pointing out that the man had consumed the cigars in the normal fashion. To their astonishment the man sued the company.

'So GII took the man's premium?' the judge asked GII's manager of public relations.

'Yes.'

'And in return issued this policy avowing they would pay in the event of fire?'

'Yes, but it was not intended —'

'What happens when you put a match to a cigar?'

'It burns.'

'And does any clause of this policy specifically exclude a fire of this nature?'

'No, your Honour, but common sense —'

'This court, I am afraid, is interested only in the law.'

The man won the case and the press had a field day. It became fair game for everyone from stand-up comedians to newspaper cartoonists — a public relations disaster. General Insurance International knew full well that to appeal would only prolong the expense and the agony and so decided to cop it on the chin and pay the man his $10,000. It was at that point that Teschmaker knocked on the CEO's door, introduced himself and offered an elegant solution.

Teschmaker waited until the man, a frequent visitor to the United States, returned on business and had him arrested on twenty-four counts of arson. Using the man's own insurance claim and transcripts from the proceedings of the earlier trial as evidence against him, the man was convicted on all counts of intentionally burning the rare cigars and attempting to defraud General Insurance International. He was instructed to repay the $10,000, sentenced to three years' imprisonment and a fine of $50,000. But the real winner in the case was Teschmaker. With the CEO's blessing he was initiated into the ranks of the fraud division and within a year was making a name for himself as a tenacious and creative agent.

'You said you were following someone who was following Jane,' Sinclair said when he had stopped laughing. 'I take it you don't mean you were following my men?'

'No. I didn't even see them.'

'Care to tell me who you were following then?'

'So you can send Mr Edwards and his friend around?'

'No. So I can understand what the hell is going on.'

'Sorry, but I still don't know.' Teschmaker refilled the glasses. 'He's a Romanian and he's involved in something. I think he was following your wife because she was there.'

'What?'

'I don't think he has a clue who she is.' He realised he was asking for rather a large suspension of disbelief. But fortunately his mind was working better than his body. 'His extracurricular activities have been causing a bit of a problem for the embassy and I've been employed to file a report.' Not bad, he thought, almost plausible. 'Obviously they couldn't use one of their own people as he would recognise them,' he added for good measure.

If Oliver Sinclair was sceptical he didn't show it. 'I can pay.'

'I never doubted that.' Teschmaker wanted to laugh but his ribs were aching again. He gritted his teeth. 'Maybe we can come to an arrangement, but I would need your full cooperation.'

'You have it.' Sinclair moved his hand slightly and allowed the build-up of ash to drop from the tip of the cigar. 'Tell me what you need to know.'

Teschmaker knew he was about to make the wrong decision and for all the wrong reasons. Though he couldn't put his finger on it, every professional instinct was telling him not to trust Sinclair. Not to have anything to do with his messy affairs. Was it something he had said that sounded odd? Or was it simply his overwhelming self-confidence? It irked Teschmaker, worried him, and yet he couldn't stop himself.

'Everything about Jane. I want to know everything about her.'

'This is everything you need.' From behind the bar Aleksandr Shlyapnikov handed over the manila folder. 'The embassy staff is pretty stable.'

'Stable?' Teschmaker asked. 'In what way?'

Shlyapnikov laughed. 'I think it's an economic thing. They can't afford to rotate their staff in the way most embassies do. These people have all been here since Ceau¸sescu was overthrown.'

'Banished for life.'

'Somehow I don't think they would consider it like that. The life here is much better than in Bucharest.'

That was understandable, Teschmaker thought as he flipped open the folder. He ran his eyes down the list of names. Whoever had done the job for Aleksandr Yefremovich had been pretty thorough. Listed alongside was the make and numberplate of the car they were officially listed as using. Only five names out of the thirty or so had a car beside them. Times were obviously tough in Romania. There was no mention of a Ford.

'There is a list of their pool cars on the back.' Shlyapnikov leaned over and flipped the page. 'Six of them, but from what I understand only two are in running order. One of them isn't even registered.'

'There's no Ford, Aleksandr Yefremovich.' Teschmaker glanced down the list again.

'Sorry,' Shlyapnikov grunted and ambled off to the freezer for a bottle of vodka. 'You didn't ask about any

Ford,' he said when he returned. 'You must be more precise, Martin.'

For a while they sat and drank; single icy shots accompanied by slices of dill-flavoured gherkin and spicy sausage. Later, as he cautiously navigated the steps down to the street, Teschmaker turned and called out: 'A Ford. Precisely a black Ford.' Behind him he heard Aleksandr Yefremovich laugh.

Despite the amount of vodka he had consumed Teschmaker was up at dawn, prepared to devote the day to getting a better idea of Jane's routine. Now familiar with the cars she drove, he could afford to take more care and so he parked further along the road but still in sight of her house. There was no sign of life. He spent the time reviewing the information he had garnered from her husband. Was he still her husband? Oliver Sinclair had described it as a temporary separation. Was he fooling himself? According to Sinclair, Jane had been the one to suggest they spend some time apart. He claimed he had shown her the photographs and demanded an explanation. None had been offered. Simply said she couldn't talk about it and that it would be better to part for a while, like she was punishing herself, he had said. And the photographs? No matter how Teschmaker put together what he knew about Jane, the images simply didn't fit. Five photographs. None of the other people in the shots were identifiable but neither were they the same people. Five photographs and the only common denominator, apart from the activities, was Jane.

And what about Sinclair? There was something about his determination to get to the person who had mailed him the photographs that didn't quite ring true. Nothing, Teschmaker had to admit, that he could pin down, but rather a vague feeling that maybe Sinclair wasn't being totally straight with him. Sinclair had sworn Jane had never shown any inclination towards S&M. Quite the reverse. A couple of times when he had suggested something like it she had told him flatly that she wasn't the slightest bit interested. Apparently that had changed. When, how and why?

'What about *your* infidelities?' Teschmaker had asked. 'Surely most women wouldn't have put up with such behaviour?'

'So you're an expert on my sex life?' Sinclair retorted.

'There have been rumours . . .'

'What can I say?' Sinclair shrugged. 'I have my needs.'

Teschmaker laughed. 'You've always been like that?'

'Aren't most men?'

'Maybe.' Teschmaker thought about it. 'No, maybe not. Probably most men would be happy just to be loved.'

Sinclair groaned. 'What are you, Martin? Some kind of old-fashioned romantic? I got all the love I could stand from my mother.'

'So what do you want from women?'

'Excitement? Forbidden fruit? Jesus! I just like a good screw.'

'You like to conquer? Is that what you're saying?'

'I know it's not fashionable to admit it, but I reckon that's about it.'

'Not fashionable? It's bloody antediluvian. So you're hooked on the illicit? Is that what you're telling me?'

Oliver shook his head morosely. 'I have no idea what I'm telling you, Martin. I don't even know why I told you. I guess I could spout a lot of psycho-babble about how our first sexual experiences shape the way we are for the rest of our lives, but that's a bit too touchy-feely for me. I just think we all have needs and everyone has different ways of satisfying them.'

'And Jane? She has needs?'

'She had her study, then her work.'

'Investment advising?'

'If only that was all.' Sinclair scowled. 'She was perpetually on call to Foreign Affairs and every other bloody bureaucratic body that can't sort itself out.'

'Really?'

'Oh yes.' Sinclair sounded bitter, jealous. 'Jane's speciality is defence procurement policy assessment, especially in relation to the former Soviet Republics. She not only did her day job but she was up half the night advising government about Uzbekistan's military budget, Kalashnikov confederalism, how much Ingushetia spends on ground forces or preparing a paper for some conference. Oh yes, that's my girl — not so great in bed but ask her to churn out fifteen thousand words on problems in methodological analysis and she's hot to trot.'

To Teschmaker that had all sounded as foreign to the Jane he was piecing together as the photographs were. But then, maybe not. After all her 'day job' as Sinclair had termed it was involved with investment opportunities overseas. And he remembered that Jane's business partner Sarah Norrby had said Jane specialised in the Eastern European region. What was it about that area of the world that fascinated her? But Teschmaker couldn't make the connection. He checked his watch. It was after nine. No sign of Jane. An hour later he gave up for the day.

It was the same the following morning. No car, no Jane, no nothing. Teschmaker decided it was time for a break from the entire business. He did his laundry, defrosted and cleaned out the refrigerator and shopped for groceries. But by late afternoon his distraction therapy was wearing a bit thin. Time and again his mind came back to the enigma that was Jane Sinclair/Jane Morris. Somewhere there must be a thread of logic running through it all.

In an attempt to clarify his thoughts he turned on his computer and made a list in chronological order of everything that had happened since he set out to contact her. It didn't tell him anything. Jane appeared to like S&M, had left her husband and hated Teschmaker. Why she hated him, he still had no idea. It dawned on him that his anger at her had diminished, replaced, surprisingly, by a sense of enjoyment at the mystery of it all. He reread what he had written, looking again for a pattern. Nothing. Finally he switched the computer off, acknowledging that it had been a futile exercise. There was nothing that he could do now until she resurfaced. The knowledge rankled, the forced inaction bothering him. Then he realised that there was something he could do. He made himself a quick snack, drank a coffee and headed for the car.

Forty-five minutes later he was driving slowly past the entrance to the country house he had followed Jane to a few days earlier. As he'd expected, the house was in darkness. Teschmaker drove on another hundred metres and found a place to park the car; well off the road, out of sight of passing traffic. He locked it and, not wanting to have a set of keys jangling in his pocket, tucked them behind the front left wheel. It was a clear crisp night; scattered cloud and free from the light pollution of the city, the stars burned sharp and bright. Away towards the horizon a sliver of new moon was sailing up the sky.

At the gate Teschmaker found the padlock securely in place, so he climbed over and, avoiding the gravel drive, made his way silently on grass towards the house. A flight of steps, cracked concrete, an upturned urn and dead shrubs. Nothing. The large front door looked solid — too solid to attempt a forced entry. He moved around the building, pausing to check the dilapidated shed on the side. Outside the broken fingers of an inverted harrow pushed up through tangled weeds, while inside an ancient tractor, stripped of its engine and tyres, sat up on blocks — an abandoned artifact from an earlier age. A misshapen horse collar hung from a rusted hook on the wall. Nothing of interest.

Behind the house he found a collapsed tank stand alongside of which a newer and smaller one had been built. Between the stand and the stump of an ancient tree was a neat pile of chopped and stacked firewood. Teschmaker picked up a piece and brought it to his nose. It was freshly cut, still exuding the resinous smell of pine. For a second he was a boy again, stacking the firewood at the holiday shack at Keynes. His father, fingers wrapped in mittens, getting another log ready for the crosscut saw. 'Just push, don't pull,' his father would bark and Martin would grasp the cold steel handle and push until his arms ached. He had loved those moments. Cutting, stacking amidst the smell of fresh sawdust that fell like brown snow on the frosted ground.

Maybe Jane planned to restore the house and was preparing to spend some time in residence. He replaced the firewood and was about to continue his circumambulation of the house when he noticed a dark shadow on the stonework. Set back under a low stone lintel that had been designed to give some protection from the elements was a wooden door, held shut by a single latch. Teschmaker expected it to be secured on the inside by a bolt, but to his surprise the latch clicked up and the door swung open. He stepped inside, leaving the door open behind him.

There was very little light so he paused to let his eyes adjust to the dim surroundings. The atmosphere inside the house was musty but not unpleasant and several degrees warmer than the cool night outside. Teschmaker found he was standing in a hallway. To the right and left were open doors. Straight ahead of him the hall ended at a larger door. This, he surmised, must be the main entrance at the front of the building. Taking care not to bump into anything he guided himself along the hallway, peering into the rooms on either side. They were all empty. No furniture and, from what he could see, no decorations. The hallway walls appeared to be covered with wallpaper, but when he stepped into one of the adjoining rooms his groping hand came into contact with raw hessian. He approached the front door where there was a great deal more moonlight spilling in from glass panels in the door and small round windows on either side. To the right a stairway led up to the top storey. It was as he turned to the stairs and reached out for the bannister that he sensed he wasn't alone. His heart rate accelerated and he peered up into the shadows. Nothing . . . but then he saw a figure in the darkness. Someone was sitting on the edge of the balcony at the top of the stairs, back resting against the stair post.

'You should have knocked.' The voice, almost a whisper, sounded petulant.

Teschmaker couldn't determine the gender of the speaker. He took a breath and stepped back. 'I didn't want to disturb you.'

'You haven't come to replace me?' There was a pleading quality to the tone.

'No. I was just having a look around.'

'You were checking on me,' the voice whined and the person stood up and opened a door. Soft light flooded the balcony and Teschmaker could see that the speaker was a man. 'Everything's in order. See for yourself.' He beckoned for Teschmaker to come up. 'When am I going to be relieved?'

'Tomorrow,' Teschmaker said firmly and made his way up the stairs. If the man assumed him to be someone else then he wasn't about to correct him. He was a peculiar-looking individual: shorter than Teschmaker, very slim, his face as effeminate as his voice sounded. His hair was extremely short, as though it been shaved and only recently grown back. He was dressed in a pair of odd black pantaloons, tied at the waist in the manner of pyjama trousers. He wore no shirt, just a simple waistcoat above which was a studded collar.

'Now tell me what's been happening,' Teschmaker demanded.

The man nodded and lowered his eyes as Teschmaker crossed the landing. He held the door wide, waiting for Teschmaker to precede him into the room. As Teschmaker stepped up beside him he couldn't help noticing that the man appeared to have waxed or shaved every hair off his arms and chest.

'Nothing,' the man replied. 'Nothing's been happening.' He looked down at his feet as Teschmaker came level with him.

The man is scared of me, Teschmaker thought. Everything about him showed it: the half-whispered tone, the lowered eyes, the body language, the submissive attitude.

Teschmaker stepped through the door into a large room lit by two oil lamps. The one on the table by the door was a hurricane lamp; the other, at the far end of the room set back in a small stone alcove, was more ornate, an old-fashioned mantle under a purple glass shade. It appeared that this storey was in its original condition. The wooden ceiling and floors looked as though they had once been polished, the only sign of damage a fine web of spidery cracks across the plastered walls. A single carpet runner, old and threadbare, traversed the length of the room.

'You would like a cup of tea?' The man followed him into the room and quietly shut the door to the landing behind him. 'It wouldn't be any trouble. I have to make him some anyway. He likes his tea about now.'

'Yes, tea,' Teschmaker said, thinking that while the man was preparing it he would have a chance to look around the room. Then he realised what the man had said. 'Where is he?'

'Through the door.' He indicated towards the far end of the room. 'There's no fresh milk —'

'Black. I have it black,' Teschmaker snapped. He didn't normally speak to total strangers that way but there was something irritating about the obsequious and ingratiating tone of the man. Suddenly things clicked into place and he knew instinctively where this man fitted into the picture. Everything about him suggested that he would enjoy being tied up and disciplined; Teschmaker was sure he was the man in the first picture with Jane. Teschmaker decided to test out his intuition.

'Tell me the name of your master,' he demanded.

'I haven't done anything wrong,' the man whined.

'His name.'

'Master Francis. I thought he would come and get me —'

So the man was not the slave of whoever was in the next room. 'What does Master Francis call you?'

To Teschmaker's amazement the man sank to his knees, stared at the ground and mumbled something. He looked so soft and pathetic; at the same time the glow from the oil lamp painted his skin in burnished tones.

'Speak up!'

'Viola. Master calls me Viola.'

Teschmaker repressed his disgust. 'He likes to play on you?'

'Yes.'

'Then, Viola, make the tea and bring it through to me.' He spoke more gently and reaching out his hand stroked the man's hair. The man winced beneath his touch, as though anticipating this small tenderness was a feint and would be followed by a blow.

'How should I address you?' Viola asked timidly, still on his knees.

'Martin. My name is Martin.'

He turned and strode down the room, attempting to give the impression that he knew what he was doing. In the light of the second lamp he saw a makeshift mattress beside the door. Obviously this was where Viola slept. Hearing a noise behind him Teschmaker turned and looked quickly back down the room, fearing that the man might not be convinced by what he himself felt was a less than persuasive performance. But he need not have worried. Viola was crouched over a small gas stove and was filling a kettle from a plastic water bottle.

'Not too strong,' he said.

'No, Master Martin.'

Hiding his grin, Teschmaker grasped the door handle and turned it. The door opened away from him and he found himself in a smaller room lit by a single hurricane lamp, the wick turned down so that it gave out only a small amount of light. This room, in contrast to the previous one, was fully furnished.

Against one wall stood a wardrobe; the other held a casement window, beneath which was a bed. A man, sensing or hearing someone enter, struggled up into a sitting position in it.

Teschmaker walked quickly over to the lamp and turned it up. The man in the bed looked terrified. He was old, probably seventy or eighty years of age. The face had been full once but now loose skin hung from his cheekbones and the frightened eyes were set back in deep sockets. Wisps of long silver hair hung in disarray at the back of the man's head, the front of which was almost completely bald. As Teschmaker lifted up the lamp and moved to the bed the man cowered back against the pillows, his hands clutching at the sheets.

'*Tak oni poslali tebe*,' he said slowly, his voice surprisingly deep and strong given his demeanour and age. But what startled Teschmaker most was that the man was speaking fluent Czech. They have sent you. It was a statement, not a question.

'*Znáš me?*'

'No, I don't know who you are, but I know what you are.'

'*Co jsem?*'

'You are a killer. You are shit, just like all the rest.'

The man seemed to have shrugged aside his earlier fear. He reached out a hand and grasped the metal bed frame and pulled himself up into a more upright position. 'You might as well do it now. All of the others are dead, and not even that will stop them.'

It wasn't making any sense. Teschmaker put the lamp down carefully on a small bedside table. 'I didn't come to kill you.'

The man laughed, a dry hollow laugh that set off a fit of coughing. Seeing a glass of water on the table, Teschmaker picked it up and held it to the man's mouth but his hand was brushed away.

'Well, if you didn't come to kill me, you might as well leave. You are wasting what little time I have left. I have said everything I am going to say and I can't remember anything more.'

As though suddenly tired the old man lay down again, but he kept his eyes open, watching Teschmaker closely as he pulled a chair up to the bed. 'I'm sick of all the questions and I just want to be left alone.'

Teschmaker looked around the room, seeking something that would make sense of what he had stumbled into. An old man in fear of his life, hidden away in a ramshackle house in the country. A prisoner? Was he being kept here against his will? Was the other man, the peculiar Viola, acting as a guard? It hardly seemed feasible. His musing was interrupted by the sound of the door opening behind him. He turned to see Viola entering, carrying a tray neatly arranged with two cups of tea and a plate of digestive biscuits.

'Your tea, Master Martin,' Viola murmured as he placed the tray on the dressing table. After passing Teschmaker his cup, he glided over to the bed and, moving the lamp to make room, put the second cup of tea on the bedside table. He took a couple of tablets from a small bottle on the table and handed them to the old man then passed him his tea. 'Come on now, sit up, take your tablets and have your tea while I fluff up the pillows.'

'Stop fussing,' the old man growled in perfect English. 'You know I hate being fussed over.'

'You speak English?' Teschmaker didn't bother to hide his surprise.

'Of course I speak English.' The man turned his scowl from Viola to Teschmaker. 'It appears you do too.'

'Mr Morris speaks very good English, don't you, sir?' Viola said softly. 'When he wants to. However most of the time he jabbers away in foreign languages.'

Teschmaker's head was in a spin. Could this Mr Morris be Jane's father? He looked at him, trying to conjure up his childhood memory of the man. But as hard as he tried he couldn't remember what Jane's father had looked like. But the fact that the man was here, in what Teschmaker assumed was a house belonging to Jane, was compelling. It had to be her father.

Having swallowed the tablets, the old man sipped his tea with obvious enjoyment, no longer looking fearful or haunted as he had only moments before. Teschmaker turned to Viola. 'Leave us. I want to talk with Mr Morris while I drink my tea.'

Viola finished plumping up the pillows and with a courteous nod of his head left the room.

'How long is it since you have seen Jane?' Teschmaker asked, but the old man appeared not to hear him.

'I helped with the lilies.'

'What?' Teschmaker had no idea what Morris was talking about. Then he realised the old man was not even addressing him. He was talking to himself, searching for something inside.

'The lilies. Such lilies that had never been dreamed of, but then nobody had any idea what gardeners we were. But it killed them. Every one of them. Bouquets? You can't imagine the bouquets. Without the mirrors it would not have worked. You think it was my fault? Such gardeners: Greenglass, Alberto Garcia, clever little Marcia. So good with her hands. Jacob Sedov — he loved my little flowers. So many of them. Each in their own way a talented gardener. None of them would have died if it wasn't for my damned flowers. Do you know that?'

His hand trembled as he clattered his cup down on the bedside table. He looked at Teschmaker with a sudden blaze of hatred.

'Do you think I wouldn't tell you if I knew? Of course I would, but I don't know. I never did. Marcia Zanda, Yakunin, Guy Greenglass, Georg Bella, Hugh Cowgill . . . too many dead gardeners. All I did was train them. I gave them my little flowers. I didn't know they would kill them.'

Just as suddenly as the anger had swept over him it vanished and the old man sank, drained and shaking, back into the pillows. 'You know what you would see if you could look into those mirrors?'

Teschmaker wasn't certain that he was the one being addressed but he answered nevertheless. 'No. What would I see?'

'*Mrtví vstanou z hrobu.*'

The dead rising from their graves? The old man was demented, Teschmaker realised, and paranoid, his mind haunted by ghosts of his own making. Yet that didn't explain why he was here, locked away in this house. And how long had he been here? And speaking Czech — is that where he had vanished to all those years ago?

Teschmaker got wearily to his feet and, draining his tea, put the cup back on the tray. One last shot, he thought. 'Good night, Mr Morris,' he said quietly and then added in Russian, '*Spokoinoi nochi.*'

'*Desvidanja*,' the old man replied automatically. So he also spoke Russian.

'Maybe we'll talk again.' But if the old man heard him he made no reply. Teschmaker left the room and shut the door quietly behind him.

Viola scrambled to his feet as he saw Teschmaker come out of the old man's room. 'Would you like more tea, Master Martin?'

'No. I have to return to the city. Tell me what the medicine is for.'

'I'm not sure. I think it's supposed to help his memory but . . .' He paused and glanced around as if he was about to break a confidence and wanted to make certain nobody was going to reprimand him. 'But I think it makes him a bit silly and sends him to sleep.'

'He sleeps a lot?'

'Sometimes he pretends . . .'

Well, the craziness obviously wasn't faked. Teschmaker moved to leave. Then he stopped. 'Oh, one other thing, Viola . . .'

'Yes?'

'Thanks for the tea, it was very nice.'

Teschmaker walked down the stairs with the distinct impression that behind him on the landing Viola was blushing with pleasure.

CHAPTER ELEVEN

B ack at home Teschmaker was about to call Oliver Sinclair when the phone rang. It was Aleksandr Shlyapnikov.

'You remember the black Ford?'

'Yes.'

'It's a cheap long-term rental.'

'And . . .' Teschmaker knew how Aleksandr Yefremovich liked to string things out. It was already late and he was impatient to get on to Sinclair.

'Laverov . . .' Shlyapnikov paused as though the name should mean something to Teschmaker. 'Konstantin Ivanovich Laverov.'

'He doesn't sound very Romanian,' Teschmaker snorted.

'That's the whole point.' Shlyapnikov laughed. 'He's a Russian *muzhik* — a real man, an old-fashioned *homo Sovieticus*. Laverov was raised on the three staples: Communism, *pelmeni* and vodka. He was the KGB chief for the Moscow Military District, but things changed faster than he could and Konstantin Ivanovich found himself seriously out of step with the times. In Moscow the dominant species isn't *homo Sovieticus* any more, or even *homo sapiens*, but *homo Mafioso* —'

'But what is he doing here?' Teschmaker interjected. 'And why is he hanging out with the Romanians?'

'Patience, Martin.'

Teschmaker heard something that sounded suspiciously like Shlyapnikov throwing back a shot of vodka.

'When they changed the KGB to the FSB he decided to retire, but apparently Sergei Stepashin, who was in charge at the time, persuaded him to stay on in some kind of advisory role. I don't know if that is still the case but the story I hear is that he is working from the Romanian Embassy so that not even his Russian colleagues know what he's doing.'

'And how did you find this out?'

There was a muffled laugh at the other end of the phone. 'My friends have friends and their friends told them.' He laughed again. 'Then I rang up the Russian Embassy and asked the receptionist —'

'The receptionist?'

'Sure. Why not? You know what it's like these days — *khozyaina nyet*.'

'Nobody is in charge?'

'Exactly. And she told me everything I needed to know,' Shlyapnikov said triumphantly. 'Mind you, she is a regular at the restaurant — she rates my *pelmeni* as better than any she's had in Moscow.'

'I'd have to concur.' Teschmaker shuddered at the thought of the number of times in Russia he had been confronted with inedible *pelmeni*. 'But, *Bozhe moy*! My God! Where's the security gone?'

'To feed the stomach the mouth has to open.'

'Is that an old Russian saying?'

'No, my friend, I just made it up.' Shlyapnikov laughed at his own joke. 'But that's it, I'm afraid. Nothing more. My reading is that the man is on government business.'

'Thanks, Aleksi, you've been a great help.'

'It's nothing. Come and eat again soon, Martin.'

'I will. *Spokoinoi nochi* — good night.'

So this man, Konstantin Ivanovich Laverov, was a not-so-innocent abroad, operating out of a friendly embassy in order to keep his own people in the dark about his intentions. Well, that had only been partially successful. Even if the Russians didn't know what he was up to, they knew he was in town. But doing what? It was a fair bet that Jane's father was the key. He spoke Czech like a native and when Teschmaker had switched to Russian, Mr Morris had replied without hesitation. But why would the Russians have an interest in an old man who was obviously not in full control of his faculties? And why did Jane keep him locked away in the countryside? Too many questions — too few answers.

He glanced at his watch: almost eleven. He picked up the phone again and dialled the number Oliver Sinclair had given him. To his surprise it was picked up immediately.

'Oliver, it's Martin Teschmaker.'

'Good, I was just about to phone you.'

'You were?'

'Jane is back in town. I was looking after Mel and —'

'Mel?'

'Melanie Louise, our daughter.'

'Okay. And?'

'Jane came around. I thought she was going to pick Mel up. I mean, that's what she normally does.'

'But not this time?'

'No.' Sinclair paused as though gathering his thoughts. 'She asked if I would mind keeping Mel here for another night. Apparently she has something on tomorrow evening. I thought you should know.'

'Sure,' Teschmaker replied. 'You want me to keep tabs on her?'

'You have a problem with that?'

Teschmaker forced the smile off his face so that his pleasure at this development wouldn't be apparent in his voice. 'I told you, I'm not —'

'A private detective.'

'But in this case —'

'I suppose you could . . .'

'Make an exception.' Teschmaker laughed at the verbal tennis rally. 'Do you know where or when?'

'Zilch. You'll have to start from scratch. Now, you were ringing me?'

'Yes. I need a bit more information.'

'Shoot.'

'Jane's father . . .'

'Sydney Morris?'

The surprised tone was all the proof Teschmaker needed that Sinclair had no idea that Jane's father was still alive, let alone sequestered away in the country.

'Yes. What do you know about him?'

'Not a hell of a lot. Some kind of physicist, wasn't he?'

'A long time ago.'

'Probably dead now,' Sinclair said.

'Didn't Jane ever say anything about him?' Teschmaker realised that he was going to have to push if he was to get anything. Chances were that Oliver Sinclair knew nothing.

'A no-go area.' Sinclair sounded wistful. 'I raised it with her early on but all she would ever say was the stuff that is in the public record.'

'Which is?'

'I had one of my assistants dig up what there was. Apparently Morris had some kind of ideological problem with capitalism. He defected to the Soviets back in the sixties. There was a bit of huff and puff about it at the time but after that he faded from view. A report a couple of years later claimed that he was working on the Soviet nuclear program. It was never verified.'

'And he never made contact with his daughter?'

'Never. I doubt that she would have welcomed it.'

Teschmaker wondered if he should tell Sinclair that he had seen Sydney Morris, but decided against it. The nuclear angle was interesting but . . .

'Tell me, Oliver, do you think Jane's interest in the Eastern Bloc countries has some kind of connection with her father?'

'I thought that once. But even with all of her contacts and language skills she's never tried to find him, as far as I know.'

'Could she have done so without your knowing?'

'Probably,' Sinclair snorted. 'But why would she keep it from me?'

Teschmaker let that one go. As far as he could make out there were a great many things that Jane had failed to mention to her husband. But there was nothing to gain by pointing that out at this particular juncture. 'Okay, I'll be in touch.'

'Hang on. Why the questions about Jane's father?'

'Nothing really. It turns out the man following her was a Russian. I just wondered if there was a connection.'

'And is there?'

'No,' Teschmaker said. 'I don't think so.

He hung up and reached for the bottle of scotch and poured himself a drink. Start from the centre and work out — isn't that what he always did? Hell — he laughed out loud. Out where? There were threads leading in so many different directions. A spider web spun by a psychotic spider. And somewhere in the web was Jane. For a moment he played with the notion that she might be the spider. No, she was not spinning this one. Jane was caught in the web just as surely as . . .

He shook his head and tossed down the remainder of the drink. Had he been about to say that he too was caught in the web? No, Teschmaker reassured himself. I'm simply an observer. And I have no investment in any of this other than the enjoyment of playing the watcher. In the end it was probably all about sex. Jane was simply having an affair and dabbling in bondage. But how did the Russian fit in? Had he taken the photographs? No. That made no sense at all. Or Viola's master — what had he called him? Master

Francis. Now he was a definite candidate for the role of fetishistic photographer. Good old-fashioned sex and bondage. Not his cup of tea. But it obviously did it for some. What had he read somewhere? *I seek the love that is more cruel than pain.* He ran the thought around for a moment and wondered, as he poured another drink, if love without pain was love at all?

The following evening, just on dusk, Teschmaker drove over to Charlottewood and positioned himself in Haycroft Avenue ready to follow Jane. All afternoon the humidity had been rising, dark clouds massing in the west. As he waited the wind picked up and the temperature began to drop as the first rain squalls swept across the city. It was a mixed blessing. Rain made a tail harder to spot but also made the job of tailing somebody that much more difficult. He started the engine and rolled the car a little closer to Jane's gate. So far the summer had been dry, with clear days and unseasonably cool nights, but after a burst of warmth it looked as though the weather was going to swing around to the south-west and turn really nasty. Even as he thought it, he felt the car buffeted by stronger winds and in the distance lightning illuminated swollen clouds.

'Damn.' Teschmaker swore out loud as the car windows began to fog up, forcing him to roll down the side window. Rain blew straight in and he rolled the window up again, buffing at the windshield with his hand. This was a night to spend at home. He corrected himself: 'home' was a concept hardly applicable to the emptied-out shell he was living in. But it was in many ways a more comfortable existence than that which he had shared with Gwenda. Her infidelities — and his — had made a mockery of their marriage for many years. Thankfully he was pulled from that depressing thought by the intrusion into the dark street of a set of headlights. As the car turned into Haycroft Avenue he was briefly washed by its lights. Without pausing the car drove past and turned into a tree-lined driveway two houses behind him. A false alarm.

There was still no sign of movement at Jane's house. Had she gone out straight from work? Hardly likely, but he had to admit he really had no idea. Face it, he lectured himself, you have not the slightest evidence on which to base any presumptions about Jane. She was even more of an enigma now than when he had started with the discovery of the photograph from their childhood.

Outside the rain bucketed down and a flash of lightning nearer at hand was followed by a percussive clap of thunder that was close enough to make him flinch. In the holiday shack at Keynes he and his father had always counted the seconds between 'flash and crash'. 'A fascination with thunder and lightning is a fascination with your own fear of death,' Alexi Teschmaker had once said. The young Martin hadn't really understood at the time.

Still nothing from Jane's house. He glanced at the clock on the dashboard. Was it really nearly nine? Or was the clock faulty? He knew he couldn't risk turning on the interior light but then he remembered that the glove box had a small light that came on when it was opened. He pressed the catch and peered at the dial of his watch. The car clock was slow: it was nine fifteen.

Twenty minutes later, just as the car was getting cold enough to make him consider turning on the motor and running the heater for a few minutes, a light switched on at the front of the house. It was only a glimmer over the wall but enough for him to know that someone was preparing to leave the premises. But five minutes passed and there was no sign of movement. No car backed out; and the gates remained firmly shut. Another false alarm. Now the rain was drumming on the roof with such ferocity that he became concerned it might turn to hail and damage the car. Between flash and crash there was now no time to count anything. Far from depressing him, the intensity of the storm had a strangely energising effect. Teschmaker felt all charged up. Coinciding with the lifting of his blue mood, a yellow Volvo turned into the street. Unlike the previous vehicle that had homed itself like an obedient pigeon, the Volvo was cruising slowly, looking for somewhere unfamiliar. So, she was being picked up?

Teschmaker's guess was right. As the car drew level with the gates of Jane's house they opened and a figure, bent almost double against the rain, scuttled through. The rear kerbside door opened and the person got in. For a moment the Volvo sat there, then pulled out slowly and did a U-turn. Where the hell did anyone go to just before ten at night?

Teschmaker knew he had a problem. There appeared to be few other cars on the road and this late on a wet night he was going to stand out like — what was the expression his father had always used? Like tits on a bishop. Checking his lights were off, he turned on the engine and eased the car into gear. Fortunately the weather was so foul that the Volvo was taking its time, cruising slowly back in the direction of the city. Hopefully its rear window would be fogged up and the driver more worried about the elements than being followed; nevertheless he knew he couldn't take a risk. He kept the lights off and stayed well back. Now the rain was coming in sheets; even in normal circumstances he would have had difficulty seeing where he was going. To compound the problem it appeared that the street lights had been knocked out by the ongoing electrical storm. Ahead the traffic lights near the Charlotte River Bridge were blinking on and off in amber distress.

Teschmaker knew that if they took the Belmont ramp onto the Mitchell Freeway he would have to use his lights, and silently prayed there would still be enough traffic at this time of night to allow him at least minimal cover. He was in luck. As he swung onto the ramp a late-night delivery van and a small sedan sped past in a flurry of spray. Teschmaker switched on his lights and crossed into the freeway lane behind the yellow Volvo. After a few minutes the sedan changed lanes and sped away, but the van stayed put, seven or eight car lengths behind the Volvo with Jane inside. At least I hope it's Jane, Teschmaker thought. He really had no way of knowing.

Overhead the lightning was heading inland towards the hills. The rain was probably also on the decrease, but tucked as he was behind the spray from the van it was hard to judge. He turned the wipers on full and swung into the outside lane. But to his dismay the tail-lights of the Volvo veered off down an exit in the other direction. Teschmaker slammed on the brakes. It was too wet and the car slid sideways; for one sickening moment he thought he was going to hit the rear of the van. Behind him another car was forced to brake and for a split second he saw it in his rear-view mirror, slewing sideways and heading for the guard rail.

Somehow Teschmaker managed to keep control of the BMW and slid behind the van towards the exit ramp. Suddenly he was heading into the dark. He fought for control as the car bucketed over the low end of a concrete hump that divided the highway from the exit ramp. With more good luck than skill he found himself heading down the exit without hitting anything or smashing the sump on the road divider.

'Fuck this!' he swore, more to let off steam than at anything in particular. The road curved around to the left to where a set of traffic lights controlled the entrance to a major road. Before he had time to work out where he was he saw that the lights were red and that he had no option other than to pull up directly behind the late-model yellow Volvo. Fortunately the driver had not turned on the rear demister, affording Teschmaker a slight amount of protection. You are getting too paranoid, he told himself, they have no idea they are being tailed. He rolled up close enough so that he was hidden from the wing mirrors. Unfortunately he had no view of the people inside and so was still uncertain if Jane was on board or not.

As the lights went green the Volvo turned right and headed towards the city by the secondary roads. Why they should be taking this route was unclear to Teschmaker, but he dropped back as far as he dared and breathed a sigh of relief as another car overtook him and slotted in between them. They passed through a light industrial suburb that was unfamiliar to Teschmaker. It had seen better days: old fibro sheds, grimy two-storey buildings, their windows broken or boarded up.

Five minutes later he followed the Volvo left into the outskirts of the Russian Quarter. The car that had been acting as a buffer continued on towards the city centre so he was feeling exposed again. Fortunately the rain had increased and visibility was poor. The Volvo slowed down and pulled into the kerb and Teschmaker stopped too. Switching off his lights he peered through the downpour, trying to work out exactly where he was. To his right was a warehouse; to the left a row of lock-up garages with rusted roller-doors and padlocks. Further down the road he spotted a landmark he recognised: the Guzenko Parking Station. No, he corrected himself, the rear of the parking station. He took the city road map from the glove box and, holding it up so that he could read it in the light of a street lamp, located himself at the top end of Nikolayevsky Street. The street ran parallel to Guzenko. He remembered one of his Russian friends explaining that Nikolayevsky was a prominent émigré in the early 1930s and publisher of a Menshevik broadsheet. He had been honoured with the street name after surviving an attack by the NKVD.

It was never a busy street even during the day so Teschmaker was surprised by the number of parked cars. Ahead of him the Volvo had switched off its lights. There was nothing for it but to get out, though how he was going to walk casually along the totally exposed street without coming to someone's attention he had no idea.

Act now, think later, he joked lamely as he buttoned his coat to the neck. Cursing himself for not having an umbrella in the car, he stepped out into the rain. After locking the car, he crossed the road to where the buildings afforded him a slight respite from the prevailing wind. He was also further from the street lights there. He walked quickly along the pavement until he was opposite the parked Volvo but he had been too slow. There was no sign of the car's occupants. The street was completely deserted and, to make matters worse, the rain was even heavier than before. There was no way he was going to stand on the street like a drowned rat. He looked around for somewhere to shelter. Just a few steps to his right there was a recessed doorway leading into a wholesale furriers. Teschmaker climbed the steps and found himself in an ideal position for observing the other side of the street.

There were twenty or thirty cars parked either side of an unprepossessing office block: six storeys of brick sporting a large, unlit neon sign announcing the place to be the home of Mlad Fashions. Teschmaker wondered how many years ago the company had vanished. The street level was given over to a computer repair business. According to a dilapidated real-estate board, the entire building was 'ripe' with potential. Give it ten years, he thought, and the place will be all trendy inner-city apartments.

He waited for quarter of an hour but there was no sign of anyone going in or out of the building. A quick stroll-by, he decided and, turning his collar up, crossed the road. There was no front entrance, other than to the securely locked computer repair shop. Teschmaker paused and looked up and down the street; he appeared to be the only person in the vicinity. This late at night, in this area and particularly in such inclement weather, he would have been surprised to see another soul. He moved to the side of the building and came across a narrow entranceway between the buildings. A walkway — cracked paving and weeds — led to a side entrance. A small amount of illumination was provided by a low-wattage light positioned above a door in the side of the building. For a moment he considered walking down to it, but decided it was not worth the risk. He knew there was little hope now of finding out if Jane was inside other than by waiting in the increasingly cool night. Then he thought of a more constructive option.

Going quickly back to his car he rummaged around until he found a scrap of paper and a felt-tipped pen. He walked back along the row of parked cars jotting down the numberplates. If nothing else he could get an idea of who these people were. By the look of the cars — a couple of Jags, several Beamers and an assortment of Volvos, Mercs and Saabs — they were a pretty well-heeled bunch. He put a small star beside the licence number of the yellow Volvo he had tailed from Jane's place.

Teschmaker was about to cross the road to work his way back along the other side when he heard voices coming from the alleyway. He ducked quickly behind a car and crouched out of sight. He couldn't make out what was being said but the tone was less than amicable. Someone was yelling abuse. There was a scream and then the sound of a door being slammed. Teschmaker waited for a couple of minutes and then, hearing nothing further, decided to risk taking a look. He strode quickly to the gap between the buildings, intending to keep walking if there was anybody still outside. But a quick glance revealed the narrow pathway to be empty.

He was about to return to the task of jotting down the licence numbers when out of the corner of his eye he saw something move on the ground. Halfway down the alley a man was struggling to his feet. Teschmaker held himself back. There was no point in getting involved. Whoever it was was obviously not too badly hurt as he had managed to get to his feet and was now stumbling up the laneway towards him. He was about to slip back across the road and out of sight when the injured man looked up. Even in the dim light Teschmaker could see that someone had made a real mess of his face. The man was bleeding profusely from the nose, lip and a cut above one eye. Then Teschmaker recognised him — the strange character he had encountered in the country house.

He stepped forward and took the man's arm. 'Viola, what the hell have you got yourself into?'

For a moment the man looked at him, uncomprehending eyes blinking wildly. Then he pitched forward. Teschmaker grabbed at him but succeeded only in ripping the man's shirt as he fell to the ground. Shit, he thought, what in God's name am I supposed to do now?

He knelt down beside Viola and rolled him over. 'Come on,' he said quietly. 'I'll give you a hand.'

All the offer elicited was a long groan but the man was still conscious, so Teschmaker pulled him up and supporting his weight half walked, half dragged him out of the lane and onto Nikolayevsky Street. 'Come on,' he repeated gently. 'Let's get you out of here.'

Slowly they made their way to his car where, with a bit of pushing and shoving, he managed to get Viola onto the rear seat. He turned on the interior light.

'Shit!'

The man had been pretty well messed up before they dumped him out the side door. The cut above his eye was superficial but there was a nasty gash in his scalp and his bleeding nose showed no sign of abating.

'What on earth did you do to deserve this?'

Viola opened his eyes and mumbled something.

'What?'

'You,' Viola said. 'Your fucking fault.'

'Me?' Teschmaker tucked an old newspaper under the man's head. There was no point in getting blood all over the car. 'I didn't do this to you.'

'They found out that you had tricked me.'

'They beat you up because I came to the house?'

'They beat me up,' Viola whimpered. 'But they'll kill you.'

Satisfied that he could do nothing further to staunch the bleeding, Teschmaker shut the rear door and went around the car to the driver's side. He slipped behind the wheel and started the motor.

'I'll take you to my place and get you cleaned up,' he said. None of the wounds looked like they needed stitching and, anyway, the last thing he wanted was the complication of having to explain Viola to a hospital matron and then, inevitably, the police.

If his tiredness and the wet conditions weren't enough, the thought of the police caused him to drive very sedately. Teschmaker thought it unlikely that any traffic cops would be out on a night like this but he would rather err on the side of caution than take the risk. Outside the weather was deteriorating, a second storm front was coming through and jagged bolts of forked lightning split the night with increased frequency. It was twenty minutes before midnight.

There was a vehicle in his driveway. Teschmaker parked in the street and made a quick dash through the rain to the limited shelter of the overhanging garage eaves. The first thing he noticed was the damage to the car: the maroon Mercedes was missing a wing mirror and sporting serious-looking body damage all along one side. The door on the driver's side no longer appeared to open and Norman, dressed in a rather sodden business suit, was holding the passenger door open as Edwards slid across the front seat.

'Evening, Mr Teschmaker,' Edwards said. Like Norman he was dressed in a suit but his was in a considerably drier condition. He moved quickly under shelter, followed closely by Norman.

'Late night?' Norman grinned. 'Rough weather for it, but.'

'Fuck off,' Teschmaker said. 'And get your car out of my drive.'

Edwards shook his head sadly, as though he was a much misunderstood individual resigned yet again to being denied a fair hearing. 'Understandable attitude, sir.'

'Absolutely,' Norman concurred.

Teschmaker began to wonder if it really was a grin on Norman's face or some congenital affliction. 'If you don't mind pissing off.'

'Apologies all round.' Edwards seemed determined to make some sort of personal breakthrough. 'We overstepped the line last time. Our fault entirely.'

'Absolutely. Overstepped the mark,' Norman added for clarity.

'Which part of "fuck off" don't you understand?' Teschmaker spoke as slowly and as patronisingly as he could.

'As I said, it was a misunderstanding. Mr Sinclair told us to come around and give you a hand. Offer our services.'

'We were going to stay well behind you tonight,' Norman said, 'but you lost us on the freeway.'

'Nice bit of driving, I must say.' Edwards looked ruefully at his car. 'Better than mine.'

'Straight into the guard rail . . .'

'My own fault entirely.'

Teschmaker grinned as he recollected the split-second view he had caught earlier in the night of the out-of-control car on the slippery road. 'Let me get this straight. You say Sinclair sent you to assist me?'

'Absolutely.' Norman nodded. 'Back him up, that's what Mr Sinclair said, right, Mr Edwards?'

'Right.' Edwards extended his hand in anticipation of a breakthrough in the hostilities. 'One of us fore and aft, *medio tutissimus ibis.*'

'Oh really?' Teschmaker laughed at the image. '*Nemo repente fuit turpissimus*,' he said and held up his hands in capitulation. 'If I have to walk "in the middle" of you two, I want you either side — no offence meant, Mr Edwards — but not fore and aft.' He turned and gestured to his own car. 'Well, you can start by getting the body out of the back.'

'Jesus!' Norman swore quietly. 'You knocked off someone?' He looked at Teschmaker with renewed respect.

'No. He's alive, just a little beaten up.'

'I never took you for the type . . .' Norman started but stopped as a noise came from the street. As though responding to being mentioned, Viola staggered out of the car. If anything he looked even worse than he had earlier. The blood from his nose and the cuts above his eye and in his scalp had all contributed a generous amount of blood to the ripped shirt, giving him the appearance of someone terminally wounded.

'Give him a hand while I unlock the door,' Teschmaker said, then in case Norman had the wrong idea added, 'And be gentle with him, he's not one of the bad guys.'

He unlocked the house and held the door wide as they brought Viola in. 'Viola, this Norman and Mr Edwards.'

'Gerard.' Edwards raised a questioning eyebrow in Teschmaker's direction. 'Viola, was it?'

'Viola. I think it's a nickname. We haven't known each other that long. There's a bathroom upstairs.' He led the way.

'Come on, pal,' is Norman spoke gently. 'We'll soon get you cleaned up.'

Viola looked terrified but he didn't resist.

In the bathroom Teschmaker lowered the toilet seat and they sat Viola down. 'Here.' Teschmaker tossed Edwards a towel. 'I'll get the bed in the study ready. I haven't got much stuff, but what there is is in the cabinet under the sink.'

'Not a problem. Norman, get the first aid kit from the car,' Edwards ordered.

He gave Teschmaker the impression of someone who was used to taking charge in an emergency. Probably trained in the forces, he thought.

By the time Teschmaker had prepared the bed, the other two had cleaned most of the blood off Viola's face. They then helped him to his feet and eased off the remnants of the shirt.

'Christ! Take a look at that.' Edwards screwed up his face in disgust. 'They've beaten the shit out of the poor bastard.' He turned Viola around. His back was covered with welts, ridged with tiny corrugations. 'What the hell did they use on you?'

'I deserved it,' Viola mumbled, turning his face to the floor in shame.

'Nobody deserves to be beaten like that.'

'I did,' Viola insisted.

'Come on,' Teschmaker interjected. 'We can talk about it in the morning.'

After they had Viola lying down, if not comfortable, they met in the kitchen. Teschmaker poured the remnants of his scotch into three tumblers and apologised for the lack of chairs, while Norman, still looking like a drowned rat, removed his jacket and hung it from a hook on the back of the door.

'I never did understand what happened to all your furniture,' Edwards said.

'I dumped it after my wife jumped ship.'

'Too many painful memories —' Norman began sympathetically.

'No. She had lousy taste and the stuff never suited me.' Teschmaker shrugged dismissively. 'Now, what's the story? You guys were following me on Sinclair's instructions. Doesn't he trust me?'

'Of course he does. He just wanted to make sure you had some backup.' Edwards drained his scotch in a single gulp. 'He thinks there's some funny stuff going on with his wife and he figured you might need some assistance.'

'We're to take orders from you,' Norman added.

This elicited a frown from Edwards. Obviously he hadn't been about to mention that, preferring a more equal partnership.

Teschmaker handed the scrap of paper to Edwards. 'Well, first thing in the morning you can start on this list of licence plates. They were all parked outside the building that Jane visited tonight.'

'What was it?' Norman asked. 'A party?'

'I think that depends on your definition of "party". You have seen the photographs?'

Teschmaker was uncertain how much Sinclair had divulged to his hired muscle. But he needn't have worried. The grin on Norman's face said it all.

'A bunch of very sick puppies,' Edwards said quietly.

'Not your cup of tea?'

'I have no problem inflicting pain, Mr Teschmaker, but I do so in a strictly professional manner.'

'I know.' Teschmaker grimaced at the memory.

'Sorry about that. I hope it won't get in the way of our —'

'Mr Edwards, I think that under the circumstances —'

'Gerard.'

'Gerard, under the circumstances I think we'll pretend that it never happened.'

'Appreciated, Martin,' Edwards beamed.

'Absolutely,' Norman added. 'Abso-bloody-lutely.'

CHAPTER TWELVE

Teschmaker found himself wandering through a rock maze. Gigantic slabs of red granite set either side of an obsidian path, but unlike stone in the real world it was alive. At each twist and turn he watched as the rock flowed like lava to reform in new shapes, to open new pathways and block the old. It seemed sentient, its malignant intent to send him forever in circles; holding, too, the potential to close in at any time and crush him. He tried running but the faster he moved the quicker the rock shape-shifted and moulded itself into new obstacles. Somewhere he could hear the clink of a stonemason's hammer and chisel. I must find this person, he thought, but as if in response to his thought the obsidian beneath his feet changed its consistency to the tackiness of tar that sucked him down and he knew he would sink. The clink of the hammer grew more insistent and summoning all his strength he threw himself sideways. It took him a moment to focus before he realised he was on the floor of the old master bedroom and the phone in his study was ringing. He had slept uncomfortably on the floor and his body ached in protest as he staggered to his feet and made his way through the hallway to the study. From the bed Viola flashed him a malevolent look and rolled towards the wall.

Teschmaker grabbed the phone. 'Yes?'

'Is that Mr Teschmaker?' It was a woman's voice, a slightly foreign accent.

'Yes.'

'I'm Irene, Mr Sinclair's personal assistant.'

'Yes?'

'Mr Sinclair asked me to ring to tell you that he has some important information for you and he wonders if you could meet him in two hours' time.'

Teschmaker glanced at his watch. It was just after nine thirty. 'Tell him I'll be there,' he said.

'He would rather not meet in the office. He asked if you would mind meeting him at the kiosk and flower shop at the Western Gate at Freeholm.'

Freeholm. The suggestion struck Teschmaker as strange. 'Freeholm cemetery?' The cemetery only had one public entrance, known as the Western Gate as it was located on the spot where the city's original western gate had once stood.

'Yes. He always visits the cemetery on the anniversary of his mother's death. I can contact him if that's not suitable for you.'

'No, it's not a problem. You can tell him I'll be there.' Teschmaker hung up the phone and turned to Viola. 'How are you feeling?'

'Well enough to go home.'

He didn't look it. Norman and Edwards had done a fair job of cleaning him up, but he was still pale and washed out. Against the white skin, the cuts and bruises appeared worse than they probably were. He was also sporting a black eye.

Teschmaker sat down on the bed beside him. 'Do you live alone?'

Viola nodded.

'Then I want you to stay here for a few days.'

'Why?' He sounded alarmed but he turned back from facing the wall and curled himself up in a foetal position. 'What will Master Francis say?'

'I'm not going to tell him.' Then a thought struck Teschmaker. 'Do you want to go back to your master? Is that what you want?'

Viola's hand shot to his neck, his fingers probing then dropping limply away. A tear rolled down his cheek. 'He's not my master any more. He's taken my collar away.'

Of course. Teschmaker wondered why he hadn't noticed before that the collar was gone. 'I'm sorry, I didn't realise the significance of the collar.'

'I don't belong to anybody now. There's nobody to look after me.'

Viola's lips were trembling and Teschmaker mentally urged him not to cry. He was finding the man difficult enough to deal with without the added stress of his emotional baggage.

'Then if Francis is not your master now it's none of his business.'

'But he would be very angry that I'm with you.'

'I think I can deal with that. You can stay here,' he said gently, 'but Viola, I need you to help me. I need to know why Francis had Sydney Morris hidden away in the country with you guarding him.'

'I wasn't guarding him.' He looked at Teschmaker in disbelief. 'Would you ask me to guard anything?'

'Okay, I used the wrong word. What were you doing with him?'

'Mr Morris is a sick old man. I was giving him his medicine and looking after him.'

Teschmaker still couldn't make sense of the scenario. 'But why out there? Why not in the city where he could get medical attention?'

'Master Francis told me that there is no cure for what Mr Morris has and that the country air is better for him.'

'Locked up in that room? Come on!'

'Truly. That's what I was told.' Viola looked pained that he should be disbelieved.

Teschmaker decided to take another tack. 'How long has he been there?'

'I don't know. There is another man who stays with him most of the time. I just fill in when he has to go away.'

'Who is the other man?'

'I don't know. Master Francis doesn't introduce me to people. But I have seen him a couple of times when he visited to ask Mr Morris some questions.'

'Really?' This sounded hopeful. 'What kind of questions?'

Viola rolled his eyes as though Teschmaker should know the answer. 'They were gabbling on in some foreign language, and anyway they made me wait outside and only come in when they wanted tea. I remember thinking that the man was very angry with Mr Morris.'

'Why was that?'

'He was shouting at him and banging his hand on the bedside table. It was not very nice.' Viola screwed up his face at the distasteful memory.

'Does Mr Morris's daughter visit him?'

'I didn't even know he had a daughter,' Viola replied meekly, apologetic for his lack of knowledge. 'I've never seen a woman there.'

'We'll talk more about this later, Viola.' Teschmaker got up from the bed and straightened the covers over him. 'You get some rest now. I'm going out for a while. You'll be safe with Gerard and Norman.'

'I don't like them.'

'Sorry.'

Teschmaker turned to walk out of the study then stopped. Maybe it didn't hurt to be a little softer. 'I'm making a quick coffee, you want one?'

'Tea. I only drink tea.'

'I'll ask Gerard to make you one.'

After coffee and a slice of toast Teschmaker began to feel a little more human. He asked Gerard to keep an eye on Viola and went out to his car. Norman was sound asleep in the back seat of the Merc and for a moment Teschmaker was tempted to wake him, but decided against it. The ground was still very wet underfoot but, apart from a few ragged remnants of cloud, the day was looking better than he had expected. The wind had downgraded itself to a northerly breeze and the air felt clean and freshly washed.

Even though he drove slowly north-west along the road that followed the meanderings of the Charlotte River, Teschmaker still made good time. He arrived at Freeholm with fifteen minutes to spare before the agreed rendezvous. There were several cars in the parking area, none of which looked like something that Oliver Sinclair might drive. Teschmaker had assumed that Oliver would already be at the cemetery paying his respects, but it seemed this was not the case. He looked at the locked vehicle-access gates and wondered if someone with Sinclair's money was able to drive inside the grounds. Probably, but the ground staff would have left the gate open for his return.

Graveyards had never been high on Teschmaker's list of priorities, but neither had he a particular dislike of them, so he filled the time with a stroll through the plots nearest the gates. He had only visited the cemetery a few times before. Aleksandr Shlyapnikov's son had died many years ago and Teschmaker had twice accompanied the old man and stood uncomfortably by while his friend placed flowers on the grave. It was completely overgrown; even the headstone, a distinctive slab of purple marble, was partially obscured by long grass. On the first occasion Teschmaker had offered to give him a hand weeding the plot, but Aleksi had turned on him angrily and told him not to touch it. He never offered again.

Teschmaker had not asked the Russian what had happened to the boy, but from the little that Shlyapnikov had volunteered it appeared he had been thirty-two years old at the time of his death some twenty years before: a man really, not a boy. Shlyapnikov had only mentioned his son on a couple of occasions and Teschmaker couldn't recall Zoya Nikolayevna ever speaking of him. He racked his brain trying to remember the young man's name, but it escaped him. Anyway, the grave was further in, in a newer section, and he had no inclination to walk that far on this particular morning.

An area to the north had been Freeholm's first burial ground, used by the city's earliest inhabitants some two hundred years before. It had been closed and then, just over a century and a half ago, had reopened. None of the graves from the initial period remained, but the oldest of those around the Western Gate were from the reopening period. Folklore had it that the original graveyard had been abandoned after the Charlotte River burst its banks in the devastating flood of 1809, at a time when the city was not much more than a country town struggling to establish a foothold in the swamp beneath its feet. Coffins had floated to the surface, so the stories went, and drifted down the town's main street to the Western Gate where the receding waters had left them high and dry. The town priest decreed that the good Lord had ordained that the place where the coffins rested was to be the new cemetery. As an added precaution he quietly had every subsequent coffin drilled with enough holes to make sure the dead never rose again.

Teschmaker crossed the footbridge over the river that still ran like liquid history through the cemetery. Today that history was clouded, opaque, a consequence of the overnight rain, and there were no iridescent flashes from the large fat trout that could usually be seen from the bridge. He walked on and found himself in front of one of the older and more ornate marble memorial stones. Monica Opazo. The name was clear but time and the elements had erased dates and epitaph. Teschmaker gave her one: 'She loved the Schottischer Dudelsack.' He laughed out loud at the absurdity his mind was capable of. Well, it was better than having no epitaph. She had probably been one of those hardy pioneers who had tramped through the mountain passes to settle on the coastal fringe, living to a ripe old age on a diet of swamp berries, honey, swedes and wild mountain trout. Their descendants proudly referred to themselves as swampies, though the use of the term had now expanded to cover everyone from derelicts to gypsies.

Teschmaker nearly missed the next grave. The remnants of a foot-high metal fence struggled to be seen through the dense mat of weeds and thistle. A feral poppy had gone to seed and wild briar was devouring the tombstone. Stepping over the remains of the fence, he knelt and gingerly closed his hands around the weeds obscuring the small headstone. The foliage was cold to his touch, still wet from the previous night's storm. Feeling that there were no thorns or prickles in his grasp, he tugged the weeds away. The revealed headstone wasn't fancy — a field stone propped above a grave that had long since been swallowed by the relentless seasons. But around the sides of the stone there still clung a wreath, braided from barbed wire and decorated with leaves of beaten metal. In places the strands had rusted or corroded away but enough remained to display the skill of the long dead metalworker. In the centre of the stone was hewn: *Elena Dymond sleeps here. Born 1807; murdered 1828. The Lord will avenge.*

Teschmaker squatted back on his haunches. For some reason he felt himself touched by the unkempt grave and its stubborn survival. What story lay beneath the dirt and stones? Who was Elena Dymond? By whose hand had she been plucked from life? There was something about the wreath of cruel barbs that moved him. Had her parents commissioned that? No, he thought, more likely the gesture of a lover. There was no mention of a husband. Did Elena really sleep, or was she a driven soul amongst the legions of hungry ghosts?

'Do you think the Lord *did* avenge her?'

Teschmaker started and turned to find a slightly plump, middle-aged individual standing at the edge of the grave. Despite the warmth of the morning the man was wearing a heavy coat, as though he expected the previous night's storm to return.

'It's kind of sad, don't you think?' Teschmaker responded.

'Life is often short and cruel. In a cruel life, shortness can be a blessing.' The man spoke wistfully, his voice deep with a pronounced Slavic accent. He was wearing rather old-fashioned wire-rimmed glasses which he pushed back at the bridge of his nose. His hair was full, its darkness flecked with a peppering of silver.

'But she didn't get to choose.' Teschmaker stood up and stepped back over the broken fence. 'And she will never know if she was avenged.'

'Ah, so it is the unfinished, the unknowing — that is what moves you?'

The man opened his coat and took out a silver cigarette case. With a practised one-handed gesture he flicked it open and proffered it to Teschmaker.

'I usually only smoke when I am abroad,' Teschmaker said half-heartedly, but wavering only a second, took a cigarette.

'I'm under doctor's orders to cut down. So I share.' The man's laugh was pleasant. 'So do you often spend time uncovering old murder victims?' The man produced a lighter and held it out for Teschmaker.

'No. I'm just filling in time. I'm meeting someone.'

'I'm afraid your friend won't be coming,' the man said quietly.

For a moment Teschmaker thought he had misheard. The man was looking at him, waiting for a response. 'What?'

'Mr Sinclair. Oliver. No, Mr Teschmaker, I'm afraid he won't be coming along.'

'He sent you?' Teschmaker was confused. 'Sorry, I'm not clear what you mean.'

'Mr Sinclair doesn't even know about this meeting. You see, I owe you an apology. I indulged in a slight amount of dishonesty so that we could meet. Why don't we go and sit down and have a chat over a cup of coffee?'

'So the message wasn't from Sinclair's secretary?' Teschmaker flicked the half-smoked cigarette away. There was no way he was going to drink coffee with this man.

'Personal assistant. I asked my colleague to say "personal assistant".'

'She did.'

'It was imperative that I got to speak with you.'

'Then speak.'

'You wouldn't like a coffee?' The man looked genuinely disappointed, almost hurt by the anger in Teschmaker's reaction. He shrugged. 'Let that be. I just wanted to warn you that following Jane Sinclair is not a healthy occupation. This is not personal, Mr Teschmaker, simply a — what is it you say — a word in time?'

'And just how is this anything to do with you?' Teschmaker didn't bother to hide his anger at the implied threat.

'Jane Sinclair's security is my number one priority.'

'Security!' Teschmaker snorted. 'And you know something about security?'

'I pride myself on it.' The man drew deeply on the last of his cigarette and dropped it on the ground.

'And if I decide to ignore your warning?'

'Mr Teschmaker, I am sure you're a good man. Believe me, I have no grudge against you. But if you don't desist I will probably have to kill you.'

Teschmaker was about to walk away but he knew he couldn't dismiss the man as a crank. The tone of his voice was casual but, perversely, that made the threat credible. Then, just as quickly, Teschmaker realised what was happening. The mist cleared from his eyes and he knew who the man was.

He turned back to him with the biggest grin he could muster. 'Of course we should have coffee. There is much I want to ask you.'

This caught the man off guard. Instinctively his

hand came up to his coat but Teschmaker was faster. He shot his hand out and grasped the man's wrist. 'No. Not a good idea. Enough dead people here without us adding to the list.'

He slid his hand inside the man's coat and removed a small pistol. 'I'll look after this, if you don't mind.'

Teschmaker stepped back and released the man's wrist. 'So, Konstantin Ivanovich, shall we have that coffee?'

The colour drained from the man's face as though someone had pulled the plug on his bloodstream.

'You are working with them?' He spoke slowly, his face suddenly contorted by a mixture of fear and bewilderment. 'It can't be.'

'No, it can't be.'

'Then who? I thought you were just a stalker who had stumbled accidentally —'

'And you were right. You must learn to trust your instincts.' Teschmaker laughed, more to relieve the tension he was experiencing than because he found it amusing. 'I'm nothing more than an old friend trying to find out what Jane Sinclair has been up to. Now, tell me who you thought I was working for.'

But Laverov shook his head. 'I must know how you know my name. Not even my own —'

'Not even your own people in the embassy? Sorry, Konstantin, everyone seems to know who you are and that you are operating out of the Romanian Embassy. What they don't know is why.'

Teschmaker realised he was flying on empty. There was only so far he could take the pretence and he knew full well that a bluff was also something one could fall off. But as long as he had the advantage he was going to wing it. He started back across the footbridge towards the coffee kiosk. Laverov quickly fell into step beside him.

'They know I'm at the Romanian Embassy?'

'Yes.'

'Then Rusak knows.'

Time to stop bluffing. 'Who's Rusak?'

'You really don't know?' Laverov had regained some colour but the confusion still lined his face.

'You want me to lie to you and say I do?'

'He is Mafia. Big-time Mafia. The boss of the bosses.'

'Big scum is still scum.'

'No!' Laverov spat the word out. 'No, he is not scum. He is educated. He gave up an elected position in the Duma to follow *biznes* interests.' There was a beat, a hesitation, as he decided just how much information he should divulge. Then Laverov said slowly, 'He is a dangerous man, that's all you need to know.'

They arrived at the kiosk and took a table as far from the counter as possible. There were only a couple of other patrons: two elderly women, middle-Europeans, black dresses, black scarves. Something about them suggested that they were cemetery regulars. Black crows, *twa corbies*, Teschmaker thought, enjoying the vicarious thrill of having outlived those who lay beyond the walls.

He waited until the coffee arrived then accepted the proffered cigarette. 'I didn't enjoy the last one. So, Rusak?'

'Oleg Vasilyevich Rusak. He likes to kill. Personally. Hands-on. He is impatient. Instead of waiting to build his interests he simply co-opted people to him, and those who opposed him he killed. He has his hands in everything from banking to the black marketeers and grey area traders, the *shushara* and *tolkachi*. But his big thrill is arms dealing. He would sell guns to the Chechens if they could be trusted to pay.'

'You've lost me.' Teschmaker inhaled on the cigarette, enjoying what felt like partaking of an illegal substance. 'What the hell has this got to do with Jane? Or, for that matter, you? What's your game, Comrade? What's your big thrill?'

For a moment Laverov stared at the end of his cigarette, watching the paper burn and the ash lengthen. Opposite him Teschmaker had taken a paper napkin and was absentmindedly cleaning a spot from the table. What did he want? What did any of them want? Contentment, maybe. Peace and quiet. Was that a universal thing? Did the man across the table want the same things? Or did he want order and certainty? Laverov mused as he watched Teschmaker fold the napkin and place it neatly beside his cup. The man's fussiness irked him. He looked Teschmaker straight in the eye. 'I just want to make it through to retirement age in one piece. Then I want to find a house near a salmon stream in a forest with good mushrooms.'

Well, you couldn't beat that for an ambition. Teschmaker stubbed out his cigarette and carefully moved the ashtray to one side. Salmon and mushrooms sounded pretty good, but none of this was taking him any closer to understanding what was going on. As if reading his thoughts Laverov started to speak.

'Jane's father, Sydney Morris, came over to us years ago. Not for money, not for notoriety. I think he genuinely believed that Communism was the only way forward.'

'He wasn't alone in that,' Teschmaker said, thinking of his father's friends who had marched and agitated with the closing of every mine, the lock-outs in the factories and the seemingly endless disputes on the docks. They had all died disappointed but unrepentant, and since then nothing much had changed. Capital had triumphed, there was no God but the dollar and the new puritans, the economic rationalists, would happily sell advertising space on their mothers' coffins. 'At least they believed in something other than profit.'

'Foolish dreams.' Laverov smiled. 'But I agree with you. And Sydney Morris had a dream, even though both he and his dream were corrupted in the end.'

'It must have seemed less than foolish to him at the time. He left his wife and child behind —'

'In order to do what?' Laverov ground out the butt of his cigarette and pushed his glasses back up his nose. 'He was young and bright, at the top of his field. Sydney Morris could have picked up research work at any lab he wanted. A couple of years and he would have been old enough to have been considered for a chair at a university. He was so far ahead of his colleagues. The tragedy is that he thought to use his science to bring peace and yet ended up working on Soviet armaments. The type of —'

'Doing what?' Teschmaker immediately regretted the interruption. He should have let Laverov continue, but it was too late, he had stemmed the flow. Laverov looked at him with narrowed eyes for the second time, reassessing just how much he should say. What is it, Teschmaker wondered, that he is afraid to tell me? Afraid? No, that was probably the wrong word. Laverov was simply being cautious.

'What about you, Laverov? Who are you? Military Intelligence? KGB, or whatever they call themselves these days?'

'The FSB? Nothing so grand, I'm afraid. Just a humble policeman.'

Teschmaker didn't believe him for a minute, but he knew there was nothing to gain from pursuing it. 'So why is everybody getting so excited about Sydney Morris?'

'For a long time I had never heard of the man. Nobody had. He was kept out of the limelight, locked away in one of the closed research cities, the science gulags. A couple of years ago I was working in an archive repository, trying to analyse the contribution made by foreign scientists to the Soviet era. I had Sydney Morris's name and little else. But then I discovered that almost everyone who had worked with him had passed away.'

He paused for a moment and concentrated on lighting another cigarette.

'I thought Morris was dead too. But, as I later found out, he had quietly slipped out of the country during the confusion of the Gorbachev era. It was probably what saved his life.'

'He came back here?'

'No. Not at all. I don't think he ever had any intention of coming home.'

'Then what happened?'

'He had been preparing a retreat, a bolt hole if you like, in the Czech Republic. He must have considered himself tucked out of harm's way in the countryside outside a quiet little spa town called Mariánské Lázně —'

'Marienbad?' A long time ago Teschmaker remembered having sat through Alain Resnais's murky and perplexing film, *Last Year at Marienbad*.

'Yes, just over the border from Germany. From what I have managed to piece together, it seems that Rusak or his men flushed him out and brought him here, or he ran and they followed.'

Teschmaker shook his head. 'No. Slow down, I'm not with you. What the hell has your Mafia man got to do with Sydney Morris?'

But Laverov appeared not to hear him. He was lost in the maze of his own thoughts, fitting some imaginary jigsaw together — a jigsaw in which the pieces did not match.

'All the old-timers were gone and, by some crazy twist of fate, only Morris remained. The Professor. He knew them all. He trained them.' Laverov paused and looked at Teschmaker, suddenly comprehending what he had said. 'You don't understand? Of course not. There is no way you could. Don't you see, even I don't know.' He sighed and his shoulders slumped as though he had run out of energy. He lowered his voice. 'See those two?' He nodded in the direction of the two old women. 'They would understand better than either of us. What we are talking about is secrets from beyond the grave. Rusak must think he can dig whatever he's after out of Sydney Morris.'

'Fat chance,' Teschmaker snorted. 'The old man is completely gaga.'

'You have talked to him?' Laverov demanded, suddenly energised again.

'Yes, but he's lost it —'

'Where? You must tell me where he is.'

'Hang on!' Teschmaker protested. 'I'm just as interested to know about this. What is it this Rusak wants to find out?'

'I can't tell you.' Laverov's eyes burned into him. 'You have to tell me where Sydney Morris is,' he repeated vehemently. 'Look, we have a man in Rusak's inner circle —'

'Then ask him.'

'I would, but we have lost contact. I don't even know if he is still alive. That's why you must help me.'

Stick to your guns, Teschmaker told himself. 'No deal. This isn't a one-way street.'

There was a long silence, then Laverov shrugged. 'With you or without you, I'll find out. If you change your mind, you have obviously worked out where to contact me.'

He stood up and wrapped his coat tightly around himself. 'Goodbye, Mr Teschmaker.'

'Wait a moment.' Teschmaker reached out and held the sleeve of his coat.

'What?'

Teschmaker released the man's coat, took the pistol from his pocket and handed it to Laverov. 'Here, you might need this. Just in case you still need to kill me.'

'Thank you.' He took the gun and slipped it into his pocket. 'Just walk away, Mr Teschmaker. There is nothing in this for you.'

What about Jane, he was going to ask, but decided against it. He watched as the Russian walked out into the morning sunshine and over to his black Ford — the black Ford he had failed to recognise when he drove up. After Laverov had driven off he turned his attention to the cup of coffee that sat untouched in front of him. It was cold and bitter.

After a while he realised he was sitting there thinking nothing. His mind seemed to have gone into hibernation, retreating from the mass of contradictions that surrounded him. Concentrate, he told himself. Do what you do best. Work with what you know. Start with something small and nail it down.

It was good advice. Having resolved to treat the whole messy business like an insurance investigation, he shoved Laverov from his mind and drove back into town.

It took him less than an hour to check on the ownership of the yellow Volvo and the small rural property in the Landsbury Valley. Gormenghast belonged to someone by the name of Francis Abelard Grice; so did the Volvo. A further check turned up another interesting fact. It seemed that Mr Grice was a small-time property developer who owned several blocks of apartments in Hitchon and a property in Nikolayevsky Street.

Teschmaker always enjoyed the tingling sensation in his spine when his instincts started to respond. And in this instance he knew his instincts were right. He drove along Nikolayevsky and stopped opposite Grice's piece of real estate. It was the Mlad Fashions building.

'Get that little snivelling creep away from me.'

Gerard Edwards was not a happy man. He had been waiting for Teschmaker when he returned, sitting on the front doorstep, chain-smoking.

'You and Norman had a falling out?' Teschmaker tried to sound solicitous.

It obviously failed. Edwards rolled his eyes heavenward and, getting to his feet, stumped off down the drive. Then he turned and snarled at Teschmaker in desperation. 'No, Mr Teschmaker.' It was amazing that he could make Teschmaker sound like an expletive. 'No, it's not fucking Norman. It's that slimy little Viola. I swear, if he calls me "sir" one more time, I'll clock the cunt.'

'Pity. Respect is in short supply these days.'

'Respect?' Edwards snorted. 'Don't give me respect. Respect, I understand. It's grovelling that gets up my nose.'

'Live and let live.'

'Yeah? Well, I don't call that living.'

Edwards came back to the front step. 'Listen, all I'm asking is that you don't leave him alone with me. I can't be held responsible . . .'

'Sure, Gerard. I think I get the picture.' Whatever buttons Viola was pushing in Gerard Edwards, they were certainly getting a response. 'I'll have a word to him.'

That stopped Edwards in his tracks. 'No. I don't mean . . . What I'm trying to say is . . .'

'Yes?' Teschmaker smiled cruelly. 'What is it you're saying?'

'Nothing.' Edwards scowled and handed over a piece of paper. 'The car registrations you wanted.'

'Thanks.' Teschmaker decided it was not the right moment to reveal that he had checked the only one that really seemed to matter — the yellow Volvo. He moved towards the door but Edwards, obviously flustered, took his arm.

'Look, don't go telling Viola I was complaining. It would make things even worse. Just don't put me in charge of looking after him.'

Teschmaker was about to observe that one should confront one's fears, but before he could decide on how that might be received Norman came to the door. He had white powder, chalk or something, all over his hands.

'Phone for you, Mr Teschmaker.'

It was Oliver Sinclair.

'Any progress?'

'A little.' Teschmaker still had the feeling that Sinclair was playing a game with him. He decided to put him on a slow drip-feed. 'I think I've found the place where the photographs were taken.'

'And?'

'Do you know the Mlad Fashions building in Nikolayevsky Street?'

'No.'

'Jane went there to some sort of club. She went with a man named Francis Grice.'

There was silence for a moment then a forced laugh. 'You don't muck around, do you! Well done, Teschmaker. Well done.'

'I can't really do much more, so I'll send you an invoice for my time.'

'Now hang on,' Sinclair growled. 'I want a good deal more than that —'

'Sorry, that's it. I said I would find out what was going on and it seems pretty clear that I've delivered. Oh, and one other thing. Your personal assistant . . .'

'Yes?'

'Her name is Irene, right?'

'Yes, but I don't understand what the hell that has got to do with anything.'

'Just don't talk to me on this phone. I think it's probably been tapped. Mine as well, most likely. I'll send the invoice.' He hung up before Oliver could protest.

Teschmaker realised he was very hungry and that the smell coming from the kitchen had a lot to do with it. He walked through to find Norman and Viola serving up a batch of muffins while a sour-looking Gerard Edwards was making a pot of tea. Happy families.

CHAPTER THIRTEEN

Ambassador Panyukov took a lot of convincing. 'You want to phone who?'

'The President,' Laverov insisted tiredly. He had waited until late in the evening before driving up to the Ambassador's residence, uninvited, unexpected and, so it appeared, unwelcome. The security detail had failed to convince him to leave and in the end had reluctantly woken the Ambassador.

'Come to the embassy tomorrow and one of my staff will put your request to the people at Moscow Centre.' Panyukov glanced out the window at the rain. There was no way he was going out on a night like this to deal with some spook with delusions of contacts in high places.

But Laverov stood his ground. 'I want access to the Dome and I want to phone the President now, not tomorrow. Now.'

'I'm sorry, but I don't know of any Dome.'

The look on Panyukov's face betrayed him. He was clearly shaken. The Dome did not officially exist.

Nobody was supposed to know about it, certainly not some complete stranger turning up in the middle of the night. Nobody was allowed inside the Dome except the chief communications officer, the head of station intelligence and the Ambassador. In practice, the Ambassador — a man with a distinct distrust of even his own spooks — rarely used the secure facility. He thought of himself as a cultured man, a new Russian, and as far as he was concerned Moscow Centre was akin to Leonardo da Vinci's golden mean — decidedly off-centre. On top of that was the worrying report he had received the day before that Vladimir Putin was intending to merge his security bodies into one organisation with powers that appeared, on the face of it, identical with those of the old KGB. Yeltsin had gone a long way towards breaking up the agency but this initiative came amid signs that Putin — who spent sixteen years in the security service, including five years as a spy in the former East Germany — was on track to give his former KGB colleagues more influence. Not only was it planned that the internal security agency, the FSB, the SVR, the foreign intelligence agency and FAPSI, the electronic surveillance body responsible for bugging operations, would be merged, but of just as much concern was the suggestion that leading the new organisation would be FSB head Nikolai Patrushev, and Sergei Ivanov who ran the powerful security council. They were both veteran KGB men, both friends of Putin. Maybe, the Ambassador thought, it was time to consider a quiet retirement.

Laverov handed Panyukov a piece of paper. 'Ring this number at the Centre and ask if Lynx has authorisation to ring the Chief.'

'Lynx?'

'A code name; the President's little joke.'

Twenty minutes later Laverov was being chauffeured to the embassy; the Ambassador a changed man.

'I must say, I didn't realise you chaps were still so involved.'

He's trying to claw back a bit of credibility, Laverov thought, save a bit of face. Poor sod. He decided to be generous. 'Mostly trade stuff these days. Run of the mill. We keep an eye on what the multinationals are up to. Try and sniff the wind for the opportunity to steer trade in our direction. That sort of thing.'

'Important work,' Panyukov said gravely. 'Damn difficult times.'

'And we keep an eye on loyalty,' Laverov added mischievously.

'Yes, there's a few back home who could benefit from a dose of that,' the Ambassador deflected obliquely, wondering if he could organise a move to Canada.

The station chief obviously kept tabs on the Ambassador because he was waiting for them at the embassy.

'You're working late,' Panyukov remarked glibly.

'I thought you might need me . . .' He turned to Laverov and extended his hand. 'I'm sorry, I don't believe we've been introduced.'

'We haven't.' Laverov ignored the hand.

The Ambassador, who was having difficulty suppressing a smile, patted the station chief on the back. 'Very commendable turning up like this, but we'll be fine. I'm just taking our guest through to the Dome.'

'But, Excellency, I must protest —'

'And I insist you run along,' Panyukov snapped. 'This is important and can't wait.'

'It is highly irregular.' The station chief looked angry and flustered at this incursion into his territory.

'Your comments are noted.' The Ambassador turned to Laverov. 'Please, follow me.'

Laverov waited until the Ambassador had left the room before dialling the number. It was answered immediately.

'What is it, Laverov?' the President asked tersely.

'Clarification, Mr President.'

'Yes?'

'It seems that I may be close to one of the devices.'

'Excellent.'

'The two major players are present.'

'Very good.'

'But . . .'

'What?'

'I take it that the destruction of the device is acceptable as a last resort?'

'Yes. If it can be salvaged all the better, but it must be destroyed rather than allow possession by any other players. Clear?'

'Yes, Mr President. There is also the question of several peripheral players —'

'In the endgame there are no peripheral players. I hope you understand that.' The President allowed a second's silence then added softly, 'You, of course, are an exception, Konstantin Ivanovich.'

'Thank you, Mr President.'

* * *

'I trust the President is well?'

Laverov repressed a smile. He had seen similar expressions on the faces of dogs waiting at the foot of a table for scraps. 'He sends his warmest greetings,' he lied.

'And . . .' the Ambassador's fishing expedition continued, 'everything is satisfactory?'

Satisfactory? A mission that started with the opening of a few boxes in a locked room in Moscow would end with the deaths of several people who probably had no idea why they should die. This was satisfactory? 'Completely.'

'Excellent!' Panyukov beamed. 'Well done!'

No, he thought as he picked up his car from the Ambassador's residence and drove off, it was far from satisfactory. The endgame, as the President had succinctly put it, was still far from clear. He didn't know the exact whereabouts of the device, there had been no contact from the so-called 'man on the inside' and the major players seemed to be going in circles. His instincts told him he was missing something. His body told him it was sleep.

He had only been out of bed a matter of minutes when the phone rang and Sinclair's voice barked at him.

'Saturday, Teschmaker.'

'What? What time is it?'

'Listen. Jane's babysitter just rang me to say Jane is going out again on Saturday.'

'The babysitter is on your payroll?'

'Just a backup . . .'

'Oliver, the answer is no.'

'It's not no at all, damn you. Now listen to me —'

'No! Oliver, I am not following Jane around just to give you some lurid description of how she gets her kicks.'

'Will you shut the fuck up! That's not what I'm asking. I want the man who took those photographs. I want that slime ball. You deliver him. Name, address, whatever . . . and that's it. End of story. Okay? I'll pay you whatever you ask . . .'

'I don't want money.'

'What then?'

Teschmaker realised that the idea of having a look inside the world Jane was drawn to was actually quite enticing; it was Oliver he disliked.

'Okay. I'll do it, but this is the last time. After Saturday you can find someone else. Is that understood?'

'Clear as a bell. Be in touch.'

Sinclair hung up the phone and turned to the man sitting on the other side of his desk. 'Not a problem.'

'He'll be there?'

'Trust me. He'll be there, and then he's all yours.'

'Can I play with him first?'

'You can do what the fuck you like as long as he ends up dead.'

You've just done something stupid, he told himself as he scrubbed the kitchen bench and replaced the cooking utensils that Viola had put away in the wrong drawer. How the hell are you going to get into this damn place?

Behind him Viola was being petulant. 'I did clean up already, you know.'

'Good. I just want things in their proper place.'

'And everyone says *I'm* fussy . . .'

'Listen, Viola, do you mind if I pick your brain?'

'Of course I could have just left things —'

'Viola! This is important. Is Master Francis really Francis Grice?'

'Doctor Francis Grice. Yes, but a lot of the others use scene names.'

'Do you know their real names?'

'Most of the time they wear masks . . .'

'What for?'

'It's the trademark of this group.'

'So not every bondage and discipline scene does that?'

'No . . .' Viola hesitated and corrected himself. 'Well, maybe sometimes, you know, like for special occasions.'

'So you're saying you don't know most of their names and you haven't a clue what most of them look like?'

Viola blushed and looked downcast at his failure to deliver. 'I know what their bodies look like.'

I bet you do, thought Teschmaker. 'I need some names and descriptions.'

'May I ask a question?' Viola kept his eyes on the floor.

'Viola, for Christ's sake! I'm not your frigging master.'

'No, sir.'

'So what did you want to say?'

'Well, if I knew why you wanted to know, then maybe I could help.'

Teschmaker realised that he had no chance of pulling off the stunt he had in mind without Viola's help. 'I'm going to the meeting on Saturday to see if Jane is there her own volition, and I also want to have a close look at your Master Francis.'

The look on Viola's face showed that he thought it a particularly stupid idea. 'They would spot you as vanilla straight away.'

'Vanilla?'

'You know, *straight*. These people aren't life-stylers, they're all serious players or twenty-four-sevens. They would deal with an intruder very . . .' Viola hesitated, unsure of what word to use, '. . . seriously.'

'Then you'll have to make sure I fit in.'

'But —'

'And you can start by not speaking gobbledygook. What's a twenty-four-seven?'

Viola shook his head distractedly, unable to conceive of even the possibility that Teschmaker would attempt such a thing. 'Life-stylers are people who are into the scene for a hobby. Twenty-four-sevens are twenty-four hours a day seven days a week.'

'Full time?' Teschmaker couldn't imagine what that would entail.

'Yes, the serious players will usually be a dom and a subbie . . .' He glanced up and spotted Teschmaker's look of non-comprehension. 'A dom is the dominant or top in the relationship. A subbie is the submissive or bottom. I'm a subbie,' he added with a look of pride on his face, then continued shyly, 'I think you would make a very good dom, Master Martin.'

'For this particular exercise I think it would be the best choice.' Teschmaker kept his face straight. 'So, can you think of any dom who looks even vaguely like me; that is, if I wore a mask?'

Viola hesitated, his face screwed in concentration. Then he grinned. 'Doctor Orpheus, but he's a strange one.'

'Strange?'

'Yes. He's a silent watcher. He's a dom but he keeps to himself most of the time.'

'Do you know his real name?'

'I'm sorry.' Viola looked as though he might burst into tears.

'Could you find out?' Teschmaker asked gently.

'I could try.'

Five minutes later Viola returned from a whispered telephone conversation with a look of triumph on his face. He shoved a piece of paper into Teschmaker's hand. 'Doctor Orpheus.'

Teschmaker looked at the name. 'Adrian James Wright. Seven Greystokes Close, Belmont.'

'He's not really a doctor like Master Francis, though he would like to think he is.' Viola smiled. 'Actually Orph does look a lot like you. I think with a bit of training you could probably get into the Chambers.'

'Chambers? That's what they call the place I picked you up from — the Chambers?'

'The full name is the Chambers of Pain, but you know what it's like, people always abbreviate things. Don't you just hate that?'

'What do I need to get in?'

Part of him hoped Viola would tell him something that would make the idea impossible to put into action. It was not that he was particularly worried about what these people might think of an intruder, rather that there was no guarantee the risk would lead to any tangible outcome. It was entirely possible that Jane was a willing and active participant. And Francis Grice? With any luck he might be the man behind the camera, but there was a big gap between a hunch and delivering proof to Oliver Sinclair.

'You'll need to get his tool kit and his mask —'

'Viola, let's be sensible here. There is no way that people are going to think I'm this man.'

'With respect, there are a lot of people and the lights are low —'

'It would have to be pitch black and the minute I open my mouth —'

'Ah!' Viola clapped his hands gleefully. 'Master Martin, Doctor Orpheus hardly speaks to anyone. Some nights the most you'll get out of him is a grunt.'

'So I have to grunt now, do I?' Teschmaker failed to keep the sarcasm out of his voice. 'Great! Just great.' He shook his head. 'No. There has to be another way. Surely I can be a guest from out of town.'

'True. But you would need someone to sign you in and that way you would be drawing attention to yourself. Everyone would be interested to see what your particular kink was. It would never work.'

Viola was probably right. Maybe he should abandon the idea and look for another strategy. 'What were you saying about a tool kit?'

'Everyone has one. Doctor Orpheus has an old black Gladstone bag. Very gothic.'

'But what's it for?' Teschmaker was struggling to keep up. Every time Viola opened his mouth there was something new to take in.

'All his toys. His canes and floggers and —'

'Jesus. Can't I just get a bag of my own and rent a whip or something?'

That sent Viola into a fit of giggles.

'I don't get the joke, Viola.' Teschmaker made it sound like a threat. 'Now, come on, work with me on this. Can I rent something? Don't you guys have a shop that sells this stuff?'

'Of course,' Viola agreed but was shaking his head at the same time. 'Only a vanilla would do that. These players have their stuff custom-made. Some of them design it themselves. No, if you are going into the Chambers, you'll need to go as Doctor Orpheus and you'll need to be carrying his tool kit.'

'Fine! And what do you suggest I do with Doctor Orpheus while all this is going on? Knock him out and tie him up? Get real!'

'I know some very good rope work,' Viola said.

But Teschmaker wasn't listening, he was already thinking ahead. Would it be possible? Would he really be able to walk in and act as though he knew what was going on? Three days was an extremely short space of time in which to make himself not only conversant but comfortable with a scene that sounded as weird as anything he had come across.

'Edwards!' he called. 'Get your keys, we're going for a drive.'

He pocketed the piece of paper with the address on it. 'We'll do a drive past. Viola, you and Norman see if you can get some food happening.'

'I'm not your wife,' Viola mumbled.

'What?' Teschmaker asked.

'I said we'll make something nice, sir.'

For once luck seemed to be favouring Teschmaker. He and Gerard Edwards found Adrian Wright's house in a situation that could not have been better. The low-set bungalow, situated at the end of a small cul-de-sac, was obscured from the nearest house by a line of trees and a dense hedge. They parked and, after Teschmaker had grabbed a clipboard from the back seat, made their way on foot up the concrete drive to the front door. 'No security,' Gerard whispered. Teschmaker nodded in agreement, pressed the doorbell and stepped back.

After a moment there was the sound of a bolt being slid back and the door opened. Viola's description had been accurate. The man standing in the lamp-lit hallway was five foot ten or eleven and, like Teschmaker, of light build. The receding sandy-coloured hair looked to be an exact match. The man appeared perplexed, surprised to see anyone at his door at six thirty in the evening.

'Yes?'

'Good evening, sir.' Teschmaker stepped forward. 'Derek Copper from Star Security Systems. Your wife made an appointment for us to consult with you on your home-security needs.'

The man looked even more puzzled. 'I'm afraid you must have the wrong address. I don't need a security system and I certainly don't have a wife.'

Teschmaker consulted his clipboard. 'This is number seven?'

'Yes . . .'

'Well, that's what the office gave me. Number Seven Wyndham Close.'

The man beamed and stepped through the door. 'Now that's your problem. This isn't Wyndham Close. That's the next street. This is Greystokes.'

'God, Cooper, that's the second time this week.' Gerard moved into the light. 'Sorry about that, sir. Sorry to trouble you.'

'Not a problem,' the man said affably. 'Back the way you came and turn left. You can't miss it.'

'Don't count on it,' Gerard laughed.

'Well?' Teschmaker asked as they got back in the car.

'Piece of cake. The bolt can only be used when he's at home. The lock is a Grigson standard barrel I could open with a butter knife.'

'And no wife to worry about.'

'We could have dealt with her as well.' Gerard sounded wistful.

'So I guess Saturday night is party night.' Teschmaker's voice sounded far more confident than he felt. But there was no point in being apprehensive now. There would be plenty of time for that on Saturday.

When they arrived back at Teschmaker's house they found that while Viola had done wonders in the kitchen, Norman had also been busy. The previously empty downstairs living room now sported a table and four chairs. To Teschmaker's amazement there were place settings and even a candle in the middle of the table.

Norman and Viola greeted them nervously, like two kids having their parents to dinner for the first time.

'Nice.' Gerard appeared to be gritting his teeth. 'Where the hell did this stuff come from?'

'I had a friend drop it over.' Norman frowned, suddenly aware that he might have stepped out of line.

'It's very sweet of you.' Teschmaker wasn't certain that 'sweet' was the right word to use in relation to Norman, but if the ear-to-ear grin on the man's face was anything to judge by it seemed to have hit the mark.

After a remarkably good meal of poached rainbow trout, steamed vegetables and couscous, Teschmaker beckoned Viola to follow him. 'We'll leave those two to finish the wine.'

Viola looked troubled. 'What is it?'

'Relax. I just want to have a talk with you.'

'Oh.' Viola still looked dubious but he followed Teschmaker up the stairs to the study.

'We saw your Doctor Orpheus —'

'He's not mine,' Viola interjected.

'Okay. But what I was going to say is that we think we can go ahead for Saturday. You were right, he does look a little like me and if you are also right about the low lights —'

'Just candles,' Viola reassured him, then added, 'It's quite exciting, isn't it? Your first time . . .'

Teschmaker was irritated by Viola's tone but he stopped himself from showing it. 'We'll see.'

He poured himself a scotch and offered one to Viola, but he declined. 'If I'm going to pull this off on Saturday, Viola, I'm going to need your help.'

'I've told you I'll do everything I can.'

'Well, you can start by telling me how you became involved in the scene in the first place.'

For a moment Viola looked at the floor then he crossed to the desk and picked up the spare glass. 'May I change my mind?'

'Of course.'

Teschmaker poured him a generous slug and was astonished to see Viola down it in a single gulp.

'Do you really want to hear the whole story?' Viola asked.

'The truth, the whole truth and nothing but the truth.'

There was a pause and then Viola whispered, 'So help me, God.'

CHAPTER FOURTEEN

'My name was Dominic Healy and I was fourteen the year that I discovered for true and certain that God wanted me. Have you any idea how hard it is for someone that age to explain to an adult that they know what they're doing?'

For the first time since they had met, Teschmaker saw Viola's sloe-black eyes burn with an inner fire.

'I tried so hard to make them understand. I did everything I could. But no matter how I explained it, they didn't hear me. I felt like I was the only person with a voice in a world of deaf people. I tried to show my parents how dedicated I was, but just as they couldn't hear, they couldn't see. But I was determined and so I spent every spare moment in church. I went to St Sebastian's every day and knelt on those cold hard flagstones, and they were hard. Back then I wore short pants and I would come out with my knees red and sore. But the more it hurt the stronger my conviction grew and I would kneel in front of the statue of Jesus and look at those wounds and I knew. I knew that we had all gone wrong because we didn't understand how he had suffered. It was so clear to me, even at that age, that unless we understood the real meaning of suffering, we could never be saved. I read that we had to be born in the blood of the lamb and I knew it was true. I wanted that blood so much. If I could have traded places with Jesus I would have. I dreamed of it, night after night . . .'

He lapsed into silence, his eyes shut, but his eyelids and lips quivered with the intensity of his remembered vision. Teschmaker watched, dumbfounded by the outpouring, bewildered by the depth of the pain he could sense beneath the words. He tried to remember himself at fourteen but all he saw was Jane. Had she been his epiphany?

'More than anything I wanted to be crucified. I could imagine the sensation of the nails pressed against my hands. Then the dull thud of the hammer and the explosion of pain. And my legs . . . I would lie in bed and imagine that my legs were bound and the nail would go through the skin, then flesh, then bone of one leg and then into the leg beneath. When I was in the church I found I could shut my eyes and imagine it so strongly that my body would twitch and I would cry out.'

'Jesus, Viola!' Teschmaker had done everything not to interrupt, but couldn't help himself.

'No! Don't you see?' Viola rubbed wildly at his face; strong raking strokes. Teschmaker reached out, but Viola was lost in his own catharsis.

'I couldn't understand why they were so proud of the agony of Jesus and yet couldn't tolerate my small pain. I was too real for them and they couldn't deal with it. They didn't want me! The priest, of all people, should have understood, but he didn't. In the end he told me I must stop coming to the church because I was disturbing his congregation. Me! Disturbing them from their comfortable prayers, their petty little confessions. I begged with him, I pleaded and promised I would do anything if only he would let me keep coming. But it did no good.

'I had heard stories of a group of ascetics who suffered for Jesus and so I ran away to find them . . .'

Two days before his fifteenth birthday Viola caught the weekly ferry out to Gissing Island, ten miles off the coast. In the early days Gissing had been a whaling station; some years after it was abandoned, a reclusive order of monks took it over as an ideal place to lock themselves away from the wickedness of the world. The order — the Brotherhood of the Righteous — was, in its idiosyncratic manner, attempting to follow the teachings of the eighteenth-century mystic Josip Slootmeyer. According to Slootmeyer, the world was a bad dream created and maintained by habituated sin, and the aim of the spiritual journey was to dissolve this delusion of reality and reveal the kingdom of God which was the true universe. The methodology was simple: in order to 'wake up' from the dream the flesh had to be punished; and so, over the years, the monks on Gissing became masters of fleshly mortification. When the young Dominic Healy arrived, they welcomed him with open arms.

The first few months were some of the happiest in his life. Dominic's days were filled with instruction in understanding the mystic writings of Josip Slootmeyer and contemplation. The instruction reinforced his view of suffering, and the monks' sole focus of contemplation, the agony of Christ crucified, was the bitter-sweet nectar his thirsty soul had been seeking. There was also the revelation of self-flagellation.

'You will find it a difficult step to take,' cautioned the abbot. 'But he who walks the path of the flagellant walks the path of the Lord.'

He laid the wooden-handled flogger on the escritoire. 'Pick it up, Brother Dominic.'

It was the first time he had been addressed as brother and, determined to live up to the honour bestowed upon him, Dominic stepped forward and firmly grasped the rough wooden handle. The dozen or more strips of leather were bound to the wood with copper wire and a single thong of thinner leather was attached through a hole in the handle. As Dominic slipped his hand through the thong he experienced a surge of energy and felt his face flush. In his hands, he knew with absolute certainty, he held the weapon to drive out Satan. Not only would he be purified, he would also be emulating the Lord Jesus. Had the Romans not whipped our Lord on his dreadful journey to Golgotha? Had they not raised great welts on his body? Had they not drawn blood? And as Jesus had suffered, so too would Dominic.

'Brother Dominic, there is another matter . . .'

Dominic struggled to pay attention. 'Yes, Father?'

'It appears that the authorities on the mainland are concerned about your disappearance.'

'No, Father!' Dominic cried out. The rush of energy he had been feeling drained away in an instant. No, they could not take him back. This was where he belonged. 'Please, Father —'

'Brother Dominic! Control yourself.' The abbot strode around the escritoire, his face darkened with anger. 'I can't stop them taking you from the abbey. You are under age . . .'

Dominic fell to his knees and prostrated himself. His mind was spinning in confusion. Why had the abbot called him brother and given him the whip if he had to leave? 'Father,' he wailed, 'I would rather die —'

'Silence!' The abbot stood above him and glared down. 'Now, listen. I believe you have the calling but you cannot be seen here. I understand that they will come on the regular ferry service next week. When they arrive you will not be here so I will not be placed in the position of having to lie. Tomorrow Brother Simon will guide you through the caves to Stormcliff Cove on the ocean side of Gissing. There is a small stone hut there, cold and rough, but it will serve. Many years ago it was used as a lookout for the whalers. Brother Simon will visit you every week to bring provisions. But you will observe strict rules.'

'Anything, Father,' Dominic said gratefully.

'You will pray, and discipline yourself with renewed vigour.'

'Yes, Father.'

'You will spend no more than one hour a day outside, and never if there is a passing ship. You will not light a fire at any time.'

'No, Father.'

'You will obey Brother Simon's instructions for they shall have come from me. And when I consider the time right, I will send for you. Do you understand?'

'Yes, Father.' Dominic kept his face to the ground, but he sensed the abbot bending over him and felt a hand on his shoulder.

'Now get up, Brother.'

Dominic clambered to his feet. His feeling of gratitude was overwhelming but he had no idea of how to express it, so he simply stood, tears streaming from his eyes, the flogger clenched tightly in his hand.

'I have great hopes for you, Dominic.' The abbot was standing very close, his voice a terse whisper in his ear. 'Do not disappoint me.'

'No, Father.' No, he wouldn't let the abbot down. Neither would he betray his vocation.

The three months Dominic spent at Stormcliff were a constant misery juxtaposed with flashes of bliss. For much of the time he was hungry, and for all of it he was cold. The tiny single-room stone cottage was too low for him to be able to flagellate while standing so he spent hours on his knees.

After the first few days he found that the whip's leather tongues were too soft so he devoted many hours to experimenting and modifying them. First he cut them thinner and then he knotted the ends, but it still was not satisfactory. He complained to Brother Simon, who listened sympathetically and returned the following week with a very different instrument. Instead of flat strips, the leather tapered from pencil thickness down to braided tips.

'But it is too long for me,' Dominic protested.

'Then I shall assist.' Brother Simon smiled kindly and indicated that he should kneel.

Dominic had never experienced such pain as those first dozen or so strokes. But then his cold skin warmed up and he found himself calling to Jesus as Brother Simon put his considerable strength into developing a rhythmic fore and backhand. Suddenly he was transported — the floor beneath his knees was not the floor of the hut at Stormcliff Cove but a Roman cell, and Brother Simon transformed into a cruel Roman centurion. Beneath the lash it was the body of Christ that was suffering. A web of welts sprang up and flowed with holy blood. The leather was sodden with blood and yet nothing could stop his spirit flying high and free in triumphant glory. And the pain had gone, replaced by such peace, such harmony, that words were insufficient to express it. Instead he felt music rising through him, swelling in a slow crescendo; the rhythm of the whip joining that of his heart until they beat as one. And as the blows rained down on him with increasing intensity he found himself singing one of the old hymns from his childhood: *My heart is weak and poor / Until it master finds / It has no spring of action sure / It varies with the wind; / It can not freely move / Till thou hast wrought its chain; / Enslave it with Thy matchless love, / And deathless it shall reign.*

Over and over he sang until he felt himself floating away from the pain. Finally, exhausted and dripping with sweat, Brother Simon knelt and washed the blood from his back.

The days between Brother Simon's visits were miserable. No matter what he did, he was unable to emulate the ecstasy of those intense sessions.

At the end of the three months Dominic received permission to return to the monastery, where Brother Simon indicated that he would be disposed to visiting Dominic's cell on a regular basis. It was common for the monks to join one another in prayer and night-time vigils, and given the cell walls were built of thick granite they knew that, if they were discreet, there was little chance the other monks would learn of their ritual. In order to make it easier for Brother Simon, Dominic constructed a large wooden cross and installed it in his cell, bolted to the wall. At the end of each arm of the cross he placed large tallow candles, so that there would be suitable illumination.

When Brother Simon arrived he would tie the naked Dominic face-in to the cross with lengths of coarse hemp rope and together they would sing, '*Bend me, bend me to Thy will, / while in Thy hand I'm lying still.*' Then Brother Simon would strip to the waist and commence the flogging.

From time to time he would walk to Dominic's side to inspect the results of his work. It was during one of these inspections that he noticed Dominic's arousal and from then on would administer some stinging blows to the offending member with his hand. Through all of this, Dominic, having attained a state of grace, continued to sing hymns or psalms. The first time Brother Simon saw him ejaculate during a flogging he punished him so severely that he was unable to sleep on his back for a week.

Two years elapsed before the event that brought this stage of Dominic's life to an end; two years during which Dominic delved deeper and deeper into the mysteries of what he termed his 'holy agony'. Then one day he was summoned by the abbot and introduced to a stocky bearded individual whom he had seen on Gissing from time to time.

'The doctor tells me he has never examined you, Brother Dominic. You will accompany him to your cell.'

'Of course, Father,' Dominic said.

The man smiled, picked up a black bag and followed him out the door. 'It's just a checkup.'

The doctor didn't speak further as they walked back across the courtyard to the low-roofed building that housed the cells. As they entered the room he glanced at the imposing cross bolted into the wall, but if he thought it strange he kept his thoughts to himself. He placed his bag on the bed and instructed Dominic to undress.

'Your back is a mess,' he said curtly.

'Flagellation is part of my calling —' Dominic began.

'I understand about self-flagellation, young man. The welts are vertical. You, on the other hand, have horizontal welts from your back down your buttocks to your legs. That is not self-flagellation.'

'Please, you mustn't say anything. Brother Simon would get into severe trouble with the abbot.'

The tears flowed down Dominic's cheeks and he threw himself to the floor and held the doctor's feet, imploring him to not give them away.

The doctor knelt and gently took the boy's face in his hands and tilted it towards him.

'Your back is festering. I am going to ask the abbot to release you into my care until it is properly healed.'

He stroked Dominic's cheeks and wiped away the tears. 'Being flogged is important to you, isn't it?'

Dominic nodded, knowing he would endure anything as long as he could continue his quest.

'Then trust me. I will not betray Brother Simon to the abbot.'

'Thank you,' Dominic sobbed. 'Thank you so much.'

The abbot took some persuading, but in the end Dominic was given permission to leave Gissing on the return ferry. As soon as they arrived on the mainland, the doctor took him to his palatial home in the suburb of Lakeside and installed him in an almost perfect replica of his cell on the island.

Like that cell, although the rest of the house was lit electrically here there was only a single candle. The doctor lit it and watched for a moment as it burned, its flame straight and pure, undisturbed by any movement in the air. He ordered Dominic to disrobe and lie on the bed, then proceeded to rub an antiseptic ointment onto his back and buttocks. 'This will soon mend,' he said. Then, to Dominic's horror, he felt the man attach something to his neck.

'What are you doing?' Dominic turned and sat up.

The man was standing at the end of the bed holding a chain, the other end of which was attached to a collar around Dominic's neck.

'I am going to train you.' The man smiled sweetly and tugged at the collar, jerking Dominic forward.

'Gissing was just an apprenticeship. You can forget all that nonsense about Jesus. From now on I am your master. You will serve me without question and in return I will initiate you into realms of pain and humiliation you have never dreamed of.'

Instead of protesting and struggling to free himself, to his absolute amazement Dominic felt himself shiver with excitement. He saw that he was stiffening in arousal. He slid from the bed onto his knees and bowed his head in total submission. 'Yes, Master.'

The doctor glanced at Dominic's erect penis and shook his head. 'I am afraid I will also have to restrain your hands. Under no circumstances are you to touch yourself without my permission. Is that clear?'

'Whatever you say, Master.' Dominic blushed.

'And you will refer to me as Master Francis.'

'Yes, Master Francis.'

'I shall call you Viola. Do you understand? From now on you have no other name.'

Master Francis delved into his bag and removed a set of leather manacles. Pushing Dominic's hands behind his back, he quickly buckled them to his wrists. 'You may rest tonight but tomorrow I will start your training and I will require total obedience. Any sign of resistance and you will be punished severely. I hope I make myself clear?'

'Yes, Master Francis.'

Though his arms ached from being restrained behind him, Dominic eventually fell asleep, but it was a sleep visited by troubled dreams. He fought battles with demons and angels for a prize that eluded all of them: the body of Christ. Then it was his own body, finally where he had always wanted it — nailed to the cross. When he awoke in the first light of dawn he knew that something had died in the night.

Dominic had gone and Viola, stiff and cramped, his arms aching intensely, was alive and ready to serve his new master.

The horror of Viola's story unsettled Teschmaker. His sleep was disturbed by dreams that twice during the night shocked him awake. Neither time could he recall what he had dreamed. Finally he slept deeper and this time the dream stayed with him, strange but not horrifying.

Teschmaker stood on the outside of a circle of people. It was a garden party, elegant, expensive. Beyond the large marquee manicured lawns and hedges ran away to a horizon of thick forest. He felt isolated from the group; their faces grimacing practised niceties and well-rehearsed wit. He looked down and saw his clothes were worn and stained with dirt, his shoes covered in dried mud. He felt rather than heard the voice.

'Why not?'

It didn't seem strange that the voice, if that was what it was, should come from the beautiful mare that stood so close behind him.

'Because . . .' Teschmaker began, and was about to say that it had been his father's chaos that he feared. But instead he looked into the large dark eyes — eyes so large he saw himself reflected in them.

'He let his feelings rule him.'

He stepped away from the horse with a sudden fear of this irrational intimacy.

'Feelings?' The horse moved closer and rubbed its nose against Teschmaker's back.

In front of him some of the people turned and eyed him with suspicion and distaste, while behind him the horse moved closer, bringing its head over his shoulder.

'Come.'

The horse pushed with its head and suddenly, powerless to resist, Teschmaker found himself astride the mare and moving through the crowd. Then with a powerful surge forward they were over the stone wall and off across the fields. But it was not the ride or the horse that seduced him but the sensations that swept through him. He became one with the animal and felt . . .

'I feel . . .'

'And I.' The horse's thought now his own. 'A Centaur knows no closer bond.'

So sweet. So indescribably sweet.

He dreamed and became aware it was a dream and fought to stay asleep; to stay at one with this being which he loved so improbably, so deeply. But failed. He awoke feeling cheated.

After breakfast, while Viola instructed Norman and Gerard on the best way of restraining Doctor Orpheus, Teschmaker roamed the house, unable to concentrate on any one task. For a while he watched the intricate rope work.

'It seems a very complicated way of going about things,' he commented.

But was immediately rebuked by Norman. 'Viola says that doing it this way will make him think it was somebody from within the group.'

Viola had a point for, as far as Teschmaker could see, no normal person would use a single piece of rope in such a manner. But he had to admit when he returned twenty minutes later that the end result was very impressive. Norman and Gerard had tied Viola in a foetal position, arms behind his back, with the rope work laced from crutch to neck. He murmured his acknowledgment of their accomplishment and resumed his pacing.

For a time he sat at his computer and pulled up every note he had made about Jane Morris. Then he logged on to the internet and found the photograph of her with Oliver that he had first seen what now seemed a very long time ago. He stared at the grainy image and knew that whatever it was she was involved with didn't matter. He was, if anything, more attracted to her now than when he began his quest. Back then it had been sheer curiosity and a way of taking his mind off the sudden loss of self-esteem he now reluctantly admitted he had experienced at the time of his redundancy. But that curiosity had grown, fuelled by a feeling that there was unfinished business between them. Her anger at him and . . . She was beautiful. Maybe it was nothing more than lust, impure and complex.

As he turned off the computer he noticed his hand was shaking and realised again why he so hated introspection. If he felt such disquiet at examining his own life, how must Viola feel? It was, he thought, a wonder that Viola had emerged from his trials and tribulations even mildly sane. He could not begin to imagine what effect such experiences would have had on himself. And Jane — was there something in her past that he had overlooked, some event that had set her on the path to bondage and submission? He found himself at the back door, gazing out at the weeds that had sprung up to claim the remains of Gwenda's once-neat garden. Maybe we are all capable of voyaging down those paths and are restrained only by circumstance. Without Gwenda, would he have sought out more exotic pleasures? No. He shook his head, no. But maybe he had sought out Gwenda as an antidote to the chaos that his father's drunken binges had wreaked upon his childhood. He remembered his mother standing in a doorway screaming at his father, 'Go away, you've made my life a fucking hell.' Had he? Or had she, in her turn, sought him out to fulfil whatever promise she thought life had in store for her? Where did it end? He knew with sudden bitter clarity that nothing he could do would alter one bit of any of it. Damn Viola! The man's story had struck a nerve and catapulted him deep into his own head. It was no place to be — the outside world was bad enough.

Teschmaker returned to the kitchen, scrubbed the benches and made a pot of tea. There were still half-a-dozen muffins left over from the previous afternoon and so he buttered them and gave each a neat dollop of guava jelly. After the tea had brewed he loaded everything he needed onto a tray and took it through to the lounge room.

'Norman is sooo good with rope,' Viola exclaimed excitedly, his eyes shining with pride at his pupil's handiwork.

Teschmaker looked at the scene before him and wished himself miles away. He felt like an exile in his own home. I don't know these people, he thought, suddenly homesick for anywhere else: for a doss house, a park bench or the gutter. *La nostalgie de la boue*. I'll get a babysitter and go out to the pictures. It was an insane thought but he was tempted; the notion of these intruders in his home as children was very close to how he felt. But he was feeling drained as well; weary, exhausted by everything. Maybe he should pack the whole thing in, sell the house and move to Europe. But even as he thought it, he knew he wasn't ready to settle anywhere. Contentment was a country for which he had never had a visa. He sat on the edge of the table and placed the tray in front of him.

Sensing Teschmaker's shift in mood, Gerard looked up from the trussed-up form of Viola and rolled his eyes. 'Time was when people were happy to spend the evening watching the television.'

'*Tempora mutantur*, times change,' Teschmaker said and yawned. 'Take a break for tea.'

On Saturday morning Viola woke Teschmaker with the news that Oliver Sinclair was downstairs, impatient to see him.

'Make him some coffee while I get dressed,' Teschmaker mumbled and headed for the shower. Stupid bloody time of the day to be calling. He glanced at his watch. It was quarter to nine. He had intended to get up early and spend some time going over the plans for the night ahead with Norman and Gerard.

By the time he had shaved and showered he was feeling slightly more human. The smell of fresh muffins greeted him halfway down the stairs.

'There is no need to cook every morning, Viola.'

The poor man looked instantly crestfallen; damn him, he had no right to make Teschmaker feel guilty in his own house. But he backpedalled. 'I mean, toast would have been okay.'

'Don't knock it.' Sinclair spoke with his mouth full and he had crumbs on the corners of his moustache. 'Best muffins I've had in a while.'

Emboldened by the praise, Viola placed a buttered muffin in front of Teschmaker. 'Wholemeal. It keeps you regular. Coffee's coming up. I had to make a fresh lot.' He rolled his eyes as if to say, *I made your coffee but these peasants drank it all.*

'Fine. Whenever you're ready.'

Teschmaker pulled up a seat and turned to Sinclair. 'Well, what — other than Viola's baking — brings you here so early, Oliver?'

'You and your paranoia. What the hell was that about Irene and my phone being bugged?' Sinclair washed the muffin down with a gulp of coffee.

'Did you have your phones checked?'

'No, of course I didn't. Costs an arm and a leg. I'd need a bloody good reason —'

'I had a phone call from someone claiming to be your personal assistant, Irene. She said she was setting up a meeting between us —'

'It sure as hell wasn't on my instructions.'

'Does she have a slightly foreign accent?'

'No. Believe me, it wasn't Irene.'

'As I found out when I turned up.' Teschmaker picked at his muffin; it did taste good.

'Who?' Oliver snapped impatiently.

283

'A Russian spook.'

Oliver put down his coffee cup slowly. 'Now, I know that something pretty weird is going on with Jane, but would you care to explain to me what the hell a Russian spook has got to do with anything?'

'Might have been an idea to keep us informed.' Gerard sounded miffed.

'Shut up, Edwards. Teschmaker knows what he's doing.'

'I just meant —' Gerard tried to claw back some ground but was dismissed with a gesture from Oliver.

'I'm trying to understand it myself.' Teschmaker paused and accepted a mug of coffee from Viola. 'Thanks. I think the more important thing is that this Russian not only knew that you and I were in contact but had Irene's name.'

'Irene's not a state secret.'

'No, but he could have simply made up a name. I wouldn't have known. I think it was his way of showing me that he had the bases covered. I don't think the man's a fool.'

Teschmaker shrugged and took a sip of his coffee then turned to Gerard. He didn't want the man offside, especially as getting into the Chambers was going to require his expertise. 'I didn't have anything concrete to share with you and I didn't want to speculate about anything at that stage; it would only have muddied the waters.'

He turned back to Oliver. 'The Russian isn't interested in Jane.'

'Then what's he after?'

'Jane's father.'

'But isn't he dead? I always assumed he must be by now.'

'Seems not. I'm doing some digging around and I'll brief you as soon as I have something. Now . . .' Teschmaker put down his coffee and got to his feet.

'Okay. I have things to do.' Oliver obviously wasn't happy but appeared resigned to the fact he wasn't going to learn any more at the moment.

'Like getting your phones checked and sending someone over here to sweep this place.'

'Are you really serious?' Oliver looked dubious.

Teschmaker nodded.

'Twenty seconds in the microwave and they'll be just like new.' Viola smiled and handed Oliver a paper bag. 'I've wrapped them in greaseproof paper.'

As soon as Oliver Sinclair was gone Teschmaker outlined the plans for the day. Norman and Gerard were dispatched to procure Adrian Wright's tool kit and to make certain that Mr Wright would not be attending the evening function at the Chambers.

'You don't trust Mr Sinclair, do you?' Viola didn't look up from his cleaning of the kitchen benches.

'What makes you say that?' Teschmaker looked at Viola with mild astonishment. The idea of not trusting Oliver was not even that firmly established in his own mind. But Viola was correct: he had been guarded with the man. Maybe it was rebellion. He had never trusted the rich; not because of any ideological belief on his behalf, but because of the vague notion that anyone who had amassed that kind of wealth must have bent the rules. His father had once told him that compliance was the treason of the upwardly mobile. Teschmaker had never really understood what sort of compliance his father had meant. Compliance with the status quo and the death of idealism? His father had been living — and dying — proof of the antithetical position. He had rebelled at every moment of his downward spiral; a railing rallentando against capitalism and hotel closing hours.

'You didn't tell him what you are going to do tonight.' Viola sprayed disinfectant around the sink and began to scrub far harder than necessary.

Teschmaker laughed out loud. 'Viola, for fuck's sake! He knows I'm going, that's enough. I don't even know what I'm going to do tonight.'

'Ah, but I can help you.' As if to prove his determination to assist, Viola wrung the neck of the dish cloth. 'As soon as Norman and Mr Edwards get back with Doctor Orpheus's tool kit we can begin.'

'You seem a little too keen to help, Viola.'

For the first time in the conversation Viola raised his eyes and looked directly at Teschmaker. 'I've always fancied the smell of vanilla, Master Martin.'

'Then you'll have to wait until I get back from doing the shopping. What do we need?'

Viola produced a neatly folded square of paper. 'I've made a list. We've got the meat, so it's only really vegetables and some green apples for the sauce.'

Teschmaker took his time. He did the shopping and then, although he disliked the local shopping centre, opted to linger over a coffee, putting off returning home. A few years back, the village — as the locals called it — had been a conglomeration of small shops and boasted the best coffee this side of the CBD. But then the developers had moved in and the Gower supermarket had spread out like a cancer, transforming itself into Gower shopping town. The small traders had been squeezed out, replaced by small boutique shops with low ceilings and high rents. The independent traders, gobbled up by franchise holders, employed teenage staff done out in ridiculous uniforms whose idea of service was a scripted response: 'Hello, I'm Marlene and I hope you're having a *truly* wonderful day.' The smile was as uniform as the teeth would be once the orthodontic work kicked in. Teschmaker mumbled that he just wanted a coffee, but still had to sit through a recitation of the virtues of the morning's *special* pancakes. He repeated his desire for coffee a little more tersely and was rewarded with a mantra of Italian. He waited until Marlene had got to macchiato and interrupted her. 'I'll have a flat white, thanks.' Flat was how he was feeling. The idea that in a few short hours he was going to be venturing into the ludicrously named Chambers of Pain was not one that he relished. Should he abandon the idea? Why not? After all, who was he doing this for?

His coffee arrived. 'I've given you *two* special almond kisses.' Marlene beamed through the metalwork on her teeth. Teschmaker waited until she had retreated and glanced around. She was obviously liberal with her kisses as every other patron had benefited from her special largesse. He let his previous train of thought meld with the current and imagined Marlene strapped to a metal frame, being whipped. It was a mildly pleasant thought. He nibbled at one of Marlene's kisses and turned his mind back to the evening ahead.

On the plus side was the notion of seeing Jane, albeit in a bizarre setting. He wondered what she was doing now. Was she looking forward to an evening of libertine indulgence, or fearing it? There was also the possibility that she wouldn't be there at all. There had been nothing in the photographs Oliver had given him to indicate that it was a public affair. Maybe the entire thing had been a setup — a few people brought in to give the photograph a sense of veracity. On the other side of the ledger was the impression he had gained from Viola that, despite Francis Grice's penchant for cruelty, he would not have played with Jane if she wasn't a willing participant. Played — that was the word he had used. Viola was insistent that he had never been present while Jane was around. 'Master Francis knows how jealous I get' had been his response to Teschmaker's probing.

Teschmaker realised that he would be unable to resolve the question of Jane's role in things until he had spoken to her, or seen with his own eyes that she was a willing participant or otherwise. That being the case, he knew he couldn't renege on the decision to go ahead with the masquerade. Having arrived at that conclusion he started to worry that something might have gone wrong for Gerard and Norman because, if he had any chance at all of pulling off the charade, he needed Adrian Wright's tool kit. He abandoned the remains of his coffee and one of Marlene's special kisses and headed home.

Coming into the kitchen with the groceries is usually the most mundane of experiences. Or at least it should be. Teschmaker took one look at the trussed body of Adrian Wright and knew that he had a choice: stay and admire the rope work, or turn around and walk away. A long way away. Preferably overseas and for a considerable length of time.

He took a deep breath and put the supermarket bags down on the sink. Mild, he told himself, adopt a mild tone.

'What the fuck is he doing here?'

It came out a little too high-pitched and definitely far too panicky. It wasn't within a bull's roar of mild. His words appeared to have no effect on Viola and Norman.

'Couldn't leave him.' Norman didn't even look up from whatever he was involved in.

'Is he alive?' The man seemed, at the very least, to be on the dead side of comatose.

Viola giggled. 'He's having a little nap.'

Time to be firm, Teschmaker told himself. He saw what Norman and Viola were doing; saw it, but didn't understand and couldn't bring himself to ask. Then he had another thought. 'Where's Gerard?' At least he would get some common sense out of Edwards.

'Upstairs, he said he was going to have a shower,' Norman volunteered. But he still didn't look up and not for a second did he lessen his concentration on the job at hand. For a moment Teschmaker watched the two men and then plucked up the courage to broach the subject of their attentions, albeit from a lateral direction. 'Is that the meat for dinner?'

'Rolled shoulder of pork,' Viola clarified. 'I hope you remembered the apples.'

Apples? Of course he had remembered the apples. Daft thing to do, buying apples when you could get damn good apple sauce ready-made in a bottle. There is a man dead or unconscious on my kitchen floor, tied up like a Sunday roast and two deviants doing strange things to meat. Teschmaker took a deep breath and decided to try a lighter note. 'Call me silly, call me wacky, even call me zany, but hey, I don't get it.' He was struggling to keep the sarcasm below critical mass.

'What?' Norman glanced over his shoulder.

'Can you explain to me in words of one syllable what the fuck you two are doing sticking coloured needles into our dinner?'

Norman and Viola exchanged a glance as if to confirm that silly, wacky and zany weren't even in the same ballpark.

'The needles are not coloured. The needles are metal. The plastic knobs on the ends of the needles — they're the coloured things. It's where they connect to the end of a syringe.' Viola stretched, rotating his neck and exercising his back as if he had been hunched over the shoulder of pork for far too long. 'You can leave the shopping, we'll put it away.'

Teschmaker knew that tone of voice. It was the same one his mother had used. *There, there, run along and play, this is adult time.*

'He's showing me some needlework,' Norman explained. 'See. He's pushed all the needles just under the skin and left the coloured ends in a circle —'

'This pattern is called the Rose of Pain.' Viola's eyes

were gleaming. He held up the meat so that Teschmaker could admire their handiwork.

On the floor Doctor Orpheus gave a long low groan. Viola glanced at him apprehensively. 'Maybe I should tell Gerard that he's coming round?' He looked questioningly at Teschmaker.

'No, I will. And while I do, get those bloody needles out of our dinner and get it in the oven. Norman, give him a hand.' He spun on his heel and executed what he hoped was a dignified exit.

He pounded up the stairs, furious with himself for allowing his home to be taken over by such maniacs. Sick! That's what they were. As he reached the top of the stairs he came face to face with Gerard coming out of the bathroom. He was naked but for a towel wrapped around his waist. For some inexplicable reason this was the final straw for Teschmaker.

'I hope you can explain what the hell is going on?' he exploded. 'Why is Adrian Wright here? I thought we had decided you would do what was necessary to incapacitate him. I don't recall saying you should bring him here. What the hell do we do with him now that he's seen this place?'

Unperturbed by the outburst Gerard removed the towel and gave his hair a quick rub.

'Relax, Teschmaker. He was unconscious and blindfolded.'

Relax? Sure, I always relax in the presence of naked men. Edward's tattoos were not confined to his arms but snaked across his chest and down his stomach like a roadmap leading to . . . Teschmaker looked down at the floor. 'But why bring him here?'

'We got in easy as pie but unfortunately he was . . . er . . . how can I put this delicately? He was with someone. A young boy. And it looked as though he was expecting other people as well . . .'

'So?' Then the penny dropped. 'You mean *with* like I think you mean with?'

'Yep.' Gerard curled his mouth in distaste. 'He was screwing the kid on a couch in his lounge room. Fucking pervert.' To Teschmaker's relief he tucked the towel back around his middle.

'Jesus! So what about the kid? Did he see you?'

'No. He was face down. Never knew what happened. I gave our Doctor Orpheus a little tap and Norman grabbed the kid.' He turned and gestured to the study. 'He's in there.'

Shaking his head in disbelief, Teschmaker strode past him and swung the door open, hoping that somehow this was all a sick joke. He swung the door open and took a step back. The boy, no more than seventeen or eighteen years of age, was expertly tied to his office chair, the blanket from the bed wrapped around his shoulders, the pillowcase doubled over as a blindfold.

Teschmaker stepped back and quietly shut the door. Thinking time. He needed thinking time. This was getting way out of hand and there was a glaring absence of exit signs. For a moment he considered ringing Oliver Sinclair and telling him to get his men as far away from him as possible, but even as he thought it he knew it was never going to happen. He remembered seeing a documentary about buffalo or wildebeest who had strayed into a swamp. Of those who kept going straight ahead a few made it to safety, but those that hesitated or tried to backtrack were sucked under and drowned in the mud. He began to appreciate how they must have felt. In certain circumstances, oblivion must be a blessed relief. But he knew that it wasn't a choice on offer. They had come a long way down this road now and there really was no feasible option other than pressing ahead. Okay. One problem at a time.

'Have you any idea what those two are doing in the kitchen?'

'Needlework. Viola said it was important. Not my scene, I'm afraid I get a bit squeamish.' It must have suddenly dawned on Gerard that Teschmaker was seriously pissed off, for his tone changed. 'Look, let me get some clothes on and then Norman and I will get our two guests out of harm's way and into the spare room. We've got a few hours up our sleeve and we had better use it to check we have you all set for this evening. Okay?'

Yes, it was okay. Just. Mind you, Teschmaker thought, it felt good to let Gerard run things for a while. The tiredness he was feeling was, he knew, due to the accumulation of days of tension and the unfamiliar experience of sharing his home. He remembered how often it had happened during his childhood. When other kids had come to stay it was always fine for the first couple of days, but any longer and the tension would build to the point where he ended up detesting them.

Not for the first time he wondered why Sinclair had offered Norman and Gerard's services. At the time it had seemed an act of generosity from a man who could afford such gifts. But now Teschmaker wondered if it didn't have the potential to become something of a poisoned chalice. No, he dismissed the thought. Norman might be a tad strange and Edwards a bit of a thug, but if you were liberal with the definition they could be described as well meaning.

He turned to Edwards. 'Sorry I shouted, Gerard. I'm feeling a little strung out.' It came out lame as hell, but Gerard caught the drift.

'The tool kit is on the table downstairs. Have a look through it. I'll bring you a belt of scotch.'

Teschmaker was about to say that it was far too early, but stopped himself. It was the right time for a scotch; if anything it was a touch late.

Eventually his hand was rock steady. Viola looked into his eyes and nodded. 'Yes, Master Martin. Do it.'

Teschmaker looked down at the point of the needle and rolled it over so the bevelled edge was facing upwards. He inhaled deeply then halfway through the exhale held his breath and pushed the needle beneath the surface of the skin. He pushed it almost its full length then angled the point up so it broke through the surface. Slowly he removed his hand. The rosette formed by the red plastic needle handles was perfectly centred around Viola's nipple.

'It's beautiful.' Viola sounded breathless and there was no doubt about the sincerity of his awe.

'You think?' Teschmaker sounded as tentative as he felt.

'Truly beautiful.' Viola's face was flushed. 'You're ready, Master Martin. You had better go and get changed. I'll pack up the tool kit.'

'What about the needles?' Teschmaker asked softly.

'I'd like to keep them in for a little while. That is, if you don't mind.'

'Of course.' Teschmaker found himself whispering as the intimacy of what he had just done suddenly hit him. For half an hour he had been concentrating totally on Viola's breast, not with any homosexual eroticism but a sweet, calm caring. He tried to think of something to say that would distance him from the feeling, but his mind was a blank so he turned and walked slowly from the room. He knew that something profoundly strange had taken place and, for some reason, he didn't want to break the moment. For two hours they had gone through the weird assortment of implements — toys, Viola had called them — in Adrian Wright's tool kit. Then Viola had brought up the issue of needlework.

'It's Doctor Orpheus's signature piece. You'll have to practise.'

At first Teschmaker had refused point blank, but Viola had gently insisted and then removed his shirt.

'Here,' he said. 'You can practise on me.'

Viola's instruction had been as tender as it was thorough. He took Teschmaker through the swabbing with alcohol, needle choice and the actual method of inserting them under the skin. But the revelation Teschmaker was having trouble coming to terms with was the mental space he found himself in. He tried to rationalise it, telling himself it was a by-product of his reduced breathing rate and meditative concentration. But the rationale didn't fully explain the floating feeling and heightened awareness he was experiencing.

'Dom space,' Viola explained. 'Just like a subbie can get into sub space.'

'Like the religious ecstasy you told me about when you were flogged?' Teschmaker's previous incredulity was slipping away.

'Exactly.' Viola smiled, then added wickedly, 'You may even find you enjoy this evening.'

CHAPTER FIFTEEN

Teschmaker had Gerard drop him off at the Botanical Gardens end of Nikolayevsky Street just after 10 pm. Although, according to Viola, some people would arrive as early as eight o'clock, his advice was to wait until things began to warm up. 'Nothing much happens before ten, they just stand around and socialise, and that's the last thing you need.'

Teschmaker couldn't agree more. His nervousness had been increasing all evening and in a way it was a relief that the waiting was over. He had half convinced himself that he probably would not even make it past the front door. And even if he did, there was a distinct possibility that Jane would not be there. One thing was certain. He would have no trouble recognising Master Francis. Viola's description — bald, moustache, silver mask and a silver-handled whip — suggested he would be hard to miss.

He thanked Gerard and told him he would take a taxi home. Gerard offered to wait outside, but

Teschmaker insisted that it was more important he keep a close eye on Adrian Wright and the boy. Kidnapping was bad enough; the last thing he wanted was for one of them to come to more serious harm.

Gerard protested that they would be fine, but sensing that the fewer things Teschmaker had to worry about the better, reluctantly agreed. He waited while Teschmaker took the tool kit from the rear seat, then did a U-turn and headed back towards Gower.

The evening was pleasantly warm and though down on the street there was only a hint of a breeze, above him the few clouds were drifting slowly towards the south. He was five blocks away from the top end of Nikolayevsky Street but was glad of the walk. He patted his pocket to double-check his mask was still there, then picked up the bag and strolled slowly towards his destination.

Back at his house he had packed and unpacked the tool kit several times until Viola had been satisfied he knew where every last item was and how it was stored. Despite the fact that the contents of the tool kit were alien to him, Teschmaker had to admit that Adrian Wright had a very tidy mind. Each of the floggers was velcro-sealed inside a strong plastic bag, which in turn had external velcro strips that allowed it to be attached to the inside of the tool kit. In his head he reviewed the inventory: whips around the outside, studded leather wrist and ankle manacles at one end. Under them the heart-shaped paddle, solid leather. In the middle were the containers of nipple clamps, a pair of evil-looking breast clamps, clothes pegs, rubber gloves, condoms . . .

'For Christ's sake, Viola! He can't need all this stuff,' Teschmaker had said the first time it was spread out in front of him. He picked up a strange object with a tail of horse hair. 'What the fuck is this?'

'A butt plug.'

Teschmaker dropped it quickly. 'You mean that someone . . .'

'They wear it sometimes for the whole night.' Viola picked it up, straightened out the tail and placed it neatly back on the table. 'Look, these are the same but without the tail. And this is for CBT.' He held up a stainless-steel tube with a clasp that looked like bent teeth from a comb. Several heavy metal rings were clipped to the side of the instrument.

To Teschmaker it looked like a surgical instrument you might find in the operating theatre from hell. 'CBT — Competency Based Training?'

That broke Viola up completely and he laughed so hard he had to sit down, hugging at his sides to stop the pain. 'That is *such* a vanilla thing to say,' he managed through tears of mirth. 'CBT is shorthand for cock and ball torture.'

Teschmaker shook his head, speechless.

'The tube hinges open and then clamps shut around —'

'Enough! I get the picture.' He took the clamp and weighed it in his hand. 'So what's the socket for?' It looked like something you would plug a headphone into.

'It's a connection for a TENS machine. Usually it has contact pads . . .' Viola saw he was way ahead of Teschmaker so he backtracked. 'A TENS machine is used in electric play. It delivers a variable charge,' Viola explained patiently. 'Normally the contact pads — one positive, one negative — are put on a subbie and the Master or Mistress operates the controls.' He frowned, remembering something difficult. 'I've heard that you can put the positive pads on one person and the negative on the other and then . . .' He blushed, hesitating. 'Then they make love and the charge is felt through anywhere that is . . . lubricated.'

Teschmaker had tried to imagine the sensation, but couldn't.

He was now only two blocks away from the alleyway that led to the side entrance. Stay calm, he told himself. You'll walk in, have a look around and walk out. Simple. Another part of his brain was telling him a completely different story. In his hand, the tool kit felt a great deal heavier than it had back at the house. He forced his mind to concentrate on reviewing its contents. What was it that Viola had told him? You always warm somebody up first. Warm them up? It sounded deceptively friendly considering he had been talking about the floggers.

'This large heavy one, it's very thuddy — not much sting but a lot of noise. Use this to warm people up. Because of the noise you can fuck with people's minds.'

'How do you mean?'

'Probably fifty per cent of pain is in the mind, so if you use something that makes a lot of noise then the subbie feels you are doing more than you actually are. Some people play a lot of mind games. Anyway, you'll see what I mean tonight.'

Teschmaker had felt totally out of his depth;

inadequate and stupid. No, he told himself, there is no reason why I *should* have known all this stuff. He'd picked up another whip with a yellow handle and a very long tail. 'This one?'

'It just plain hurts.' Viola's eyes were shining again. 'But you need a fair bit of skill to use it. The leather is harder and thinner. You should try it out.'

'Damn it, Viola, I'm not going to whip you, okay?'

'I meant on the back of the chair,' Viola protested innocently.

And so for half an hour, under Viola's eagle eye, he had lashed with both forehand and backhand strokes at a kitchen chair to which Viola had obligingly tied a pillow. After the first twenty minutes it had seemed like a pretty normal thing to be doing on a Saturday afternoon. Then they had returned to the tool kit. A quiver of canes; a single-tailed whip; the viper — a single piece of thicker leather split like a snake's tongue — an evil version of the old school strap. 'It produces a beautiful welt that lasts for days,' Viola informed him. Ropes, cuffs, leather and steel . . . Teschmaker had struggled to take it all in.

'Now . . . ooh . . . this brings tears to my eyes just to look at it,' Viola whispered. 'Oh, that's gotta hurt.'

'This?'

'It's called a scourge — a chain flogger. Those tiny metal balls really get the claret flowing.'

'Hang on.' Teschmaker was confused. 'I thought that blood was a no-go area.'

'Usually. Most groups have a no-blood rule, so they have a safety system, a word or phrase to let the dom know that it is getting a bit much and to stop. But the

Chambers of Pain people were brought together by Master Francis because they were all established edge players — people who like to go to extremes. The edge is where most groups stop but with Master Francis it is where they begin.'

It was not a comforting thought.

At the end of the laneway that led down the side of the building to the Chambers, Teschmaker reached into his pocket and fished out the mask. It was, in fact, only a half mask: black leather outlined with silver studs. In addition to a strap that fastened at the back there was another thin strip of soft leather that passed either side of the bridge of the nose, over the crown of the head and joined the other strap at the small buckle at the back.

'It's meant to stay securely in place, no matter what you might do,' Viola had said in a reassuring tone. Teschmaker, however, was a long way from feeling reassured about anything. He had adjusted the straps before leaving home and thankfully it slipped on easily now and simply required tightening. He stepped back as a man in a business suit brushed passed him. He too was carrying a tool kit, looking for all the world like a slightly overweight, middle-management executive on his way home from work with his gym bag, ready to pump some iron or hit the squash court.

'Good evening.' The man had a pleasant, educated voice. Confident. Normal.

Teschmaker gave him a slight nod and, picking up his own bag, followed him down the alley. Of course the man sounded normal. What had he expected? That these people would speak like a cross between Hannibal Lecter and Quasimodo? It's too late for fear, he told himself sternly.

The door was open and so he stepped over the sill and found himself in a dimly lit reception area. In front of him the man in the business suit stood at a small window fitted with thick steel bars behind which sat a man dressed in the uniform of an SS officer. The hat-check clerk, Teschmaker thought, in an attempt to forestall the rising sense of panic. The SS officer ran his pencil down a clipboard and, finding the name he was after, ticked it off.

'Lord Eros, welcome.'

'Thanks, Commandant. See you inside?' The man sounded hopeful.

'Yes. We've nearly got a full house, including a busload of kinksters from out of town. I shouldn't be stuck up here much longer.'

Lord Eros turned to Teschmaker and winked. 'Full house, eh, Orpheus? And some fresh meat, should be a good night.'

Teschmaker repeated his curt nod and, hearing Viola's voice in his head, remembered to grunt for good measure. It seemed to do the trick.

'That's the spirit!' Lord Eros beamed.

Teschmaker thought he had never seen anybody less evocative of Eros than the plump individual hurrying down the stairs that led off from the right of the lobby. He turned back to the SS officer. 'Evening.'

'Ah! Doctor Orpheus, glad you made it. Dog Dirt was looking for you. Probably wants you to take him for a walk. I told him that he'd be locked in the kennel if he got too pushy. He liked that a lot.' The man laughed shortly and ticked his clipboard.

He was about to say something else but his laugh had triggered what sounded like a nasty bronchial cough and so Teschmaker grunted and made his way to the stairs. He felt a little light-headed at having made it past the first hurdle so easily, but as he went down the steps the feeling evaporated.

The basement of the building appeared to be cut from solid rock and he experienced the first onslaught of claustrophobia. He had never suffered from such a fear before but the unevenness of the steps and the closeness of the walls combined to fill him with unease. He put out his hand to steady himself and the stone felt cold and damp to his touch. It felt dead. He knew it was an irrational thought, but knowing did nothing to mitigate the tomb-like atmosphere and his sense of dread. He realised he had stopped, so he took a deep breath and forced his feet forwards.

Ten steps down he came to a landing from which the stairs continued down at right angles. Fortunately he could now see what he assumed must be the main entrance to the Chambers: two stone pillars cut in relief from the surrounding stone. Above the pillars, on a massive stone lintel, was carved what Teschmaker recognised as a quote from St Augustine: *Ama et fac quod vis*, Love and do what you will. Given the location, he thought, it could just as easily have been from Aleister Crowley. The Great Beast, as he liked to be known, would have felt quite at home here. As a teenager Teschmaker had read an account of Crowley's exploits at the Abbey of Thelma in Sicily, where he had gone after leaving the Society of the Golden Dawn. Teschmaker remembered it well because he had been severely castigated by his lower-sixth English master for including a reference to Crowley in an essay. His defence — that WB Yeats had also been a member of the Society — had done nothing to ease the severity of the reprimand. Ironically, he had been caned for arguing his case.

Teschmaker stepped through the door and found himself in a small but stunning replica of a basilica, complete with a row of colonnades on either side, running the full length of the chamber and ending in a polygon-shaped apse. He felt he had stepped back into the Dark Ages. There was not a single electric light, the entire space lit by a series of large candles burning in niches cut into the walls. Viola had assured him that the lighting would be dim, but this was brighter than he had expected. As his eyes adjusted he could see relatively clearly. There were forty or fifty people milling about, and so for a moment Teschmaker stood, taking it all in.

Even more stunning than the architecture were the furnishings; a medieval torture chamber was the nearest comparison he could think of. Large posts were set into the floor at regular intervals. At the top of each a solid spike secured the chains that were being used to constrain the men or women attached to the posts. They were not being whipped; as far as Teschmaker could make out, they had simply been left there, much as one might leave a horse hitched to a rail. To his right though it was a different story. A huge naked man was strapped into a contraption that resembled a dentist's chair, except that it was built from large, roughly polished slabs of timber. His chest, wrists and ankles were restrained by broad leather straps with large buckles. Several men and women were standing around watching as a woman, in nothing but a black miniskirt, applied what looked like shaving cream to the man's extremely hairy upper body. Teschmaker sauntered over and attached himself to the rear of the group, trying to catch some fragment of conversation that might enlighten him as to what was going on. But the onlookers were engrossed and, apart from the odd murmur of appreciation, were silent.

Viola had warned him to expect a wide range of fetish wear, but nothing he could have said would have prepared Teschmaker for the impact of seeing it in these surroundings. He glanced at the large woman beside him. Her enormous breasts were forced up and out by a black corset and she appeared to be wearing nothing else. No, he looked down at her feet, she was wearing riding boots. Sensing his attention the woman turned and smiled. Her mask was a work of art. Though it must have been lined with something, the outward appearance was all peacock feathers.

She leaned over to Teschmaker and whispered, 'This should be fun.'

He grunted his agreement and turned his attention back to the man in the chair. The cream substance now not only covered his chest and stomach, but all down the length of his widely spread legs. The miniskirted woman was moving around him, checking something. Then, satisfied all was in order, she took a couple of small white towels and laid one across the man's face, the other across his genitals. She gave two more towels to members of the crowd and, keeping one for herself, motioned for the onlookers to step back. As she picked up a small taper and moved to the nearest candle and lit it, the onlookers moved back another step. In a single movement she spun back to the bound man and touched the taper to the cream on his ankles. In an instant the man vanished beneath a sheet of flame. The crowd gasped and then, just as quickly, the people with towels moved forward and wiped the remnants of the flames from the now totally hairless body.

'I'll stick to my razor,' someone quipped and there was a ripple of laughter.

'Nice work, darling,' the woman in the feather mask called and then turned back to Teschmaker. 'Honestly, I don't know where she gets such hairy specimens.' She gave a deep-throated laugh and moved off.

For Teschmaker it was a great relief to see so many other people cruising as he was. His biggest fear had been that he wouldn't know how to behave, but watching seemed to be a totally acceptable activity. It was a voyeur's paradise, if pain was what turned you on. The dull thwack of a whip caught his attention and he followed a leather-clad couple to one of the small alcoves off the main hall. Here the light was even dimmer, a single guttering candle providing the only illumination, but it was more than enough for him to see a man being strapped to — what had Viola called it? — the pain-tree. The cruciform shape was constructed from solid timber. The man — naked, arms and legs spread and manacled — was also attached to the device by a D-ring on his collar that hooked onto an additional beam that ran upright from the centre of the X formed by the crosspieces. His neck now forced up, the man looked far from comfortable. I suppose that would defeat the purpose, Teschmaker thought bleakly. Having satisfied himself that the subbie was correctly secured, the other man — the dom — turned and nodded at the two or three people who had joined Teschmaker to watch the proceedings. He crossed to the rear wall and pulled a whip from his bag. As he shook it to free the dozen or so strips of leather he moved back to the pain tree and, whispering in the subbie's ear, held the whip out for him to see. The man flinched, eliciting a murmur of approval from the onlookers.

For a couple of minutes the dom simply stroked the subbie's back in a strangely gentle and loving manner, running the strands of leather all the way down to his buttocks. Then he took a step back, twirled the whip and with a grunt landed a powerful blow. There was a yelp from the subbie and a gasp from the crowd. Seemingly oblivious to the restrained man's pain, the dom built into a rhythm of harder and harder blows. Most of the strokes were aimed at the buttocks, but from time to time the dom switched focus and laid into the subbie's back or legs.

'Good colour,' someone said quietly.

Teschmaker, mesmerised, nodded. Then he realised that the remark was a reference to the subbie's buttocks, which had indeed taken on a red glow. The flogging continued until the dom was dripping with sweat and the subbie twitching with the pain of every blow. Then, just when Teschmaker had decided that he would move on, there was a sigh from the now much bigger crowd of onlookers. The subbie had suddenly gone limp, hanging from his restraints, his head rolled to one side displaying a look of beatific pleasure.

'Sub-space,' came the whisper from behind Teschmaker.

'Well done, sir!' exclaimed someone else.

The dom turned and, wiping the sweat from his brow, bowed to the crowd. 'Took some doing tonight. I swear that man has a Teflon arse.' This was greeted with laughter. The dom beckoned to someone behind Teschmaker. 'Ah, Commandant! Care to keep him warm while I get a drink?'

'A pleasure.'

The man in the SS uniform who Teschmaker had seen upstairs stepped through the crowd. He shook his head at the proffered whip. 'I'd rather use Satan, if you don't mind.' He pulled a short, evil-looking whip with a metal handle from his belt.

Deciding that he had seen quite enough, Teschmaker turned to leave. He glanced around him but there was no sign of Jane or Francis Grice. He decided to continue his tour and then exit before he gave himself away. So far it had gone better than he had expected, but he didn't want to push his luck and find himself exposed or, worse still, having to insert needles into someone in order to maintain his pretence.

It was then that he noticed the small surveillance camera high in the corner of the room. Back in the main hall he found three more, spaced along the length of the room. A quick check confirmed that there was one in each of the alcoves. For a second he paused and took in the sight before him. A large naked woman was strapped to a table. Two people were dripping hot wax on her stomach while a third was attaching clamps to the flesh around her nipples. Teschmaker squirmed in involuntary sympathy and then had to confront the thought that she was probably enjoying it. Above him he noticed that the camera was moving. So, they were capable of tracking and focusing. Which meant of course that the images were being manually operated, rather than simply recorded to video.

Taking his time, Teschmaker ambled around the main room, following the path of the cable above his head. It ran the length of the room and then down the wall where it vanished near the entrance. Damn! The control room must be entered from somewhere else, probably the office upstairs. Then he saw the door behind the first of the tall columns. Fortunately the column hid it from the view of the nearest camera so he walked over and, assuming an air of authority, tried the handle. To his surprise it was unlocked and he slipped through and shut it quietly behind him.

Teschmaker found himself in a darkened stairwell. He paused, letting his eyes adjust to the light. The atmosphere was airless and unpleasantly claustrophobic. From somewhere above him came a slight glow; just enough to illuminate the concrete steps. Cautiously, he made his way up the narrow stairs until he came to a landing where a small shielded light shone faintly above a strong metal door. Unfortunately this one had no handle on the exterior.

Teschmaker was about to turn and retrace his steps when a flare of light caught his eye and he realised that in the gloom he had failed to see the panel of darkened glass that ran from floor to ceiling beside the door. He stepped back into the shadows and watched. For a moment he could see nothing but the faint flicker of a bank of monitors. Then the flare was repeated and behind the glass he had a clear and unmistakable view of the profile of a man lighting a cigar. Teschmaker blinked and squinted through the dark. In that one instant every feeling he had about the way this whole game was being played unravelled, like a ball of wool at the whim of a kitten. Then the match was extinguished, plunging the control room into darkness.

Teschmaker was certain that his eyes had not played tricks on him, but about everything else he was suddenly not so sure. The man behind the cigar was Oliver Sinclair.

Sinclair was a player? It didn't make a scrap of sense, at least not in the scenario Teschmaker had imagined was unfolding. He decided to call it quits and go home.

He made his way down the stairs and out into the main hall, but just as he was heading for the exit he felt a tap on his shoulder. Startled, he turned to find himself confronted by the SS officer, Commandant. Looking hot and sweating profusely from his exertions, the man grinned at him.

'The boss has a little bit of work for you. Something you'll really enjoy.'

Teschmaker grunted and followed the man who, not waiting for an answer, had turned on his jack-booted heels and stridden off down the length of the main room. They passed through the apse and turned right. The Commandant held a door open for Teschmaker.

'Bit of a treat,' he beamed and ushered Teschmaker in front of him. 'I hope you don't mind waiting a moment. I'll be along with the others directly.'

The room was totally black except for a large stainless-steel table in the centre of the floor. The only source of illumination was a bulb high in the ceiling. Teschmaker noticed another row of small spotlights, but there appeared to be no switch for turning them on. The floor felt slightly springy beneath his feet and when he bent and pressed his hand against it he found that it, like the walls and ceiling, were covered with sheets of black rubber. There was, he noticed, an almost total absence of sound in the room, the acoustics providing an oppressive silence.

Stepping back into the shadows Teschmaker glanced around and located not one but two cameras on the walls and, to his surprise, a small microphone hanging in the darkness above the table. There was something about the room, something that nagged at him. Then it occurred to him that this was probably the room in which the photographs sent to Sinclair had been taken. Mind you, he thought, it also seemed likely — given Oliver Sinclair's presence in the control room — that he hadn't been sent them at all. But if not . . .? And then he remembered the night Sinclair had come to his house with the bottle of wine. Something he had said: *You weren't even in the country when these photographs were taken.* So Sinclair must have known when they were taken. An unintended slip? Or part of the elaborate game he appeared to be playing? Teschmaker couldn't untangle the competing possibilities.

'Doctor Orpheus!'

Teschmaker turned. The Commandant was holding the door open for another man to come into the room. 'I don't believe you have met Oleg?'

Unlike everyone else Teschmaker had seen so far, this man was not wearing a mask. He was a solid individual in his early forties, dark cropped hair, a flattish Slavic face with a livid scar running diagonally across his left cheek. The muscles emerging from the arms of his tight black T-shirt looking as though they had enjoyed more than a little steroid inducement. He nodded curtly at Teschmaker.

Teschmaker gave a grunt and moved further out of the light to lean against the wall. So what were they were doing here? S&M porn videos? Again his mind went back to the man he had witnessed in the control room. What was Oliver Sinclair's role in all of this? Was he excited by the pain? The sex? Or simply the profits? Teschmaker still couldn't make sense of the puzzle of the photographs. It seemed unlikely that Sinclair had been sent them by person or persons unknown, but what possible motive could he have for constructing such an elaborate scenario? And why the hell would he want to involve Teschmaker in it? Maybe he was trying to establish an alibi in case something went wrong. Teschmaker filed the line of questioning away for later examination.

Whatever was coming up next, it didn't look as if it involved whipping. Oleg and the Commandant were threading manacle straps through holes in each of the four corners of the table. The door opened and for a moment Teschmaker thought it was some kind of joke. Two men dressed in what he could only think of as mock-Grecian robes entered the room, followed by two more carefully carrying a red-hot brazier.

The Commandant indicated that the brazier should be placed beside the table. Crossing to the wall, he turned a handle to open a small window high up, presumably to allow the fumes to escape.

'Line up.'

The order was curt and promptly obeyed by the men, who formed a row along the opposite wall. Sensing Teschmaker's bewilderment, the Commandant smiled. 'All will be revealed, Orpheus.'

He went to the door and returned with a bucket and a long metal shaft, the broad end of which was covered with a velvet cloth. 'Master Francis has excelled himself this time.'

Teschmaker shrugged and grunted. None of it made any sense.

The Commandant turned to the nearest camera. 'I think we are ready.'

Up in the control room someone flicked a switch and the single bulb was replaced by two softer lights centred on the surface of the metal table, the spots focused so that it appeared to float against the black. The remainder of the room contracted into darkness. A couple of seconds passed and then, as if in response to a secret cue, the four men, now almost invisible in the gloom, started to sing. The robes may have been Grecian but the song was medieval Latin. Whoever they were, Teschmaker had to acknowledge they were superb. The four voices — two tenors, a countertenor and baritone — melded as one, threading notes together in flawless harmony.

'Virgo flagellatur, crucianda fame religatur,
Carcere clausa manet, lux caelica fusa refulget.'

As the singing continued the door opened and Teschmaker felt himself tense up as he recognised the man from Viola's description: bald, moustache, silver mask and a silver-handled whip in his left hand. With his right hand Francis Grice led a gagged and blindfolded woman. Teschmaker was in no doubt that this was Jane. She was dressed in a loose white shift. As she passed in front of him, Teschmaker saw that the gag was a rubber ball in her mouth, held in place by a leather strap buckled at the back of her head. Everything about her demeanour suggested she was not a willing participant.

No, Teschmaker corrected himself, that was simply his projection. He was certainly in no position to judge her motives. For all he knew, she and her husband were involved in some complex sexual mind games that he had no experience of and, he realised, didn't really care to know about.

'Good evening, Orpheus,' Grice murmured as he led Jane to the table. Teschmaker took an involuntary step further back into the shadows. The less Grice saw of him the better, he thought. For a moment he contemplated simply slipping out the door and leaving, but there was something compelling about discovering what was about to unfold. His arm touched the wall and he leaned back against the cool, clammy, rubber surface.

When Jane reached the table the Commandant and Oleg came forward and lifted her onto it, pushing her face down and quickly attaching the straps to her ankles and wrists. The cotton shift was ripped away leaving her naked; though there were a few welt marks on her buttocks, her back looked completely untouched.

Grice walked alongside the bench, casually running the thongs of his whip down her skin. 'Poor Jane. Whatever am I to do with you?'

He flicked the whip lightly across her back. There was no overt aggression or force in his action but Jane flinched and struggled against the restraints, a muffled noise escaping from the gag as she shook her head vigorously.

'Jane, Jane ... All I needed was a little bit of cooperation.' Grice sighed as though remembering some great sadness. 'I warned you it would end in tears.' He reversed the whip and slid the handle gently up between her legs. 'I suppose I could give you to Oleg here; he has such an appetite and really is a bit of a brute. Would you like that?' For a moment he pressed the metal harder against her. 'No. I think not. You might enjoy it.'

He turned and peered into the dark, looking for Teschmaker. 'Tell me, Orpheus, do you like my choir? Trained them myself. Don't you find the old songs inspiring?'

Teschmaker grunted.

'Do you understand all that old Latin?'

'No.'

'Pity. Such a sign of culture, I always think.'

Grice sighed again and idly stroked his fingers down Jane's spine. For a moment he listened to the music, eyes shut, swaying gently.

'*The maiden is beaten, is bound, with a hunger to be tortured, remains in a closed prison, the heavenly light shines forth abundantly.* That is just my rough translation, but apt, don't you think? Particularly apt.'

He straightened up as though he had come to a decision. 'Jane, I think I have to teach you a very big lesson. Then maybe you will do as you're told.'

He turned to Oleg. 'Hold her head up.'

Grice beckoned to the singers to come forward; without missing a note they lined up at the head of the table. He gestured again and they turned to face the wall.

'Commandant, their tunics, if you please.'

And as the Commandant stepped up to the singers, Grice crouched and brought his head down beside Jane's and, as Oleg tilted her head towards the singers, he slipped the mask from her face. At the same time the Commandant walked along the row of men and pulled the loose tunics from their shoulders.

It took every bit of control that Teschmaker possessed not to gasp out loud. Each of the men had been branded. Burned deep into the flesh on their backs was the single word: SLAVE. He wanted to turn away but he couldn't, so he stared, revolted and fascinated at the same time. He tried to imagine the pain and the long agony they must have endured while the scar tissue healed. And the humiliation. Not a name, not even a number, but a single debasing word.

On the metal table Jane was thrashing against the restraints, flailing her head from side to side. Oleg grabbed her and held her firmly as Grice picked up the metal rod and, holding it in front of her, removed the velvet cover. For a moment Teschmaker thought the branding iron was the same one that had been used on the singers, but then Grice turned it slowly in front of Jane and he read the word he had in store for her: SLUT.

'Poor Jane,' Grice whispered. 'And it could all have been avoided. Oh well . . .' His tone changed, no longer soft but harsh and abrupt. 'Do it, Commandant,' he ordered.

They placed the brazier in front of Jane and left the mask off so that she could see what was happening. While the brand was being heated, Oleg rubbed oil into Jane's back and laid a folded towel alongside her.

'Such a pity about that back, don't you think, Doctor Orpheus?' Grice walked over and leaned casually against the wall beside Teschmaker. 'I suppose you would like to rescue her?' There was no change of tone, the line delivered with a barely perceptible tinge of sadness. 'Is that what you are here for?' As Grice stepped right up close Teschmaker felt the metal of the pistol, cold against his arm.

'I'm not sure —' he began.

'Really, Mr Teschmaker, do you take us for complete fools? The Commandant informed me we had someone pretending to be Orpheus the minute you walked in.' Grice paused and watched as the singers returned to their original positions in the dark, still singing. He gestured casually around the chamber. 'So, what do you think of my little playpen?'

'I think you are a very sick individual, Grice.' Teschmaker tried to back away but found himself in a corner, the pistol pointed unwaveringly at his stomach.

Grice smiled disdainfully and patted Teschmaker's arm. 'Pity you are not going to stay around. I would have rather enjoyed punishing you for your rude intrusion into our privacy. However, I understand others have prior claims on your time.' He kept the pistol against Teschmaker's side and with his other hand beckoned Oleg over. 'I take it you two haven't been introduced? Oleg, this is Mr Teschmaker.'

'The Commandant did the honours earlier. A pleasure. I have heard so much about you.' Oleg grinned, his Russian accent guttural and thick enough to cut with a knife. 'I hope you don't mind waiting while we complete our modest little production?'

'I'd have your head in the brazier if I thought I could get away with it, Rusak,' Teschmaker sneered.

The Russian looked surprised. 'So you know who I am? I am impressed.'

'You're low-life Mafia scum.' Teschmaker shrugged and then added in Russian, 'A pig must have fucked your mother.' It didn't come out quite right and he wasn't sure if it should have been dog rather than pig, but he had obviously got the tone right.

'*Khuilo! Eb tvoju mat.*' Rusak lashed out. Grabbing Teschmaker's throat and holding him up against the wall, he drove his fist into his stomach. As Teschmaker gasped for breath Rusak released his neck and let him crash to the floor. '*Ebaniy v rot!*' The kick was aimed at his groin but missed its mark and smashed into his arm.

'Enough!' Grice stepped in and pushed Rusak back. 'There will be plenty of time for pleasure later on, Oleg. We are keeping the lady waiting.'

'Okay, okay.' Rusak raised his hands in capitulation, then leaned over and dragged Teschmaker to his feet. 'Nobody calls me scum and insults my mother, understand?' he whispered. '*Pizdez*. Later, okay?'

Rusak released his grip. Unable to breathe properly, Teschmaker slid slowly down the wall. He struggled to get air into his lungs and gingerly ran his fingers down his arm. It felt like it was broken.

'Now, Mr Teschmaker, I am going to leave Oleg to keep you company. Please don't do anything to upset him because we certainly don't want any disturbances while we attend to Mrs Sinclair.'

Handing the pistol to Rusak, Grice turned and went over to the brazier, gesturing for the Commandant to lift the branding iron so he could see it. It was red hot.

'Perfect. Well, Jane, it seems we are all set for your big moment.'

He took the handle of the brand and showed it to her. But although she kicked and pulled at her restraints a couple of times, it seemed to Teschmaker that all the fight had gone out of her. Horrified, he watched as Grice moved round to her side. For a second he stood there, then he nodded to the Commandant to join him. Grice positioned the brand above Jane's back and slowly brought it down low enough for her to feel the heat. As she squirmed against the manacles and choked on the gag in her mouth, the Commandant flipped open the folded towel and reached his hand down into the bucket beside the

CHAPTER SIXTEEN

The weather had undergone as abrupt a change as Teschmaker's fortunes. The balmy summer evening had been replaced by a sudden southerly storm. As they emerged from the Chambers it appeared that the rain had been set in for a while. Wild gusts were curtaining down Nikolayevsky Street, sweeping paper and plastic detritus before them. Already the gutters were overflowing, their contents heading for the stormwater drains that would take them under the city to where the Charlotte River would be cascading down to the lake. It was not a good night for a drive in the country but Teschmaker realised he wasn't going to be given a choice in the matter.

'We will speak English,' Rusak instructed as he pushed Teschmaker into the back seat of the Mercedes waiting for them at the end of the alley. 'Because my driver doesn't.'

'I wasn't feeling like a chat.'

'But we have so much to talk about.' Rusak made a show of laying the pistol on his lap. 'Now, please, your seatbelt. I would hate that you had an accident.' It seemed that he didn't consider the possibility of an accident very likely as he made no attempt to do up his own belt and contented himself with lowering the armrest between them.

The car moved off and for the first few minutes they drove in silence. As they circled the Botanical Gardens and headed out on the Airport Freeway, Rusak lit a cigarette and lowered his window slightly. It seemed that the smoke at least would be given an opportunity to escape.

'So, I am curious, Teschmaker. You know my name.'

'Yes.'

Teschmaker was feeling decidedly flat and the idea of engaging in chit-chat with a man who seemed not only intent on killing him but capable of doing so was not appealing. He stared ahead, but the windscreen wipers were working overtime and the visibility was zero. A view was out of the question. For a moment he pondered the problem of escape. He thought of movies where, at this point, the hero would wait for a slow corner then fling open the door and roll free. He always hurt himself slightly — usually a twisted ankle that added tension to the ensuing chase through the woods. The hero would limp and stumble, fighting his way through dense undergrowth, and the villains would be right on his heels, torches in one hand, guns in the other, cursing the visibility and getting closer every moment. Eventually the hero would trip and as he lay in the sodden leaf litter the villains would run right beside him. One always stopped, as though sensing him, and just at the moment when he was about to be discovered the other villain would hear something and call. The hero would be safe — for the moment. Much as Teschmaker liked the scenario, he knew that the electronically locked car doors and the absence of a handle on his side made it all a little difficult.

'So, how do you know me?'

'A friend in intelligence showed me a photograph of you in Moscow. Said you were a big cheese.'

'A what?'

'He said you had been in the Duma but now you were an important boss.'

It could have been true. Teschmaker knew it would appeal to the man's vanity. Rusak would want it to be true. So it would be.

'I told Mr Sinclair that you were with intelligence. He said you sold insurance.' Rusak laughed. 'I should have bet with him.'

'You are a friend of Sinclair's?'

Teschmaker wondered if they would be lucky enough to have a road accident. He slipped his hand onto the seatbelt clasp, just in case. His mind was flipping all over the place and in a sudden moment of clarity he realised this man was going to kill him. This friendly chat — it was not about information; this was because it didn't matter what was said, because . . . well, it didn't matter. Scared, Teschmaker thought, I am really scared.

'We are in *biznes*.'

'I thought you were working with Grice?'

Rusak snorted. 'Grice is a stinking little pervert. He is nothing.' He lowered the window a little further, flicked the butt of the cigarette into the night and raised the window again, trapping the smoke inside. 'Sinclair set him up. Paid for everything.'

Teschmaker inhaled deeply, wondering if passive smoking would steady his nerves. 'But the building — I was told that Grice owned it.'

'And who told you that?' Rusak's smile went from ear to ear. He was obviously enjoying the joke.

'The records say it belongs to his company . . .' But as he said it he realised how deeply he had been misled.

'Exactly, and Sinclair owns his company.'

'So you and Sinclair are in *biznes*.' Teschmaker echoed the Russian slang. 'He provides the product and you provide the market. Very cosy.'

'Much more, Teschmaker. It is the new world order — East and West in partnership. Video is only a little hobby. We make money make money. We are serious players.'

Rusak sounded as though he believed it. And Teschmaker imagined that it was probably true.

'So what do you do apart from pornography, Rusak? Arms? Drugs?'

Rusak looked genuinely hurt. 'Teschmaker, I told you. I am a businessman. I deal in money. I facilitate its movement.'

Well, Teschmaker thought, that was probably true as well. There were so many ways to make money by moving currency around. He peered through the window. His guess that they were heading out to Grice's country house looked like it had been right on

326

target. They had passed the airport exit and were on the Daleborough road. It also appeared that they had come through the worst of the storm, the rain on the windscreen now little more than drizzle.

'Does Jane Sinclair know about your *biznes* with Oliver?'

'Jane?' Rusak looked at Teschmaker as though he was crazy. 'Oliver and Jane hate each other. If it wasn't for his enormous fortune I am sure he would have been rid of her before now. You see, he was worried she would claim half his assets and I am afraid Oliver could never allow that. So they remain married and nobody is happy. This situation distressed me so much.'

'Really?' Teschmaker didn't veil the sarcasm, but it appeared to sail right over Rusak's head. 'And Jane and Grice? What's going on between them? Why the performance tonight?'

'You really don't know?' Rusak shook his head in disbelief.

'I have no idea.'

For a moment Rusak paused, fished another cigarette from his packet and lit it. 'Actually, it was my idea. Jane was proving very difficult for Oliver and for me. I needed her to assist me with a small problem and she was most uncooperative. So I found a way of putting some pressure on her and Grice decided to exploit it to get her down to the Chambers. Sinclair saw what was happening and agreed that it was just what he needed.'

'I'm sorry, I don't understand.' Teschmaker felt that if this was the executive summary, then he wasn't executive material. 'What did you and Sinclair want from Jane?'

Rusak smiled. 'Different things. Sinclair just wanted her to disappear, but I had another agenda. You have met Jane's father, yes?'

'You know I have.'

'Well, he has information I need. Jane was helping me jog his memory.'

'Why would she help you?'

'Because I said I would kill her father if she didn't. She was very understanding of her position. I also mentioned how much it would upset me to have to hurt her daughter.'

Teschmaker looked at the man with absolute revulsion, knowing that if he had the opportunity he would not hesitate in killing him. 'You are a total bastard, Rusak.'

The smile didn't move from the Russian's lips. 'But one who enjoys his work.'

'What information were you after from Jane's father?' Teschmaker asked.

'Not your affair.' Rusak straightened up in his seat as though the conversation had suddenly veered down paths that were off limits. He renewed his grip on the pistol.

'So why didn't Jane institute divorce proceedings herself?'

'Because Jane made one mistake.' Rusak chuckled. 'Ironic, really.'

'Why? What mistake?'

'After all those years of putting up with Oliver's infidelities, she had an affair herself. Such a brief little

328

romance, but unfortunately Oliver found out and collected all the evidence. Jane wrote some very graphic letters that, unfortunately for you, don't mention any name, just "darling" and "beloved".'

'Why unfortunate for me? I have nothing to do with her. So Oliver was . . . what?' Teschmaker failed to see how this had anything to do with the photographs, or the Chambers or Grice. 'He was going to blackmail her?'

'No!' Rusak seemed to find the notion immensely amusing. 'No, Teschmaker, don't you see? Oliver had all the cards but he didn't know how to play the hand. So I came up with a wonderful scenario. You were putting pressure on her. There are some pretty graphic photos of Jane with your fingerprints all over them.'

'Me? Why the hell would I do that?'

'Because you wanted her to leave Oliver.'

Teschmaker let himself sink back in the seat as the jigsaw slowly assembled itself in his mind. But some pieces didn't fit. 'But Sinclair didn't even know me.'

Rusak didn't reply. He finished his cigarette and for a few minutes ignored Teschmaker altogether. He stared out the window into the darkness, all the time toying with the pistol on his lap. Then, after they had passed through Daleborough, he touched Teschmaker on the arm.

'It hurt me to see Oliver so worried. "Why continue a situation in which two people are so unhappy?" I said to him. "Wouldn't it be better if at least one of you is happy?" Of course he agreed. Why not? It is logical. So I said to him, "Then let us make you happy."'

'Very public-spirited of you.'

'So I told him that he should kill his wife. So simple. But it seemed he hadn't the heart for it and so I told him I would arrange it.' Rusak shrugged. 'What else are friends for, huh? And then we found you. That was a very beautiful moment. You just turned up and started stalking her. The right man at the right moment. It was perfect. It was as though we had scripted you. You were having this torrid affair with her. She writes you the love letters. You find out that she and Grice have been playing in the Chambers. You see the photographs and in a fit of rage you demand she leaves Sinclair immediately. She refuses, you kill her and then, in remorse, you kill yourself. It is like a poem. You were made for each other. Her husband is heartbroken, of course, but he is comforted by the fact he still has their daughter and his millions. Oliver thinks it an elegant solution.'

They travelled the rest of the journey in silence. When they arrived at the house, Rusak handed the pistol to the driver and instructed him to take Teschmaker upstairs. The man who emerged from behind the wheel turned out to be as solidly built as Rusak, but with a look about him that suggested he had spent a lot of time in one of the armed forces. He prodded Teschmaker forward.

They were met at the bottom of the steps by another of Rusak's Russians. Even in the low light spilling from the house, Teschmaker could see the man was the complete opposite of the driver. He was as slim as a shadow, gaunt, sallow-cheeked. His hands were long, thin-wristed. His long hair, black, streaked with grey, was tied back in a ponytail. A wraith. A junkie? He looked at Teschmaker, his expression open and curious, then turned and took the steps two at a time. The fitness didn't square with addiction.

'How is the *bzdenok*?' Rusak asked.

'He sleeps, he farts, he doesn't talk.' The Wraith stood at the stop of the steps and shrugged, then added, '*Mne eto vs'e osto'eblo.*'

'How bored you get is not my concern,' Rusak growled, then softened. 'I'll see if I can find you some more books.' The man shrugged again and led the way upstairs.

'What zoo did you get these guys from?' Teschmaker asked. 'Were you all in the army together?'

'Army?' Rusak snorted. 'The army is for arselickers.'

'Really? I'm disappointed. I was guessing you got your scar in Grozny or Afghanistan.'

Rusak stopped on the landing and turned to Teschmaker, the disfiguring scar exaggerated by the angle of the light. 'I got this in Moscow. In a bank.'

'What happened? Walk into the door?'

For a moment Rusak looked as though he was going to hit him, then he relaxed and smiled. 'No, Teschmaker, not a door. A friend of mine overestimated the amount of explosive and underestimated how strong the metal on the safe was. The damn thing disintegrated. Fucking Soviet workmanship.'

'Blowing up bank vaults doesn't sound like part of the working brief of someone elected to the Duma. Must have been after you resigned?'

'No. Before. Getting elected to the Duma is a very expensive undertaking.'

Teschmaker clamped down on his impulse to laugh and the driver, following a cue from Rusak, pushed him through the door into the top room.

Teschmaker hadn't taken more than a step onto the carpet runner when he felt the hand on his shoulder. Rusak spun him round and smashed his fist into his face. Teschmaker didn't even see the blow coming and went down hard, hitting the side of his head on the floor. Rusak looked at him for a minute then gestured for the driver to drag him to his feet.

'Nobody insults my mother, Teschmaker.' He spat in his face. 'I'm sorry that I can't have the pleasure of killing you now. But I can wait. We have a little drama to play out. You know, Teschmaker, I have always enjoyed the theatre. What about you? You enjoy a good comedy? No? Tragedy, perhaps?'

Teschmaker tried to speak but his head was reeling and he couldn't get his jaw to move. He tried to focus on Rusak's face but there was blood or spittle in his eyes and his head kept lolling to one side. The driver pushed him onto an old settee beside the wall. Rusak came over and looked down at him.

'The final act of this little drama is going to be most enjoyable and you have a starring role. Unfortunately, just after you kill Jane you will also be dead. But we want a great performance from you. So I suggest you rest while you can.'

Rusak slipped a cigarette into his mouth and waited while the Wraith lit it for him. 'You don't know Ilya Ivanovich, do you? No, I didn't think so. He speaks good English. He is an educated man, a scholar, a poet. It is a pity you will be dead for I know nothing better than to sit and listen to him read poetry. Like me, he also loves the theatre. But he is a harsh critic. I once saw him strangle an actress whose performance was less than pleasing to me. So, no theatrics while I'm away. I want a great performance and I will be very angry if there is the slightest hitch, the slightest *nakladka*, okay?'

Teschmaker didn't bother to react to the threat. He had the distinct feeling that if he moved his head even slightly he would vomit, so he remained motionless as Rusak and his driver left. His arm still throbbed from the blow earlier in the evening but, thankfully, the side of his face had gone totally numb. The blow to his face had been hard, but it was probably his head hitting the floor that had concussed him. Rusak was right, he decided, this was not the right time for theatrics.

After a while the nausea subsided and he let his eyes move around the room. Only one of the oil lamps was lit, creating a small pool of yellow light, while the rest of the room swam in perpetual twilight. The Wraith came over and pushed a cup of something warm into his hands. Teschmaker realised they were trembling but no matter how he concentrated was unable to avoid slopping the hot liquid down his shirt. He waited until his hands steadied and brought the mug to his lips. It was tea; hot and sweet. He managed a mumbled 'thank you' which Ilya ignored.

The Russian waited until Teschmaker had finished the tea then took his cup and indicated a single mattress on the floor by the door to the adjoining room where, Teschmaker assumed, Sydney Morris was still being held. He struggled to his feet and, though he was still feeling very unsteady, managed to make it without falling over. Theatrics, he thought, I do need some theatrics. But he made the mistake of letting his eyes close and though he told himself that he was just resting, he went straight to sleep.

It was some hours later when he woke. He realised that he must have rolled onto his injured arm and the pain had dragged him from the chaos of his dreams. He was happy for the reprieve. He had been lost, not in some pseudo reality, not in memory, but in an abstract realm of shapes and grainy images; everything too big for him, too wide, too tall, too black. Each time he tried to steady the images in a desperate attempt to recognise what they were, the grainy phantoms dissolved into individual dots and swept over him like blackened hail or showers of lava. At times he felt himself falling in a colourless maelstrom; the very absence of colour threatening in itself. Vertigo competed with a paranoia intensified by the lack of any recognisable or tangible threat. It was a dream he had endured before, or maybe the recognition was simply part of the dream. He wasn't certain of anything until the pain rescued him and delivered him back to the world of colour and solidity. Teschmaker lay still for a moment, letting his eyes feast on his surroundings; even in the dim light, the faded colours of the room seemed rich and satisfying. The pain in his arm was diminishing, the sharp twinges replaced by a dull but constant ache. He raised his head and looked down the length of the room. The Russian was hunched over a book in a wicker chair by the door, the one oil lamp on a table by his side. There was also something on his head. Teschmaker squinted and saw that it was a set of headphones, the cord running down to a portable CD player lying on the floor at his feet. Teschmaker lay back, wondering which he preferred — the grey phantoms in his head or this wraith-like individual by the door. He decided that, for the time being at least, he preferred the latter.

'Is there a toilet I can use, Ilya Ivanovich?' He addressed the man politely in his best Moscow Russian. It had no effect at all so he decided to risk an insult. '*Ty mne van'ku ne val'aj.*'

This time he caught Ilya's attention and the man pushed the headphones off. 'What did you say?'

Fortunately for Teschmaker the man hadn't heard anything over his music, so he repeated the polite version of his request for a toilet.

'Through the old man's room.' Ilya didn't bother to get up. He replaced the headphones but didn't return to his reading. He kept his eyes firmly on Teschmaker as he got gingerly to his feet.

Finding the door to the next room ajar, Teschmaker pushed it gently open and looked in. Sydney Morris was asleep, an oil lamp glimmering beside the bed, its wick turned right down, the arc of light spilling onto his face and washing it in a warm glow. The old man looked far better than he had on the previous occasion; colour in his cheeks, less marasmic.

Teschmaker tip-toed past the sleeping man and found the door to the bathroom off to the right. When he returned, the old man was stirring, his eyes open.

'Hello Mr Morris.' Teschmaker, not wanting to alert Ilya, crossed the room and crouched beside the bed. He kept his voice low. 'You probably don't remember me —'

'Nonsense. You're another one of those people that came to interrogate me.'

'No. I came and spoke with you. But I'm not with them.' Teschmaker wondered just how selective the man's memory was if he remembered his visit but couldn't recall whatever it was that both Rusak and Laverov wanted from him. 'Mr Morris, I'm a friend of Jane's. I want to help you, but I can't unless I know what it is everybody wants to talk to you about.'

'Everybody's a friend of Jane's when they want something from me.' The old man brushed a thin wisp of hair out of his eyes. 'What about me? What about what I might want?'

'And what is that?'

'Tea. I would like a cup of tea.' The old man's eyes sparkled. 'And a pretty young thing to come and change the sheets and tidy this place up. I'm sick and tired of this place. It's a *bardak*!'

'A brothel?'

Sydney Morris looked at him for a moment, searching his memory. Then it dawned on him. 'Of course. You are the young man who spoke passable Czech. And a word or two of Russian?'

Teschmaker nodded. 'I'll see if I can talk Ilya Ivanovich into making tea.'

'That *khokhol*? *Da na ego na khuy* — to hell with him. That *pizd'uk* couldn't make tea with a tea bag and hot water.'

336

'That bad, huh?' Teschmaker smiled. 'I'll see what I can do.'

He went back into the main room and found that Ilya hadn't moved from his position on the chair by the door. But, just in case Teschmaker had been entertaining any ideas of trying to leave, the Russian now had the pistol prominently displayed on his lap.

'Mr Morris would like a cup of tea,' Teschmaker said. He waited until the headphones came off and repeated the request. But it appeared that the Wraith was not in a mood to oblige.

'*Mne po khuy* — I don't give a fuck.' He slipped the headphones back in place and gestured to the small stove and the kettle. 'I will have tea also.'

'What did your last slave die of? Devotion?' Teschmaker asked quietly.

'You like this?' Ilya said loudly and thrust a CD case at him. 'That's me!'

'You think?' It would need one of those warped mirrors in a sideshow to make Ilya look even vaguely the same shape as Meatloaf.

'No. Bat out of hell.' Ilya grinned at his own perceived cleverness.

'Of course. You're a bat out of hell. Must be very nice for you.'

'What?' the Russian shouted, competing against the noise of the music in his ears.

'Great. Splendid!' Teschmaker shouted back and, feeling he had done enough bonding for the time being, set about making the tea under Ilya's watchful eye. The Russian's head was moving in time to the music and, disconcertingly, every now and then he would sing along with the lyrics.

After a time the batteries in the CD player expired. Frustrated, Ilya yanked the headphones off and, tucking the pistol in his belt, stood up and stretched. He walked over to where Teschmaker was proving that the old adage about watched pots was doubly true of kettles. Ilya hunkered down beside the little stove and warmed his hands. For a while he didn't say anything. Teschmaker thought they must look like a couple of soldiers around a campfire. He remembered Rusak's remark about the actress and wondered if it was to be Ilya's job to kill him. Death seemed such a bizarre outcome. No, he dismissed it, that had been just talk. He lifted the lid from the kettle and cautiously dipped his finger in the water; it was only a degree or two above tepid. As he replaced the lid he felt a nudge and twisted around to see the bottle that the Wraith was offering. He took it, drank from the bottle, wiped the rim and passed it back.

'*Ostohuitel'no*! Excellent.'

'He who dies from vodka does not die in vain,' Ilya intoned slowly, then drank and lapsed into silence. After a while he rocked on his heels and grinned at Teschmaker. 'I have not always been a bat out of hell. I used to listen to classical and jazz. But times change and the people with them, yes?'

'Yes.' Teschmaker took the bottle again. The vodka was raw and strong and he felt it register in his brain before it seemed to have had time to reach his stomach. It was peculiar, he thought, that they should be like this — the killer and his victim, caught in this sepia moment. There was a timelessness to the scenario. He imagined the door opening and a photographer coming in with a large plate camera. The moment of comradeship would be captured in the silver salts — the small fire flaring white, the gaunt Ilya, enveloped by shadows, and himself . . . But his fantasy didn't seem to run to self-inclusion. He recognised the mood, the rising melancholia, and the fact that the previously taciturn Ilya Ivanovich was wanting to talk and would need little encouragement.

'Tell me, Ilya Ivanovich, how do you come to be so far from your motherland? And what is a poet doing with a man like Rusak?'

There was no reply, but the bottle came his way again. As he was already feeling light-headed, he drank cautiously. It had been a long time since he had eaten and Teschmaker knew it was important that he remain alert. Simply because his mind couldn't envisage his own mortality didn't mean he wasn't going to grasp any opportunity to remove himself from the situation. Then Ilya began to speak.

'No one ever reached the climax of vice in one step . . .'

'A few years ago, just after I had graduated, a friend of my father's rang and said he could get me some work. He said he knew of somebody who wanted a handyman to take care of a dacha outside Moscow. The idea appealed to me, so I applied and got the job. I didn't meet the owner, but one of his men gave me a key and instructions that I was to do any repairs and always have the house ready for the boss to arrive. I asked who it belonged to but was told very firmly to mind my own business.

'So I set out and found the dacha, located in the forest beside the Moscow river just the other side of Kubinka. It turned out to be a beautiful modern dacha, not traditional at all, but open plan divided by sliding screens. It felt the way I imagined a Japanese house might. The windows had more glass than I had seen in a single building before — triple-glazed floor to ceiling on the side facing the river, and many smaller windows on the others. There were three small guest rooms out the back and a big master bedroom with wonderful views up a flight of stairs off the living room. At the centre of the house was a huge stove built from stone, with a fireplace front and back and a small bread oven built into one side. But best of all, the house was full of books. Not just Soviet but English, American and foreign ones, in languages I couldn't understand. There were all the great poets: Mandelstam and Blok, Mayakovsky and Pasternak. Of course I knew these well, but there were others; forbidden gems that I had heard of but never seen. A copy of Akhmatova's *Requiem*, Tarkovsky's *Before the Snow*, Fazil Iskander's *Mountain Paths* and even a tattered original of Vasily Belov's *My Forest Village*. There were other books too; books with pictures. Can you imagine, a book full of photographs of Harley-Davidsons? Another one of nude women, from every race on earth. I swear I had never seen anything like it.

'It was late spring and the forest was bursting with life. I would walk out every day into a wonderland of berries, mushrooms, wildflowers and the noisiest birds on the planet. Every now and then a fighter would take off from the military airfield at Kubinka. Sometimes they flashed overhead while I lay in the long grass near the river spitting out sunflower-seed husks. For a few minutes the forest would be silent, as though every bird had glimpsed the red stars on the wings and fled in terror. After a time they would start again, tentative at first, regaining their voices, and soon the cacophony of birdsong would reign until another silver bird roared into the air.

'I had been there only two weeks when I met her. Her name was Anna, but she told me everyone called her Anechka. She was about my age, narrow blue eyes, high cheekbones and her hair in plaits like an Uzbek girl. Around her neck was her Pioneer scarf. She had knocked on my door and seemed surprised to see me. After I explained why I was at the dacha, she told me that the owner had said she could have some of the baby potatoes from the garden and some dill. I hadn't explored the vegetable garden properly, so I went out with her and together we discovered that there were only a handful of potatoes big enough to eat. We talked for a bit and then she asked if I would like to come over later and share the potatoes. I had planned to spend the evening exploring the library, so I left it open.

'"Well," she laughed, "if you want to, you can find me."

'I returned to the library. Much later I realised I was hungry. I remembered the woman's invitation and, without any real idea of where she lived, I set out in the dusk. Fortunately I found a path that took me directly to her small cottage, less than half a kilometre from the dacha. It was small and pretty and wouldn't have looked out of place in a melancholy Turgenev landscape. Anechka welcomed me in and, after ordering me to take a seat, returned to stir a pot of borshch as red as the scarf around her neck. A scarf, I was to learn in the next few days, that she never took off. Even though the evening was warm she had lit a fire, and a battered old samovar was bubbling away in one corner of the room. I had brought a bottle of vodka and we started on dill-pickled cucumber and then had huge bowls of borshch soaked up with fresh bread. I couldn't have eaten another thing, but I jokingly asked her what had become of the potatoes and she clapped her hand over her mouth in horror.

'"Oh, God! I forgot all about them."

'She got up from the table and ran over to the samovar. I had never heard of anyone doing such a thing but, as she said, why waste the water? To this day I cannot drink tea from a samovar without imagining I taste potatoes. A couple of times I asked her about the owner of the dacha, but she avoided answering, or said something vague about him kindly letting her stay in the cottage in return for doing odd jobs for him every now and then. To my delight, that was the only thing she was reticent about and we became lovers. I was not particularly experienced with women, but Anechka was a great teacher, and kind enough to tell me that I was going to graduate with distinction.

'The summer came, the weeks went by and each day I worked at keeping the dacha spick-and-span, and in the evenings I continued my lessons with Anechka.

One night we made love on the banks of the river. For the most part it was wild and rocky, but in the middle there was a deep channel which, in the moonlight, became a ribbon of silver set in onyx. I told her that we should swim out and let it float us all the way to the monastery at Zvenigorod.

'Anechka laughed and said that she had always dreamed of visiting a monastery but she would rather wait until winter when we could skate. I promised her that one day we would go. I remember that night very clearly because the following morning the owner arrived with two of his colleagues. They were intending to stay the week and so I was moved into the smallest of the back rooms for the duration. I was not a great student of politics, but I recognised the owner as a minister in the Duma. His friends, or maybe they were business acquaintances, were very different. Rough men. The Slob and the Weasel, I called them. One fat and lazy; the other skinny and jumpy, always looking over his shoulder as though someone was about to attack him. They seemed to be a little in awe of the owner and always waited until he suggested something, never volunteering anything themselves. A lot of the time they were locked in discussion in the living room, but on the final night the owner asked me to go and tell Anechka that she was invited for dinner. I was pleased to get the chance to see her as I hadn't had an opportunity since the men arrived.

'The party started well. I worked in the kitchen, but I could hear that there was a lot of laughing, singing and drinking. Anechka had smiled at me when she arrived, but distantly, as though she was wary of showing the feelings we shared for each other. Then I noticed that Anechka and the Slob were missing. I must have been very naive in those days because I didn't guess what was going on. After dinner the owner moved from the table to sit beside the fire and asked me to make some coffee. When I brought it in I saw the Slob was back but now the owner had vanished. There was still no sign of Anechka. Then the Slob asked me if I wanted a turn.

'"A turn? How do you mean?"

"With the little *pizda* upstairs." He leered at me, watching my reaction.

'The other man, the Weasel, ran his fingers through his slicked-back hair and laughed. "Not 'til I have had her." He was very drunk and had been singing raucously through much of the evening.

'I felt nauseated. Was that what she was? And all that time she had been playing me along. I sat in the kitchen, alternating between anger and self-pity. I helped myself to the vodka and was on my third glass when I heard the argument break out. I went into the living room to see what was happening and found the owner and the Weasel shouting at each other, but what was more horrifying was that the Weasel's hands and shirt were covered in blood. The owner suddenly realised I was in the room and, turning to me, ordered me to follow him upstairs. I'll never forget that sight.

'Anechka's body was sprawled across the bed, one leg dangling to the floor. She was naked except for her beloved scarf, a patch of red at her pale throat. She had been stabbed a dozen times or more in the chest and

344

stomach and there was blood everywhere. On the floor, lying in the blood, was a small knife. I thought I was going to faint.

'"Help me get her out of here," the owner ordered.

'I was feeling too numb to resist and so between us we managed to get her body down the stairs. The Slob was sitting by the fire, his head in his hands; the Weasel, grinning nervously, had poured himself a brandy. The owner told him to give us a hand but the man just shook his head and gulped at his drink. But the owner took out a small pistol and ordered the Weasel to help me carry Anechka's body through the forest to the river.

'"The bitch had no right to bite me," he whined in protest but put down his drink and reluctantly took Anechka's wrists.

'"No!" I said. "I will take her."

'I pushed him out of the way and scooped her up in my arms. For a moment the owner looked at me oddly, as if wondering why I would do such a thing. Somehow I think he suspected why, but he didn't say anything. He shrugged and gestured that the Weasel should accompany us.

'The short walk through the forest was the worst time in my life. So often in the previous weeks I had walked there, Anechka's hand in mine, or her arm around my waist. Now I was carrying her and I could feel her still-warm blood soaking into my shirt and against my skin. Tears blurred my eyes and it was all I could do to stop myself from laying her body down in the leaves and howling like a madman. In the end it was just as well that the Weasel came with us, for the river bank was treacherous and I did need a hand to step over the river stones. Slipping and sliding we waded out through the shallows to the channel in the middle of the river and there we let her go. As we stood and watched, she twisted and floated away into the dark and I imagined the Cossack, Stenka Razin, sacrificing his beautiful Persian girl to the Volga way back in the seventeenth century. In that moment I knew how he must have felt.

'Then the Weasel spat after her. "Fucking whore!"

'I don't understand what happened next, for I had never reacted like that before. Something must have snapped inside me, for I sprang at him and grabbed him around the throat. I realised that the owner was standing there with his pistol, but I didn't care if he shot me. I think I would have welcomed it. But he didn't. He just watched as I strangled the man. When he went limp, I dropped him in the deep water. For a second I wanted to pull him out. Not to attempt to revive him, but because it seemed unfair on Anechka that she should have to share her river with such a man. But he was gone.

'For a while we stood there. I don't know what the owner was thinking, but I imagined I could hear distant cloister bells and was picturing Anechka fulfilling her wish to visit the monastery at Zvenigorod.

'We walked back to the house in silence. The Slob, white and shaken, insisted that they return to Moscow without delay but the owner just shook his head and sat. I thought he had forgotten about me, and it was a long time before he seemed to become aware of my presence again. I must have looked a sight — my face streaming with tears, my shirt and trousers streaked with blood. The owner poured me a drink and then said that he was sorry about what had happened to Anechka and that I must not worry about him turning me in to the police. He would take care of everything. And he did. Later he offered me a job and I have worked for Oleg Vasilyevich Rusak ever since.'

Teschmaker stared into the steam rising from the kettle but drew no comfort from it; the mundane vapour seemed like some malignant miasmal mist. He wanted to say something but words were suddenly inadequate. And he was confused by the flow of feelings that had washed over him despite Ilya's almost monotone recitation of the story. But the sadness and pain dragged sound from him — a whisper.

'Ophelia. I had a picture in my head of Ophelia. A red Ophelia in a black landscape.'

'Floating down the river.' Ilya took a long swig of the vodka and handed the bottle to Teschmaker. 'I had a dream for years that she wasn't dead, that she had crawled ashore somewhere.'

'Ophelia. Guided by naiads.'

'Covered in weeds . . .'

'Floating between willow roots . . .'

'Brushing against the rubbery stems and pads of waterlilies.'

'Cuckoo flowers, celandines . . .'

'Duckweed clinging to her arms.'

'Fronds of water crowfoot caressing her as she floats . . .'

Ilya struggled to his feet and recited slowly:

'There is a willow grows aslant a brook,
That shows his hoar leaves in the glassy stream;
There with fantastic garlands did she come
Of crow-flowers, nettles, daisies and long purples
That liberal shepherds give a grosser name,
But our cold maids do dead men's fingers call them:
There, on the pendant boughs her coronet weeds
Clambering to hang, an envious sliver broke;
When down her weedy trophies and herself
Fell in the weeping brook. Her clothes spread wide;
And, mermaid-like, awhile they bore her up:
Which time she chanted snatches of old tunes;
As one incapable of her own distress . . .'

Ilya sighed, wrested the bottle back and drank deeply. 'You're right, tovarich, she was my Ophelia.'

He seemed deeply satisfied and lurched unsteadily to fetch a small tin of tea and a jar of sugar. 'However . . .' He stood still, holding up a finger for added emphasis, but momentarily lost his train of thought. Then, regaining it, proclaimed triumphantly, 'I don't think I am Hamlet.'

'No,' Teschmaker agreed lugubriously, aware that he was now quite drunk and rather enjoying it. 'But you could be, Ilya, you could be.'

'And so could you!'

'We could both be —'

'Two Hamlets are better than one!'

Ilya collapsed in laughter. When he recovered, he produced a packet of tobacco and proceeded to display his ability to roll a cigarette with one hand. 'You know Rusak will kill you.'

'So he says.' Teschmaker found himself giggling at the prospect.

'It would be better if I do it.'

Teschmaker took the proffered cigarette. 'Why?'

'Because I like you and I am very expert at this thing. You wouldn't feel anything.' He fished a lighter from the packet of tobacco and with a surprisingly steady hand lit Teschmaker's cigarette and started to roll one for himself.

'That is very kind of you,' Teschmaker said.

He decided to give up on making tea for Sydney. He leaned over, turned off the stove then rose and weaved his way to the door. Sure enough the old man had gone back to sleep. He turned and made his way back to the settee where Ilya had seated himself. He slumped down beside him and inhaled deeply on his cigarette. 'I would do the same for you.'

The combined effects of too much alcohol, a hit of nicotine and no food were ganging up on him. His mind drifted off for a while; then he marshalled his concentration and was about to say something to Ilya about food when he realised the man was asleep. On the floor beside him lay the empty vodka bottle. Beside it was the pistol. Teschmaker smiled. It was good to have everything in the right place. He stubbed out his cigarette and lay back. For some strange reason he felt safe. The room was a cocoon in which only good things happened. It was outside that was dangerous. In the minute or so before he fell asleep he thought about escaping, but decided it would be much better to do it in the morning. It would be light and, after all, he would want to say goodbye to his new friend Ilya.

CHAPTER SEVENTEEN

Teschmaker awoke to find Ilya standing over him proffering a cup of tea. He tried to sit up but his body rebelled. He reached out and grasping the back of the settee pulled himself upright. 'What time is it?'

'Nearly midday,' Ilya said. 'You snore very loudly.'

'Sorry,' Teschmaker mumbled and took the tea. His head was aching and his eyes struggled with the concept of focus.

'There is some porridge if you want it.' Ilya pointed to a pot on the gas stove. 'I think it's still warm.' He returned to his chair by the door.

Teschmaker hadn't previously noticed the small window set in the wall by the door. It was now open, the curtains pulled back, and the sunlight streaming in afforded enough light for Ilya to read by. 'What are you reading?'

'Words, words, words,' Ilya grunted and held up the book for Teschmaker's inspection. But his eyes still refused to focus and he learned nothing other than the book was a small hardcover volume with a title in gold-embossed Cyrillic script. Teschmaker helped himself to the lukewarm porridge and then made his way to the bathroom. He had been intending to talk to Sydney Morris again, but the old man was sound asleep, an empty cup and bowl on the bedside table.

It must have been about four o'clock when they heard the car. Teschmaker had dozed off again and Ilya, having finished his book, was attending to Sydney Morris. At the sound of the vehicle, Teschmaker sat bolt upright. Up until that point he had been content to nurse his still aching body and head gently back from the previous night's abuses. Now he was suddenly awake and painfully aware of a sinking feeling in the pit of his stomach. A couple of minutes passed and then Ilya, who had reclaimed his pistol, opened the door to admit Rusak. To Teschmaker's surprise Rusak was followed by Jane Sinclair. Alarmed, his mind flashed back to Rusak's claimed intention that he should kill her. Just talk, he told himself; you can talk your way out of this. He didn't believe it. He turned his attention to Jane. There was nothing in the woman's demeanour to suggest she considered herself to be in any kind of danger. Wearing a dark blue ankle-length dress and a white cardigan, she looked particularly ordinary — a woman out visiting, not one attending her own execution.

Jane glanced at Teschmaker with a look of disinterest, then addressed Rusak. 'Shall we get on with it?'

Rusak held up his hand. 'In a minute. Introductions first.'

He turned to Teschmaker. 'Of course you know Mrs Sinclair. Jane, this is the man who was stalking you. I promise you he won't trouble you any more.'

Jane didn't react at all, but turned on her heel and went through to her father's room.

'You have a reprieve, Teschmaker,' Rusak said quietly. 'But then, so does Jane.'

'Good, then I'll get out of your way.' Teschmaker wondered if it was really going to be that easy. The look on Rusak's face suggested otherwise.

'Temporary reprieve. I have decided to give Jane one more chance to jog her father's memory. After that . . .' He shrugged and followed Jane, shutting the door behind him.

'Well, that was good — for a moment.' Teschmaker grinned weakly at Ilya. 'I don't suppose you would consider just standing back and letting me leave?'

Ilya simply mimicked Rusak's shrug.

'Oh well, I thought it was worth the try. We don't have any more vodka, do we?'

This time Ilya didn't even bother to respond, just turned away and took up his position by the door.

It was over an hour before the bedroom door opened and Jane and Rusak emerged. It was plain from the look on Rusak's face that he hadn't got what he wanted. Several times Teschmaker had heard raised voices, usually Rusak's but, on one occasion at least, Jane's.

'We'll be back to clean up this mess this evening,' Rusak snapped at Ilya as he strode to the door, ushering Jane before him. She looked angry and frustrated. Just as she was about to step out onto the landing, she pushed past Rusak and came back into the room. Without hesitation she marched up to Teschmaker and slapped his face. It happened so quickly and took him so much by surprise that he didn't have time to duck or fend off the blow.

'I don't know what's going on in your sick little brain, but fucking keep away from my family.'

The vehemence of her words stung Teschmaker like a second blow.

Behind her Rusak guffawed. 'After tonight she won't be worrying about you at all, will she?' He held the door open for her and followed her down the stairs.

'So what happens next?' Teschmaker asked after they had heard the car drive away.

'You heard Mr Rusak.'

'Clean up the mess? What mess?' Teschmaker didn't really need an explanation but was in need of a good dose of denial. Unfortunately Ilya had no such need.

'You and Sydney Morris. We have been here far too long. This business would have been so easy if that stupid old man had half a brain left.'

'What the hell are you after? What can an old man know?' Teschmaker didn't bother to mask his anger.

'Too much,' Ilya replied blandly. 'The old man knew too much, but, sadly for all of us, he can't remember.'

They sat in silence for a while. Then Ilya got up and lit the oil lamp. 'I'll make some food. You like baked beans?' He didn't wait for a reply. 'I hate them.'

'Why?' Teschmaker asked after a while.

'Why what?'

'Why everything.' He laughed dryly then added as an afterthought, 'Why do you think she slapped my face?'

Ilya looked up from the little stove. 'Because she likes you. Some things I see only with my poet's eye and these things I don't tell Oleg Vasilyevich. I think she was once your Anechka. I am right, yes?'

'How the hell could you tell that?'

'Because she pretends you are nothing when she comes in. Then, when she leaves, she does like the American music says — "Love hurts". So she hurts you to show you this thing.'

'She is my Anechka?' Teschmaker shook his head. 'No, Ilya, she is not my Anechka but sadly it appears she may well become my Ophelia.'

'So you will be a *real* Hamlet,' Ilya said softly.

After they had eaten Teschmaker tried to have another conversation with Sydney Morris, but got no further than on the two previous occasions. For a moment it occurred to him that the old man was not as senile as he appeared and was playing a game with him. If he could only say the right thing, Teschmaker felt he could elicit a meaningful response; but he realised it was hopeless. If it was a test he had no idea of the subject. He had no glimmering of what he was hunting for and even less of what might prompt the old man's memory. Anyway, why should he succeed when it seemed that even his own daughter couldn't get through to him? No matter how he pushed, the old man kept up the meaningless gobbledygook about flowers and gardening. Whatever it was that Rusak wanted, it certainly had nothing to do with horticultural pursuits.

Teschmaker said goodnight, with a dark sense of foreboding that he would never see the old man again. He might not see anyone if he didn't figure a way out of his present situation.

Ilya had obviously sensed Teschmaker's line of thought and had the pistol on his knee. He was withdrawn, morose and uncommunicative. Much as he knew he should be concentrating on his own fate, Teschmaker's mind kept turning back to Ilya's story. It was a bizarre set of circumstances that had brought the man to his present position. The twists and turns of fate had given killer's hands to a man with the heart of a poet. In another universe they might have become friends, yet there seemed only one way out of his predicament now and that was past Ilya.

He searched the room, desperately looking for some makeshift weapon. Could he light the stove on the excuse of making tea and somehow use it against the Russian? Even as he thought it, he knew it was not in his make-up. Yet he was just as sure that he wasn't going to give up without some kind of fight. And so he went — around in circles.

It was some time after 10 pm when they heard the car returning. Ilya looked as tense as Teschmaker was feeling. Both men got to their feet but kept their distance from each other. Ilya gestured with the pistol that Teschmaker should get back against the side wall. Feeling like a trapped animal, he reluctantly obeyed. It seemed to take an eternity before they heard a noise downstairs and then footsteps on the stairs.

The door opened and Jane came in looking drawn and pale. She took in the situation at a glance, went straight up to Ilya and pushed down the barrel of the pistol. 'He's to come with me. Rusak wants to talk to him in town.'

'I have strict orders —' Ilya began but Jane cut him off abruptly.

'You're to give me the gun and I am to escort him to Rusak. You are to stay and keep an eye on my father, and I swear, if anything happens to him, I will come back and kill you.'

She didn't wait for another protest but turned to Teschmaker. 'You, downstairs. I'll be right behind you and, believe me, I would love an excuse to shoot you.'

'I'm sorry, I can't allow it until I hear from Rusak.' Ilya stepped back, his fingers tightening on the pistol. 'It is more than my life is worth.'

But Jane was not to be put off. 'And just how much is that Ilya Ivanovich?' She stood directly in front of him and held out her hand.

Teschmaker sensed the momentary hesitation and the flicker of doubt in his eyes.

'Ilya, Jane has told you that the order comes from Rusak,' he said quietly and moved away from the wall and stepped up to the Russian. For a second they locked eyes.

Then Ilya turned to Jane. 'Be careful of this man. He is more dangerous than he first appears.' He passed her the gun and put his hand on Teschmaker's shoulder. 'You leave me only the role of Yorick.'

Teschmaker grinned. 'I think not, and I am no Horatio.'

'For Christ's sake!' Jane exploded. 'Will you two shut up? We have to hurry.'

Teschmaker needed no further prompting and headed down the stairs with Jane close behind him. At the bottom he glanced back at Ilya standing on the landing, feeling that he should say something, but the Russian just shrugged and turned away.

Outside sat Jane's VW Golf. 'Get in,' she snapped. 'And tell me what the fuck that was all about.'

'I really don't know,' he said truthfully.

'He knew I was bluffing.' She looked totally perplexed. 'Here, put this damn thing in the glove box.' She handed him the pistol and, without another word, started the car and drove down the driveway and out onto the road, not stopping to close the gate.

'So why did you come back?' Teschmaker asked, just as bewildered. He checked that the safety catch was off and opened the glove box, but what little room there was was taken up by a robust-looking flashlight, so he slipped the pistol into the pocket in the side of the door.

'Not because of you, so don't get the wrong impression.' She glanced at him and he could see by her expression that she was telling the truth.

'Then why?'

'Because the rules have changed. That bastard has my daughter.'

'Rusak?'

'Of course Rusak. Who the hell did you think I meant?'

'Look, I haven't a clue what all this is about,' Teschmaker protested.

'Haven't a clue is right. Why the hell were you following me?' She didn't wait for a reply, her anger driving her on. 'You know they were on to you from day one.'

'I was just interested in finding out what had become of you. What kind of person you had turned into.' Teschmaker knew it sounded weak. He also knew it was more complex than that, but now didn't seem to be the right time.

'You didn't have to stalk me to —'

'I wasn't stalking you. Jesus! I know it sounds silly, but you *are* Oliver Sinclair's wife and from what I could find out you keep an extremely low profile. How was I to know if you even remembered who I was?'

He stopped and stared at the road ahead. After what he had been through he was damned if he was going to justify himself to this woman.

'Remember you! You're the bastard that fucked up my life from day one; of course I remember you. The only reason you're here is that I hate you marginally less than Rusak. It's just that everything is so screwed up and now I'm at my wits' end. I don't know how long I can keep going and there's nobody else to turn to . . .'

For a moment he nearly confronted her with all the questions he had about why she hated him so much, then decided that this was definitely not the right time. All he could think of was to get as far from her anger as possible.

'Then just stop the car and let me out. Go to the police.'

'Police! Oh, for Christ's sake, Teschmaker, you really are stupid. I have been blackmailed, compromised and gone through hell in order to stop my father being killed or exposed and to avoid losing custody of Melanie. Oliver has photographs of me that he will give to the media if I breathe a word of this to anyone.'

'I know, I've seen some of them.'

'Yes? Well, I bet he hasn't shown you the choice ones.'

'But why did you go along with it? Why did you let yourself be compromised?'

She shot him a sideways glance. 'You don't have children, do you?'

'No.'

'Then how the hell do you think you can judge me?'

'I'm not —' Teschmaker began, but she was in full flight.

'I could have dealt with anything — public ridicule, shame and disgrace — but I was damned if I was going to let Oliver walk away with everything. It wasn't even the money. The bottom line was I couldn't deal with losing my daughter and her trust. How do you think she would feel about the mother that exists in those photographs? How would she feel about a mother who's betrayed her own father? And all the time I was pushed further and further into Grice and Oliver's disgusting little games, thinking that if only I went along with it I'd find a way out. But instead I got deeper in the shit.'

'And now . . . What on earth are you going to do?'

'Not me, *we*. We are going to get my daughter back.'

'You don't really think they'll harm her?'

'They won't as long as they still think there's a chance they can get what they're after. The problem is that once they have it, everybody else becomes superfluous.'

'And what's that? What are they after?'

'Something my father knows.'

'I meant exactly.'

'For Christ's sake! If I knew that I wouldn't be in this mess.'

Teschmaker was confused. Hadn't she been visiting her father to find out something? She must have known what they wanted. 'You mean, you don't even know what they are after?'

'No. I mean, I know it's something to do with his work . . .' She glanced at him again. 'You do know what he was doing?'

'Only the bare bones. From what I've pieced together, he defected to the Soviets years ago and was working on their nuclear program.'

'Yes. But it was something that happened at the end of his career. Or something that brought his career to an end — I can't be certain which. Apparently he was working with a small team of specialists on a very secret project. From what I can gather, the other team members are all dead and Rusak thinks that my father can tell him about the project.'

'What's Rusak got to gain from it? I thought he was up to his neck in rackets or something.'

'He is,' Jane replied. They had been driving fast and already the lights of Daleborough were twinkling in the distance. 'But whatever this project is, it must have produced something worth an absolute fortune because Rusak is desperate to get his hands on it. He told my father he would kill me if he didn't cooperate, and told me he would make my father suffer if I didn't convince him to give Rusak the information he wanted.'

'I'm beginning to think that Rusak's answer to any problem is to kill someone.'

Jane glared at him. 'It's no joke.'

'I'm not joking,' Teschmaker said flatly. 'You never found out anything?'

'Nothing. Believe me, I've spent days going over this with Dad but all I get is muddled stories of gardeners and —'

'Bouquets and little flowers?'

'He told you?'

'Yes.'

'Well, at least he's consistent,' she said bitterly.

For a couple of kilometres they drove in silence, Jane concentrating on the twisting road and Teschmaker trying to stop his mind racing in the chaos of confusion that threatened to overwhelm him. After a time he came back to their present predicament.

'Surely you don't think that Oliver will let Rusak harm Melanie?'

'Oliver doesn't know. He thinks she's with me and Rusak has made it crystal clear that if I breathe a word to Oliver then Mel will suffer.'

'So what do we do now?'

'Well, I don't think we have a hope in hell of finding where Rusak has Mel, so we have to organise a trade.'

'Sure. And what exactly have you got to offer?' He was too exhausted to hide the sarcasm. Jane simply ignored it.

'We have to find out what the project was and then swap the information for Mel.'

'Fine.' For a moment he had thought she might have a feasible plan of action. 'Let's do it now and then I can get home to bed.'

That did it. Furious, Jane pulled the car to a screeching halt at the side of the road.

'Listen, you bastard. You don't have a choice in this. In case it hadn't dawned on you, you are now in some of the photographs and I can't tell you how much Oliver gloated when he got your fingerprints all over the others. One bloody slip-up and you're there on the front pages, as a pornographer and blackmailer. I'll go down as well, but I'll bloody well drag you with me. If they ask, I'll say that, sure, Teschmaker was the one who arranged all that sick stuff. Now spare me all the sarcastic crap and work with me.'

'Okay,' he surrendered, but it wasn't good enough for Jane.

'Okay? Is that all you have to offer?' She glared at him.

For a fraction of a second he considered telling her that Rusak's real agenda was for them both to end up dead, but he resisted. 'Look, I'm sorry. I'm really exhausted and not thinking straight. I promise you I'll help.'

For a moment she eyed him suspiciously, then pulled back onto the road again. 'I'm tired too, Teschmaker. I have been for months. I want it to be over, but I can't stop until I have Mel back. After that I don't give a shit what happens between Oliver and me.'

'Sure, I understand. What about your father though?'

'I nearly brought him with us, but he's probably better off there. They certainly won't hurt him until they get what they're after. We couldn't look after him and work this out too. I'm sorry if it sounds cruel, but this is partly of his making, and Mel is my first priority.'

'So what do we do once we get back to the city?'

'Go to ground until we've worked out how the hell we're going to tackle this. I can't go to my house and Rusak will have his men swarming over your place.'

'So?'

'My partner, Sarah Norrby, is in Europe for the next six weeks. She gave me her key so that I could pop in and keep an eye on the place. It's ideal — nice and secure and with separate bedrooms.'

The last comment struck him as unnecessary. The notion hadn't even entered his head. Another time and in a different situation it might have, but now all he wanted was food and sleep. 'Fine,' he said. But he shot a glance at her. She was still angry and still attractive. No, she was beautiful. For an instant he thought he could see the young girl he remembered from years before. Jane must have sensed his train of thought.

'I've changed. Changed far more than you could ever imagine, Teschmaker, and not all for the good.'

He was going to respond, but his attention was suddenly attracted by a flash of light. Someone was coming up behind them, moving fast. He swung around in time to see the red and blue lights on top of a police car switch on. The car's headlights flashed and its siren screamed at them.

'Shit!' Jane hissed. 'What the hell . . .'

She slowed down and began to pull over but the police car overtook them and continued on towards the Airport Freeway in pursuit of other quarry. 'Christ! I hate it when they do that. For some reason I immediately think I'm guilty of something.'

Teschmaker saw she was trembling. 'Even when you're not.' He laughed; not that he saw anything funny in the situation but as a reflex discharge of tension. 'I felt the same. Why do you think we automatically assume our own guilt?'

'Because, deep down, it's true. We *are* all guilty. It's just a matter of degree.'

'Guilty of what?'

'Let's hope we never find out.'

They drove on in silence. As they entered the city Jane headed east on the Ring Road and then took the Lincoln exit. Teschmaker remembered following her around the CBD.

'Where did you learn to drive the way you do?'

'You mean my ducking and weaving?' It was the first time she had smiled at him.

'One of the first times I was on your tail you damn near gave me the slip.'

She shrugged. 'Oliver insisted that I learn. He hired some outfit that trains drivers for government and corporate clients. You know the sort of thing — ex-SAS guys teaching wealthy types how to avoid kidnap and assassination.' She shot him a look. 'I guess I failed, huh?'

'Not at all. Actually I was impressed. But it did make me more curious about you.'

Jane didn't reply. A couple of minutes later they pulled into the car park under the newly renovated Dansen Brewery.

For decades the old factory had lain empty, except for a period during the eighties when the squatters had moved in. A fatal fire in what had been the riverside office section had put an end to the squatters. Another ten years passed before the developers moved in and turned it into a very trendy address, complete with internet cafés, bars and designer clothing outlets. Though the original plum-coloured brick facade remained, the inside was themed in lime-washed blues and yellows with raw steel and old machinery parts. 'Industrial Chic' the reviewers had cooed and, despite the post-industrial price tags, the units had sold out in a month. Sarah Norrby's was on the top floor and would have had a great view of the river if the city's building code hadn't been flexible enough to absorb kickbacks from other developers who, despite the city's genesis in a swamp, had bribed their way up to fifteen storeys.

'Hope you can stand slumming,' Jane said with heavy irony as they entered the apartment.

The vast expanse of polished Baltic pine was patched tastefully with several tribal rugs. Teschmaker wasn't sure which tribe but he guessed that whatever the original artisans had been paid it would have been the wrong side of the decimal point on the price tag.

The masks on the walls seemed to indicate that Ms Norrby was either a very extensive traveller, very wealthy, or both. Teschmaker plumped for the latter option. When it came to cultural plunder, he had to admit that her taste was exquisite.

'No, I always feel at home in museums of folk art. Mind you, I assume you are used to living in such luxury.'

'Money and taste were mutually exclusive in Oliver's case.'

'What about his house?'

'I rest my case.'

'But surely it wasn't as bad on the inside?' Teschmaker asked as she led the way through to the kitchen — a sea of stainless-steel benches and appliances.

'Seriously gross. I told him Hugh Hefner and Larry Flynt wouldn't have been my first choice as interior decorators.' She caught the look of disbelief on his face. 'The place was like a bordello, right down to breast-shaped, pink toilet deodorisers.'

'Ouch!'

'Enough. I'm famished. I'll open the wine. Can you do something with eggs and whatever you find in the vegetable drawer?' She turned and peered at him. 'I take it you can cook?'

'One Spanish omelette coming up, madam.'

He executed a mock bow and immediately felt foolish. Fortunately Jane had turned away to open the small wine fridge.

Teschmaker knew he was running on the remnants of adrenalin. The last . . . How long had it been? Only a couple of days? It seemed far longer. The last couple of days had drained him and he was ready to crash out. But hunger was competing with his desire to switch off the world and hibernate. He took a deep breath and set about the task at hand.

Jane passed him a glass of wine and retreated to the lounge to make some phone calls. From the snippets he heard, she appeared to be ringing contacts in Moscow. She came back ten minutes later and he could tell by the look on her face that she had hit a brick wall.

'I thought I could call in some favours,' she explained. 'But nobody wants to go near it. Apparently Putin has just done a big reorganisation of security and anyone working in a sensitive area has their head down.'

'I thought there was a whole new industry in releasing files from the bad old days?'

'There was. Past tense.'

In the end the meal and the wine were fine but they both ate mechanically, in silence. Teschmaker knew it was only partly the tiredness. Jane's anxiety about her daughter was visible in her face and her body. She hunched over her plate, pushing at the meal with her fork.

'Sorry,' she said quietly as she left half the food on her plate. 'I guess I just can't eat.'

'I understand.'

'No, you don't,' she replied, but there was no anger in her voice, just emptiness.

She stood up. 'I'm going to try and sleep. We'll talk in the morning.' She gestured to the far end of the main room. 'There's a bed made up in there. It has an en suite. Just help yourself to the towels and things.' She took her plate and glass over to the sink.

'We'll sort this out, Jane,' Teschmaker said in an attempt at reassurance. But she just kept walking towards her bedroom. She probably didn't believe him, he thought, but then why should she? He didn't.

PART THREE

CHAPTER EIGHTEEN

Teschmaker awoke to what under other circumstances would have been a glorious morning. The sun was streaming in, reflecting off the polished floors and bathing the bedroom in a golden glow. Struggling against his instinctive desire to roll over and go back to sleep, he forced himself to sit up. For a moment he rubbed at his eyes and squinted out through the windows. Reluctantly he got dressed, opened up the French doors onto the balcony that ran the length of the apartment and went out into the sunshine. The sun was already well above the buildings and between them he caught a glimpse of the sparkling waters of the Charlotte flowing away to his right. The air was soft and balmy.

A coffee and the papers would be the ideal way to spend the next hour, he thought. Then he realised he could smell coffee. He wasn't sure if it was coming from the kitchen or one of the apartments below, so he walked along the balcony to where the double doors to the main room were latched back. He went in and found Jane dressed in jeans and a T-shirt, squeezing an orange in the kitchen.

'Good morning, what's for breakfast?'

She didn't bother to look up. 'I don't know. What are you making?'

'Sorry I asked,' he replied frostily.

'I'm not playing wife for anyone, okay?' She stood at the bench and drained the glass of juice.

'Fine by me.' Teschmaker shrugged. 'I'll just go down to one of the cafés and get something to eat.'

'I thought we were going to decide what to do —'

'When I've had breakfast. Is there a key? I'd hate to put you to the trouble of opening the door.' He immediately regretted saying it, knowing it was petty, but he was in no mood to keep butting heads with Jane. If she wanted to maintain the antagonism, then so be it.

'There's a key on a stand by the door.'

Damn her, he thought, but avoiding eye contact he located the key and unbolted the door. 'I'll be back.'

Teschmaker had a coffee and bagel at the Café Dansen. Despite the unimaginative name both were superb. After what he had been through he felt like a tourist visiting normality. The clientele were mainly young office workers and students. It was hard to imagine that they were inhabiting the same world. Yet it was his own experiences that seemed surreal. He imagined attempting to describe the preceding forty-eight hours to any of them. They would have thought he was mad.

He considered having a second coffee, but knew it would be partly to frustrate Jane and realised it was unworthy of him. The task at hand seemed impossible but putting it off was not the answer. So he paid for the breakfast and headed back upstairs.

'I'm sorry about snapping,' he said as he walked in.

'No, it was me.' Jane's expression, partly sheepish, was completely unconvincing.

'So?' He moved to sit opposite her at the kitchen table.

'I'm really afraid I did the wrong thing last night,' she began.

'Rescuing me?' Teschmaker laughed.

'No, leaving my father behind. I thought it would be easier for us to work this out without him, but I can't do it. I can't leave him there. And if he is here at least Rusak can't keep grilling him about the project.'

'And there is an outside chance we might get him to remember something other than bloody flowers.'

Jane shook her head. 'I'm still not sure about that.'

'What? About all that gardening stuff? How do you mean?'

'I don't know . . . Anyway, we have to get him out of there.'

Teschmaker didn't think much of that idea. They had what — two people and one pistol? Then it occurred to him that there might be a way.

'Listen. If we can't come up with a trade then we have to go on the offensive.'

'You mean, go after Rusak?' It was obvious from her expression how little Jane thought of that particular notion.

'Can you think of any other options?'

'No. But you and I against —'

'What about Oliver's men? Norman and Edwards.'

Jane looked blank. 'Who are they?'

Teschmaker explained about his first unpleasant experience with the two men. The sticking point, as he saw it, was one of loyalty. 'It all depends on the extent of Oliver's arrangement with Rusak. What's his involvement with this stuff about your father's project?'

Jane thought about it for a moment before she spoke. 'I don't know, but my gut feeling is that he's unaware of it. Oliver's dealings were always through Grice until recently. He had a different relationship with Rusak, a long-distance one. Oliver and I met Rusak some years ago in Moscow. My understanding is that they developed a reasonably long-standing business arrangement —'

'Producing S&M porn for sale in Eastern Europe?'

'Yes. Oliver had dabbled in it for years but didn't have the contacts in the Eastern Bloc before meeting Rusak. No, the more I think of it I'm certain Rusak's agenda with my father is outside of their business dealings.'

'And you haven't told him?'

Jane shrugged. 'I don't talk to Oliver if I can avoid it and Rusak made it clear right from the beginning that my father would be hurt if I said anything to anyone.' She paused, thinking it through. 'I think that somehow Rusak learned of whatever my father had been involved with and tracked him down to the Czech Republic.'

'So Rusak brought your father here. Why?'

'A last-ditch effort to get something out of him. He discovered that he had a daughter and thought he could use me as a lever. He told my father I would suffer if he didn't cooperate and . . . Well, you get the picture.'

'Okay. And, just so I have this clear, Oliver and you —'

Jane held up her hands. 'Stop! Look, I don't see what this has got to do with getting my father back.'

'Jane, there's only you and me, right? Now, if we want to enlist the help of Edwards and Norman then we're involving Oliver. He'll know about it the minute we approach them.'

'So?'

'So we have to involve Oliver.'

Jane snorted. 'Just great! And he tells Rusak and they have a welcoming committee waiting for us.'

'No. Not if you tell him about Mel.'

Teschmaker got up and went round to her, unable to deal with the distress in her face. He knelt down beside her and took her hands in his. She didn't resist. 'I'm really sorry about what's happened, Jane, and I have no right to tell you what to do. Maybe taking out Rusak is too big an ask, but Norman and Edwards could get your father back, believe me.'

But Jane was slumped over, fighting back the tears.

'I'll make you a cup of coffee.' Without waiting for an answer he got up and, feeling suddenly as if he had overstepped some invisible line, went over to the bench and began to rinse out the coffee plunger. Jane didn't say anything but when he turned he found that she had her face buried in her hands. Her body was shaking.

There was a box of tissues on the end of the bench, so he pulled out a couple and put them down in front of her.

'Listen. You said that you were pushed into all of this because you were fighting with Oliver over custody of Melanie, right?' Jane just sniffed and reached for the tissues. He went back and got the whole box.

'And you say that Oliver knows nothing about this project stuff — it's outside of his deal with Rusak about the videos. So if Oliver is willing to go to the lengths he has done to prove you aren't a fit mother to have custody of Mel, then logically it seems to me that he's going to go ballistic when he hears that Rusak's kidnapped her.'

'Maybe.' She sounded dubious.

'You find it hard to see that Oliver really loves Mel?'

'Of course, I'm sure . . .' Jane sniffed and picked up another tissue, 'I'm sure he loves her, but he treats her like a possession.'

Teschmaker shrugged. 'And you know all too well how hard he'll fight to keep his possessions. Melanie is the key to the way you're behaving and it'll be the same for Oliver. The video deal will seem unimportant to Oliver compared with getting his daughter back.'

'But I told you, he doesn't know . . .' Then it dawned on her where this was leading. 'Who's going to tell Oliver? You?'

Teschmaker shook his head. 'No. I think you should tell him.'

He could see by the look on her face that she didn't like the idea. He turned away and hunted for the coffee.

'In the freezer.' Jane sounded defeated.

Teschmaker busied himself making the coffee. Behind him Jane's inner turmoil was palpable.

When she spoke again, he sensed the fire had gone out of her. Her voice was soft and almost monotone. 'Oliver and I clashed right from the very beginning. The trouble was, I was young and excited by him. He was so immensely confident and I blamed myself for not always meeting his expectations. There was also a seductive element to the tensions between us. At first I thought it was because we were such high-spirited beings and it was inevitable we would spar like that. But then I realised I didn't have the energy or the desire to keep it up. I started giving in to his demands, I did things I've never forgiven myself for. And, right from the beginning, there were Oliver's other women. Stupidly, I justified it by convincing myself that no one person could satisfy a man with such enormous appetites. So for a while I tried to ignore them. But it was very difficult to ignore it when his dalliances ended up in the news or the gossip columns. Oliver delighted in the notoriety, not once expressing remorse or asking my forgiveness — and in the early days I would have given it.

'Just when I had decided that I couldn't take it any more I found I was pregnant with Mel, and for a short time things improved. I guess I thought that becoming a father had changed him. For almost two years we had the nearest thing to a normal relationship. Oliver was attentive and spent all his time with me. But then, about five years ago, he got involved with Grice, and at the same time his sexual demands on me became more and more perverse. I still don't know why I went along with him, but I was scared and didn't know how to stop him. Then he went too far. I remember feeling so dirty, so soiled, that all I wanted to do was kill myself. It was only the fact that I had Melanie that stopped me. So I told him I wanted a divorce. Well, that sparked the most horrific fight and he told me that if I ever talked of divorce again he would take Melanie away from me forever. I capitulated and we agreed on an uneasy truce. I got a separate house and started my business with Sarah. Slowly, over the next couple of years, I began to regain my own life but instead of easing the tensions it got worse. Oliver was paranoid that I was going to take off with Melanie, and convinced me that he could do so any time he wanted.

'Then he showed me some photographs he had taken of me secretly. I can't tell you . . .' Jane stopped, suddenly choked by the memory.

Teschmaker put a cup of coffee in front of her. She looked up at him through teary eyes and mumbled thanks. She sipped it cautiously then slid it away, determined to complete her story.

'He showed me the photographs and told me he'd sent a copy to his lawyers and that they were going to start an action to claim custody of Melanie. I became hysterical. I told him I'd do anything he wanted as long as he didn't take her away. Unfortunately, as you know, he found a way of humiliating me even more . . .'

Her voice trailed away and she reached for the now lukewarm coffee. 'I seem to be making a habit of not finishing the things you give me.' She smiled weakly.

'It doesn't matter. I think I can deal with it.' Teschmaker returned the smile.

'But I will complete what we've started. I'll go and see Oliver.' Jane dabbed at her eyes and then said quietly, 'I'm not used to anyone being kind to me. I don't know how to react. How can I thank you, Martin?'

You fucked up my life once before. You think I'm going to forget that? He looked at her, wondering if this was the moment to raise the issue that had been bothering him. He decided he might not get a better chance.

'Why did you say that I'd fucked up your life?'

'Oh shit, I wondered when that would come up.'

'Well?'

'Forget it. It was just an instant reaction.'

'Fine. Don't tell me. I'll keep on helping you and you keep on being a prize bitch.'

'For fuck's sake, Teschmaker!'

'Sorry. That was out of line.' Leave it, he told himself, it isn't worth fighting over at this point in time.

But Jane looked at him for a moment and shrugged. 'For years I blamed you for my father leaving.'

'Why? I had nothing to —'

She held up her hand to silence him. 'You remember the night Dad caught us?'

'We weren't really doing anything.'

'I know. But he exploded at me like you wouldn't believe. Two days after that he vanished.'

'Oh Christ, and you thought . . .'

'I thought it was your fault. I know it's not true, but when you phoned all that stored-up anger came out and I rang back and dumped it on you. I had it worked out intellectually, I guess I never dealt with the emotional baggage.'

They sat in silence for a while then Teschmaker reached out and touched her hand. 'You know, your father must have been so tense in the lead up to his defection and catching us like that would have really hurt. Knowing that he wasn't going to be there for you. It's no wonder he got so angry. I think if you asked him now he'd tell you that it wasn't about us at all.'

Jane smiled bleakly. 'I did ask him.'

'And?'

'He couldn't remember a damn thing about it.'

Fifteen minutes later Jane was ready to leave.

'I'll be back as soon as I can. I'll ring you if I run into any problems. If you go out, take the key.' She shot him an anxious look. 'You are going to stay, aren't you?'

'Sure,' Teschmaker replied. 'I'm not planning on going anywhere.'

Despite the fact that she dreaded visiting Oliver, Jane knew that she really had no other option. She needed him on side.

And Teschmaker? It had been good to have someone to talk to but he was still a stranger. Yes, they had been children together but that seemed a lifetime . . . *was* a lifetime away. And he was weak. Right now, as much as she despised Oliver, she knew that he would be decisive. Mind you, his strength was a double-edged sword. It was fine when it was working for you but, as she knew from bitter experience, he had no compunction in using it against those close to him.

It had been over a year since she had entered Sinclair Towers but Andrews, the doorman, maintained his poker-face and swung the door open. 'Morning, Mrs Sinclair.'

'Good morning, Andrews.'

'If you'll allow me the pleasure I'll escort you to the private elevator.'

'Thank you.'

They walked through the foyer and instead of going left to the public elevators he led the way to the right of the security desk. A young boy, uncomfortable in his uniform, straightened up and quickly opened the door.

'Top floor for Mrs Sinclair,' Andrews snapped.

'Welcome to Sinclair Towers.' The boy recited it as if it had been drilled into him. Jane imagined that he probably said the same thing to Oliver. Fortunately that was where the script ended and they ascended the tower accompanied by only the slight whir of the lift.

Andrews had obviously decided it was best to cover all bases, for Oliver was waiting for her as the door opened. His face was wreathed in a broad grin.

'Have a pleasant day,' the boy said as the doors shut behind her.

'You should have rung first,' Oliver said softly. 'I would have alerted security.'

'Sorry to disappoint you, Oliver. But then I've made a career of that, haven't I?' She matched his soft tone, determined not to let him faze her. 'I see you're still setting the trend in corporate dress codes,' she said disdainfully. 'At least you must still be buying your own shirts, or has your latest tart developed your supreme lack of taste?'

The shirt looked as though it had started life in Tahiti but been under the influence of LSD ever since. She walked past him and straight into his office.

'Well, you certainly seem to have regained a bit of your old spark.' Oliver laughed as he caught up with her. 'Come to mend the bridges, or fences, or whatever it is one mends?'

'No. You trampled the fences years ago and I recall several notable bridge burnings. Sorry, Oliver, I come not to praise Sinclair but to bury him.'

She sat carefully on the edge of the calf-leather chair, making sure that she didn't allow herself to slip back into it. Years before Oliver had boasted about how he'd had the office furniture designed to put his visitors at a psychological disadvantage.

'Many have tried, believe me,' Oliver said and sat himself behind the desk.

'Can we stop playing games now? I really need to talk to you.'

'But I was just warming up,' he began, then realised she was no longer joking. 'What is it? I can only spare a few minutes.'

'This will take as long as it needs to sort out.' She knew she couldn't put off the moment any longer. 'Oliver, your friend Rusak . . .'

'Yes, what about him?' He shifted in his chair, suddenly uncomfortable. There was something in Jane's demeanour that unsettled him and he didn't like it. He glanced at the clock on the wall behind her. He really did have things to do. But still Jane didn't speak. 'Damn it, Jane! You know how busy I am.'

'Too busy for your own daughter?'

'What do you mean?'

Jane took a deep breath and launched in. 'Rusak has taken Melanie.'

'What do you mean?' Oliver was confused. 'You mean, out for the day? To the pictures —'

'The bastard has kidnapped your daughter — our daughter.' Jane stood up, grabbing the front of the desk to steady herself. 'That fucking evil little Russian shit says he'll kill her if I don't do what he says. He already has my father, Oliver, and unless you agree to help me, our fight over Melanie will not matter one iota. We could both lose her, Oliver.' She realised she was shouting but it was too late to stop now. 'We have to get her back. If you help me, then I promise you she can live with you, whatever you want, but I don't want our little girl killed. I need you to say you'll help me.'

The blood drained from Oliver's face. He tugged at his moustache for a moment then grabbed the phone. 'I'll kill that fucking Russian —'

'No!' Jane screamed and reaching across the desk grabbed the phone and ripped it from his hands. 'No, you can't say anything. Not yet.'

Oliver had never seen Jane like this. For the first time in their years together he was unsure of what to do, what to say.

'Okay. Tell me exactly what's happened and we can work out what to do.' He went round the desk and gently took the phone from her. After replacing it, he leaned across and pressed the intercom. 'Irene. Something's come up. Cancel all my appointments and absolutely no calls.'

'But what about the gentlemen from Zurich? They're already in the boardroom —'

'Get rid of them. Make something up.' He took his finger from the button and straightened up.

Jane looked at him and for the second time that day did something she hadn't done for several years. She burst into tears.

Rather than being therapeutic, Teschmaker found the sudden inactivity bordering on the intolerable. He hunted through the apartment but although there was a bookshelf of brand new books he decided that he was too agitated to read. He thought of going back to bed, but even as he thought it knew that he would never sleep. In the end he decided to take refuge, temporarily, in domesticity. He would prepare a meal. Teschmaker had no idea what condition Jane would be in after her encounter with Oliver, so he played it safe and opted for comfort food.

After scouting the pantry he pocketed the apartment key and went down to the street in search of provisions. As he had feared, there was no supermarket or even a general store, though the restaurants and bars were a mini United Nations of obscure third-world cuisines. Maybe cooking was out of the question and they would be better to go out for a Taste of Mali or a Mongolian Barbeque, or live dangerously and book a table at what sounded like a gastronomic oxymoron — Basil's Baltic Treats. Fortunately, just as he was about to give up, he noticed a small blackboard on which a chalk arrow directed him to the Village Delicatessen. The owner was a garrulous individual who, after labelling Teschmaker as 'not from round these parts', went on to describe himself as a 'swampy'. Teschmaker escaped half an hour later with a bag of vegetables, a packet of frozen oxtail and more local history than he cared to know.

Back in the apartment he prepared the vegetables for the stock while the microwave made short work of thawing the oxtail. It wasn't until the casserole was bubbling away that he noticed the flashing light on the answering machine. The message was from Jane. *Don't worry. Having lunch with Oliver. Back later.* Well, he thought as he started to peel the potatoes, it was just as well he was cooking dinner.

Later he polished the benches, cleaned up the cooking utensils and then lay down on the couch intending to watch television and catch up with the news. He didn't get as far as switching the TV on and slept soundly until he was woken by the sound of the key in the door. He glanced at his watch. It was four thirty.

'Something smells good,' she said as she came in. 'Pity I had lunch.'

'It'll keep. How did you go?' he asked.

'Better than expected. I think if Oliver had his way, Rusak would be dead by now.' Jane put down her bag and went through to the kitchen. 'I'm just putting the kettle on. Do you want tea or coffee? I ended up drinking a bit too much with lunch.'

'Coffee would be great. Lunch must have been very cosy.'

Jane popped her head around the door. 'No, Teschmaker, just civil. Though I must say I was surprised by the way Oliver behaved. Instantaneous civility.'

Teschmaker stretched and got to his feet. 'So what did he say?' He went through to the kitchen and sat at the table.

'It was all I could do to stop him going after Rusak straight away, but when I explained the situation with my father he agreed to hold off.'

'Did you ask him about Norman and Edwards assisting us?'

'He raised it before I had time to. He said he had a couple of people and you should have seen his face when I asked him if he meant Norman and Edwards. He asked how I knew and so I told him about you. For some reason he thought you were out of the picture.'

'I bet he did,' Teschmaker said, but decided again against telling her that it had been planned that she would be too.

'The strangest thing was the change in Oliver. Once it sank in that it was his daughter in danger, he started saying how sorry he was about the way he had treated me. It was as though he blamed himself.'

'Well, it was his fault —'

'Of course, but I mean the whole thing. Not just Melanie, but way back. Everything.' Jane put out the coffee cups and sat while she waited for the kettle to boil.

'And you believed him?' Teschmaker didn't bother to veil his cynicism.

'Yes. I wish you could have seen him. It was as though Melanie being at risk suddenly put everything in perspective.' She shot a look at him. 'Don't get me wrong. I'm not going back to him. In fact, he agreed that we had come to the end of the road, but at least we aren't going to fight over Mel any more.'

'It sounds too good to be true. But what about your father? When do we try and free him?'

'We don't,' Jane said as she got up to switch off the kettle and make the coffee. 'Norman and Edwards will handle it this evening and bring him back here.'

'Just the two of them?' Teschmaker said dubiously.

'Sorry, I'm sure it wasn't a reflection on you, but he said it needed professionals.' Jane turned back to him. 'Black or white?'

'Black, no sugar.' It worried Teschmaker that even if Norman and Edwards managed to rescue Jane's father, they were all still a long way from finding anything that could be used to get Melanie back safe and sound. There was something at the back of his mind that he had been meaning to ask Jane about, but each time something else came up. As they took their coffee out onto the balcony he decided to raise it. 'Jane, do you have much of a memory of your father before he defected?'

She looked at him, surprise in her eyes. 'That's an odd question. Why?'

Teschmaker shrugged. 'Just curious. Not having a father around was something we shared, remember?'

'I was thinking about it last night before I went to sleep. Your father was ill or something?'

'He drank. He was an alcoholic. He'd take off on these binges and then go into hospital or a boarding house. But he was at home from time to time, though Mum couldn't stand the sight of him after a while.'

'At least you knew where he was.' Jane stared out through the buildings towards the river. 'My father was there one day and gone the next.'

'Did you know why?'

'No, not for ages. For a while I thought he must have died. It's all pretty hazy now, but I think that just after he left there were several occasions when people came and searched the house. I remember throwing a tantrum and accusing some man of killing my father, and Mum took me upstairs and explained that Dad wasn't dead but had gone away and the men in the house were going to help find him and bring him back. That was the worst thing.'

'How do you mean?' Teschmaker asked.

Jane continued to stare resolutely away into the distance. 'It would have been easier if he had been dead. For years I had this fantasy of him walking up the drive and coming home.'

'But you knew where he was?'

'No. Mum refused to talk about it. You remember what she was like — stubborn as hell. When she made her mind up about something that was it. She'd decided that the best way to protect me was to keep the truth hidden. She was so ashamed; in fact, I think it's what killed her eventually. His betrayal was her betrayal. She thought she should have been enough to —'

'Like you with Oliver?' Teschmaker interjected.

'Like mother, like daughter?' Jane thought about it for a moment then nodded. 'I guess.'

'So when did you find out about what your father had done?'

390

'First time I applied for a job with the Department of Foreign Affairs. I went through the usual vetting and then a couple of very smooth gentlemen took me aside and asked me how often I was in contact with my father. I told them they were nuts and that I didn't even know if he was alive, and to my amazement they didn't believe me. Eventually they told me that he was still alive and in the Soviet Union. They said he was a traitor. It was a hell of a way to find out. And, of course, I didn't get the job.'

'Too much of a risk, huh?'

'Something like that,' she said flatly, then laughed. 'Mind you, after I'd made a bit of a name for myself in strategic analysis they were falling over themselves to offer me work. I let them hire me as a consultant and made the bastards pay through the nose.'

She drained her coffee and got to her feet. The air was beginning to cool down and in the dusk the streets between the taller buildings were deepening canyons of shadow.

'Before he went away,' Teschmaker persisted, 'did he spend much time in the garden?'

Jane leaned on the balcony rail and looked at him quizzically. 'Gardening?' Then it dawned on her what had prompted the question. 'Oh, you mean all that stuff he goes on about, the flowers, bouquets and the gardeners?'

'It does seem strange that he's fixated on it.'

'I thought about that as well, but he never liked gardening. Mum once told me that she had an argument with him because he wanted to concrete around the front of the house so he didn't have to waste his time mowing the lawns. So I guess the short answer is no.' She held out her hand for his coffee cup. 'Finished? I'm going inside.'

Teschmaker nodded and handed it to her. But he remained seated, looking out over the city. 'I'll be in shortly.'

For the first time in ages he felt like having a cigarette. Sometimes he found they helped him concentrate, or so he told himself. But he resisted the urge to go downstairs to buy a packet. For a few minutes he sifted through everything he knew about Rusak, trying to find some connection to Sydney Morris. It just didn't gel. Apart from the fact they had both lived in Russia in the Soviet days, there was nothing. Their worlds would have been totally separate. The world of the Mafia meets that of the nuclear researcher? Hardly. And there were years in age between them. Sydney Morris had probably retired long before Rusak's short stint in the Duma. He certainly hadn't even been in the country when Rusak left the parliament to take up his dubious career in *biznes*. But their worlds must have intersected somewhere. Why had Rusak gone to the trouble of seeking out Morris in some obscure village in the Czech Republic? Teschmaker's ruminations were cut short as Jane poked her head around the corner of the door.

'Oh, by the way, Oliver told me to tell you that he really is sorry about having misled you. He says he'll find a way of making it up to you.'

'That's big of him,' Teschmaker snorted.

'I think he meant it. Honestly, Teschmaker, this has hit him like a brick. Don't get me wrong, the man is an absolute bastard, but his one and only redeeming feature is that he adores Mel. As he said, he would kill anyone who hurt her.'

Jane went back inside and he returned to his musing. While it was true that the threat to Sinclair's own daughter had probably pulled him up pretty damn quickly, Teschmaker wasn't about to forget that the man had contrived a scheme to kill his wife and him in order to have total custody. Teschmaker had always been suspicious of conversions on the road to Damascus. He went inside, shutting the balcony doors behind him.

'You don't feel like eating yet, do you?'

Jane shook her head. 'Why?'

'I've got a friend in the Russian Quarter who might be able to shed some light on Rusak. It's a long shot, but I think we should try everything.'

'You can take my car. I'm going to stay here until I hear how Oliver's men got on.'

'Fine,' Teschmaker said and then changed his mind. 'Actually I won't take the car. It's likely I'll have a couple of drinks and I wouldn't want to put any dents in it.'

Jane laughed. 'You could hardly make it any worse. The Saab is a different matter but the Golf is already a mess.'

'Thanks, but I'll walk. It's not all that far and I feel like I've been cooped up for days. I'll take the key so I can let myself back in.' Then he remembered something else. 'The casserole in the oven should only need a little warming and there are some spuds in the pot on the stove that I was going to mash.'

'Thanks, Teschmaker. I'll help myself if I get hungry.'

He let himself out and went down the stairs to the street. Entering the first bar he came to he bought a packet of cigarettes. The sun had gone now and the earlier cool breeze had developed into a distinct chill. Teschmaker lit a cigarette and set out through the streets, melding with the flow of people making their way home. He had no doubt that by now Rusak would have his people out looking for him, but he felt confident that he was reasonably safe in a crowd. He was less confident about Jane's belief in her husband's change of attitude. It was, Teschmaker thought, a distinct possibility that the first thing Sinclair had done was alert Rusak as to Jane's whereabouts.

As he had expected, Restaurant Shlyapnikov was closed. Aleksandr Yefremovich ran it more out of tradition than necessity and, giving into the constraints of old age, only opened from Wednesdays to Saturdays. The clientele were almost exclusively émigrés who frequented it more out of habit than anything else. No, that wasn't quite right. Zoya Nikolayevna still made the best stroganoff this side of St Petersburg.

Teschmaker went around the side of the restaurant and climbed the stairs to the family's apartment. He rang the bell and a moment later the door opened and he was warmly greeted by Zoya Nikolayevna. Her plump girth was encircled by a slightly grubby apron and there was flour on her hands and a solitary white streak across her wrinkled brow.

'He's in the kitchen, come on through,' she said and bustled Teschmaker in the front door. 'As you can see,

I'm baking. Just in time, it would seem. You are all skin and bones.'

'I'm fine,' Teschmaker retorted.

'Then you'll have a *fine* appetite.' Zoya made it sound like a command. She prodded him in the ribs. 'Unless you think I'm too old to be trusted at the stove.'

'No, I just don't want to put you to any trouble.'

'Trouble? Isn't that we are put on this earth for — to get you men out of trouble? That worthless peasant inside is nothing but trouble and do I complain? All day he plays chess against himself and at night I get no rest. The stupid man yelps in his sleep like a dog that has had its tail stepped on.'

She shuffled along the corridor and pushed open the kitchen door. 'Aleksandr Yefremovich will be glad to see you.' She nodded to where her husband was hunched over a chessboard and went back to her mixing bowl.

'Ah, Teschmaker, *Bozhe moy*! You have come just in time.' Shlyapnikov struggled out of his chair and embraced Teschmaker, kissing him on both cheeks. 'Sit down, sit down. See what I am reduced to?'

'I've heard, playing yourself at chess. It doesn't sound so bad.' Teschmaker noticed the half empty vodka bottle beside the chessboard.

'But I lose.' The old man drummed his gnarled fingers on the edge of the table. 'I'm playing like some dumb Vanya.'

'Let it rest for a while then, I've come to talk.'

Shlyapnikov looked up, arching his bushy eyebrows. 'Talk, is it? Then we had better go to the other room.'

He pushed back his chair and gripping the table for support got to his feet again. 'Zoya, can you bring a bottle and glasses through?'

'The boy wants to talk and you want to drink.' She wiped her hands on the apron. 'Rubbish is what you'll be talking.'

Shlyapnikov inverted his palms, protesting his innocence. 'See what I must endure?'

'Tush! Teschmaker knows the truth, Aleksandr Yefremovich. Now both of you get out of my kitchen before you ruin my cake.' She handed two shot glasses and a bottle to Teschmaker. 'Don't let the old fool drink too much.'

'I'll do my best,' he laughed and followed the old man through to the lounge room. In all the years he had been visiting, he had only been in the room a couple of times and it was immediately obvious that it was used very little these days. Slowly over the years the couple had retreated to the kitchen, leaving behind only the stains of memory. Dust covers were draped over all but two of the chairs and most of the pictures had been long removed, bequeathing only faint outlines where the frames had once rested — the ghosts of paintings. Above the small gas fire was a single smoke-darkened icon. Teschmaker tried to imagine the couple in their younger days. Had they entertained in here? Or had it been a quiet sanctuary from the hustle and bustle of the restaurant? He realised he couldn't visualise it because in his mind the couple had always been old.

Teschmaker put the bottle and glasses down on the coffee table and took the box of matches that

Shlyapnikov was holding out. As he bent to light the gas he heard the clink of bottle on glass.

'I get cold, even on warm days.' Shlyapnikov sat in his chair, inclining his body towards the fire. 'You know, I grew up in a place were we had winters like you would never believe. Months of snow and cold that could freeze you to the bone. And on clear still days the frost would fall from the sky and you wouldn't even see it till it started to build up. But I don't remember feeling this cold.'

'Here's to warm memories,' Teschmaker said, taking the glass that Shlyapnikov had filled to the brim. He held it up in salute and then drained it. The old man did the same and watched as Teschmaker refilled them. Then he launched into a rambling story about the village where he had grown up. Though his family came from Moscow they, along with twenty other families, had been 'rewarded' for their patriotism by being moved into more spacious houses after Stalin had liquidated the previous inhabitants. The kulaks had vanished into history in such a hurry that the newcomers found the beds made, remnants of meals on the tables and, worst of all, the skeletons of the livestock that had starved to death still tied up in the barns.

Just as the story was coming to an end, Zoya Nikolayevna came in with coffee and slices of cherry cake. The slices were huge but Teschmaker could tell by the smell emanating from the kitchen that a replacement was well on the way. 'Why are you talking about that place?' she demanded. 'How many times must the poor boy hear about our miserable childhood?'

'It's the first time I've heard about it.' Teschmaker came to his host's defence.

'Well, I bet that he doesn't tell you that within a year every one of those families had forgotten their working-class lives back in Moscow and was going around putting on airs and graces; no better than those halfwit kulaks before them who got what they deserved. But I'll tell you what they had really become — country yokels.'

'Nonsense, woman. I would have never chosen to marry a yokel.'

'Chosen?' Zoya Nikolayevna snorted. 'My father beating you with a stick until you said you would make an honest woman of me? You call that chosen?' She winked at Teschmaker and, satisfied that she had scored a direct hit, retreated to the kitchen.

'That woman — she is like pepper vodka.' Shlyapnikov beamed at Teschmaker. 'Rough on the throat but warms the heart.' He pushed the coffee to one side and refilled the glasses. 'So, since it is forbidden to bore you any longer with my reminiscences, what did you want to talk about?'

'I wanted to ask you about some Russian words.'

'But your Russian is very good.'

'Passable at best. However, I think I'm missing something.' He paused and took a sip of his coffee, aware that he had better leave the vodka alone for a while. A couple more shots and he would be incapable of exploring what he'd come for, and even less capable of understanding any explanation Shlyapnikov might have. 'I've a friend who is suffering from some kind of dementia. I have the feeling he's trying to say something but every time I talk to him he goes on about flowers and gardening. And not just with me. He does the same with his daughter.'

The old man laughed. 'Well, I'm sorry but I'm not a brain doctor. Maybe he just likes flowers.'

'Little flowers, bouquets, gardeners ... He seems particularly fond of lilies. You're probably right. It just seemed strange because his daughter said he had never shown any interest in gardening in the past.'

Teschmaker sighed, picked up the slice of cherry cake and took a bite. It was rich, moist and delicious. 'Zoya Nikolayevna has surpassed herself.'

He was about to reach for his coffee again when he sensed a shift in the mood. Shlyapnikov had straightened up and was studying him through eyes that had been reduced to slits; shadows under the bushy eyebrows.

'Tell me exactly what words he used.'

'You mean in Russian?'

The old man nodded.

'But he was speaking English.'

'Then in English. I just want to know what the hell you are talking about.' Shlyapnikov's words were slurred but Teschmaker could feel the tension in his voice.

'Little flowers, lily, bouquet and gardener or gardeners, I'm not sure which.'

The old man picked up his glass and drained it in a single gulp. His hand was trembling. 'A gardener with a bouquet? *Liliya*, *buket*, *tsvetok* and *sadovnik*.' It appeared to Teschmaker that Shlyapnikov had withdrawn and was talking to himself. But then he felt the man's eyes blaze at him. 'You are talking about a Russian, right?'

'No. Not at all.'

'Pah! Then it is nothing.' He waved his hand as if to dismiss Teschmaker. 'You get this man a good doctor is what I say.'

'But he spent most of his adult life working in Russia.'

Shlyapnikov didn't appear to have heard. He shifted his weight even further forward on his chair and gazed into the fire. For a while Teschmaker thought he had nothing further to say. Then he heard the old man's voice. He was speaking so quietly it was only just audible.

'I think it was back in 1967 when Andropov became KGB chairman. He took the new Department V of the First Chief Directorate and gave them orders to instigate what he termed "special actions of a political nature". And at the same time he instructed the Line F officers in the KGB residencies to locate possible targets and suggest strategies. While this was happening, Department V set up a number of sabotage and intelligence groups, or DRGs as they were known. There had been so many stuff-ups in the past that they decided on one set of code words for use in all operations. That meant that if an operative was lost, he could be replaced without the new man having to go through any training as he would already know the codes.'

The old man lapsed into silence, his eyes still staring intently at the fire. Teschmaker, sensing where the monologue was heading, wanted to prompt him but he held his tongue. After a time, Shlyapnikov heaved a great sigh and continued. 'In DRG parlance, a *sadovnik* or gardener was a saboteur. *Liliya* was the act of sabotage. The little flower or *tsvetok* was the detonator and the *buket* was the explosive device. There were other terms too. *Zaplyv* or splash was the actual explosion, *doroshki* were the landing zones for dropping in a team or equipment and beehive, *ulya*, was the name given to an operational base.' He turned to Teschmaker. 'All this is dated information and defectors have long since revealed the sorry history of Department V's incompetence, but I would say that if your friend is talking about these things, even now, then he should be very careful.'

For a moment Teschmaker just sat and stared into the fire, attempting to imagine Sydney Morris involved in sabotage. Sabotage of what? Where? But it didn't fit. The man had been a scientist, not an active agent. But then, what did he really know about Jane's father? Maybe the KGB had decided to utilise the fact that English was his first language.

He leaned over and gentle nudged Shlyapnikov's shoulder. The old man appeared to have nodded off. 'Would the DRG have used foreigners for that kind of work?'

'Many times. Over the years Department V did all kinds of work using both illegals and citizens of the target countries.' The old man rubbed his eyes, reached for another glass of vodka and began a long and complex explanation of the structures within the KGB. According to Shlyapnikov, the First Chief Directorate got a large increase of funding and staff in the late

1970s and Directorate S, which ran the illegals, was reorganised with Department V being swallowed up by Department 8. Teschmaker found he had tuned out, but he sipped the last of his coffee and sat politely while Shlyapnikov's monologue meandered through everything from shipping arms to the Irish Communists and operations with the Sandinistas, to tracking down post-war defectors in Australia. After a time the old man stopped talking, and shortly after Teschmaker realised he was sound asleep. He quietly put down his cup and went out to the kitchen where by the delicious aroma he judged the baking had been a success. Zoya Nikolayevna had just pulled the cherry cake from the oven and was gently removing it from the tin.

'Asleep, is he?' Zoya shook her head. 'More and more that's what he does. Drink and sleep.'

'With respect, he is an old man,' Teschmaker began, but the old woman was having none of it.

'And that should excuse him? Do you see me drinking? The old fool drinks to forget the past and ends up wallowing in it. Russian melancholy is a disease. If he had been half a man we would have had children to look after us in our old age. Let me tell you, there were times when I thought I should just go out and make a baby with someone else.'

Teschmaker was confused. 'But I thought you had a son who died?'

'Pah! The old fool told you that?' Zoya rolled her eyes. 'He got himself involved with sponsoring this kid to immigrate. Fine choice he made. Some young punk who wanted nothing to do with us and Shlyapnikov didn't see what was happening. I warned him, but he didn't listen to me. He bent over backwards to get the boy set up and all the time he was just being used. And of course the next thing we know he's involved with a bunch of crooks and gets himself killed.'

'I'm sorry. I always thought he was your boy.'

'Better having no children than one like that. I didn't grieve for him.'

'It seemed to affect Aleksandr Yefremovich . . .'

'He liked him, but he couldn't see that he was bad news. Enough.' She wiped her hands on her apron. 'I had better go and get the old man into bed before he falls out of his chair. You should come and eat on Wednesday. I'll cook something special for you.'

Teschmaker thanked her and let himself out into the now dark and deserted street. He started in the direction of Lincoln but then, changing his mind, found a phone box and rang the Romanian Embassy. After concluding the call he made his way to the back bar of the Dredger's Arms and settled into an alcove with a beer and cigarette. Thirty minutes later he saw the man walk in.

For a second Laverov seemed hesitant, peering through the smoke haze, then he saw Teschmaker and came over.

'I thought I had heard the last from you,' he said as he took off his coat and slipped into the seat opposite.

'So did I, Mr Laverov. But I decided it was time we had a talk.'

Laverov gestured the approaching waiter away and turned his attention back to Teschmaker. 'I really don't see the need for that. The affairs I am involved with have nothing to do with you. You are far safer keeping a long way away from this.'

Fair enough, Teschmaker thought, but the man had lost little time in getting from Lakeside to the city. He didn't say anything for a moment but aware that he had a stomach full of cake, coffee and vodka sipped cautiously at his beer.

'You should take my advice and stay right out of this.'

'You could have said that over the phone.'

'You said you wanted to ask me something,' Laverov retorted.

Teschmaker pushed the packet of cigarettes across the table. 'Take them back to Russia with you. I'd hate to see you go home empty-handed.'

For a moment Laverov looked nonplussed, then he smiled and picked up the packet. 'Okay. Maybe I have been a little too hasty.' He opened the packet and took out a cigarette. 'My doctor says he hopes they kill me.'

'I'd change doctors,' Teschmaker snorted.

'He is being kind. He knows the work I do and thinks it would be an easier way to die.'

Teschmaker reached over and lit the Russian's cigarette. 'Maybe he has a point.'

'You have no idea how things have changed. I tell you, Teschmaker, if I could turn the clock back I would do it. Under the old regime at least we knew who the enemy was. There was something comforting in knowing that if something went wrong, if something broke down, the Party would tell us it was always the fault of the Americans. An enemy is something to treasure. But now? You would not believe the way people are acting. There are Russians but no Russia. We inhabit the country but don't even own it any more. Everyone is out for themselves.' He drew deeply on the cigarette and tilting his head back blew the smoke out towards the ceiling. 'Without the Party there is no unity. Before, it was the Party that held us together. The Party blamed the Americans and we all hated the Party. But it was that hate that made us a nation.'

'Oh, come on,' Teschmaker scoffed. 'You didn't hate the Party.'

'Trust me. It was true. And I should know, I was a member of the Party.'

'But now you have democracy and capitalism —'

'Listen! Democracy does not suit the Russian temperament. We are a nation who deep down wants to be told what to do. We want a father —'

'A Czar?' Teschmaker drained his beer and wondered whether he should have another. He decided against it.

'Yes, and not this capitalism. We do not do it very well. You see, we do not know where its limits lie and we are a people who need limits as much as we need a leader. If we know where the boundaries are, we may well argue and brawl about it but in the end there is still a boundary. With capitalism, we think that the only answer to our problems and the limit to our abilities is the dollar. We have embraced capitalism like a madman embracing a bear. But the bear will crush us.'

'So why are you chasing ancient ghosts?'

Laverov looked startled then, regaining his composure, smiled broadly. 'Ah, but you have no idea what I am chasing. And I can tell you, it is certainly not a ghost.'

Time to play the bluff, Teschmaker thought. He reached over, retrieved a cigarette and, pausing before lighting it, said casually, 'So tell me, Comrade Laverov, are you after the gardener or the bouquet? The *sadovnik* or the *buket*?'

'I'm afraid I have no idea what you're talking about,' Laverov replied coldly and stubbed out his cigarette.

'Fine. I'm sorry to have wasted your time.' Teschmaker slid along the seat and got to his feet. 'If I don't see you again, have a good trip home.' Without pausing he turned and started towards the door.

'You're a fool if you walk away,' Laverov said loudly enough to be heard over the buzz of conversation in the bar.

Maybe, Teschmaker thought, but he kept walking. For a moment he thought that Laverov was going to follow, but as he went through the door he saw the Russian signalling to the waiter for a drink. He set out in the direction of Lincoln, walking slowly, savouring his victory. It didn't matter that he hadn't received an answer to his question because, although it had only been an instant, the look on Laverov's face had been sufficient to tell him he was on the right track. For so long he had felt as though he was wandering a maze, lost and directionless. Now, though still in the maze, he had a sudden glimpse of the forces governing its design. And maybe — just maybe — it would be enough. He tossed the cigarette away and picked up his pace, suddenly looking forward to getting back to see Jane.

*   *   *

The temperature dropped fast. The skies had cleared and the earlier chill had turned to an unseasonable cold. Teschmaker wished he had taken a coat, but the day had been balmy and he hadn't given it a thought. Now it was as though winter had returned. He paused on the edge of the business district, debating whether to take a cab. But the streets were deserted and he realised that it could be a while before a taxi cruised through the now dead heart of the city. Above him, in the strip of sky visible between the darkened buildings, the stars burned fiercely, while at the northern end of the street he thought he could see mist rising from the waters of the Charlotte. He breathed on his hands and saw that even his own breath was steaming. He plunged his hands deep in his pockets and strode on.

It took another fifteen minutes before he saw the squat silhouette of the Dansen Brewery building. Teschmaker was just approaching the entrance when a movement in the shadows opposite caught his eye. For a second he thought it was Rusak and he felt himself tense.

'Evening, Teschmaker.' Gerard Edwards stepped into the light. 'Sorry I startled you.'

'You've taken to hanging around on the streets now?' Teschmaker noticed that Edwards had taken the precaution of wearing a thick coat.

'Sinclair's orders. Seems he's decided to stop playing games with Rusak and pay some attention where it belongs. He's got me keeping an eye on Mrs Sinclair and her father.'

'Oh shit! I'd forgotten about that. How did you go?'

It was true; he had been so absorbed in his own venture he hadn't given a thought to how Norman and Edwards might be making out. A couple of blocks away a car turned into the street. Teschmaker felt a hand on his arm and Edwards guided him back into the shelter of a darkened doorway.

'It went fine. Not a problem. There was only one of Rusak's goons guarding them.'

'Them?' That didn't make sense. There was only Sydney Morris. 'How do you mean?'

'The old man and a tall fellow with a ponytail, all tied up, don't know why. He was a real mess. He wouldn't have gotten far.' He paused as the car cruised slowly past them.

'You mean Ilya? The poet?'

'Is that what he was?' Edwards watched as the car disappeared down the road towards the river. 'A poet. *Etiam disiecti membra poetae.*'

Teschmaker looked at him in horror. 'They killed him?'

'*Even when dismembered, the limbs of a poet.* Something I picked up at university. No, they didn't kill him but he was very badly beaten. We dropped him off at the hospital.'

Teschmaker felt relieved, surprisingly so considering that if Jane hadn't intervened Ilya could well have ended up killing him. 'And Jane's father?'

'Sydney Morris is fine. Far better than Jane expected. It seems the new guard had forgotten to give him his medication so he's not half as dopey as Jane had seen him before.'

'Well, I had better go up and see how she's coping. Are you going to be lurking around all night? Or is Norman going to relieve you?'

Edwards shook his head. 'No such luck. Norman and Viola were off out somewhere and Sinclair reckoned I could handle it. Mind you, I think Rusak is going to be extremely angry when he sees what we did to his goon.'

Teschmaker didn't really want to know but felt he should ask. 'What did you do?'

Edwards shrugged. 'We didn't have an option. The man refused to let us in. I'm afraid Rusak's boys are going to be a little miffed at me for it. I killed him.'

'*Oderint dum metuant.*' Teschmaker smiled. '*Let them hate, provided that they fear.* Something *I* picked up at university.' He was about to walk away when a disturbing thought crossed his mind. He turned back to Edwards. 'By the way, what happened to my unwelcome house guests?'

'I killed them and left them out for garbage collection . . .' Edwards stopped, aware that Teschmaker didn't seem to appreciate his attempt at humour. 'We dumped Orpheus and the boy back at his house with a gentle warning about what would happen if the newspapers learned of his activities. He's pissed off but basically undamaged.'

'Basically?'

'He may have bumped his head getting out of the car.'

Teschmaker crossed the road, let himself into the apartment building and climbed the stairs. Earlier in the day he had been sceptical when Jane described Sinclair's change of heart, but the fact that he had organised Edwards to keep an eye on the place struck Teschmaker as a pretty good indication she may well have been right in her assessment. He checked his watch. It was ten forty-five. He slipped the key into the door as quietly as he could and opened the lock. He needn't have bothered because as he opened the door Jane got up from a chair in the lounge room and came straight over to him. She looked as though sleep was the last thing on her mind.

'I thought something had happened to you,' she snapped and pushed past him to lock the door, slamming home the security bolt with more force than was necessary.

Teschmaker felt like a schoolkid caught sneaking home after staying out too late, but he realised that there was more to her anger than just his lateness. Jane looked as though she was ready to explode. 'Sorry,' he said lamely. 'It took longer than expected.'

'You should have rung me. I've got more important things to do than worry about where you are.'

'I said I'm sorry.'

He moved around her into the kitchen; the place was a mess. A dirty wine glass, bread crumbs everywhere, three dirty plates had been abandoned on the bench, the cutlery scattered around them. Instinctively Teschmaker reached for a cloth to wipe up the mess, but the coffee plunger had been tipped into the sink and the cloth was covered with coffee grounds. Picking it up he began to rinse it under the tap.

Jane strode over and ripped it out of his hand. 'And for Christ's sake, stop cleaning up after me! You're like a fucking housewife!'

Staggered at her outburst he watched as she threw the cloth on the floor. Too stunned to retaliate, he let the cloth lie there, drew a deep breath and said as calmly as he could, 'Now, if you don't mind I'm going to get something to eat.'

'You'll have to make toast.'

'You ate all the food? I made a whole stew.' Teschmaker turned and stared at her. She was leaning against the kitchen door, the look on her face one of pure anger.

'So? I didn't know what time you were coming back. You could have eaten out for all I knew. I had to feed my father and Oliver's men.'

'Yes, Edwards told me they got your father . . .' He stopped, trying to work out what else was going on. 'Jane, I realise you're stressed about your father and Melanie —'

'Stressed!' Jane blazed. 'I am worried out of my fucking mind. Do you know that they killed someone tonight?' She didn't wait for Teschmaker to respond. 'What do you think Rusak is going to do to Melanie now? I have no idea where she is and Oliver's animals have just made the situation worse. They kill one of Rusak's men and then they tell me to relax. And to top it off, you waltz in, start fussing around like a fucking obsessive compulsive and then expect me to have a meal ready?'

'I never said that.' Teschmaker struggled to stay calm. 'I'm quite happy to eat toast.'

'Well, after you've had something to eat maybe you'll tell me what you were doing. Obviously drinking was part of it, just like your stupid father.'

'Are you quite finished? Or are you going to go on like this all night? I'm perfectly happy to go somewhere else. I can book into a hotel and come back in the morning when you've calmed down.'

He strode to the front door and picked up the keys. Damn the woman, this was not his affair and he certainly didn't have to put up with being castigated when he had been trying to assist.

'You'd do that? You'd walk out and leave me with this?'

The vitriol and disgust in Jane's voice was too much for Teschmaker. He spun around and only just stopped himself from hitting her. Instead he took her by the shoulders. 'Listen, Jane. I can come or I can go. But I'm not staying to be abused. I'm trying to help so either you let me do that or I do walk out. And one other thing, don't insult my father like that.'

But she wasn't ready to capitulate. She shrugged herself free of him and stormed out of the kitchen. A couple of seconds later he heard the door to her room slam. For a moment he thought of going after her, but knew there was nothing he could say to placate her. 'Great,' he said to himself. 'Just great.'

He went back into the kitchen but after looking around at the empty pots and dirty dishes piled up on the bench decided that he no longer felt hungry. He wanted a cigarette but knew that would mean going out into the cold on the balcony and so abandoned that idea as well. Then it came to him why he felt so churned up by Jane's outburst of anger. It was like being married — all arguments and no sex. To his surprise, Teschmaker found himself smiling at the notion, but realised as he did so that it wasn't entirely accurate. With Gwenda the battle had always been conducted in icy silence, the most tangible evidence of her disapproval being her withering looks of scorn. And the sex? What there had been of it had been dispensed rather than shared and always clinically performed as though it were a burdensome task rather than an act of pleasure.

He bent down to pick up the dishcloth but stopped himself. Obsessive compulsive? What the fuck was that supposed to mean? I'll show her obsessive fucking compulsive, he thought grimly, and with a single sweep of his arm brushed the dishes from the bench onto the floor. For some strange reason the act gave him intense satisfaction. Fuck the mess! I'm sick of tidying up after everyone. For a second he had a flash of the chaos his father had lived in, the filth and broken-bottle squalor. Not me, he thought; but no more cleaning up either. And he knew as he thought it that it was true: all of his adult life, even the nature of his work, had been about cleaning up other people's messes.

Teschmaker turned his back on the wreckage and walked through to the darkened lounge room and took a bottle of scotch and a glass from the drinks cabinet. He knew he had already had enough to drink but decided he no longer cared. Deliberately he avoided the coaster and with a sense of liberation put the glass straight onto the coffee table. It will need to be wiped now, part of his mind scolded. Fuck off, the other part responded. In that moment he saw with absolute clarity that his life had been all about appearances. Carefully he and his mother had wallpapered over every crack his father had caused in their middle-class facade. Keeping up appearances, his mother would stress. Upholding standards. A place for everything and everything in its place. And inside? In him? The same pattern. Cover the cracks, keep the exterior 'ship shape' — another of his mother's phrases. Well, not any more. He dipped his finger in the scotch and licked it. If he ever got out of this mess . . .

For several minutes he sat in the dark nursing his glass, feeling pleasantly numb. Each time his mind began to replay the day's events he gently pushed the thoughts away and sipped at his drink. It was good scotch, a single malt with a mellow peaty tang and a hint of seaweed, probably from some godforsaken island. Maybe that's what he should do: pack up and find himself a cottage in the Hebrides, or the Orkney Islands. The idea of hibernation seemed like a good option. He imagined himself walking on windswept beaches, hunting the drift for salt-bleached firewood. Or going for long hikes amidst tarns and craggy rocks before returning to a crackling fire and a bowl of steaming soup.

Teschmaker had drifted so far into his fantasy that he didn't hear the door open. And when he did hear the voice, he thought it was his imagination.

'Would you mind if I joined you?' the voice repeated.

Teschmaker sat forward and looked around at the figure silhouetted in the wedge of light that spilled from the bedroom.

The man stepped forward. 'Sorry, I didn't mean to startle you.'

It was Sydney Morris. He wore pyjamas and was pulling a dressing gown around his shoulders. Teschmaker got rather groggily to his feet. 'It's fine. I just dozed off for a moment.' He put his glass down on the coffee table and went to the cabinet to get another. 'I take it you would like a scotch?'

'Yes, thanks. I'm afraid my previous hosts didn't run to such luxuries, preferring to keep me doped up.' He walked over to the lounge and sat. 'You're Teschmaker, right?'

'Yes.' Teschmaker nodded and then, unsure of how much the old man remembered, added, 'I visited you a couple of times.'

'I know. And I should apologise for being so vague with you. I wasn't clear what your role was, or who you were working for, so I stuck to the script I'd developed for dealing with Rusak.'

Teschmaker poured a scotch and handed it to Sydney. The transformation was remarkable. There was no sign of his previous incapacity, and though the hand that accepted the drink shook a little, the eyes that followed him were sharp and alert. 'Well, you had me well and truly fooled.'

'A matter of self-preservation, I'm afraid. My memory isn't all that good these days, but I certainly don't have any problems other than too many miles on the clock. I was living in the Czech Republic for a while and one of my neighbours had Alzheimer's. And when Rusak came on the scene, I thought it was the best defence. Unfortunately the drugs Rusak's people forced into me made it very difficult. I wasn't even making sense to myself a lot of the time. You probably thought I was a babbling idiot.' He peered at Teschmaker. 'I can't say that I remember you as a child, but from what Jane has said you appear to have turned out all right.'

'Really? I gained the impression that Jane saw me as a meddling pain in the arse.'

'Somehow I think that marrying Oliver Sinclair has made her a bit wary and certainly sharpened her tongue. Nevertheless, we are in rather a nasty bind now that Rusak has my granddaughter, Melanie. You know, I've never seen her.' The old man lapsed into silence, sipping his drink and looking at Teschmaker as though waiting for a solution to his problems.

Teschmaker topped up his glass and came back to his chair. 'I don't really understand what's going on. But from what I can piece together, Rusak is after information from you about something you were involved with back in the Soviet Union. If I knew what that was, then maybe we could come up with a way of dealing with him.'

'I'm afraid I can't help. You see, it's not a matter of my memory; I simply don't have the information he wants.'

'So why does Rusak think you do?'

Sydney Morris put down his glass and pulled the dressing gown tighter. 'When Rusak bought his way into the Duma he came across some information that related to KGB activities during the Cold War. Rusak has a well-developed nose for opportunities and, sensing that the information could be worth a lot, used his position to gain access to files of the personnel involved. After he left the Duma, he removed the files and set about tracing the people. I was the only one still alive. He refused to believe that I didn't know what he wanted, and still does.'

Sydney Morris paused as they both heard the door to Jane's bedroom open.

For a moment Jane stood in the doorway, watching the two men sitting in the darkened room, then came over and sat beside her father. She avoided looking at Teschmaker but even in the dim light he could tell that she had been crying.

Sydney patted her knee affectionately and then continued. 'I had worked on a very sensitive project and though it was unusual for the science people to have any knowledge, let alone contact, with the operational teams, the technical problems necessitated my being involved in briefing and training. I spent several months with these people and became very fond of them and so when Rusak told me that they were all dead, I was devastated. Alberto Garcia, Jacob Sedov, Marcia Zanda, Guy Greenglass, Georg Bella, Andrei Yakunin, Hugh Cowgill. All dead.'

'The dead gardeners,' Teschmaker said quietly. '*Sadovnik*.'

Sydney Morris peered at him suspiciously. 'Who told you that word?'

'You did. The first time I came to see you. Whatever they had given you must have been doing something because you mentioned the names of the saboteurs.'

'Maybe I wasn't as in control as I thought.' There was a momentary look of confusion on his face. 'What else did I say?'

'You didn't seem to make any sense at the time, but along with the gardeners, you did talk about the lilies, the bouquet and the little flower or *tsvetok*.' He sensed Sydney Morris suddenly stiffen. Jane also picked up on the mood change and looked directly at Teschmaker for the first time since she had come into the room.

'Hearing the words is one thing, Mr Teschmaker, but I'm wondering how you come to know what those words signify.' The previously soft tone had evaporated in the face of the old man's sudden suspicion, to be replaced by an abrupt terseness.

'I went out tonight and spoke with a Russian friend, a man who has studied these things all his life. He explained to me about the DRGs, the sabotage teams, and the code they used. Relax, I'm on the side of the angels.'

'Are you?' Sydney Morris looked as though he was far from convinced. 'I suppose I really don't have any choice but to trust you. Jane does and so that will have to suffice.'

Teschmaker looked at Jane but she had gone back to assiduously avoiding his eyes.

Sydney Morris took his daughter's hand and decided to continue. 'After I had trained the teams they were dispatched to the target countries, and once they had set up bases the devices were delivered to them. It was the lowest point of my life. The only way I could deal with it was to believe that the devices were simply a deterrent and would never actually be detonated. I understood that I would never see the people I had trained again, but I thought that was because our paths would never cross. But when Rusak told me . . .'

His voice choked and he reached for his glass. He gulped at the scotch and turned to Jane. 'It was as if I had killed them. I had no idea . . .' He stopped as he struggled with the memory. 'I knew I hadn't killed them, but I felt responsible. From what I now understand, it seems that once they had put the device in place they were killed so that the exact locations were known only to very few people at Moscow Centre. As the years went by I took some comfort in the thought that my original belief was right and not one of the devices would ever be detonated. Then in 1997 General Lebed told the world that we had lost track of a large number of them. It had been so long since they were planted that most observers were sceptical about Lebed's comments, doubting that the weapons ever existed. It was an understandable reaction, but I knew he was telling the truth. And in fact I was relieved, because if there was nobody left alive who knew where the devices were, then at least my team's deaths had achieved something. In the larger scheme of things, it was arguably a small price to pay for the fact that the devices could never be detonated or fall into the wrong hands. However, Rusak is a very determined man. He believes that if he can get his hands on one of these devices he could sell it for millions. Fortunately, I don't know where any of them are.'

Teschmaker could hardly believe what he was hearing. He recalled the fuss over General Lebed's comments, but also remembered how quickly the issue had been dismissed. 'Sydney, are you saying that you worked on the nuclear suitcase bombs?'

'Suitcase . . . I wish that people wouldn't call them that. I was good at my work, but nobody could make one that small. The devices I designed were about the size of one of those old-fashioned trunks that people used to travel with.'

'But we *are* talking about nuclear explosives?'

'One kiloton.'

'And they're planted in different countries around the world?'

Sydney nodded. 'I wasn't briefed on the politics, but it seemed clear that they were to serve a double purpose. Threat in the first place, and if that was not enough they could be used as an extreme means of sabotage if the need arose.'

Teschmaker tried to remember what he had read about the devices. The Chechen leaders had claimed to have possession of two of the missing bombs, and he vaguely remembered a claim by the Palestinians of having found several, but neither claim had ever been substantiated or, in fact, given much credence. They were probably bluffing. Then he remembered something else he had read.

'Sydney, suppose Rusak did locate one, would it still function? I thought one of Yeltsin's advisors had said something about the half-life of some of the materials being a factor?'

'The tritium? No, that story surfaced later. The man you're referring to is Alexei Yablokov, who used to be Yeltsin's science advisor. He validated the existence of the bombs but the Russian military went on the defensive, denied their existence and then claimed that if they existed at all they would be dangerous because of deterioration.'

'And?' Teschmaker prompted.

'Nobody knows. As the core decays, a slight amount of americium contamination is created, but it tends to stabilise the plutonium rather than seriously impact its explosive power. Storage and retrieval of the weapons would be hazardous because of accumulating radioactive helium gas, but really it would be in such minute quantities that it would matter little. All of which means nothing in terms of a terrorist's use of the weapons. I think the issue was raised as a ploy to deter anyone who had one from using it.'

'And if they did? What kind of destruction would it cause?'

'One kiloton?' The old man sipped his drink and then shut his eyes as if savouring the flavour. 'It would destroy a major inner-city area. Huge loss of life and, because they were not built to be clean, massive radioactive contamination. But the point is that if one should fall into the hands of a terrorist group or one of the Russian fascist organisations, they don't actually have to detonate it. The threat alone would be sufficient.'

Teschmaker looked at the old man in the pyjamas and dressing gown, glass of scotch in one hand, the other clasping his daughter's hand — it was hardly an image anyone would associate with the designer of the weapons they were discussing. 'Why in God's name did you make them, Sydney?'

'Intellectual pride,' Sydney answered, with only a momentary hesitation. 'Because they told me it was impossible to create a reaction with such small amounts of material. I had been working at Krasnoyarsk-45 on another project and in my spare time was struggling with the theory of miniaturisation. It was almost a hobby, until one day I heard that all work in that area had been discontinued because it was deemed to be impossible below a certain limit. I worked up my theory and presented it, and a couple of months later I was transferred to the design laboratories at Chelyabinsk-70.'

Teschmaker noticed the sudden animation in Sydney's voice. Despite what he was describing, the old man was obviously proud of his achievements. For her part, Jane was looking at her father with a mixture of bemusement and horror. Teschmaker thought of interrupting Sydney but he was in full flight, reliving what he clearly saw as his scientific triumph.

'The brief was to come up with something that Soviet Army Intelligence Units, the GRU, could transport with relative ease. Much of the preliminary work had been done but it had hit a brick wall. Finally my team came up with a device that was a mere 60 x 40 x 20 centimetres. We worked from the premise that the smallest possible object would be a single critical mass of plutonium, or U-233. An unreflected spherical alpha-phase critical mass of Pu-239 weighs 10.5 kilograms and is 10.1 centimetres across. But of course a single critical mass cannot cause an explosion because there is no fission multiplication. But as little as ten per cent more can produce explosions of ten to twenty tons.'

Teschmaker was struggling to keep up. 'But isn't that a reasonably small yield?'

'Of course, but far more dangerous than conventional weapons because of the intense radiation emitted. A twenty-ton fission explosion, for example, produces a very dangerous 500 rem radiation exposure at 400 metres from burst point, and a hundred per cent lethal 1350 rem exposure at 300 metres. But we were going bigger than that anyway. But that wasn't the point of what I was trying to do.' Sydney waved his hand at Teschmaker, indicating that he didn't want any further interruptions. 'Listen. The whole concept of critical mass is dependent on the density of the fissile material and the type of neutron reflector. High explosive implosion can compress fissile material to greater density, thus reducing the critical mass. A neutron reflector reduces neutron loss and reduces the critical mass at a constant density. But in all the previous experiments they'd found that adding explosives or neutron reflectors to the core added much more mass to the system than it saved. My idea was to use a thin beryllium reflector, and I was able to show that with one of even a few centimetres thickness, the radius of a plutonium core was reduced by forty to sixty per cent of the reflector thickness. There was a limit of course, and a point at which increasing the thickness of the reflector began to add more mass than it saved. But we had the problem beaten. With all the components — plutonium, beryllium reflector, high explosive and triggering system — we had a package below fifteen kilograms.' Sydney stopped and looked at Jane, his face flushed. 'Two years it took, but I did it.'

'Why?' she whispered. 'Why would you do such a thing?'

'Because it was possible. I didn't think it would ever be used.'

'You must have known . . .' Teschmaker began.

'How could I? I existed in a laboratory with other scientists, we were excited by the research . . .' He faltered. 'Later, much later, when I was given the job of showing the teams how to assemble and arm the devices, then I was concerned. But I was still convinced that they would never be used, except as a threat.' He took Jane's hand again. 'I know I was wrong.'

'How could you do it?' She removed her hand, her lips pursed tight in disgust. 'You, who knew better than anyone what devastation it could cause.'

Her father just sipped at his drink, his hands shaking gently.

'So you don't know where they are?' Teschmaker asked.

Sydney shook his head.

'Then we have nothing to offer in return for Melanie.' Jane's voice was flat and lifeless. The last vestige of hope gone.

But Teschmaker wasn't ready to give up. 'Rusak must have been sure you knew, otherwise he wouldn't have spent so much time tracking you down. And why bring you here? Was that just because he thought threatening Jane would make you talk?'

The old man thought about it for a moment then held out his glass for a refill. 'It didn't take too much intelligence to look at the make-up of the teams and then deduce where the likely targets were. America, of course, probably California, New York, Texas, Montana and Minnesota. Paris, London, Geneva and Brussels.' He paused again, as though struggling to bring himself to keep going.

'And?' Jane prompted.

'Well, I suppose you should know. They have one of the devices planted here.' He sat back in his chair, his head tilted back, his eyes peering up into the gloom.

'But that doesn't make any sense,' Teschmaker protested. 'This city isn't important. It's certainly never been home to anything of remotely strategic or military significance.'

'No? Then let me tell you you're wrong. The very first of the devices was sent here and Rusak knows it. He told me that it had been done to ensure my loyalty, but he was wrong about that. They knew they had my cooperation. My understanding is that if they ever needed to demonstrate to the West that they had such capabilities, then although a detonation here would be horrific, it would be far less provocative than an explosion in upstate New York, say.'

'Then why not tell Rusak where the damn thing is and let him take it away?' Jane's eyes were blazing and she got up from her seat, unable to contain her fury. 'You leave it here and we are all at risk —'

'And he takes it away and sells it to the Russian fascists or a terrorist group?' Sydney sat forward and looked at her. 'Jane, the simple truth is, I don't know where it is. It is so small, and anyway, without the remote detonator it is worthless.'

'Surely a remote would be relatively simple to make?' Teschmaker asked.

'Oh for God's sake, drop it! Give it up, Teschmaker. Can't you see it's over?' Jane looked totally exhausted, her hands folded tightly across her chest as though trying to keep in her remaining energy.

But Sydney shook his head. 'Each one is coded and sequenced in such a way that only the designated remote can trigger it. The remote control boxes were to be cached separately so even if I knew where the device was . . .' He collected himself and struggled to his feet. 'I'm truly sorry, I can't tell you any more. I have to sleep now.' And without another word he ambled back into the bedroom and shut the door.

Teschmaker watched him go, wondering bitterly how the man could live with himself. Or how he could sleep, knowing what he had unleashed all those years ago. Certainly he could never have anticipated that it would manifest itself in such a direct way — here, with his daughter and grandchild.

Behind him he heard Jane exhale loudly as though she had been holding her breath. Teschmaker reached out and gently touched her arm. But she didn't react, instead moving away from him to the cabinet.

'It's a nightmare.' Jane shuddered and poured herself a scotch. 'I want to hate him so much, but I can't. All those years spent wanting him to appear again — but not like this.' Nursing her drink she went through to her bedroom and returned with a blanket and a pillow. 'I gave your bed to my father. But you should be all right on the settee.' She placed the bedding down and turned to go.

'Jane, I'm sorry about before —'

But she cut him off with a wave of her hand. 'Forget

it. I'm stressed out of my mind about Mel, and when they told me they'd killed someone it hit me just how out of control this mess has become. I blame myself. I thought I knew what I was doing and that I would be able to pull out. But that was when it was just a nasty fight with Oliver. Now I realise how deep in the shit I've put us all.'

'You shouldn't blame yourself,' Teschmaker began lamely.

'She's my daughter, Teschmaker. My daughter.'

'We'll figure something out.' He tried to sound confident but knew even as he said it that confidence was a foreign language to her in this moment.

Jane shrugged and went to her room.

Teschmaker finished his drink and went through to the kitchen to wash the glass. His foot crunched a piece of broken crockery. In the morning, he told himself. I'll clean up in the morning. Back in the lounge he stretched out on the couch and pulled the blanket up over himself.

For what felt like a long time he lay unable to sleep, his mind going over and over Sydney Morris's horrific story, trying to understand the kind of person who could justify such experiments as a theoretical challenge. It was incomprehensible to him that anyone could engage in such work without confronting insurmountable ethical problems. And actually teaching the teams how to arm these devices . . .? It was years ago, and the times were different, he rationalised unconvincingly. He tried to imagine the Cold War mind-set, the fear and paranoia that must have infected those who had worked in the closed cities, whose only view of the world was shaped by Soviet propaganda. Could he, in the same situation as Sydney Morris, have done what Morris did? The answer, he had to admit, was yes.

Finally he drifted off to sleep, his head still filled with troubled images. Huge cold steel walls pressed in on him. Grey shapes, phantoms in dark uniforms, watched. And somewhere, always out of reach, a solid shape, a trunk, that Teschmaker knew he must open even if to do so meant death. Voices called to him. Hands, rising above thick swirling mist, reached out for help, but he was unable to save them. More voices, softer now, both distant and near, telling him to turn back. But he couldn't move. The mist solidified around his legs and ankles and sent a numbing cold up towards his heart. He began to sink and knew as he did so that the mist was poison waiting to claim him. Below, his legs corroding, flesh dry and dead, flaking away to reveal bones bleached and white. Long dead. Another voice, pleading. Somewhere a scream descending into darkness. Black ice replaced the steel and deep within it he could see the faces of the dead contorted with pain and terror. Eyes frozen open. He looked around and in every direction stretched a vast plain of black ice. Not all the bodies were yet encased and from the ice, as from the mist before, a limb, an arm, a hand reached up, striving to evade the inevitable. The air itself was beginning to freeze and he held his breath, knowing that if he allowed such cold inside he would succumb, his throat and lungs crystallising, shattering. He called out — the sound became mist, poison. And he realised that as he sank he too would become part of this dark vaporous world. The voice again, closer. The hand that reached out not grey and lifeless but warm. Alive. And all he had to do was open his eyes and he would be free of the nightmare.

'Will you stay with me?' The hand reached out and tentatively touched his arm. Jane.

She was standing beside the couch in a plain white nightgown, her face wet with tears.

'Just for a while? Please?'

Teschmaker took her outstretched hand. It felt so warm. He followed her back to her room and, still fully dressed, lay down on the bed beside her. She rolled into his arms and clung to him as she let herself surrender to the pain and fear, her body racked by the sobs that arose from deep within. She buried her face in his neck and let them come, long low keening sounds. Animal sounds.

For a long time they lay like that, until eventually the sobbing subsided. But still she held him. Then Teschmaker felt her fingers, which had been digging so deeply into him, relax. She still held on to him but more gently now. Her fingers moved to his shirt. 'Martin, please? I want to.' And so did he. They undressed each other with care, as if both were carrying wounds that they feared to touch. She slid underneath him and guided him into her and quietly they nourished each other.

Later Teschmaker looked back on it and knew it was the most enfolded he had ever felt. For Jane too it was both reassurance and comfort. And having been replenished and comforted they began again and let themselves expand into the more familiar realm of pleasure. But they kept to softness, taking their time as though it were fragile or ephemeral, as insubstantial as an oil slick on water, swirling peacock colours that could vanish with the slightest ruffling of the calm.

Then, as she snuggled into his side, she started to talk, her voice only a whisper louder than her breathing.

'The sad thing is, I loved him so unconditionally and yet I never knew him. The father I loved so much was my own creation. I took the void that he left and filled it with my imagination. My mother had a photo album which I'd never seen her look at, and which she certainly never showed me. When I discovered it, I took it to my room and sat up late into the night studying the old photographs she had collected. They were all black and white, some quite faded, others creased and torn as though they had been rescued from an older album. They were held in place by those funny little corner things that had to be licked and stuck on the page. I remember there was one picture that I liked particularly. He and a friend were leaning against the mudguards of a chunky sports car. Their trousers were baggy and they wore short-sleeved shirts, open at the neck. I used to imagine that it was the car he had driven off in, and that one day he would return in it.

'There were other ones I liked, of him with Mum and me. But I remember thinking that those photos looked posed, as if the presence of the camera had stiffened us all. At the back of the album I found the only really candid shot. It was darker than the others, grainy, taken on a train station. My father had been at the ticket window and whoever had the camera must have called to him, for he was caught looking over his shoulder. It was the eyes. In that photo his eyes seemed cold and cruel.

'My mother must have noticed that I had my light on and came into my room and found me with the album. At first she looked as though she was going to be angry, but she just took the album away and I never saw it again. I searched the house and eventually confronted her about it and she pretended she'd misplaced it.

'As I went to sleep each night I would conjure up the image of my father standing in front of the sports car and dream that he was going to take me with him. Then after a few months I couldn't remember his face any more and I asked Mum for a photograph. We had a huge fight about it. She told me that the men who were looking for my father had taken all the photographs, but I refused to believe her. I'm not really sure what happened to them but there was never a picture of my father in the house again. So from then on I created my father from all the things I was missing. Whenever I liked something in someone — you know, an attribute or personality trait — I added it to this composite I was building. And, though I didn't sense it at the time, I started gravitating towards older men. My first real lover, when I was only eighteen, was thirty-six. He was married of course, but he had a sports car and he treated me like a daughter. When it was over I thought it was the end of the world and I blamed myself. If I'd been better he would have left his wife. If I wasn't such a clumsy lover he would have stayed with me. I was so confused by this discovery of passion and heartache that I didn't learn from it at all. In fact I repeated the same mistakes with all my boyfriends. In the end I became infatuated with one of my lecturers at university and I threw myself into my studies simply to impress him. It had no effect at all on the poor man. I doubt he knew why my work improved so dramatically. He certainly didn't know he was the main character in my masturbation fantasies. When it finally dawned on me that he was never going to respond I took refuge by going even further into my work.

'I graduated with first class honours and after the run-in with Foreign Affairs I told you about, I found out the truth about my father's disappearance. I was shattered but again threw myself into work and further study. I promised myself I would have nothing further to do with men and for almost two years it was true. Then I had an affair with a younger man, which was a weird experience for me. I'd never been on the receiving end of such unbridled adoration. He was nice enough in a gauche way. He took me dancing and he had a motorbike which I really enjoyed riding on. So I was having a good time. The affair had been going on for about a month when I was invited to give a paper to a business conference on the investment possibilities that might emerge from the former Soviet republics. I knew it was a great opportunity for me to advance my career and so I put everything else aside and spent weeks preparing. I called my presentation "Kalashnikov Confederalism and the fragmenting of the Russian Federation" and by all accounts it was a success. There was a cocktail party after my session and though I usually avoided them like the plague, I had an hour before my boyfriend could pick me up and so I went.

'I didn't notice the man straight away. It wasn't some bolt out of the blue or a cocktail-hour flirtation. I was talking to one of the other academics when I noticed him glance over his shoulder at me. I'd never seen him before. He appeared to be in his forties and there was something about him that made him an unlikely person to be attending such a conference. He was dressed casually, coloured shirt and rather crumpled linen jacket. He turned away and I remember thinking that I'd never seen such a handsome man in my life. He vanished into the crowd and for a few minutes I didn't see him again. Then I noticed he was talking to somebody by the door. I had more time to study him and on taking a second look I realised he wasn't as good looking as I'd first thought. But there was something. Then I felt this shiver go through me and my stomach churned. It was his eyes. He had the cruellest eyes — the same eyes I remembered from the photograph of my father.

'I was thrown into turmoil and tried to convince myself that it was simply because I'd drunk too much. I had been talking with someone and so I excused myself and went to the bathroom and washed my face. I recall standing there trembling in front of a mirror and rubbing off every bit of make-up. I have no idea why, other than I was scared of this man. I collected my coat and left the party straight away. As I came out on the street I saw my boyfriend leaning against his motorbike on the opposite side of the road. He waved his hand at me and started to put on his helmet. Then just a few yards along the road I saw the older man. He was standing, holding open the rear door of his car. His eyes were fixed on me but he didn't gesture or say anything. He simply stood there and waited. Without thinking I walked over and got in. There was a click as the door shut and then he went around and got in the other rear door. There was a glass partition between us and a uniformed driver. The man leaned forward and rapped on the glass and we drove off without a word being spoken. I half expected to see my boyfriend ride up alongside on his motorbike, but he didn't. I can't remember what was going through my mind other than my determination not to say a word until this man spoke. But he didn't.

'After what seemed like a long time we drove up to some high steel gates which opened as we approached. There was a short avenue of trees and then the car stopped in front of a large house. The driver got out quickly and opened the door for me and I followed the man up the steps. I have a vague recollection of someone opening the door for us, but all my attention was on the man. Not once did he hesitate or pause to see if I was following. He seemed absolutely confident that I would follow. And I, though my mind was racing with questions, obstinately stuck to my vow not to break the silence between us.

'There was a flight of stairs at the other side of a small entrance hall and he went straight up. As I followed I heard the door shut behind me, and for a second I had a rush of panic. Then I remembered those eyes and I knew that I was going to climb those stairs no matter what lay in store for me. The room we entered was obviously *his* bedroom. It had a distinctly male feeling about it. There was a jumper tossed over a chair, a pair of shoes beside a cupboard. I tried not to look at the bed, but I was damned if I was going to show this man what I was feeling. There was only a small amount of light coming in from the landing and I stood and watched as he walked to the other side of the bed and switched on a small bedside light. He'll have to talk now, I thought triumphantly. But he didn't and neither did he approach me and attempt to touch me or undress me. Instead he pulled back the bedcovers and fixing me with his eyes started to undress.

'I hesitated again, then cursed myself for doing so. I suddenly knew the rules of the game, although it was not one I had ever played or even imagined. So I locked my eyes with his and took off my coat. It's funny, the strange moments that stick in your memory. But I have this image of myself then, removing not my skirt or shoes but my watch. I unclasped it carefully and laid it gently on the bedside table, as though I was staking my claim to a piece of territory. From the other side of the bed he watched me and continued undressing. Then, when he was naked, he pulled back the top-sheet and slid into the bed, not once taking his eyes off me. I removed the rest of my clothes and slid into the bed beside him . . . and there was a beat, a second, when there was no movement and no sound. We were both holding our breath.

'We made love three times that night, neither of us breaking the silence, even to cry out in ecstasy. That enforced silence gave a piquancy and dangerous edge to each moment that was so sweet I swear I was prepared never to talk again. Eventually we slept and in the morning I awoke to find that he had gone. There was a card on the table beside my watch saying that there was breakfast downstairs and his driver would take me anywhere I liked. Just above his signature was a telephone number and the words "call me".

'I nearly fell for it. So many times over the next week I found myself with the phone in my hand, but each time I forced myself to put it down. And each time the phone rang I waited until the caller spoke before I responded. Eight days later, I was running late for an appointment when the phone rang. I picked it up and listened. Then I heard a man's voice saying, "It's Oliver. I really want to see you." We were married one month later.'

CHAPTER NINETEEN

Jane had forgotten to close the shutters on the bedroom window and the first light brought Teschmaker out of a night of restless sleep. A sleep disturbed by the unaccustomed presence of another person in the bed. For a long time Jane had clung to him then, as sleep came, she had rolled on her side, fitting her back against him. It was a delicious sensation, and yet he remained tense, not wanting to trade the pleasure of her body for his normal habit of sleeping facing in the other direction. At times he knew he was asleep, at others he wasn't certain if it was sleep or the dream of sleep. But each time Jane stirred Teschmaker awoke and placed the palm of his hand against her, for his own pleasure as much as in an attempt to ease the fitfulness he felt radiating from her.

As the darkness receded he lay looking out towards the buildings, waiting for them to take shape, but it was a morning covered with mist. In the early hours a bank of fog had rolled in from the coast and merged with the mist rising from the river and the lake, blanketing the city, blotting out the hard edges of the office blocks and towers. Teschmaker lay for a long time, watching as the fog gradually lifted and the sun appeared, weak and pallid behind high cloud. When he turned to look at Jane he found that she was lying with her eyes wide open, watching him.

'Have you been awake long?' he asked.

'Long enough to know that last night wasn't a mistake.' Her smile was sleepy and she yawned before reaching out and touching his face with the tips of her fingers. 'You?'

'What? How long have I been awake? Or do I think last night was a mistake?'

'Either.' She propped herself up on her elbows and looked down at him. 'Go on, I dare you. Tell me last night was a mistake.'

Teschmaker laughed and pulled her head down onto his chest. 'You're right. A dreadful mistake. We should have done that years ago.'

'We did everything but that.'

'We were kids . . .'

'Molester.' Jane pulled at the hair on his chest. 'I'm sure you were taking advantage of me.'

'Nonsense! Girls are much more mature at that age.' He took her head in his hands and lifted it up so he could look into her eyes. 'You were the one who corrupted me. I remember you putting my hand on your breasts.'

'I didn't have any,' she protested. 'And anyway, it was you who kissed me first.'

Teschmaker craned forward and kissed the top of her head. They lay in silence for a while and then Jane asked quietly, 'Did you ever think we would meet again?'

'Not really. I thought about you from time to time. I kept a photo taken at your birthday party. What about you?'

'It sounds terrible but I guess I'd almost forgotten about you. Once when Oliver tried to get me interested in some silly game, billiards or snooker or something, he asked me if I knew anything about it and all I could remember was that time we met in the pub when I was at university.'

'We played pool.'

'The only thing I could recall was you saying something about not putting the white ball into the side pocket. Remember?'

'Vaguely.'

'Apart from that I guess I never thought about you. Does that sound mean?'

'No. It sounds truthful.'

'Anyway . . .'

'We're here now.'

There was silence for a while. Each of them immersed in their own memories.

'Jane?'

'Mmm?'

'I need to ask . . .' Teschmaker avoided looking at her. 'You had a lover?'

'When?'

He knew by the suddenly alert tone that it was true. 'Since you were married. You wrote letters —'

'Who told you?' Jane sat up and moved away from him.

'Does it matter? I just wondered . . .'

'What? If he's still in the picture? No, Teschmaker, Oliver bought him off. The man gave him some letters I wrote.' Her tone was suddenly bitter. 'Oliver was going to produce them in court to prove what a slut I was.'

'Oliver — prove you a slut?' Teschmaker couldn't suppress the laugh. 'And a judge would take his word for it?'

'You think judges don't have a price too?'

Later they cleaned up the kitchen and took tea and toast through to Jane's father. He too looked as though he had not slept well; the trembling of his hands was markedly worse and he seemed irritable with none of the remarkable clarity he had displayed the previous evening. It was as though the effort required to explain his past had drained him, leaving him listless and distracted.

They left him to eat and took their breakfast out onto the balcony. The earlier mood of intimacy seemed to have vanished with the mist, and though the morning was now bright and clear it served only to contrast the mood of despondency that had settled on them. It was as though for a few brief hours they had escaped the context of their meeting into a small oasis, which in the night had seemed larger and safer than where they now found themselves. Jane's fleeting moments of levity were gone and she had retreated into her fears for her daughter.

For his part, Teschmaker found himself running and re-running the events of the last few days through his head. It felt hopeless. It was like turning a shapeless piece of ore over and over in his hands, running his fingers across the surface, looking for the one flaw where he could chip away and reveal some crystalline structure inside that would tell him what it was he held. And all the time he knew that he had no answers. But something was niggling at him and he knew he had to move, if only to give Jane some space.

'Can I take the car for a little while?'

She nodded distractedly. 'Sure, help yourself. The keys are on the kitchen bench.'

'What will you do?' he asked as he got up.

'What can I do?'

He had no answer so he kissed her gently and took the breakfast plates inside. He put them on the bench and left them. After a quick shave and a shower he said goodbye to Jane and went down to the car. As he emerged from the car park he looked around for Gerard Edwards, but if he was still on duty he was keeping well out of sight.

Teschmaker drove slowly around the city without any clear destination in mind. Sometime during the previous night, as he had struggled to put the pieces together, he had thought about the jigsaw pieces, the ones from Manolescu's painting, that he still retained back at his house. His fascination with them hadn't been about how the pieces could be put together, but rather the way in which the whole had become many parts. How it was possible to take a handful of the pieces and see that none of them appeared to have any relationship to the others. Yet in the night he had sensed connections between the pieces of the puzzle that now confronted him. Not between the stark, easily identifiable pieces that Sydney Morris had contributed, or the dark shapes of Rusak or Francis Grice, but somewhere else. Allowing his instincts to dictate his movement, he shifted lanes and headed out of the city. He needed space and he needed to walk.

He found that he was heading in the direction of Freeholm cemetery. It wasn't a high priority but he did want to take a quick look at the grave which Shlyapnikov had always led him to believe was that of his son. The old man would be mortified to know his wife had given away his secret, and the fact that he was unable to provide her with a child. And to lose a child that he had treated as his own — how must that have affected him? Having not had children, and never having wanted to have them with Gwenda, Teschmaker knew he was in a poor position to guess, but the way Shlyapnikov had so faithfully paid his respects to the dead young man suggested that his death had moved him deeply. He had also, Teschmaker remembered wryly, been overly protective about the grave itself.

The car park at Freeholm was crowded but he found himself a slot. He sat for a moment watching the double gates being opened for a hearse to enter the road into the grounds of the cemetery. Behind it a dozen or so people followed, walking slowly, heads bowed with grief. Out of the corner of his eye he saw the two old women in black hurry out from the kiosk and attach themselves to the rear of the procession.

They were the same women he had noticed on his last visit. Death groupies, he thought morbidly. But then, why not? The trip through the cemetery gates was the one thing they all had in common, the defining difference being the way you travelled — the living on foot and the dead with the luxury of being carried.

He climbed out of the car and set off towards the gates. For a couple of hundred metres he followed the road that the funeral procession had taken then turned left, crossing the small wooden footbridge over the Charlotte River. His memory of this part of the cemetery was of leafy shadows, but there had been extensive clearing and on either side of the path the only vegetation comprised young well-mulched saplings. A little further on he saw the reason why. Several workmen were busy cutting back the willows along the bank. They had been planted in the early days to stabilise the swampy terrain, but over the years their roots had reached out, threatening not only to choke the river but also invading the graves in search of the rich nutrients provided by decomposing bodies.

Over the other side of the bridge Teschmaker followed a gravel path to the section of the cemetery he had visited with Shlyapnikov. Here the trees were older and the morning light dappled the path with shafts filtered through birch and alder.

He rounded a corner and stopped. About fifty yards ahead of him was the slightly stooped figure of Shlyapnikov. The Russian was making his way slowly along the path, pausing every now and then to examine the graves to his right. For a moment Teschmaker thought the man's memory must be failing him, that he was having trouble remembering where the young man's grave was. But then he saw him stop in front of the overgrown grave with its distinctive purple headstone. Teschmaker decided not to interrupt the old Russian's moment of communion and moved off the path into the shade of one of the large trees. For a second he thought the old man must have sensed him, for he turned around and peered back down the path. But, having satisfied himself that he was alone, Shlyapnikov walked on, counting the graves as he went.

Teschmaker moved a little closer, but although he felt rather foolish spying on his friend, he remained out of sight. He found a good vantage point in the shadows behind a large family mausoleum and watched as the old man left the path and walked around the side of another grave. He eased himself down to sit on the concrete edging and checking again that there was nobody else in the vicinity, took out cigarette and lit it. For several minutes he sat smoking, gazing up into the branches, watching the beams of light cut through the smoke hanging in the still air.

His friend's behaviour struck Teschmaker as odd. It was almost as though the old man was ignoring the grave he usually visited, and he wasn't carrying his usual bunch of flowers. Maybe this was a result of the conversation with Zoya Nikolayevna the previous evening. Perhaps she had raised the issue of Shlyapnikov's fixation with the young man whom he had treated like a son. Teschmaker realised the speculation was getting him nowhere and was contemplating whether to go and speak to Shlyapnikov when the old man ground out the remains of his cigarette on the concrete, got to his feet and walked off down the path.

Teschmaker waited until Shlyapnikov was out of sight before he stepped out from behind the mausoleum and, returning to the main path, made his way to the young Russian's grave. Stepping over the low iron fence he crouched down in front of the marble headstone and brushed the grass to one side, revealing a name carved deeply into the stone. Grigori Vasilyevich Puzanov. Just below the name, preserved in glass, was a photograph of a young man in his early thirties. The face that looked out at Teschmaker was strikingly handsome. Blond hair combed back from a high forehead, the eyes direct and intense, the generous mouth shut firmly showing just the hint of a smile. So this was the 'almost son' — the promising young man who had ended so badly despite Shlyapnikov's best endeavours. He sensed that the old man must have had a strong emotional investment in Grigori Vasilyevich and been heartbroken by his tragic death.

Teschmaker had no idea of what he had hoped to achieve by visiting the grave, and for a few minutes the coincidence of running into Shlyapnikov had heightened his expectations. But it was, in every sense, a dead end.

Pushing the grass back in place, he stepped out of the grave site and retraced his path. By the time he got back to his car the car park was almost empty and the double gates locked. The hearse and the mourners had left, but as he unlocked the car door he saw the black crows, the two old women, returning to the kiosk. Obviously there were perks to being a funeral groupie — both of them were carrying fresh bunches of flowers and Teschmaker wondered how much the owner of the kiosk paid them for their recycling efforts. He glanced at his watch. It was just after midday. The best thing would be to go back and see if Jane had any news. But then he had an idea; a long shot, but worth checking out. He got out of the car again and went over to the public phone at the kiosk. The man he called was uncertain if he could fulfil Teschmaker's request but promised he would try. He asked for the number of the public phone and undertook to call back within the hour.

Deciding that he might as well eat lunch while he waited, Teschmaker seated himself at a table at the kiosk and ordered some food. A couple of tables away, the two black crows were spending the proceeds of their morning's flower gathering. They were sharing a huge banana split.

Jane helped her father shower and then, after ducking out to the newsagency, set him up on the balcony with a coffee and the morning papers. Next she rang Oliver but he had nothing new to offer. Feeling despondent she sat with her father for a while, her mind vacillating between her fears for Melanie and the unexpected comfort of the previous night's memories. There had been no intention on her part of inviting Teschmaker into her bed, the event surprising her as much as him. And equally surprising, she thought, was the ease with which it had happened. For so long sex had been combative or a one-sided affair, but with Teschmaker she had felt herself melt in a way she had not thought

446

herself capable of. For a moment she censured herself. How could she have done such a thing while her daughter was in danger? But even as she thought it, she knew she had been emotionally drained and had needed the physical intimacy simply to keep going. But it had been more than that. Given another time, other circumstances, she would have been excited at the prospect of starting an affair with Teschmaker. But this was not another time.

After lunch Sydney retired to bed and Jane set about tidying up. She had just loaded the dishwasher when she was startled by a sharp knocking on the door. She approached it cautiously. 'Who is it?'

'Gerard Edwards,' came the muffled voice.

Jane opened the door to find Gerard flanked by Norman and Viola. 'The three wise men?'

'Something like that.' Gerard shrugged.

'Absolutely,' Norman added and ushered Viola in ahead of him.

'I can't thank you enough for last night. Unfortunately my father has just gone back to bed, otherwise he would thank you himself.' She gestured to the couch, indicating that they should sit, but Edwards shook his head.

'You thanked us last night, Mrs Oliver —'

'Please, I'd rather you called me Jane.'

'Okay. Jane it is. Look, we just called in because I thought you should know that we think we have an idea —'

'It was Viola who thought of it,' Norman beamed.

Edwards shot him a dark look and continued. 'We think we might know where your daughter is.'

'Oh God!' Jane's face lit up. 'Where? Where do you think she is?'

'I think that she may be staying with Master Francis,' Viola began hesitantly.

'Francis Grice? Oh God, I hope she's all right.' Jane had no illusions about the kind of man Grice was and the idea that he should have anything to do with Melanie filled her with dismay. Her mind was suddenly a confusion of competing thoughts: the intense maternal instincts wanting to know where her daughter was, but the same instincts revolting against the memories she had of Francis Grice. If he had so much as laid a hand on Mel she would kill him. She looked desperately at the men. 'What makes you think that bastard has her?'

Edwards raised his hands. 'Jane, please. It's only a possibility. But it's the best one we have at the moment.'

'But why Grice?'

'Grice has a small cell in his house —' Edwards began.

'And the bastard kept Viola locked in there,' Norman interjected. 'He reckons it would be the ideal place to keep Melanie, don't you?'

Viola nodded. 'I'm afraid it's not a very nice place . . .'

Edwards shook his head. 'Let's not worry Mrs Oliver more than necessary, shall we? It is an outside chance, but we felt we should tell you . . .'

'We have to get her now.'

Edwards had anticipated that Jane would want to come along and had prepared several reasons why it was not a good idea, but Jane's peremptory tone signalled that she wasn't about to listen to anything he had to say. He had grilled Viola about the layout of Grice's house and though he had a deep-seated distrust of working with amateurs, he had to concede Viola's point that he would be able to get them in without necessitating the use of a sledgehammer. Grice may be a twisted individual, but he hardly constituted a threat to professionals with their training and experience. And if Viola was coming, then there was hardly a case for attempting to dissuade Jane. 'Fine. Then we should get going.'

Downstairs they piled into Gerard's Mercedes, still minus the wing mirror. It was not a long journey to Lakeside and they drove in silence.

Jane, in the back seat with Viola, was extremely agitated, too choked with emotion to think coherently, desperate to find her daughter and fearful of what might have happened to her. It was like driving to the scene of an accident, she thought, when all you know is that there has been an accident but have no details of how bad the injuries are.

'Next street on the left,' Viola said quietly.

Jane sensed that, for his own reasons, he was almost as nervous as she was. She leaned over and touched his arm. 'It'll be okay,' she said, knowing that it probably wouldn't.

'Absolutely.' Norman too sounded less than convincing, but he twisted around in his seat and grinned at Viola.

'I'll just drive past first,' Gerard said, glancing in the rear-view mirror at Jane, whose tension was palpable. 'Warn us when the house is coming up, Viola.'

'You can't miss it, it's the big one on the corner.' Viola pointed to a large mock-Tudor house set back from the road and partially shielded from view by two large oaks. Between the trees a narrow gravel driveway ran up to the house, culminating in a turning circle in front of a set of steps leading up to the main door. There was no sign of Grice's yellow Volvo and so, after a quick discussion, they opted for the direct approach. Gerard would knock on the door and if Grice was in, he would tell him that Viola wanted to talk with him. Then, when Grice came over to the car, Norman would restrain him while the others went inside to look for Melanie. They parked a couple of houses along from the entrance to Grice's driveway.

'What if he won't come out?' Jane asked.

'Then I'll drag him out,' Gerard said quietly and turned to Norman. 'You ready?' Norman nodded, unclasped his seatbelt and reached for a small bag at his feet. 'Okay, folks — showtime.'

The others watched as Gerard got out of the car, walked briskly back along the road and disappeared into the driveway. Almost immediately he reappeared and waved to them to come along.

'So he's not home?' Jane asked anxiously as they joined him.

'Doesn't look like it. He's certainly not answering the door.' Gerard turned to Viola, who was standing back from the others, still nervous about setting foot on Grice's property. 'You certain you know where he keeps a spare key?'

Viola nodded but showed no sign of wanting to lead the way.

'Come on then. The quicker we're in the quicker we're out.'

Gerard turned and set off up the drive again with Norman and Jane by his side. Viola followed reluctantly, a few paces behind. When they got to the house, Viola went to the side of the steps and pointed to a small clay pot containing a rather bedraggled miniature rose bush that looked as though it was fast turning into a bonsai through neglect rather than design.

'Under there,' Viola said, but made no attempt to retrieve it himself. Jane was becoming exasperated by his docility. She thought he looked paralysed by his fear of Grice and wondered just how useful he would have been had Grice been home. Thankfully that was not the case and, impatient to get inside, she brushed Viola aside and tilting the pot found the key.

'Here,' she said and held it out to Gerard. 'Now, for God's sake, let's get on with it.'

But Gerard shook his head. 'You keep the key because we're going to need you to open the door. Viola says there's an alarm on it, and if we don't want some security firm turning up we have to disable it.' He turned back to Viola. 'Are you sure you don't know the sequence?'

'I'm sorry, Mr Edwards, I never knew it. But the keypad is beside the letter-stand just inside the door. I remember Master Francis saying that he had a minute to put in the code before the alarm went off.'

'We'll have to work with that. Fortunately the meter box is on the side of the house. Norman, have you got the battery and the tools?'

'Right here.' He patted the small bag.

'Okay then, this is how we play it. I'll call out as I switch off the power, and Jane opens the door. Viola, as soon as you get in, you take Norman straight to the keypad. Jane, you stay by the door and as soon as Norman tells you he has the circuit connected to the battery, you call out to me and I'll switch the mains back on again. Is that clear?'

It sounded to Jane as though they knew what they were doing so she nodded and went up the stairs with Norman and Viola. She slid the key into the lock and waited. Beside her Norman opened his bag and passed a twelve-volt battery to Viola.

'Here, hold this and give it to me when I tell you.' He fished in the bag again and took out a screwdriver, a pair of pliers and some lengths of wire, their ends already stripped.

'Now!' called Gerard.

Jane immediately turned the key, pushed the door open and followed Norman and Viola into the entrance hall where Viola pointed to a small cream-coloured box on the wall. 'There.'

Jane watched anxiously as Norman, with ease that spoke of a lot more expertise than an honest citizen should possess, removed the face plate and deftly located and cut a set of wires. Using his own lengths of wire he quickly created a bypass and connected it to the twelve-volt battery. A small indicator light blinked red then turned green.

'It's done.' He nodded at her and Jane went to the door and relayed the message to Gerard. A moment later he strode through the door.

'No problems?'

Norman shook his head but kept his eye firmly on the green light. 'Now close the door.' The green indicator didn't even flicker as the door clicked shut.

Gerard pulled Viola forward. 'Your turn. Show us the way.'

Viola, looking less than enthusiastic, led them quickly through the house to the rear of the kitchen.

'There are stairs down from the back of the pantry,' he said, holding the door open. Not waiting for anyone, Jane pushed past into the pantry. It was a narrow rectangular area with well-stocked shelves on either side and another small door at the far end. She opened it and found herself on a platform with a set of metal steps leading down into the dark. A waft of stale, damp air greeted her as she stood still to let her eyes adjust.

'Let me go first —' Gerard began.

But Jane was having none of it. 'She's my daughter.'

Even though she had pulled the door open as wide as possible, the cellar below still looked pitch black. 'Melanie? Mel, are you there?' Her voice sounded hollow in the confined space. There was no sound.

'I need light!' she snapped at Viola. 'Where the fuck is the switch?'

'There's no light down there. But I can turn the pantry light on, that should help.'

Jane heard him move behind her but kept staring into the darkness. Then the pantry light came on and she had a clear view of the short flight of stairs and a shadow-filled room below. 'For Christ's sake! It's empty.' Her voice was choked with disappointment.

'I'm sorry,' Gerard said quietly. 'But it was worth having a look.'

Jane realised she was fighting back the tears and knew that there was nothing she could do but give way to the grief. But then she felt a hand on her shoulder.

'The cell is further on,' Viola said and moving past her went quickly down the stairs. Jane held back the tears and followed him. She was struggling to keep her composure, fighting against the memories of movies where the basement always held a corpse. She's alive, she repeated to herself, letting the words go round and round her head like a mantra.

At the foot of the stairs the room felt damp and strangely warm, and as they disturbed the still air Jane became aware of a slightly acrid odour emanating from somewhere close at hand. Then she heard it — a dull thump, as though someone was moving.

'Melanie?' Her voice now only a whisper. Behind her Norman clumped noisily down the stairs. 'For Christ's sake, keep quiet!' She glared at him as he moved to stand beside her. 'I thought I heard something.'

'Sorry,' he mumbled.

Jane's eyes were adjusting now to the dim light and in front of her she could just make out steel bars extending from the concrete floor up to the low ceiling. To one side of the cell were a couple of high-backed wooden chairs and against the side wall a wooden box seat.

'She's here,' Viola whispered from in front of her. 'In the cell.'

Jane moved up beside him, grabbed the bars and peered through. 'Oh my God, Melanie.' She let out a long sob and gripped Viola's arm. 'She's there, in the corner. Why isn't she moving?'

She fumbled her way along the bars until she located the gate. She pulled and pushed at it but it was firmly locked. Jane stepped back and threw all her weight against it. 'Melanie!' She knew she was acting irrationally, but could do nothing about it, some instinct driving her to get to her daughter at all cost. Jane felt her chest constrict. 'Why doesn't she answer me?'

'She's probably gagged. Stay here, I think I know where the key is.' Viola turned and disappeared up the stairs.

Jane threw herself against the door again, then felt strong hands pulling her away. She struggled against them, lashing out, kicking and scratching.

'Easy! Take it easy,' Gerard barked. 'You'll hurt yourself.' He eventually felt her relax as he held her firmly against him. 'You can't break it down, Jane. Wait for Viola.'

'What if he can't find the key?'

'Then we'll have to think of something else.'

Jane didn't find that very reassuring. Unable to stop herself she slipped out of his grasp and pushed her face hard against the bars, repeating her daughter's name. There was still no reply from the shadowy form in the corner.

Viola appeared at the top of the stairs, holding the key in his hand. 'Got it,' he said.

It took a couple of fumbles before he managed to insert the key into the lock, but then there was a click and the cell door swung open. Jane pushed him aside and ran to the small figure huddled against the rear wall of the cell. To Jane's horror, Melanie was naked, curled in a foetal position. 'Mummy's here, Mummy's here,' Jane crooned softly and crouching beside her gently rolled her over, then screamed and sprang back. The face that looked up at her wasn't human — large, inanimate eyes stared blank and unseeing from either side of a cruel beak; the entire head covered with dark feathers.

'The bastards put her in a mask,' Gerard said, kneeling down beside her. 'It's going to be okay, darling,' he said quietly and lifting the girl's head ran his fingers around the back of the mask, searching for the buckle. The girl suddenly came to life, writhing in his arms.

Jane, regaining her composure, squatted down and scooped her into her arms. 'I'm here, Mel. We'll soon have you out of here.' But Melanie didn't respond.

Jane clung to her daughter, shutting out the thoughts of what might have happened to her. The idea of Grice forcing her to undress was horrible enough. She couldn't face the thought that he might have touched her ... or worse. One thing was certain — Grice would pay for this. No matter how long it took, Jane knew that she would exact her revenge. 'I love you, Mel,' she whispered.

Gerard eased the strap free and as he slid the mask carefully over Melanie's head, Jane helped her into a sitting position. 'I'll go and fetch a blanket from upstairs.' Gerard stepped away, gesturing to Viola and Norman to move back into the basement and leave the two women alone.

For a moment Jane thought that Melanie didn't recognise her but then the girl looked up, blinking and shaking her head. Then, as recognition came, she gave a half-hearted smile before burying her head in Jane's breast and breaking into sobs of relief.

'You'll be fine, now, darling,' Jane said, hoping it was true. God knew what she had been through and how such an ordeal would affect her. She stroked her hair over and over and after a time Melanie's sobbing subsided, but still she didn't let go of her mother. Jane could feel her shivering in her arms.

'Here, give her this.'

Jane hadn't noticed Gerard come back down the stairs. She took the glass of water from him and held it to her daughter's lips. 'Here, darling, drink this.'

To her relief, Melanie sat up and took the glass. Her hand trembled but, obviously thirsty, she gulped the water down. She passed the glass back and gratefully accepted the blanket, wrapping it around her shoulders and sitting with it hugged over her knees.

'I'm sorry, Mum —'

'Shh dear, we'll get you home now.'

'I didn't mean to cause so much trouble. He told me you wanted him to bring me into town to your office.' She looked at Jane, imploring her to understand.

Jane wasn't sure she wanted to hear what had happened to her daughter, but knew her well enough to know that she needed to talk. 'You're safe now, that's all that matters.'

'He brought me down here and took my clothes away. I thought he was going to . . .' Melanie's lip quivered, she couldn't bring herself to put it into words. The tears welled up in her eyes and she wiped them away with the back of her hand. 'But he tied me up and just looked at me. Then I started screaming and tried to kick him and he said I had to be punished. He brought that bird mask down and put it on . . .' She shook her head wildly as though trying to rid herself of the memory.

Jane felt a hand on her shoulder. 'We have to get her out of here,' Gerard said quietly. But as he did so there was a sharp metallic click and Jane suddenly sensed that something had gone wrong. She looked through the gloom to where the others waited in the basement. Norman was backed against the wall, while Viola crouched in the corner, his face a mask of terror. As Gerard moved out of the cell to join the others, she saw what they were all staring at. A glint of light flashed off the metal barrels of a sawn-off shotgun. Behind it, at the top of the stairs and silhouetted against the pantry light, was Francis Grice.

'Nice try with the alarm,' Grice sneered. 'But the security company noticed the power outage and checked with the electricity company who told them that there had been no power cuts in the area for weeks. Fortunately they had the presence of mind to ring me.'

Norman made a move towards the bottom of the stairs but Gerard blocked him with his arm, pushing him back against the wall.

'Glad you showed up. It'll save the police looking for you. Kidnapping and molesting a fifteen year old is not something they look too kindly on.' Gerard moved to the bottom of the stairs and held out his hand. 'Now give me the gun.'

Grice rocked with laughter, but the shotgun didn't waver an inch. 'Police? Oh, you are funny. There won't be any police, will there, Jane? Do you want to explain why or shall I?'

'You'll pay for this, Grice.' Jane got to her feet and, gesturing to Melanie to stay where she was, went to the cell door. 'By the time I've done with you, you'll wish it had been the police.'

'Oh, very brave!' Grice chortled, his face wreathed with smiles. 'I can hardly wait. Are you going to flog me?'

Peering through the gloom, he saw who else was in the basement and his demeanour changed. The smile vanished and his voice became steely cold. 'Oh dear, the truant has returned. Viola, come out where I can see you.'

Jane watched in amazement as Viola obeyed. He rose and walked slowly forward, his head bowed, wringing his hands in front of him.

'I'm afraid you have overstepped the line this time, Viola. And you know what that means . . .'

That was too much for Norman and he stepped forward and dragged Viola back. 'Leave him alone, you bastard.' But to Norman's amazement, Viola shook himself free and stepped forward again.

'I have to, Norman. You wouldn't understand.'

'Norman, is it?' Grice leered. 'Have you been playing with my Viola?'

'He doesn't belong to anyone —'

'Tell him, Viola,' Grice ordered.

'I belong to you, Master Francis,' Viola said quietly, but there was nothing subservient about the tone, it was almost defiant.

Jane looked at Viola in disgust. 'How could you?'

'Because I say so,' Grice said softly. 'Now, Viola, I don't want you hurt so come up and sit on the steps.' Keeping the shotgun pointed into the basement, he bent over and patted the step below him. 'Right here, so you can watch the fun and games. Then, when it's all over, I am afraid I'm going to have to punish you. Understand?'

'Yes, Master Francis.' Viola bowed his head and moved towards the foot of the stairs.

'You bastard!' Gerard screamed and leapt up the stairs, lunging forward in an attempt to knock the shotgun from Grice's hand. But even as he moved Grice pulled the trigger. There was a bright flash and an enormous explosion of sound reverberated in the confined space. Gerard was thrown back off the steps and through the air. He slammed into the bars beside Jane before collapsing onto the floor.

Jane's instinct was to go to Melanie, but shock and the pain in her ears from the blast immobilised her and she cowered in the doorway, peering through the smoke-filled basement at the scene of carnage in front of her. Then she moved, her instincts taking her back to protect her daughter. She glanced through the smoke at Gerard's body, still moving, twitching and shuddering, but despite the movement she knew he was dead; his face and upper chest were horribly pulped. Norman knelt beside him but turned to her and shook his head.

Jane threw herself down on Melanie in an attempt to protect her from the next shot. Nobody else moved. Even Grice looked shocked at the damage the shotgun had caused. Then, as the smoke began to clear, Viola completed his journey to the top step like an automaton obeying orders. He reached it and sat, an obedient slave at the feet of his master.

'You . . .' Grice gestured at Norman with the shotgun, 'into the cell.'

'You bastard,' Norman muttered through gritted teeth but he knew he had no option but to obey. He joined Jane in the cell and stared at the now still body beyond the bars. Jane could see he had turned a deathly pale, the blood gone from his face.

Grice lowered the shotgun and prodded Viola's shoulder. 'I think that you should lock the gate, Viola. I would hate to have your punishment interrupted. Quickly now.'

'Yes, Master Francis.' Viola rose and walked down the stairs without hesitation. As he reached the cell door he lowered his head, avoiding Norman's gaze. Then he shut the gate, locked it and slipped the key into his pocket.

Behind him, Grice came down the stairs and moved to the wooden box seat. 'You know what's in here, don't you, Viola?'

'Yes,' Viola stammered.

'No, that's not good enough. You know I like you to speak clearly and address me properly.' Grice sighed impatiently. 'Now, let's try it again.'

'Yes, Master Francis,' Viola said in a stronger voice.

'I think you should take off your shirt and hold onto the bars.' Grice grinned. 'That way our guests can see how much you enjoy being punished.'

He leaned the shotgun against the wall and as Viola, his fingers trembling, unbuttoned his shirt, Grice raised the lid of the seat and took out a long plaited whip. 'Well, it's been a while since we used you,' he said as he lovingly caressed the handle of the whip.

Jane turned her head away and pulled Melanie to her. 'Don't watch, darling,' she whispered. But as the first blow fell on Viola's back she couldn't stop herself glancing over her shoulder. He seemed oblivious to the pain, his eyes open, a half smile on his lips. Jane looked over at Norman, who was standing far back in the shadows; he too was transfixed by the scene being played out in front of them, tears rolling down his cheeks.

After what seemed like an eternity, Grice brought the flogging to a halt, but it became immediately clear that he wasn't finished with Viola. He stretched out in the chair and loosened the belt to his trousers. 'Now, Viola, show your friends just how much you appreciate your master.'

Viola unclenched his fingers from the bars, slowly, painfully, as though they had fused to the metal. If he was disgusted by what the man was proposing, it didn't show on his face. 'Yes, Master,' he said softly.

For a second he looked at Grice, who was leaning back with his eyes closed, resting from his exertions, then without another word he moved soundlessly to the wall and picked up the shotgun. Jane watched in horror as he brought it up to his shoulder, his awkwardness betraying his lack of expertise with firearms. Viola closed his eyes and pulled the trigger. There was a sharp click — then nothing.

'Oh really, Viola, how many times have I told you not to play with things you don't understand?' Grice's tone was scornful as though he knew absolutely that Viola was incapable of hurting him. 'Now, put it down.'

But Viola stood frozen, bewildered by his inability to fire the shotgun. He looked around at Norman and Jane, his eyes pleading for help. Grice's expression changed and with a look of anger he started to rise from the chair. At that moment Viola discovered the second trigger. Turning his head away, he pulled it. The blast seemed even louder than the one that had killed Edwards, and was just as deadly. Grice was thrown back, taking the chair with him. The gun clattered to the ground.

Viola put his shirt back on, walked calmly to the door of the cell and produced the key from his pocket. But then the shock of what he had done hit him. His fingers began to tremble wildly and he dropped the key on the floor and had to kneel down and scrabble about in the dust to retrieve it. Finally he managed to push it into the lock and open the cell. He walked in and up to Norman who, without a word, opened his arms and pulled Viola to him. They stood there for a long time, Viola shuddering and gasping for air as though he hadn't breathed throughout the whole ordeal.

In Jane's arms Melanie whimpered softly. Gently Jane lifted her daughter's head from her breast and pried free the fingers that were digging deeply into her arm. 'Come on, it's time we went home.' She assisted Melanie to her feet and arranged the blanket around her.

'I'll bring the car up to the door,' Norman said and moved towards the stairs, but Viola held him back.

'What about Gerard?'

'Later,' Norman said firmly. 'There's nothing we can do for him now. Help the others out and lock the pantry door.' He picked up the shotgun and taking a handkerchief from his pocket carefully wiped it free of fingerprints before tossing it down beside Grice's body.

By the time Jane, Melanie and Viola came out of the house, Norman was parked beside Grice's Volvo. Nobody said a word as they got in the car and drove out the driveway. Jane knew there would come a time when they would have to speak about it, but at the moment all she wanted to do was to get Melanie fed, washed and tucked up in bed — a recipe that she realised she also craved for herself. However, that would have to wait until she had attended to her daughter. Deciding that Mel needed to be back in familiar surroundings, she rang Oliver on the car phone. They quickly agreed that he would look after Mel while she and the others went to collect her father.

Ten minutes later Jane dropped Melanie at Oliver's house, assuring her that she would be back shortly. Driving back to the apartment with Norman and Viola, the only comforting thought she could summon up was that the worst was over. The moment she walked into the apartment, she knew she was wrong.

CHAPTER TWENTY

It had been two hours and still the phone hadn't rung. The two women in black had long gone and still Teschmaker waited. He had eaten an indifferent lunch, drunk two cups of coffee and even perused the kiosk's gift shop with its bizarre array of merchandise ranging from bereavement cards to small statues of the Virgin Mary or Jesus. He decided to give it another ten minutes and then pack it in and go back to Jane. Maybe Laverov had been unable to dig up the information he'd requested, or maybe he had never intended to. If the Russian *had* gone ahead it would probably have necessitated calling Moscow, and God only knew the bureaucratic channels he would have had to go through. And there was the problem of the time difference . . .

Teschmaker decided to call it quits. He paid his bill and left the kiosk. Just as he gave the phone a final glance, it rang. He picked it up and was relieved to hear Laverov's voice.

'So how did you go?' he asked.

'First I want to know how you came across the name Grigori Vasilyevich Puzanov.'

'Not part of the deal, I'm afraid.' Teschmaker knew by the question that Laverov had the answer he wanted. 'I asked you to find out about Puzanov; I didn't promise anything.'

'Have you any idea what you're involved with?' Laverov's exasperation came through loud and clear.

'I tried to talk to you about it in the bar and you denied any knowledge.'

'And if I said that I have changed my mind?'

'What? You no longer deny it or you will talk about it?'

Teschmaker heard a dry laugh at the other end of the phone. 'The same bar in half an hour. Yes?'

'Yes,' Teschmaker said and hung up the phone.

It only took him thirty minutes to get to the back bar of the Dredger's Arms, but by the time he did Laverov was already there, seated in the same alcove as the previous night. He was vigorously polishing his wire-rimmed glasses.

Teschmaker had no idea what training KGB officers went through before being unleashed on the world, but obviously Laverov had been absent during the class on blending in with the locals when overseas. The man couldn't have appeared more Russian if he tried. The suit looked as though it had been mass-produced in a labour camp during the Brezhnev era. All that was missing was an Order of Lenin or Red Star on the frayed lapel. The red tie was simply bad, although the mid-afternoon patrons at the Dredger's Arms wouldn't have noticed if he had been wearing a kilt. The couple of swampies propping up the bar looked as though they had been there since opening time, and the barman's attention was firmly locked on to a horse race on the small TV in the front corner of the room. Teschmaker slipped into the alcove opposite Laverov. The man put his glasses back on before speaking.

'Mr Teschmaker, I hope you appreciate that I have tried to keep you out of this for your own protection?'

'Very commendable, but I'm already in it up to my fucking neck. So let's drop the bullshit and get on with it. Did you find out about Puzanov?'

Laverov looked at him contemptuously. 'I talked to my people in Moscow and I can tell you that there is no record of anyone by that name on our files.'

'Then why bother to meet me?' Teschmaker snapped angrily.

'To stop you making a fool of yourself or getting yourself killed.'

'I can assure you I have no intention of doing either of those things.'

'At our last meeting you asked me if I was interested in the *gardener* or the *bouquet*. I must assume from that conversation that you know what those words represent?' Laverov looked at him enquiringly but Teschmaker decided against volunteering anything until he got what he'd come for. Laverov shrugged and continued. 'Well, let us say that you do know these things. Where does that leave us?'

'With a damned good reason to exchange information.'

'So you have things you can tell me. Maybe you could start with the whereabouts of Sydney Morris?'

Teschmaker shook his head. That was one thing he wasn't about to divulge. 'No. But I suggest we stop this shadow-boxing. I know about the sabotage teams. And I know what Rusak is after. So just tell me about Puzanov.'

'I told you he doesn't exist —'

'Crap!'

For a moment Laverov looked as though he was about to leave, but then his face broke into a huge grin. 'You are a hard man, Mr Teschmaker.' He dug in his jacket pocket and produced his cigarette case. He lit a cigarette and slid the case across the table. 'So, let me tell you the story. I'm afraid I wasn't exactly honest with you when we first met. I had not been investigating Sydney Morris or any of the foreign scientists; he was merely a name that came up while I was digging into Oleg Rusak's business dealings.' Laverov paused and inhaled deeply on his cigarette before continuing. 'As you know, he had been a member of the parliament and while in the Duma abused his position to gain access to a great deal of information which he subsequently used to further his criminal activities. My superiors thought it would be a good idea to take a look at the documents he accessed while in the Duma and I was chosen to undertake the task. The most surprising thing we came up with was his interest in the claims by General Lebed that a number of small nuclear devices had been manufactured for use by the GRU or the KGB.'

'And which went missing.'

'So Lebed claimed. There was a great deal of discomfort about those claims and an investigation was set up to verify them. According to what we discovered, Rusak had followed the investigation with great interest and had obtained certain documents containing the code names of the agents responsible for placing the devices in the target countries. Unfortunately, when we followed up on these teams we found that, as a security precaution, the members had all been eliminated.'

Teschmaker looked at him in disbelief. 'You mean they were killed by their own people?'

'It was the way we did things back then. There was a lot at stake and I should point out that a majority of the combat agents were nationals of the target countries and seen as expendable.'

'Oh, that makes it much more understandable.' Teschmaker did nothing to veil his contempt. Laverov ignored it.

'Then it came to light that Sydney Morris had vanished. At first it was assumed that he, like the rest of the development team, had been liquidated, but as we both know that was not the case.'

'So that's why you want to find him — to silence him and finish the job?'

Laverov ground out the remains of his cigarette. 'We don't do that kind of thing any more. At first I didn't realise that we had a problem. I went to the Czech Republic and arrived a little too late.'

'For what?'

'Rusak's people had already lifted him. The locals were not well disposed to assist me, but took great delight in letting me know that the people who had taken Morris were Russians. It wasn't much of a leap to work out why Rusak was after Morris. There was only one reason anyone would want him — to discover where the teams had been sent. Though Morris would never have been given that information, it would have been easy enough for him to work it out.'

'Sorry, I don't follow. How would he have done that?'

'Every team needed detailed instructions on assembling and placing the device, as well as arming the booby trap on each of the caches. The person responsible for that briefing was Sydney Morris. And, as I said, the teams usually included at least one foreign *agent-boyevik*, or combat agent, so once he knew their nationality he would know where the team was headed.'

'Hang on,' Teschmaker interjected, 'these devices are protected by booby traps? Doesn't that mean they could be detonated accidentally? Someone unearths one and . . .'

Laverov shook his head emphatically. 'Not possible. From what I understand, the bomb and the remote detonation device are concealed in separate locations. And each has what the documents describe as a *molniya*, a "lightning" booby trap designed to destroy the devices. All the advice I have received agrees that the *molniya* is incapable of setting off the main explosive.'

'A small nuclear explosion,' Teschmaker said quietly.

'Unfortunately.'

The two men sat in silence for a moment. Teschmaker picked up the cigarette case and took out a cigarette. It was from the packet he had given Laverov the previous evening. He lit it. 'So Rusak wants to retrieve one or more of these devices. Why? Obviously not so Russia can complete its nuclear stocktaking.'

Laverov looked at him as though he was stupid. 'Money. Can you imagine how much a terrorist organisation would pay to get its hands on one of them?'

Teschmaker shook his head. The entire scenario seemed surreal. At a pinch he could accept Sydney Morris's claim that he had worked on developing the technology purely as an intellectual challenge. But that the devices had then been manufactured and deployed — that was much harder to comprehend. And then the Russians had managed to lose them! If it wasn't so horrific it would be laughable.

'So tell me about the man who doesn't exist.'

Laverov arched an eyebrow. 'As I said, we have never had an agent named Puzanov.'

'But?' Teschmaker sensed the Russian was playing with him.

'Grigori Vasilyevich Puzanov was the cover name given to an *agent-boyevik* on one of the teams.'

'A Russian?'

'Yes. Andrei Yakunin. Now, you must tell me how you came across his name, because if there is even the slightest chance he's alive then I no longer have to rely on getting information from Sydney Morris.'

'Unfortunately he's dead. Has been for years.'

'You know this for certain?'

'Well, short of digging up his remains I'd say it's a pretty sure bet. I've seen his grave. But surely the important thing is who was on the team with him? If he was the Russian, what nationality were the other members?'

'Don't be a fool, Teschmaker. I can assume, if you have seen his grave, that we are talking about this country?'

Teschmaker nodded. 'But if we can find the other members of his team, they could tell us where this damn thing is.'

'No. I had access to every available file but most of them, especially those designated as *obektovoye delo* or target files, were destroyed to preserve security or have simply vanished. However, I did come across some copies of training schedules that had survived through bureaucratic oversight. One of them had a list of each *agent-boyevik*; though it employed the code names, it appears that Yakunin wasn't working with foreign nationals. The foreigners all had code names in their own languages, while the illegals had Russian ones.'

'Illegals?'

'Soviet citizens who had been trained to live abroad,' Laverov explained patiently.

'Sleepers?'

'Is that what you call them? Fine. Sleepers. But as I said, in Yakunin's case the code names were Russian — *Starshina* and *Zolushka*.'

'Senior and Cinderella?' It sounded like a fairytale that had gone sadly astray.

'That's all we have and there is no way of finding out if they are still alive or what their real names were. The best we can do is agree that somewhere in this city there is one of these devices and set about finding it. The chances are that it is no longer operable, but I'm not certain that Rusak would care one way or the other.'

'Why not just kill Rusak?' It seemed the easiest way out of the predicament. Teschmaker couldn't understand why someone hadn't thought of it a long time before.

Laverov smiled and took another cigarette. 'Oh that we could, but at the present time he's our only lead. If we lose Rusak we may never find the device.'

'Surely that wouldn't be such a bad thing?' If there was no way of locating the device, the threat was removed.

But Laverov shook his head. 'If we don't have certainty, then how can we respond to future threats? If some terrorist group claims to have found the device, what could any government do but capitulate? Nobody is going to try and bluff out a scenario like that, the stakes are too high.'

'I think we need a drink.' Teschmaker pushed himself up from his seat. 'What would you like? Vodka?'

Laverov screwed up his face. 'Vodka? Here, in this country? No, I'll have scotch.'

As Teschmaker went over to the bar and ordered the drinks there was a naggingly familiar feeling in his stomach, one that he had experienced several times before in his professional life. It was the smell of burned rat. He recalled his final insurance investigation, where the fact that something as seemingly insignificant as a scorched rat's corpse had been pivotal in unveiling the source of the arson. Somewhere here there was a rat's corpse — he could smell it. And then it came to him; a detail, a piece of the jigsaw. It felt right but he had to test it by placing it in the puzzle. He paid for the drinks and took them back to the alcove.

'I've had an idea. Do you mind waiting while I make a phone call?'

'I have scotch. I am happy.' Laverov grinned.

The phone booth at the back of the bar had only just escaped being vandalised out of existence, so Teschmaker was relieved when he heard the dial tone. He dialled the number and waited. Then he heard a familiar voice.

'Hello?'

'Aleksandr Yefremovich, it's Teschmaker. I need to ask you something.'

'For you, anything,' the old man chuckled.

'I need to ask you about Grigori Vasilyevich Puzanov.'

There was a silence before Shlyapnikov spoke again. When he did, all trace of humour had vanished. 'What about him?'

'I'm sorry if it's difficult for you, but I need to know if he had any particularly close friends.'

'Friends?' Shlyapnikov sounded wary. 'It was a long time ago. How would I know who his friends were?'

'Please try, it's very important.'

'Why should it be important after all these years? We should leave the dead in peace.'

'I'm afraid I can't do that, Aleksandr, there is far too much at stake.' There was no response. 'Listen, you and I have known each other for years. I promise you I wouldn't ask if it wasn't crucial.'

'It was all so long ago. Believe me, I can't remember.'

If that were true then there was nothing Teschmaker could do about it, but every instinct told him he was on the right track and so he pushed harder, knowing he must, even if it meant jeopardising their friendship. 'Then if you can't remember his friends, tell me how Andrei Yakunin died.'

Again there was silence. Then he heard a deep and protracted sigh. 'He was shot. They didn't even know who he was. It should have been me.'

Teschmaker felt a chill go through his body. 'Why should it have been you?'

'Because I was the one they wanted to kill. Yakunin was in the wrong place. It should have been me.'

'Why would they want to kill you?' Teschmaker asked quietly, but there was a click and the line went dead. For a moment he stood, hardly believing what he had just heard and attempting to make some sense of it. It was certainly not what he had expected.

He turned and looked back at Laverov, who raised his glass in a toast. Teschmaker held up a finger to indicate that he needed to make one more call. Shlyapnikov hadn't noticed when he switched the names Puzanov and Yakunin. That could only mean one thing. Shlyapnikov knew who Puzanov really was, which meant that Sydney Morris probably also knew. And if Morris knew, then it followed that he might know the names of the local people on the team.

Illegals, Laverov had called them, and what better cover for an illegal in a city with a large émigré Russian population than as one of that community. But his mind was racing ahead of him. He needed to talk to Sydney Morris and that, he smiled to himself, would also give him a chance to touch base with Jane. He dialled the number and waited, listening to it ring for what felt like an unduly long time. He was about to hang up when it was answered. Surprisingly nobody spoke.

'Hello?' Teschmaker said tentatively, thinking he must have rung the wrong number. There was no reply but he could distinctly hear someone breathing. 'Hello? Can you hear me?'

'Ah, Mister Teschmaker.' The voice was heavily accented, Slavic.

'Yes.' He felt himself freeze. 'Who is this?'

'This is Rusak, Mister Teschmaker, and I have someone here who wants to speak with you.'

There was a muffled noise and, after a pause, Jane came on the line. She sounded frightened. 'Martin? You have to do what he says.'

'Are you okay?'

But Jane, not about to depart from the lines that Rusak had instructed her to deliver, ignored his interjection. Her voice was cold and flat. 'Just do as he says and don't try to rescue us. I don't want any more deaths.'

Any more deaths? 'What deaths? Is someone dead?' He realised he was shouting but didn't care. 'Jane, for Christ's sake, talk to me.' But she was gone.

Rusak came back on the line. 'You have been meddling in my affairs, Teschmaker, and I won't forget that. What I propose is very simple. You understand that it is not these people I want —'

'How would I know what the hell you want?' Teschmaker snapped.

'I'm not a fool, I know that you are talking with Laverov. My men have been following his every move for days. He bumbles around like a drunken Vanya.'

Teschmaker turned around and looked across the room. There were more people in the bar now but they looked like the usual patrons of the Dredger's Arms: misfits, drunks, swampies and a couple of ageing hookers down on their luck. He had to acknowledge that any one of them could be working for Rusak.

'So what is it you want?'

'Stop playing games, Teschmaker. You know what I'm after and I'm afraid that your knowing that isn't good for your health.'

'You're a fool, Rusak. Nobody knows where those damn things are and that includes Laverov.'

'Well, at least I can get Laverov off my back.'

'I doubt it.' Teschmaker glanced over at the Russian, who must have sensed that something was wrong for he had lost the smile and was staring questioningly at Teschmaker.

'Oh, I'm certain I can. Now, listen. I have no desire to kill these people, but trust me — if you don't deliver Laverov to me then they will die. Is that simple enough for you to understand?'

'You hurt Jane or her father and I'll come after you and you'll wish you had never been born.' Teschmaker knew it was an empty threat but he could think of nothing better to say.

'Enough jokes. You deliver Laverov to me and I'll let these people go free. I don't care how you do it but you have four hours.' Rusak hung up.

'Fuck you!' Teschmaker slammed the phone back in its cradle and turned around to find everyone in the bar staring at him. He ignored them and went straight back to the alcove and helped himself to another of his cigarettes from Laverov's cigarette case. His hands trembled as he lit it.

'Well?' Laverov looked at him enquiringly.

'We have a problem,' Teschmaker said. 'A big problem.'

It was an hour later when they walked out into the dusk and along the road to where Laverov had parked the rented Ford. Teschmaker handed him the key to his house and garage. 'Just make sure you're not being followed,' he cautioned.

'They would have to be good,' Laverov laughed.

'Yeah? Well, I did it.'

'That was luck not skill.'

'Rusak said his men have been on your tail for days.'

'Rusak is full of shit. Maybe tonight he got lucky, but before . . .' Laverov spat in the gutter and got into his car. He started the motor then wound down the window. 'Are you sure this is going to work?'

'We'll be outnumbered, but I think we stand a chance.'

'And Rusak doesn't know that one of his men is ours.'

Teschmaker took a stab. 'Ilya, the poet?'

Laverov looked as though Teschmaker had hit him. 'How in God's name did you know that?'

'Instinct. Pity, he won't be any help.'

'Why?'

'He's in hospital. A long story. Later.'

'So it's just us then?' Laverov fastened his seatbelt and shrugged. 'Just us.'

'Can you think of anything better?'

'Lots of things but they all involve women and vodka.'

Teschmaker stepped back into the shadows and watched him drive away. There was no sign of anyone following him. *Was* he sure it was going to work? Not at all. They were going to need more than their fair share of luck if they were to pull off the hastily conceived plan. He glanced at his watch, calculating the time needed for the preparations. All going well, he could be ready in an hour, but decided to give himself some leeway and plan on two hours. He returned to the bar and rang Rusak.

'Meet me in two hours at the Freeholm cemetery car park. Bring Jane and her father.'

'I don't think you're in any position to be dictating the terms —'

'Just shut up and listen, Rusak. I'm only going to say this once. You bring Jane and her father or there is no deal.'

'A deal is two-sided, Mr Teschmaker. I have already set the terms. I give you your friends and you give me Laverov.'

'I don't think you understand me, Rusak. Forget about Laverov. You do as I say and I'll give you the location of the device you're after.'

Teschmaker would have loved to have seen Rusak's face at that moment. There was dead silence for several seconds before the Russian replied.

'You know where it is?'

'And the remote control detonator.'

'How will I know that it is genuine?'

Teschmaker could hear the barely masked excitement in his voice. There was caution there too, but it was the voice of a man who wanted more than anything to be convinced.

'Sydney Morris will verify it for you. Two hours from now, Rusak. And if you have harmed Jane or her father in any way then the deal is off.' He hung up without waiting for a reply. Well, he thought as he walked to the car, bluffing always was the easy part.

Teschmaker had only a couple of blocks to drive but he took a slow circuitous route, constantly checking his rear-vision mirror. He drove past Shlyapnikov's restaurant and then doubled back. Nobody was following him. He found a park on the other side of the road and locked the car. In light of their earlier phone conversation, he wasn't too sure of the reception he was going to get, but decided that he had neither the time nor the inclination to beat around the bush. A direct approach, he told himself. Just walk in and say what you have to.

He stepped inside the door and spotted Shlyapnikov in his usual position, seated behind the small bar. Opposite him sat another elderly man and between them a chessboard. The Russian looked up as Teschmaker came in and gestured to him to wait for a moment. He studied the board and moved a piece, said something to his opponent and then signalled through the small hatch to the kitchen for someone to take over the bar. Teschmaker had been anticipating a level of hostility but Shlyapnikov came over with a cautious smile on his face.

'I wasn't expecting you.'

'I'm sorry about having to awake old memories —' Teschmaker began but Shlyapnikov cut him off rather brusquely.

'If you want to go over that stuff again, then I'm sorry I'm too busy,' he said and turned away.

'Too busy to talk about Starshina and Zolushka?' Teschmaker said quietly.

The effect was immediate; as though someone had just driven an icepick into the old man's memory. He shuddered and slowly turned back, the look on his face a mixture of horror and amazement. For a moment he stared at Teschmaker as though seeing him for the first time and then he seemed to deflate. The tension ebbed away and the lines in his face relaxed.

'It is long past the time when ghosts should be laid to rest. I felt it earlier when you rang. You know, in all the years we have known each other you have never mentioned Puzanov before. You didn't even raise it those times when we went to the grave together. I can only assume that this has something to do with the Russian, Laverov?'

Shlyapnikov might be getting on in years, and at times he drank too much, but when it mattered his mind was razor sharp. 'Yes, Laverov is keeping tabs on an unsavoury character by the name of Oleg Rusak.'

Teschmaker watched his friend's face but there was no sign that he recognised the name. 'Rusak is after the same thing that your friend Puzanov was killed for. He has hostages and if he doesn't get what he wants I have no doubt he will kill them.'

This time there was a visible reaction. The expression about someone turning white seemed all wrong — Shlyapnikov went grey, his jaw suddenly slack, his eyes glazed. Then he swallowed and gulped in a huge mouthful of air like someone who suddenly feels there is not enough oxygen to sustain them.

'And I take it you know what it was that Puzanov was killed for?'

Teschmaker nodded.

'Have you got your car?'

Again Teschmaker nodded.

'Then I think we should go for a drive.'

Without another word Shlyapnikov led the way out the door onto the street.

'This way.' Teschmaker guided him with his arm and they walked in silence along the road to the car. Neither said a word until they had been driving for a couple of minutes. Then Shlyapnikov spoke.

'I guess I always knew the day would come when the past would catch up with me. In a way it's a relief to have someone to talk to about it. Even my beloved Zoya Nikolayevna no longer speaks of it.'

Teschmaker suddenly realised just how blind he was flying. Zoya Nikolayevna? He hadn't considered her role in any of this, but of course he had known. 'Zolushka?'

'Of course. My Cinderella. I didn't know her at all,

even though we had graduated from the same Moscow university. We met on the first day at Shon. To be truthful, I didn't think much of her. She was the only woman in our intake of just over a hundred.'

'Shon? Where's that?'

'Shkola Osobogo Naznacheniya — Special Purpose School, Shon for short. It was the first foreign intelligence training school set up by the NKVD in 1940. Apart from the workload, the place was heaven.' Shlyapnikov smiled at the memory. 'They knew that the bourgeois West would be a real shock, so they gave us luxurious rooms and evenings of music and dressing up for dinner parties. All of this just fifteen miles east of the Moscow ring road at Balashikha. We were both so young and dedicated that we protested when we were selected to come here. We thought our talents would have been better used against the main adversary.'

'The Americans?' Teschmaker glanced in the rear mirror, but they were alone on the road. 'You wanted to be sent to America?'

'At that time, of course we did. But now I see that we were far better off here. Most of those who went to America were dead within a few years. Of course, they were much more proactive, running agents and more at risk of being called home and then vanishing into the gulags. Our orders, on the other hand, were to assimilate. We were the long-term sleepers awaiting activation; the sad irony is that by the time it happened, we had been here too long. Even though we were ostensibly married, Zoya Nikolayevna and I maintained a professional distance from each other for a couple of years, but then the inevitable happened and we fell in love. It was such a good thing to happen because we literally had nobody else.'

'And then Puzanov arrived.'

'Oh no, it didn't happen like that.' Shlyapnikov took out a packet of cigarettes, lit one and rolled the window down enough to let the smoke escape. 'No. I received a message to travel back to the Soviet Union. I can't tell you how terrified I was. Of course Stalin was long dead and the Terror a thing of the past, but I agonised over it for days before I even told Zoya Nikolayevna. She was, if anything, more afraid than I was, convinced that I would never return. But in the end we decided that I would go and so I made the trip to Moscow via Finland. To my surprise and relief I was greeted like a returning hero and treated extremely well. I met Puzanov, or Andrei Yakunin as you apparently know he was called, and together we were given intensive training in situating and arming a special weapons package —'

'Who? Who trained you?' Teschmaker suddenly saw the pieces falling into place.

'Oh, I don't remember.' Shlyapnikov looked puzzled and slightly irritated by the interruption. 'Does it matter?'

'Yes,' Teschmaker insisted. 'Yes, it matters. Think hard, could one of the bomb instructors have been a foreigner?'

'The Professor?' The old man laughed. 'Yes, the Professor was foreign. Why?'

'Did you know his name?' Teschmaker had no doubt that it had to have been Sydney Morris.

Shlyapnikov shook his head. 'No, he was only called the Professor. They didn't allow us to know other people's real names. The only reason I knew that Puzanov's real name was Yakunin was because we got drunk together.'

So it had been Morris. Teschmaker visualised the pieces of the jigsaw slotting into place, but it was no longer the right analogy. There was a dreadful symmetry to the way the puzzle was coming together — each of the players connected and interconnected as if in some warped karmic tapestry. What had previously appeared as individual threads now seemed inextricably woven together, and pulling any one free had the potential to unravel all the others.

'What are you going to do?' Shlyapnikov asked.

Half an hour earlier he would have offered up the same solution he and Laverov had arrived at — to play it by ear — but now Teschmaker knew with absolute certainty that there was only one possible course of action. '*We* are going to give the bomb to Rusak.'

The inclusive pronoun didn't escape Shlyapnikov but sensing the predicament he was in, he chose not to object. 'If one of these devices falls into the wrong hands, the death of a few hostages will seem pretty insignificant. I hope you've thought of that.'

'Of course,' Teschmaker snapped. 'But if we can give Rusak the device and manage to survive, then others better equipped can put paid to any ideas he might have about selling it. Rusak would be hunted into the ground.'

The old man snorted. 'Do you really think he will leave alive anyone who knows he has the device?'

'No.' Teschmaker knew Shlyapnikov was right but he also knew he was not going to sacrifice Jane and her father. 'I didn't say this was going to be easy. I just said we were going to do it.'

The Russian grunted and lit another cigarette. 'Well, it's your funeral.'

Teschmaker shrugged. 'At least we'll be in the right place for it, won't we?'

Laverov drove slowly, giving himself thinking time. An endgame was not supposed to be like this. His endgame scenario would have had him calling the shots, not some foreigner, some amateur who, like it or not, would also have to be eliminated. He hadn't warmed to Teschmaker but he did respect the way he had put the pieces together so meticulously. Meticulous ... yes, it was the right word. There was something fussy about Teschmaker that grated on him. He remembered him cleaning a spot from the table the first time they had met; he had rubbed at it with his napkin and then folded and creased the napkin, pressing it with his hand until it looked unused. Laverov hoped that when the time came he could dispose of Teschmaker neatly, with the minimum of fuss. No, he thought grimly, Teschmaker wouldn't like it to be messy.

He glanced in the rear-view mirror. A car, a white Toyota Hilux, had been behind him for three blocks. Laverov slowed and turned into a side street. To his relief, the driver of the other car made no attempt to turn, or even slow down. Paranoia, Laverov had long ago decided, was a very healthy condition.

He returned to the main road and took a circuitous route towards Teschmaker's house. For a moment he considered calling the Russian Embassy for backup, but dismissed the idea. Rusak was sure to have his own people there. No, he admitted grudgingly, it was best to follow Teschmaker's plan, makeshift though it was. Would this man Shlyapnikov do as he was asked? It was all too flimsy, but he could think of no other way. Damn that Ilya. Why the fuck hadn't he got in touch when it could have helped? The channels were all in place. And now in hospital. How? Why? At least he was still alive. Whatever good that might do. Laverov realised his mind was racing. Slow down, he told himself, this is not the moment to get rattled. But it was too late. The Professor — it was a long shot to trust the man if he was in the condition that Teschmaker had described. He would be a liability. He corrected himself: they were all liabilities.

Laverov pulled over to the side of the road and let a stream of cars pass him. No sign, no brake lights, no deviation. It seemed he was totally alone. He opened his cigarette case and lit a cigarette. The case that had been Tarasov's. It was a long way from Kimzha; a long way from home. Suddenly Moscow seemed a very desirable place to be. If I get out of this, Laverov promised himself, I will retire completely. I will go fishing and hunting mushrooms and I will never open another box of files in my life.

After parking the car at the end of Teschmaker's street, Laverov went for a quiet stroll, only doubling back once he had convinced himself that, as far as he could judge, there was no surveillance in place. And just how good is your judgment, old man? No room for self-doubt now. No time, either. If he wanted to be in position at the cemetery he needed to keep moving. He found the garage open and quickly located the implements they would need. He stowed them in the car and headed for Freeholm. Again there was no sign of a tail.

It took him a few minutes to gain entry but having done so he was relieved to find that Teschmaker's instructions were accurate. The man's fussiness may be annoying, but at times like this his attention to detail was a definite plus. A couple of hundred metres from the rendezvous point he drove off the gravel path, then backed across the road blocking it completely. Anyone attempting to escape this way would have to drive right through the Ford.

Laverov checked his pistol and, though he hoped he wouldn't need it, the spare clip. Everything seemed ready. No, he needed another cigarette first. He lit one and set out. Even though he still had half an hour before Teschmaker was due to turn up, he erred on the side of caution, walking on the grass to deaden his footfalls and avoiding the lamplight along the path by detouring around the graves. Within five minutes he had located the rendezvous point. He walked around it, looking for the right spot to position himself, and found an ornate grave that seemed an ideal vantage point. It was in direct line of sight and the tombstone provided not only good cover but a small stone cross on top that was perfect for steadying his pistol. He had no delusions about the accuracy of pistols, but even a first-year cop could have hit his target from this position. He was ready.

For a few minutes he sat on the edge of the grave, clearing his mind of all competing thoughts. He took slow deep breaths and tried to convince himself that his heart rate was coming down. It appeared to be working for his mind focused and reminded him that he had left the other implements in the car. It was as he got to his feet that he heard the footsteps on the gravel path. Laverov took out his pistol and stood still, listening, but the footsteps had stopped. No more than a few metres away. He peered through the dark, but saw nothing. Then came a voice.

'Comrade Laverov?' It was male, Russian. 'Please, I have a message for you.'

CHAPTER TWENTY-ONE

They drove in silence, Shlyapnikov lost in his own thoughts and Teschmaker racking his brains to think of some fact, some detail that he'd overlooked which might give him an edge in the upcoming encounter. But no matter which way he looked at it, there seemed to be nothing. He hoped Laverov had made all his preparations and that he could be trusted to play his part when the time came. And Shlyapnikov. Suddenly he regretted bringing him along. There was nothing more the old man could contribute and there was every possibility he would be a liability.

Just before they arrived at Freeholm, Teschmaker pulled the car over to the side of the road. There was a service station half a mile back and if he dropped the old man there he could get a taxi home.

'It would be best if you were not involved, Aleksandr Yefremovich.'

Shlyapnikov was having none of it. 'You think you

can do this without me? Teschmaker, I started this and I will see it through to the end.'

'I'd rather not —'

'You think you are so goddamn clever? I know you well enough to know that you haven't a clue about how to deal with this Rusak.'

'You've never met him —'

'That's not the point. I can show you exactly where to find what you're after.'

'I'm sorry, Aleksandr, but you should go home to your wife. This is out of your hands now.'

'You know this, do you?' Shlyapnikov growled angrily. 'You know how I have felt all these years? It is enough that I should have Puzanov's death on my hands, and now I should have another and another? Yours and God knows who else's. And I should just go back to my wife and forget all about it? I may be old but I am not dead, Teschmaker. And what do you think that Zoya Nikolayevna would think of me if I walked away from everything we worked to do all these years? She would spit on me and call me a traitor.'

Teschmaker looked at Shlyapnikov in amazement. 'The Soviet Union is gone, Aleksandr Yefremovich. The Communist Party is dead. It's a different world now. Your wife cares for nothing but her cooking and her life with you.'

But it was as though the floodgates had opened and the pent-up burden and emotion brooked no interruption. 'No! You have no understanding. For some of us Communism wasn't about the Party, it was about ideals, and when Zoya Nikolayevna and I go to our graves it will be with an unswerving belief that the ideals were right. A fool can see that the crimes the capitalists commit rival the excesses of Stalin. In the West the gap between rich and poor is growing into a gaping hole while in the Third World millions starve and disease and ignorance spread every year. This is what unbridled capitalism has done. No, I will not betray my beliefs just so you can conveniently get an old man off your hands.'

The vehemence in Shlyapnikov's voice surprised Teschmaker. 'Okay. If you want to stay . . .'

'You have never read *Sun Tzu*, have you?'

'*The Art of War*? I've read about it, but no I've never actually read it. Why?'

'Master Tzu says, unless you use local guides you cannot get the advantages of the land.'

'Which means?'

Shlyapnikov softened his voice and smiled at Teschmaker. 'Without me you will be scrabbling around in the dirt all night.'

There was no arguing with that. Teschmaker drove on.

Five minutes later they reached the turn-off. Teschmaker slowed down and pulled into the Freeholm car park. The place was absolutely deserted and for a moment the thought crossed his mind that Laverov had let him down. Or worse, might have betrayed him. No; if Laverov had walked away it would be for reasons of self-preservation, and Teschmaker knew that if the positions were reversed he too would have had huge doubts about what they were undertaking.

'What now?' Shlyapnikov asked.

'Wait here. I'll be back in a moment.' Teschmaker reached over and took the flashlight from the glove box. He walked quickly to the gate and saw to his relief that Laverov had not let him down. The chain linking the padlocked gates had been cut. He pushed each of the gates open and secured them. He had never been here after dark and was relieved to see that there were light poles at regular intervals down the road. Through the trees to the left and right other lights twinkled. At least they'd be able to see where they were going. Now, he thought, there was nothing to do but wait. Back in the car he tossed the flashlight onto the seat and switched the interior light on to check his watch. There was just over fifteen minutes before Rusak was due to arrive.

'You haven't told me who the hostages are.'

Shlyapnikov lit a cigarette and handed it over. Teschmaker took it gratefully and as he smoked explained about Jane and her father. He was conscious of the fact that he deliberately omitted the details of his relationship with Jane, describing her only as a long-time friend. The truth was, he was confused about his feelings and couldn't have explained them even to himself. The only certainty was that he wanted her and her father safely out of Rusak's hands.

'So, how are you going to play this?'

'We get Rusak to release Jane and Sydney Morris, and when they are safely out of harm's way we tell Rusak where the device is.'

'And then?' Shlyapnikov did nothing to hide his scepticism.

Teschmaker was about to reply that he had no idea what happened after that when the car was swept by the lights of another vehicle turning into the car park. It seemed Rusak believed he was going to get his hands on the device — the vehicle was a small kombi.

'We have company. Stay put.'

He got out and waited as the van approached slowly. Rusak was being cautious, flicking the van's lights to high beam and stopping well back, leaving Teschmaker temporarily blinded. He heard one of the doors open and then a figure stepped between the headlights.

'Put your gun on the ground, Teschmaker.'

Even though he couldn't see him clearly, he recognised Rusak's voice. 'I don't have one.' He patted his pockets to demonstrate.

Apparently Rusak believed him, for he walked forward to where Teschmaker could see him more clearly. He was carrying a nasty-looking machine-pistol. For a moment he thought that there was also a smaller pistol on his belt, but then saw it was a mobile phone.

'Who's that in the car?'

'The man who can show you where the device is.'

'You didn't say anything about him on the phone,' Rusak said suspiciously. 'Tell him to get out of the car.'

'We have to drive into the graveyard,' Teschmaker began.

Rusak gestured angrily with the pistol. 'Now!'

Teschmaker stood his ground. 'Where are Sydney Morris and Jane?'

'In the van, but you won't live long enough to see them if you don't do as I say. Now tell whoever is in the car to get out so I can see him.'

Teschmaker walked back to the car and opened the passenger door. 'He wants to take a look at you.'

'Fuck him,' Shlyapnikov said stubbornly. 'Tell him I don't get out of the car to greet scum.'

'For Christ's sake, Aleksandr, he's got a gun.'

'So let him shoot me. He's not going to get what he wants if I'm dead.' To emphasise the point he pulled the door shut.

Teschmaker shrugged and went back to Rusak.

'He says if you want to see him you have to come over.' He said it as calmly as he could but the reaction from Rusak was anything but calm. He prodded Teschmaker aside with the barrel of the machine-pistol and marched straight up to the car and yanked at the door handle. Shlyapnikov had had the presence of mind to lock it.

Rusak seemed to lose control, he kicked the door and shouted in Russian. '*Poslushay ty mudack*!' For a second Teschmaker thought he was going to shoot Shlyapnikov, but then the car window came down slowly and the old man turned and smiled at Rusak.

'*Ty u menja dovye' byvaesh'sja sokoro*. You keep showing off and you'll end up in trouble — and don't call me mother fucker.'

'Who the fuck do you think you are to talk to me like that?' Rusak snapped.

'Someone who's done more for the motherland than you ever will. I wouldn't wipe a kulak's arse with you.'

Rusak ignored him and turned back to Teschmaker. 'What the fuck did you bring your grandfather along for?'

'He knows the location of the device. Now can I see Jane and Sydney?'

But Rusak wasn't listening. 'How does he know?'

'He put the damned thing there in the first place,' Teschmaker said quietly. 'We had a deal. I want to see Jane and Sydney.'

'When I see that you can deliver. You lead the way.'

'Fuck you too,' Teschmaker mouthed as Rusak turned on his heel. He went back to the car and got in.

'Thanks for handling that so diplomatically,' he said bitterly. 'That really helped.'

'You want me to be nice to some jumped-up little crook?'

'I'm out of my depth and over my head and the last thing I need you to do is inflame the situation. I agreed to you coming along because you said you could locate the device quicker than I could. Just keep your cool.'

'He's the kind of shit that gives Russians a bad name.'

'Drop it.'

'Teschmaker, the man is a criminal. He has a gun and when I show him what he wants to see, he is going to use the gun on everyone he wants out of the way. You and I will be top of the list. I find that an insane enough situation, but you asking me to be nice to him — that is truly crazy.'

It was crazy. But even though he could see no way out of the situation, he was going ahead with it. Fatalism. Did he believe he was invulnerable? It was as though logic played no part in the decision; though he could see every reason to do a U-turn and drive away he knew he wouldn't, but didn't know why. For a moment he had the unnerving feeling that he was separating from himself, calmly watching as another part of him started the car and drove slowly through the cemetery gates. Into the valley of death, he thought morbidly. No, there had to be a way — but if there was, it still eluded him. At least it appeared that Laverov was in place. He wished he'd asked the Russian if he was actually any good with his pistol. He had probably never shot anyone in his life. But at least with him there it wasn't all one-sided. Maybe they had a chance. But his descent into morbidity was running unchecked. Was this how a condemned man's mind worked? As his arms and legs were strapped into the electric chair, did he convince himself that the power would fail? Was the last thought on the gallows not of an afterlife to come but the conviction that somehow the rope would break? Teschmaker shuddered, and in an attempt to banish the images from his mind, slowed down and concentrated on driving along the narrow road between the plots. Even at this he failed. I'm driving my own hearse, he thought, and no matter how slowly I approach the grave it is still my destination.

'Can I have another cigarette?' he asked.

'You'll stunt your growth,' Shlyapnikov said dryly as he lit it and handed it over.

To his left Teschmaker saw the footpath leading to the small bridge he had walked over earlier — it now felt like a lifetime ago. A little further on the road divided: straight ahead to the newest section of the cemetery, the left fork to the older areas. Fortunately the side road was also lit by a row of street lights. He watched in the rear-vision mirror as the car behind followed him around the corner. In his mind he quickly reviewed the situation. There was no doubt that the odds were stacked against them. Rusak presumably had another of his goons in the car with Jane and Sydney Morris, and they were both armed. On his side there was Shlyapnikov and Laverov. He knew Laverov had a pistol but if it came to a shoot-out it would be no match for Rusak's machine-pistol and whatever the other man had. It was not the kind of odds he would have taken a bet on. But Jane and Sydney Morris were also part of the equation, as was the device itself.

'Are you certain you can find this damn thing?' he asked, giving voice to his concern.

'Oh yes. Trust me on that score,' the old man replied grimly and then added, 'That bastard will be sorry I did.'

As they turned the corner to the section of the cemetery that contained Puzanov's grave, Shlyapnikov put out his hand and touched Teschmaker's arm. 'Pull over here, before we get to the next street light.'

'Why not just drive up to the grave?'

'You want to get out of this alive? Then do as I say.' He turned in his seat and glanced at the van pulling up behind them. 'Pull over a bit, we need him to get past.'

Teschmaker couldn't see the point of the exercise, but moved the car to the side of the road and switched off the motor. 'I hope you know what the hell you're doing.'

'Just make sure you get Jane and her father out of the van and into your car before we go any further. And put the flashlight back in the glove box.'

There was a sudden tone of determination in Shlyapnikov's voice, as though the brief exchange with Rusak had hardened his resolve. Teschmaker decided not to argue, picked the light up off the seat and stowed it away.

'I would murder for a vodka,' the old man growled quietly. 'Okay, let's get this over with.'

Rusak watched them carefully as they got out of the car. He gave every indication of a man in command of the situation. He cradled the machine-pistol in his arms as he spoke quietly into his phone. He finished his conversation and hooked the phone back on his belt before approaching them. 'It's here?'

'Just opposite that next lamppost.' Shlyapnikov indicated along the road. 'You'll need to get your van closer. The scientists were not as clever as the propaganda would have you believe. The damn thing weighs about forty kilos.'

Rusak's eyes were alight with excitement, as though he had finally let himself believe he was actually going to get his hands on the weapon. He looked at Shlyapnikov. 'You were part of the team that hid it here?'

'For what it's worth, yes.'

'Oh, it's worth a lot,' Rusak said. 'But what I don't understand is how you are still alive. Every one of the team members is dead.'

'Not this one,' the old man said bluntly.

'How is it possible?'

Shlyapnikov squinted at Rusak, weighing him up. Then, obviously wanting to tell the story but not directly to Rusak, he turned to Teschmaker 'The other member of my team had instructions to eliminate me. Unfortunately he was unfit for the task. When the time came he broke down and told me. He knew the only way he could survive was to disappear and so we solved two problems at once. We put his name on the tombstone above the device.'

'So that's not Puzanov's body in there?' Teschmaker was stunned.

'No. We obtained the body of an old alcoholic. We simply changed the death notice and the inscription.'

'So this man, Puzanov, he is still alive?' The idea that someone else knew of the device's location obviously alarmed Rusak.

Shlyapnikov turned to him. 'Don't worry, Rusak, we are the only ones who know.' He turned back to address Teschmaker. 'I sent a signal to Moscow saying that everything was in place and that Puzanov was dead. The reply instructed me where to hide the remote control. It also specified that it should be done on a specific date. At the time I thought nothing of that. When the day came I was ill with flu and so Puzanov said he would do it. Unfortunately, because Moscow had set the time and place, it was easy for them to eliminate the surviving team member. They killed Puzanov. It should have been me.'

'But that doesn't make sense,' Rusak burst in. 'If they killed him, how would they know where the device was?'

Shlyapnikov shot him a look of disdain. 'If they

knew where the remote was they had no need to know the location of the device. The remote could activate it anywhere within a ten-kilometre radius. It was perfect security.'

'So all these years you've been visiting Puzanov's grave?' Teschmaker asked.

'I was checking that the device was not disturbed. I didn't care for Puzanov. The man was a traitor. He had orders to kill me and he lacked the guts.'

'Jesus!' Teschmaker was dumbfounded.

Something was bothering Rusak. He looked at the old man suspiciously. 'If you are such a fucking patriot, why are you giving it to me?'

'Because I don't have a choice. You're the one with the guns. Anyway, you deserve it. The damned thing has ruined my life. I figure it will do the same for you.' Shlyapnikov spat on the side of the road. 'Now shall we get on with it?'

'You two walk in front of me.' Rusak indicated with the pistol.

But Teschmaker stepped in front of him. 'No, not until Jane and her father are sitting safely in my car.'

'So they can just drive away? Forget it. The old man comes with us, she stays.'

'You can keep the keys,' Shlyapnikov said.

Teschmaker looked at him in disbelief, then realised that they weren't far enough away from the grave site to give Jane a real chance of getting away, even discounting the fact that she would have to turn the car around.

Rusak thought about it then turned back to the van. 'Dimitri.'

The side door slid open and a huge bear of a man got out. He was blond-haired with eyes as dark as deep water and just as cold. He was carrying another machine-pistol. In his huge hands, it looked like a toy. Teschmaker knew the odds were not improving.

'Bring them out,' Rusak ordered.

The man nodded and said something to the occupants. To Teschmaker's relief, Sydney Morris stepped cautiously out onto the road, followed by Jane. As they moved forward into the van's lights Teschmaker saw that Jane was deathly white, her eyes rimmed with red as though she had been crying. Her father looked haggard. Clearly disoriented, he looked around blinking, loose-jawed and mouth open.

Teschmaker moved to greet them but Rusak stepped in front of him. 'Piss off,' Teschmaker snapped and ignoring the man and his weapon took Jane in his arms. 'Are you okay?' he asked quietly.

She looked at him, her eyes cold and distant. 'No, I'm not okay.'

'I'm so sorry about this . . .' Sydney Morris began, looking down at his hands. They were shaking uncontrollably.

Rusak reasserted control. 'Enough! Dimitri, take the keys from the car and shut her in.'

The big man moved quickly to the car, located the keys and handed them to Rusak. He opened the passenger door and gestured for Jane to get in, but Teschmaker held on to her, trying desperately to think of something to give her hope in a manifestly hopeless situation.

'Come on, let her get into the car,' Rusak said impatiently.

Jane turned away. She's in shock, Teschmaker thought, as he watched her move zombie-like towards the car. As she reached it she turned, steadying herself against the door, her eyes locking with his, pleading. But there was nothing he could do or say. The sense of helplessness was overwhelming and yet . . . there was something. Suddenly his mind flashed back to the first time they had sat in the car together and he knew he had to let her know what he had remembered. 'Jane —'

'I said, enough,' Rusak snapped. 'Dimitri, get her in the car and stay beside it.'

'Don't worry.' Teschmaker knew his face was a picture of false optimism, but he hoped she would understand what he was going to say. 'Just remember the only thing you know about playing pool.'

But her face was a mixture of bewilderment and resignation as with a weak smile she allowed herself to be pushed into the car. Dimitri made a show of slamming the door shut then took up guard, leaning back against the vehicle.

Rusak nodded in approval and turned to Teschmaker. 'Mr Morris will accompany us in order to verify that the device is in an operable condition. And you . . . what's your name?'

'Shlyapnikov.'

'You will find it for me.'

'That's what I said.' Shlyapnikov looked as though it was taking all his self-control not to spit in the man's face.

'Good.' Rusak grinned broadly. 'Then let's go.' He indicated that they should walk in front of him.

'What about your van? There's no way you can carry the package.'

'All in good time. I want to see it first.'

They walked in single file, the only sound the crunching of the gravel beneath their feet and, away to the right, the frightened call and sudden flight of a night bird disturbed by the unexpected intrusion into its domain. As they came to the lamppost opposite the grave, Teschmaker caught a fleeting glimpse of a small bat darting through the feast of moths that fluttered around the light. Maybe it was the unspoken presence of death that heightened his awareness, but he was acutely conscious that his senses were working on overdrive. Even the night air seemed to be full of subtle presences, as though on its meandering journey from the coast it had collected the essences of backyards, streets, gardens and people, stealing their perfumes and scents; gathering from the graves the odours of the marshy ground and cold stone.

He remembered Laverov. With any luck the man had followed his instructions exactly and parked his car further along the road in order to block any attempted escape by vehicle. Hopefully he had located the grave and was now in position, waiting for Teschmaker to give him the agreed signal. A lot was resting on Laverov's ability to perform.

Shlyapnikov stopped at the side of the road, the nearest light casting his shadow across the grave. 'It's here.' He stood like a mourner, his hands clasped behind his back.

Rusak pushed the others aside. 'Where?'

'Under there.'

Rusak looked nonplussed, not knowing who to blame for the fact that nobody had told him the device would have to be dug up. 'So how do we get it out?'

Teschmaker looked back to his car, hoping to see Jane, but Dimitri had moved around to lean on the bonnet and obscured his view. Deciding that he would feel better with something in his hands, even if it was only a spade, Teschmaker started round the side of the grave.

Rusak moved quickly, levelling the machine-pistol at his stomach. 'Stop right there. Where the fuck are you going?'

'To get a spade. Or do you want to use your hands?' It was then, as he turned to Rusak, that he saw something he should not have been able to see. Laverov's car, just visible beyond the light of the next street lamp, was parked in the middle of the road.

Rusak followed the line of his gaze and with a smile on his lips called loudly, 'Hey, Gennadi.'

Gennadi? Who the hell was Gennadi? Even as he thought it Teschmaker felt his stomach sinking and he knew that the last hope he had been clinging to was gone. The car headlights flicked on, the motor started and as the Ford moved slowly forward, its lights illuminated what had appeared to be a shadow across the road: Laverov's body, spreadeagled on the gravel. He had not even made it as far as the grave, for the spade and pickaxe he had collected from Teschmaker's garage lay beside him.

'Oh, I forgot to tell you about Laverov. He had a bit of an accident.'

'You're fucking insane, Rusak,' Teschmaker said through gritted teeth.

Rusak laughed. 'Insane for stopping a man you set up to ambush me?'

'I told you I would give you the device. There was no need for this.'

'No? Then what was he doing waiting here? It was lucky I sent my man ahead to secure the area. This man posed a threat, so he was dealt with.'

Speechless with rage and ignoring the pistol in Rusak's hand, Teschmaker brushed past him and went over to the body. Kneeling down he felt for a pulse in the neck, even though the jagged exit wound in the side of Laverov's skull was ample evidence of his death. On the gravel lay Laverov's glasses, the lenses shattered, the frames buckled. They had been trodden on. It infuriated him to be so helpless. Behind the wheel of the Ford he could see the killer watching him, his face blank, impassive. Teschmaker took his hand off Laverov's neck and reached out for the spade, but even as he raised it he knew that if he attacked the man he would end up on the road beside Laverov. He gripped it firmly and walked back to the grave.

Shlyapnikov had Sydney Morris by the arm and was seating him a few feet away, his back up against a neighbouring tombstone. Behind Teschmaker the car motor had been turned off. Rusak called to the driver in Russian, instructing him to bring the van up. The man who got out of the Ford was as big as Rusak's other offsider, Dimitri, and just as blond.

'The bastard has been mass producing them,' Shlyapnikov murmured as he returned to Teschmaker's side.

'Let's get this over with,' Teschmaker said coldly. He blamed himself for Laverov's death. It would have been just as easy to come all in the one car, but he had thought it best to dispatch Laverov in advance. It hadn't occurred to him that Rusak would also send an advance guard to scout out the location. The man must have seen Laverov open the gates and from there it would have been a simple matter of following him, making the hit and phoning Rusak to inform him.

'Start this side of the gravestone,' Shlyapnikov instructed. 'There's a concrete lip, you need to dig about half a metre this side to be clear of it.'

'How deep is it?' Rusak stepped up onto the thick concrete wall that enclosed the grave, the pistol gripped firmly in his hands, his eyes shining with expectation. Teschmaker wondered if he already had a buyer lined up for the bomb and if so, who? It hardly mattered; if it went that far then the likelihood was that he and the others would have joined history's roll call of innocent bystanders — innocent and dead.

'I can't remember,' Shlyapnikov said.

'You're certain it's here?'

'*Bozhe moy*! You want to do the digging?' Shlyapnikov blazed. 'I've told you the fucking thing is here. Just shut up and let us get on with it.'

Teschmaker prodded around with the tip of the spade until he had located the concrete slab then began to dig through the matted weeds to the reasonably soft damp earth beneath. In a matter of minutes he was down about twenty centimetres.

'Take it easy,' Shlyapnikov cautioned. 'Just scrape the dirt away now.'

Teschmaker turned the spade around, banged it against the side of the grave to dislodge the clogged dirt and began to scrape. He hit something. Suddenly fearful, he pulled the spade away and looked to Shlyapnikov.

'Use your hands.' Shlyapnikov frowned as though trying to recall something.

Teschmaker handed him the spade and crouched down, his mind flashing up macabre images, as gruesome as they were irrational. There's nothing here, he told himself, but he half expected his fingers to plunge into rotting flesh, or skeletal remains. The earth was warmer than he had expected and he imagined he could smell decay rising, cloying in his nostrils. Cautiously he worked through the earth, sifting and discarding until his hands found the object that the spade had struck. He wished he had the tools of an archaeologist and could take his time, brushing the soil away rather than probing with his hands. But then his fingers recognised the shape and texture of the object and after working it back and forth a couple of times he pulled it from the ground. It was a glass jar, the lid rusted but still in place. Realising he had been holding his breath, he took in a lungful of air and tossed the jar to one side.

'That's the first marker,' Shlyapnikov said matter-of-factly. 'Sorry, I should have warned you. I forgot all about them.'

'Them?'

'Yes, there should be another marker down a further fifty centimetres or so.'

Teschmaker reached over and grabbed the spade. 'Anything else you've forgotten?'

Shlyapnikov shrugged. 'It was a long time ago.' He paused, then added, 'The next marker is a sheet of black plastic at the bottom of the hole. It's okay to use the spade for a time.'

'Thanks,' Teschmaker said darkly and recommenced digging. As he did he heard the sound of the van's motor. It swung past his car and its lights flashed momentarily across the grave. Then it pulled in beside them, spotlighting Sydney Morris who was leaning back against the neighbouring headstone. He looked a picture of misery, head bowed, his hands still trembling despite the fact that he was half asleep.

'Tell your man to back it up,' Shlyapnikov said to Rusak. 'The shorter distance we have to carry this the better.'

'I give the orders here,' Rusak snapped, but nevertheless conveyed the message to Gennadi who proceeded to do a rather badly executed four-point turn on the narrow road.

'There's the plastic.' Teschmaker stepped up out of the hole he had excavated.

Rusak moved cautiously forward and peered down into the dark. 'I can't see a damn thing!' He glared at Shlyapnikov. 'You had better not be playing games with me.'

'Look for yourself.' Teschmaker stood back, but Rusak waited until Gennadi joined them then handed the man his pistol.

'Cover them,' he said, then pushed past Teschmaker and stepped gingerly down into the hole. He bent over and tore some strips off the remains of what had been a folded sheet of thick plastic, then took the spade and drove it down forcefully. There was a splintering noise as the spade went deep and for a second Rusak looked down at his feet then sprang from the grave. 'For fuck's sake! It's a fucking coffin.'

'I understand that's pretty standard in graves.' Teschmaker smiled sardonically but he too stepped back as the sickly sweet smell of long-trapped air rose from the hole.

Rusak was not amused. Grabbing his pistol from Gennadi he brought it up to Shlyapnikov's head. 'Okay, no more games. Where the fuck is the device?'

If Shlyapnikov was fazed he refused to show it. 'Really, Comrade, I think you have too little faith in the skill of our motherland's agents. Only a fool would place something directly on top of a coffin.'

'How do you mean?'

'Patience. Now we have to dig forward.' He brought his hand up slowly and pushed the pistol barrel away from his skull then turned and looked unflinchingly at Rusak. 'If you stop interfering maybe we can continue.'

To Teschmaker's surprise and relief Rusak stepped back as if, despite the obvious advantages of age and weaponry, he was intimidated by the sense of authority in the old man's voice.

'Get on with it.'

Shlyapnikov turned back to Teschmaker. 'You'll have to use your hands again. The case is directly beneath the concrete lip that supports the headstone. Just in front of it there should be a board protecting the handle and locks. Let me know when you reach it.'

Teschmaker nodded and stepped back into the hole, careful to keep his feet away from where the spade had breached the decayed lid of the coffin. He realised the idea of the smell was in fact worse than the odour itself. As if he was having the same reaction to it, Shlyapnikov sat himself on the side of the grave, lit two cigarettes, and handed one to Teschmaker who took it gratefully. He stretched his back and shook his legs to ease the growing pain in his cramped muscles then looked towards the car. He could clearly see Jane's face pressed forward against the window, a pale full moon in the car's darkness, watching. He waved half-heartedly and returned to the task of clearing away the dirt. The ground beneath the concrete lip, never having been compacted, was far softer and came away easily and it only took a couple of minutes before his fingers touched something solid. He brushed the earth away and peered into the gloom. 'I've found the board.'

Shlyapnikov stubbed out his cigarette and stood up. 'Okay. Now, brush the dirt away until you can get your hands around each end.'

'Done,' Teschmaker replied.

'Now take hold of the board at both ends and pull it out slowly.'

'Why the hell do you have to be so gentle with it?' Rusak demanded.

'Because the case has been here for a very long time and I don't want to damage it.' Shlyapnikov did nothing to disguise the patronising tone in his voice.

'We'll slide it out onto the board and then open it up before taking it out of the hole. That way we can make certain it is safe for you to transport. Or do you want something that's totally useless?'

'Just get it out where I can see it,' Rusak said impatiently.

Shlyapnikov cautiously stepped into the grave and, leaning on Teschmaker's shoulder, down into the hole. 'We have to ease it out very gently,' he said quietly and, steadying himself with one hand on the earth, bent his knees slowly until he was crouching beside Teschmaker, who had positioned the board on the bottom of the hole in front of them. Together they brushed away the last of the dirt until the front of the small case was clearly visible. There were locks either side of the handle. Teschmaker reached for it.

'No,' Shlyapnikov hissed. 'Don't touch it. We have to clear the dirt on either side first so we can slide it forwards onto the board.'

It seemed overly fussy, particularly as the case looked to be robust in both design and condition, but Teschmaker didn't argue. If that was the way the old man wanted it, then so be it. And the longer they took, he thought grimly, the more time he had to think of some way out of their predicament.

Rusak peered over their shoulders. 'How long is this going to take?'

'All night if you don't get out of the light,' Shlyapnikov snarled. He waited until the man had moved back and then started working to clear a space along the side of the case.

'You know what I'd like now?' He didn't wait for Teschmaker to answer. 'A great big slice of Sharlolka Malakova. I swear that Zoya Nikolayevna makes the finest in the world. You know, Teschmaker, she is the best woman I have ever known. All these years she has stuck with me. Yes, we argued at times, fought even, but never once did she want to leave. That is something rare.'

'She's a good woman,' Teschmaker said, wondering what had brought on this domestic revelation.

'Others would have given up years ago.'

'Given up what? You?'

'No, this damn city. The first few years we hated it. We thought the best thing would be if the place sank back into the swamp. But then, as time went by, we became part of it. After the Soviet Union collapsed I remember asking Zoya if she wanted to go back to Moscow. You know what she said?'

'No.' Teschmaker cleared away the last of the dirt from his side of the case.

Shlyapnikov laughed at the memory. 'Nothing. She just went and made me a cup of coffee.' He tossed a handful of dirt to one side and looked at Teschmaker. There were tears running down his cheeks. 'You ready?'

Teschmaker nodded and as Shlyapnikov worked his hands underneath the case, he took the sides and pulled carefully. There was some initial resistance and then it came free.

'Careful,' Shlyapnikov said as they moved it forward. 'Now, let me get my fingers out.'

Teschmaker held the case until Shlyapnikov had his hands free then lowered it onto the board. It was hard to believe that such a nondescript case could be so important. With the exception of the strongly reinforced corners, it could have been any standard suitcase.

'Is that it?' Rusak sounded disappointed. 'I expected something a bit bigger.'

'The device is bigger. This case contains the remote detonation controls.'

'And the bomb? Where the fuck is it?'

'I'll tell you that once you let the others go.' Shlyapnikov eased himself into a sitting position on the edge of the hole.

That was the final straw for Rusak. He lashed out with his boot, kicking Shlyapnikov in the back, sending him sprawling sideways. Teschmaker scrambled out of the grave and helped the old man to sit up. 'You bastard, Rusak. You heard him — you'll get nothing if you do that again.'

'Stop playing games, Teschmaker. You and that old bastard have been stringing me along all night. Now, where the fuck is the bomb?'

'Screw your mother,' Teschmaker said and ignoring the gun being levelled at his head turned back to Shlyapnikov, who was doubled up, wincing with pain. Behind him he heard Rusak swear and he steeled himself, certain that at any moment he would be shot. Unfortunately, as long as Rusak had Shlyapnikov he didn't need anyone else.

Teschmaker brought his attention back to his friend. 'Are you okay?'

Shlyapnikov grimaced and ran his hands down his side, checking to see if anything was broken. 'It'll take more than a kick from that little arsehole to kill me.'

'So open the damn thing,' Rusak ordered. He was

standing just behind them, the pistol aimed at the older man. Beside him Gennadi had drawn a pistol and was covering Teschmaker.

Shlyapnikov stood up stiffly. 'You want to do it, go ahead. But if you force it open the contents will be destroyed.'

'Destroyed?'

'Part of the design brief was that if the remote control should fall into the wrong hands there must be a mechanism to render the remote inoperable if forced open.'

Rusak was unsure whether to believe Shlyapnikov or not. Then it occurred to him that there was someone else who would know.

The old man was huddled against the headstone, his head on his chest. Rusak shook him. 'Wake up, Professor.'

Sydney Morris raised his head and squinted around. He looked very ill and even more confused than previously. Rusak gripped him by the shoulders and pulled his face towards his. 'These bastards are playing games with me, Professor, so I need some straight answers.'

'What?'

'Tell me what would happen if we forced this case open?'

Sydney's face looked as blank and worn as the headstone he was resting against. 'Case? I'm sorry . . .'

'The case with the remote control. What happens if it's forced open? Would the contents be destroyed?'

Somewhere in Sydney Morris's brain the connections were made. His eyes suddenly found their focus. 'Absolutely right. Have to open the thing damn carefully.'

Rusak released his grasp, letting the old man slump back against the headstone. But Morris had more to say. 'You know there are other things in there? There's cash and a pistol. You wouldn't want to lose those.'

Rusak turned back to the others. 'Oh, very clever. You thought you'd get your hands on the pistol. Now you're going to get the damn thing open and then you're going to show me where the bomb is.'

Shlyapnikov shook his head. 'No. You release the others and then I'll open it and show you where the device is.'

Rusak shrugged. 'I think not. I'm sorry, I didn't want to do this, but it seems I've no alternative.' He waved his hand to attract Dimitri's attention. 'When I tell you, I want you to put a bullet in that bitch's head, understand?'

Dimitri, who had been lounging against the car, straightened up, patted his weapon affectionately and grinned. 'Sure,' he said.

Rusak turned back to Shlyapnikov. 'Now, are we going to open the case or do I have to kill her first? I'm happy either way, and because Gennadi here gets jealous when Dimitri has all the fun, I'm afraid I'll have to let him kill the Professor next. Am I making myself clear?'

Shlyapnikov looked down at the case and then to Teschmaker. 'You know, when you play chess there comes a time in a game when you just have to lay your king on its side.'

Teschmaker felt his stomach sink. He didn't want to understand what his friend was saying but he did, all too clearly. 'Aleksandr Yefremovich —'

Shlyapnikov cut him short. 'Just tell Cinderella that the old man delivered the glass slipper.' He turned back to Rusak. 'Okay. I'll need a torch and the smallest screwdriver or nailfile that you have.'

Rusak instructed Gennadi to look in the van. The man returned a few moments later with a small tool kit and Rusak nodded at him to show them to Shlyapnikov.

'That'll be fine, but I still need a torch.'

'You'll have to make do without one.'

'Teschmaker has a flashlight in the car. Tell your goon over there to let him get it.'

'Where is it?'

'In the glove box.'

'And a gun too perhaps?' Rusak said dismissively, then called out to Dimitri, 'See if there is a torch in the glove box.'

Dimitri looked disappointed that it wasn't the order to shoot. Keeping his pistol trained on Jane, he opened the door and bent into the car, emerging a moment later with the flashlight in his hand.

'Okay, you can go and get it,' Rusak said.

The sick feeling in Teschmaker's stomach hadn't abated. He shot a glance at Shlyapnikov, who nodded curtly and waved him away.

'He's coming over to get it,' Rusak called to Dimitri. 'Put it on the ground and keep him covered.'

'Sure, I was about to use a torch to attack a man with a pistol.' Teschmaker's sarcasm was as raw as his nerves. He reached out and patted Shlyapnikov's arm. 'Don't start without me.' But he knew what the old man was about to do, and that he would do nothing to stop him.

The distance between the grave and where the flashlight lay on the ground at Dimitri's feet was not far but it felt like the hardest journey of his life. As soon as he stepped off the grave he heard Shlyapnikov also move onto the gravel.

'Even with the torch it will be dark and cramped in the hole. Do you mind giving me a hand to move the case up onto the concrete?'

Rusak grunted and gestured to Gennadi to assist as well. As the two men stepped into the grave, Shlyapnikov bent down and started to examine the contents of the tool kit. 'There's not much here,' he grumbled.

'But you can open it?' Rusak still sounded unconvinced.

'Yes.'

He watched as the two men reached down for the case. 'Lift it gently from underneath. I don't want the damn thing damaged at this stage.'

Rusak and Gennadi lifted the case clear of the hole and lowered it carefully down onto the small concrete lip in front of the tombstone.

'Jesus!' Shlyapnikov exclaimed.

'What?' Rusak looked at him, his eyes startled and suspicious.

'I just forgot something. The stupid thing is probably not even locked.'

'You mean you didn't try it?' Rusak's look turned to

disbelief. 'For fuck's sake!' He reached down and turned the handle.

The explosion ripped him apart.

Gennadi, only slightly sheltered by Rusak's body, was smashed into the rear of the van; it disintegrated around him. Fifteen metres away Teschmaker had no time to throw himself to the ground before the shock wave from the explosion did it for him. One second he was walking and the next it was as though a bus had slammed into him from behind. Shrapnel whipped over his head and he felt the hair singe on the back of his head.

Winded and dazed he lay still, enveloped in a cloud of smoke and dust. Then he rolled to one side and staggered to his feet. It only took a glance to see how effective the blast had been. The *molniya* booby trap had lived up to its name — the area looked as though it had been hit by lightning, not once but several times. Teschmaker struggled to make sense of the chaos that had suddenly replaced the tranquil setting. The main force of the blast appeared to have gone forward and upward, taking out the lamppost and ripping branches from a tree. The remains of a body lay on the ground; something or someone was burning in the back of the van. There was another body sprawled at the foot of the grave, covered with smoking dirt and debris. Then, to his amazement, he saw someone move. Covered in ash and looking less like an elderly scientist than a witch doctor, Sydney Morris rose up from behind the neighbouring grave. Somehow the headstone he had been leaning against had protected him from the blast.

Teschmaker heard a sound behind him. He spun around, suddenly aware that he had forgotten all about Jane and Dimitri. The big Russian had a superficial shrapnel wound to the head; a line of blood ran down from his scalp into one eye. But it was not enough to stop him. He staggered to his feet, shaking his head, groggy from the blow he'd received. He rubbed the blood from his eye and, seeing Teschmaker, let out a roar and scrabbled in the dirt at his feet for the pistol. He found it and brought it up, fumbling with the safety catch. Still unsteady he fell back against the car before regaining his balance.

Teschmaker knew he only had one hope and that was to charge the man. Dimitri was three or four metres away but it might just as well have been a kilometre for all the chance Teschmaker had of bridging the distance. But it was too late to stop. He launched himself forward as Dimitri brought the pistol up again, this time held firmly in both hands. Teschmaker's body was expecting a stream of bullets but there was just a single shot. Even at such close range it was an unimpressive sound. An insignificant sound. Teschmaker hit the ground with his eyes screwed shut in fear. He heard a strange sighing next to him and then the pistol fired off round after round. This time the noise was so extreme he was deafened.

He forced his eyes open and saw Dimitri curled on the ground, one hand grasping his chest as though to plug the gaping hole bubbling blood through his fingers. His other arm was twisted backwards at an unnatural angle, that hand firing the pistol in decreasing bursts along the ground, the bullets ricocheting off the nearby graves. But there was no intelligence behind the shots, just a hand stuck on the trigger. Teschmaker waited until he was sure the last shot had been fired then got painfully to his feet. His hands were bleeding and his trousers were shredded from the force with which he had hit the gravel. With a calmness that surprised him, he walked over to where Dimitri lay twitching in the dirt and bending down, took the machine-pistol from his hand and flung it into the darkness. Then he turned and walked towards the car.

Jane sat there frozen, hands still on the pistol, staring through the hole in the shattered side window.

'I didn't have time to wind it down,' she said.

He opened the door and took the pistol from her. 'At least you worked out that I had left it in the side pocket.'

'It took me a while.' She held onto his arm as he helped her from the car.

'Come on. I think your father needs you.'

She looked wildly at him, suddenly remembering her father. 'He's alive?'

'He's alive.'

Teschmaker put his arm around her and guided her around Dimitri's now still body. There was a lot of smoke coming from the back of the van and as they approached it he realised that one of the tyres had caught fire. The designers of the *molniya* device had done their job well — the scene was one of total devastation, a fact which made the next moment even more remarkable. Teschmaker wondered for an instant whether he had finally gone mad. Through the smoke came Sydney Morris, and by his side an improbable ghost — Aleksandr Yefremovich Shlyapnikov. He looked like something out of a nightmare: his shirt had been torn away and blood was running from dozens of small shrapnel wounds to his chest, arms and face. Despite his obvious pain he was grinning like a madman.

'I thought you were going to —' Teschmaker began as Jane rushed over to her father.

'I was,' interrupted Shlyapnikov. 'But then I suddenly figured that Rusak might be stupid enough to actually try and open it himself, and there might be a way out. I was at the end of the grave and as he reached for the handle I threw myself down behind the concrete surround. I thought I was dead, but I opened my eyes to see the Professor rising from the grave.'

Teschmaker glanced at the burning van. The thought flashed through his mind that it might not be long before the fire reached a fuel line or the petrol tank. He also knew that even though they were well inside the cemetery and it was surrounded by industrial suburbs, they couldn't rely on the chance that the smoke and the sound of the explosion hadn't been noticed. Somebody might be reporting it to the police even now.

'I want to get my father home,' Jane interrupted.

'Yes, I was just thinking that we'd better be going. But I wonder what to do about Laverov's body . . .'

He turned to Shlyapnikov, who was bending over Rusak, retrieving the keys to Jane's car from the dead man's pockets.

'We leave it. It will be a good ending for him. If he is found here with the others it will eventually come out that he died in the course of his duties. Maybe he has someone at home who will appreciate his brave sacrifice . . . and his pension.'

Teschmaker didn't feel comfortable leaving Laverov but Shlyapnikov's reasoning was sound and he could think of no alternative. He knelt beside the man's body and reaching into his jacket pocket took out his cigarette case. 'I'm sure you would want me to have it,' he said quietly, then got to his feet and rejoined the others.

There was one other matter worrying him. As they walked towards the car he murmured his concern to Shlyapnikov. 'What about the bomb?'

The Russian looked at him for a moment then smiled. 'What bomb? And even if there was one, there is no way of detonating it now the remote has been destroyed. Or do you really want to come back here and dig up more of the past?'

Teschmaker shook his head slowly and opened the car door for his friend. 'Come on, we'll get you to a hospital.'

'After we get a drink.' Shlyapnikov grimaced as he lowered himself gingerly into the car seat.

They drove out of the cemetery in silence. On the main road the traffic was light, but Teschmaker kept his speed down. He tried to imagine explaining the shattered passenger-side window to a traffic cop and decided avoidance was a preferable tactic. He felt light-headed, euphoric. We're all in shock, he thought. He glanced in the rear-vision mirror at Jane and her father they were immersed in their own thoughts: Jane staring out the window; her father with his head in his hands, trembling. Beside him Shlyapnikov was attending his cuts and scratches with a now stained handkerchief. Most of the wounds appeared superficial but a deep gash on his temple particularly concerned Teschmaker. The old man had managed to staunch the bleeding but it looked as though it required several stitches.

They were five kilometres from Freeholm when they saw the police car coming towards them, its flashing lights and siren leaving them in no doubt as to its destination.

'I think we should avoid the hospital,' Shlyapnikov said. 'It will be the first place they check once they see the mayhem out there.' He registered the sceptical look Teschmaker shot at him and ignored it. 'Never felt better. Anyway, it will give Zoya something to worry about. Get her out of the kitchen.'

'You need a doctor,' Teschmaker said.

'I need a vodka. Damn doctors would take one look at us and ring the police.'

A couple of kilometres later a second police car flashed past them, closely followed by an ambulance. Jane leaned forward and tapped Teschmaker on the arm.

'The gun. What shall we do with the gun?'

'We'll have to get rid of it,' he replied.

Shlyapnikov reached down and retrieved the pistol from the floor where she had dropped it. He examined the chamber, quickly removed the magazine and tossed the unspent rounds through the hole in the side window. 'Stop at the next bridge,' he said and proceeded to wipe the gun with his handkerchief.

'I didn't know what I was doing.' Jane gripped Teschmaker's shoulder. 'I didn't even know if it was loaded. There was nothing else I could do, was there? I was just going to point it at him . . .' Her voice trailed off and she dissolved into sobs.

Her father pulled her gently back into his arms. 'What you did saved us, Jane. It's all over now and soon you'll be home with Melanie.'

Teschmaker had forgotten all about Jane's daughter. 'You got Mel back?'

'Oh God, I forgot. You don't know what happened.' Regaining her composure Jane told Teschmaker what had occurred earlier.

'Gerard and Grice are dead?'

'Yes. I don't want to think about it, it was horrible.'

The euphoria their escape had produced in him evaporated. He didn't care about Grice, but despite their initial encounter he had developed a liking for Sinclair's standover man. 'Edwards was a good man,' he said quietly.

Teschmaker turned off the main road and pulled in beside a bridge crossing the Charlotte River. 'I'll get rid of the handkerchief too,' he said and wrapped it around the pistol.

There was no light over the bridge but the faint plop from below told him that the gun was safely out of harm's way.

'Where's Melanie now?' he asked Jane as he got back in the car.

'With a very relieved and repentant Oliver.'

'Repentant? Does that mean you're going to forgive him?'

'No.' Jane reached out and touched his hand. 'No, there are some things you can't forgive.'

'What about the person who "screwed up your life from day one"?' He was going to quote her phrase accurately but held himself back in front of her father.

There was no reply. Then he felt her hand move up and gently stroke the back of his neck. The message was easy to read; later.

They were nearly in town when Jane remembered that Norman and Viola were still trussed up — bound, gagged and locked in the apartment.

'They're probably enjoying it,' Teschmaker quipped, but nobody seemed to get the joke. They rode the remainder of the journey in silence.

END NOTE

In October 1997, Dr Alexei Yablokov, a former science advisor to President Boris Yeltsin, testified before a subcommittee of the American National Security Committee about the claims made by General Lebed that only 48 of the 132 suitcase-sized nuclear weapons could be located. His main concern, however, was not for the ones which had been placed outside the former Soviet Union but for those within.

'We've got about 100 organisations of a fascist nature. These fascist organisations have got many military who know where these bombs are located, who know how to use them. And if, inside the country, there's a struggle for power and these fascists and nationalists get hold of these bombs — there is a small chance, but there is that chance, much smaller than Chechnya or Palestine — but if that happens, that will be terrible. That's why I'm talking about this, that's why tactical nuclear arms, these small nuclear bombs, ought to be destroyed as soon as possible.'*

---

* Testimony of Dr Alexei Yablokov, former science advisor to Boris Yeltsin, before the Research and Development Subcommittee of the House National Security Committee, chaired by Representative Curt Weldon, 2 October 1997.

As of October 2001 there were still a large number of portable nuclear devices missing from the ex-Soviet arsenal. According to Russian intelligence sources, there seems to be very little being done to locate them.

Sandy McCutcheon
Brisbane, October 2001

Photo by Kathy Luu

Traci Harding, best selling author of 'the Ancient Future Series', has published in excess of twenty books through through HarperCollins/Voyager Australia, Brio Books and Bolinda Audio. Her work blends fantasy, fact, esoteric theory, time travel and quantum physics, into adventurous romps through history, alternative dimensions, universes and states of consciousness. Her books have been published in several languages throughout the world.

**To find out more about Traci and her books
visit her website at:** traciharding.com

For autographed copies of Traci's books visit her store at:
allthingstraci.com.au

Get Exclusive Content at Patreon:
patreon.com/user?u=20034469&fan_landing=true

Find Traci on Facebook at:
"Mastering Your Reality with Traci Harding" Group -
All Things Traci Store - Traci Harding Fans - Trazling

Traci is also on:
Twitter: @tracharding
Instagram: traciharding_author
YouTube: youtube.com/c/TraciHardingChannel
& Redbubble: redbubble.com/people/traciharding/shop?asc=u

Books by Traci Harding

The Ancient Future Trilogy
The Ancient Future: the Dark Age (1)
An Echo in Time: Atlantis (2)
Masters of Reality: the Gathering (3)

The Alchemist's Key

The Celestial Triad
Chronicle of Ages (1)
Tablet of Destinies (2)
The Cosmic Logos (3)

Ghostwriting

The Book of Dreams

The Mystique Trilogy
Gene of Isis (1)
The Dragon Queens (2)
The Black Madonna (3)

The Triad of Being Trilogy
Being of the Field (1)